HANDCLASP
OF THE
EAST AND WEST

By Martha and Henry Ripley

Western Reflections Publishing Company
Lake City, Colorado

A Reprint Published by
Western Reflections Publishing Co.
P. O. Box 1149
951 N. Highway 149
Lake City, Colorado 81235

www.westernreflectionspub.com
westref@montrose.net

Printed in the United States
Library of Congress Number: 2008930934

ISBN 978-1-932738-67-4

Front Cover: *Red Mountain* by Bob De Julio

HANDCLASP OF THE EAST AND WEST

Prologue

Henry and Martha Ripley came to Ouray in 1877 to start Ouray's first newspaper – *The Ouray Times*. Henry and his brother William hauled their press in by wagon some 300 miles from Cañon City. The Ripley brothers had operated *The Canon City Times* for almost five years, but wanted to become part of the "San Juan Excitement." Much of the trip was over Otto Mears' just-opened toll road through Ute Territory. Henry later wrote "there was supposed to be a toll road between Saguache and Lake City – at least at frequent intervals we were held up for toll." He also swore that the only "road" from Lake City to Ouray was the faint trail made by U. S. Army wagons when they transferred the Ute Indian agency from the top of Cochetopa Pass to the new Los Pinos Agency on the Uncompahgre River.

The first edition of *The Ouray Times* was printed June 16, 1877. Henry wrote of what "a great day it was when the first paper was printed. All day long men came to the office to see how things were progressing. The first paper, as was usual for such cases, was put up for auction and sold for ten dollars.... The first paper was made as much of as the advent of the first baby, and well it might, for its travail in getting there had been long and hard."

Ripley's newspaper went out of business in 1886, in large part because of a long, hard fight with renowned editor Dave Day of Ouray's *Solid Muldoon*. Day's paper was famous all over the United States and was even said to be read by England's Queen Victoria. He printed the first issue of his paper September 5, 1879.

The *Hand-Clasp of the East and the West* is an autobiography, however the authors used a convoluted, but common practice of the time, and wrote the book replacing true names with fictional ones. One example could be using "Tom" in place of "Henry." Despite the use of fictional names, this book includes valuable, historically accurate information about pioneer life on the Western Slope of Colorado.

The Ripleys lived in Montrose, Colorado, after leaving Ouray, and it was there that they wrote this book. The Ripleys were successful farmers and ranchers in the Montrose area, and their sons even discovered a valuable mine near Ouray. Henry died before The *Hand-Clasp of the East and the West* was published in 1914.

Chief Ouray and Squaw Chipeta

1

Hand-Clasp of the East and West

A STORY OF PIONEER LIFE
ON THE
WESTERN SLOPE
OF
COLORADO

By
Henry and Martha Ripley

Published, November, 1914

Press of the
Williamson-Haffner Engraving & Printing Co.
Denver, Colorado

Dedication

To the brave men who dared,
The loving women who endured,
The children who drank in the greatness of this western life and helped make what we see today;
To the East who gave to these people the rich legacy of the forefathers, the undaunted spirit of overcoming, the spirit of doing,
This book is lovingly dedicated.

HENRY RIPLEY.
MARTHA RIPLEY.

Out where the hand-clasp's a little stronger,
Out where the smile dwells a little longer,
    That's where the West begins;
Out where the sun is a little brighter,
Where the snows that fall are a trifle whiter,
Where the bonds of home are a wee bit tighter,
    That's where the West begins.

ANON.

"*Opportunity*"

They do me wrong who say I come no more,
    When once I knock and fail to find you in;
For every day I stand outside your door
    And bid you wake and rise to fight and win.

—WALTER MALONE.

Acknowledgment

We gratefully acknowledge our indebtedness:

To Ira Monell;

To Mr. Lynn Monroe, Editor, and Mr. W. A. Berry, Manager, of "The Montrose Enterprise;"

To Mr. Frank Hall of Denver, Author of the "History of Colorado;"

To Mr. Adams, Editor of "The Montrose Press," and the newspaper men all over the Western Slope, who so kindly published our request for sketches of pioneer experiences,

And for the encouraging words from our many pioneer friends of yesterday and today.

H. and M. R.

CONTENTS

ILLUSTRATIONS

Page

Hand-Clasp of the East and West

PREFACE

Another book? Yes, another book; and as long as the sun shines on human achievement someone will write.

The question comes—more as a challenge than a demand—why this attempt when so many have been written? Fearlessly the answer is given: because we love this valley, these hills and snow-capped mountains; because the mighty developments and achievements of the past forty years are worthy to be brought to light and preserved, not only for the present, but for future generations.

Marvelous changes have taken place so naturally and swiftly that we, who are classed as old-timers—and proudly we bear the name—almost fail to realize what has been accomplished right before our eyes. So this book will be a rediscovery, as it were, of what we already know—a book of remembrances—even up to the present. To the young it will be as interesting as the story of Robinson Crusoe.

A worthy past sheds light and courage on the present and future.

The desire of the writers is to bring to each and every one not the personal aspect of "me and mine" but the impersonal outlook of the Western Slope as a whole; to bring to the thought the sense of being a partner in this wonderful accomplishment, the young as well as the aged, causing the young after its perusal to be proud they live in this progressive part of Colorado, and the oldest inhabitant to lift his or her head in pride for having been led to leave the comforts of home and association of friends to "blaze the trail" for the grand results they now behold.

And if there should come a regret, it will be that we did not enter more heartily into the great work, had been less self-seeking and more thoughtful of the welfare of those coming after; had realized that every stone removed from the highway, every tree that was planted for the beautifying of our streets, was not merely for "me and mine," but for the good of all, to exemplify the prophecy, "the desert shall blossom as the rose."

To remind us as a people what were the conditions at that time, and what they are today and will be in the future; to awaken in us the realization of our responsibility for good and blessing to all who may yet come seeking in the valley of opportunity, is the real motive for presenting this book, with its ever new story of human life and love; remembering always, it was the East which gave birth to these brave pioneers.

A PROPHETIC DREAM

I dreamed a dream!

Forty years ago I stood upon a high mountain. There spread out before me an immense valley surrounded on all sides as far as the eye could reach with mountains whose summits carried their mantle of snow the year through. Sloping down from these lofty heights to a general center were lesser mountains, all clothed with the varied greens of cedar, aspen, pine, and spruce, with many openings or parks in the mass of timber, which were covered with the choicest pasturage such as could not be surpassed. Here and there one could catch the glint of sparkling water where the numerous streams from these forests and melting snows were making their way to the valley below. This valley, many miles in extent, viewed from our distant outlook, seemed but a barren desert plain, save where these streams wound their way to the river, and these water courses were marked by a strip of green. There were no signs of animal life, though reason told us these mountain forests were alive with game and the streams abounded with trout.

Roaming this vast territory at their own sweet will, and living upon the game and fish so abundant, were a few hundred Ute Indians claiming sole ownership and retarding the march of civilization. It required no prophetic mind to see here the field of controversy between savagery and civilization, and this could not long be delayed.

No white man had a home in all this great valley, though at rare intervals individuals and small parties had made their way through, going to more distant regions. The western march of civilization was beginning to show itself above the great Continental Divide, and pushing on into the wilderness, lured by the thirst for gold, and reaching out for a larger freedom and contact with nature in the wild. Here was the place to find it.

In the higher mountains are deposits of the precious metal ores which will give employment to, and line the pockets of, many men; in the valley, agricultural land which will produce in generous abundance all the grains, fruits, and vegetables of the temperate zone, and generously supply the hardy miners in the mountains. The timbered slopes surrounding the valley provided ample timber for the making of homes as well as affording pasturage for "the cattle of a thousand hills." In addition to this, possessing a climate unequaled and where the sun makes a business of shining. All these awaiting the coming of the army of hardy pioneers and home-seekers who are looking for enlarged opportunities in the glorious West.

Time passed rapidly, as it always does in dreams, and the panorama seemed to unfold before me. A few adventurous prospectors crossed the ranges which seemed to shut off this valley of rich promise from the rest of the world, and found that which was sufficiently alluring to cause them to establish their homes in the wild and rugged mountains. The news of their discoveries went out and others began to come in increasing numbers; trails were opened and in due time developed into wagon roads. Over these roads came the prairie schooner with its loads of adventurous and determined humanity. The interests of the whites and Indians began to conflict, and, after the exasperating and apparently never-ending unwinding of red tape, the government bought out the Indians and moved them to another reservation.

The bars were now down and the incoming tide of civilization greatly increased in consequence, so that the railroad must needs follow to afford them the means of inter-communication. Thousands of happy homes were built up in the wilderness, and peace and prosperity became the lot of many a hitherto weary heart.

There were cities and towns with commodious churches and schools, and many of the advantages of the older civilization, and a happy, prosperous and contented people occupied the mountains and valleys where once roamed the Indian.

Will this dream ever come true? We will see.

HAND-CLASP OF THE EAST AND WEST

CHAPTER I

THE HOME COMING

"Hello, Dad, how are you?" The speaker was a young man just home from college. He was a manly boy, with broad shoulders and a firm grip as he grasped his father's outstretched hand.

"Well, my boy; and you?"

"Fine, father; fine. How good it seems to be home once more."

The father, a wide-awake farmer, smiled back with that satisfied look which showed the pleasure he felt in having his boy home once more. As they rode along the boy was eager in his questions after mother, sisters, Kate and Mary; and Bob, how was he getting along at school? Tom was the oldest child, and many had been the privations gladly endured that he should have the education which his father had been denied. The father was hungry for this quiet ride with his son. He fully understood from past experience that there would be little chance for him when he reached home, so he asked the question at once. "Well, my boy, what are you going to do now you are through with your schooling?"

He was hardly prepared for the prompt response, "I am going out West, father, and I wish you and mother were going with me."

"Out West?" his father gasped. There was a catch in his voice which the boy did not notice at the time, and as the horses seemed to require the undivided attention of the father just then, the subject was not again referred to. Both men seemed lost in thought. As they were rounding a curve, the son, forgetting all else, said:

"See, father! what a beautiful picture! I wish I were an artist. On one side the winding river, flowing along with scarcely a ripple as far as the eye can reach; on the other, the deep, silent woods with their sweet scents of undergrowth, and the distant twitter of birds in their love-making; and then in front, miles and miles away, are to be seen the low hills partially veiled with a smoky haziness which tells of summer near at hand. Is it not beautiful? I wish Dick—one of my school-chums—were here. He is a born artist. How he would enjoy such a scene."

The father's face cleared, and his peaceful smile shone out again. Yes, his boy loved his home too much to want to leave it; he would soon get over the notion of leaving this beautiful valley and settle down as he and his father had done, to the work left them by ancestors who had made the ruts in which they were now so contentedly working.

But just then the glad, welcoming bark of a dog reminded them that home was not far away. The horses seemed spurred on by the gladness of the homecoming as old Tige came bounding toward them, his eyes fairly shining with the pleasure of meeting his young master. Then as they rounded the corner, crossing the bridge with its archway of weeping willows growing on either side, the old home, with all its beauty, came into view. Mother, wearing her white apron, stood on the veranda; the girls and Bob running a race to see which could get to the brother first, while Tige, almost beside himself, danced and leaped from one to the other until they reached the house. There all held back, for it was Mother's turn. Yes, the world seems to stand still naturally for that moment when mother and son meet, all the weeks and months of separation forgotten; the future, with its possibilities of joy not thought of. Just "My son!" "My mother!"

The father looked at them, and again the horses needed his attention, and he led them away with tender words, which they feel but do not understand. So, to break the silence she did not enjoy, Mary said, "Tom, Mamma made a currant cake for supper!" Then they all laughed and each tried to outtalk the other, there were so many things to tell, so many things to show Tom, for he had not come home at Christmas time this year, not only that he might save expense, but his chum living near the college would not take "no" for an answer to his invitation to spend that last vacation with him and his parents.

Soon, father came in and mother left the little

group to hasten supper, for well she remembered her big boy's appetite was always good. Soon they were seated around the table; such happy, smiling faces, when Bob, with his mouth full of bread and jam, said:

"Tom, the boys downtown say they are going to put you in as president of the club next fall."

"But what if I am not here?" Tom answered.

"Why Tom, not here?" his mother exclaimed. "What do you mean?" and she put down the teapot she was holding, and a startled look came into her eyes.

"Nothing to worry you, mother dear," and father seemed to choke as he swallowed his tea.

"You bet you will be here," said Bob. "Father needs you awful bad, and we do, too, don't we Mary?"

"Yes, my doll needs mending right now; it fell off the cellar door yesterday. That is a splendid place to slide, Tom," said Mary.

"And I need you, too, Tom," said Kate, "to go skating with me this winter. Mother seems to think I am too big to go with the others. But I would rather go with you, Tom, than anyone else in the world." Her eyes glowed with the love a sister always feels for a brother of whom she is proud.

"You enjoyed the visit with your friend at Christmas?" asked mother, who was fast regaining her sense of happiness which seemed to have left her a few moments before.

"Yes, mother; I know you will love him; he's fine."

"Is he the one you spoke of as being the artist?" asked father.

"Yes, his name is Dick, and I am sure he will think our home one of the prettiest places in the world."

"Do you really think so?" asked the father, a pleased look coming into his eyes.

"He could not help it," said Tom, his face beaming with admiration. "I tell you, father, you, who have worked right here all your life, have no idea how beautiful it is, and how one who has been away rejoices to get sight of it again."

The father gave the boy a pleased but keen look, for he was puzzled. Then why does the boy want to leave it, he thought.

When supper was over and the sun, which had lingered as long as possible, as though loath to part even for a night from such a beautiful scene, had left the hills and trees still bathed in its brightness, and the father picked up the milk pails, Tom called out: "You do the milking once more, father; I would scare the cows with these city clothes. I bought me a nobby suit of overalls, jumper and all, which I can put on in the morning."

"All right, Tom, my boy!" and father went to his work with a very light heart. His boy had not changed one bit, bless him!

"Yes, mother, I can play the gentleman tonight. But give me an apron. I'll wipe the dishes while the girls hunt the eggs and console the injured doll."

And so the mother and son, as was their habit

for many years when evening dishes needed washing, took that time for a confidential chat—a heart-to-heart talk over things that seemed too sacred for the busy hours of the day; and as mother was passing her boy she put her arms around him for another kiss; then, both laughing to hide their feelings and the tears that sprang to their eyes—tears of joy—began to work and talk. Mother told of how hard father had been working, and yet in spite of it all they were not getting along as they should. It was hard to sell anything. "We don't get such crops as we used to," she said, "and I don't see why. Then the price for everything is so low. Of course, we have plenty for ourselves, but we need money for so many things. But," she laughed, "I suppose we should be content. Our forefathers always got along, with far less of life's comforts than we enjoy. But say, dear, what did you mean by your answer to Bob at the supper table? You surely are not thinking of leaving us, for, what could you do? I always thought of you taking father's place on this same farm. Let me see; this farm has been tilled by our family for four generations, and we expected our children to follow in their footsteps. Why not, Tom? There is no other way, is there? Surely you—"

"Yes, mother dear, there is another way, and tonight, when the children have gone to bed, I want to talk with you and father of something I have in mind. When is Aunt Hetty coming home? You wrote me she was visiting some friends in the city."

"Yes, dear, she was getting very restless here, and when these friends invited her to visit them for a few weeks we advised her to go, though it left so much of the work on me; but I have been so happy looking forward to your coming that I have not noticed it."

Just then the children came in, wondering what kept mamma in the kitchen so long. They gathered on the veranda to laugh and talk—that happy time when every care seems to disappear, and bedtime comes to children as a happy ending to the day.

"I love you, Tom," said little Mary as she kissed him goodnight, while Kate spoke for the whole family when she said, "Just to think, Tom! you will be here when we wake up; that is the best of all." "So long, Tom," Bob merely said. But boys seem to understand each other without words.

Then the three—father, mother and son—were left alone at last, and as they sat near the grate fire, for the evenings were still quite cool, the mother was first to speak. Womanlike, her heart was full and must find expression.

"Tom is thinking of leaving us, father. He is going to tell us now what he means to do."

"All right, my boy," said the father, as he braced himself for the ordeal. "Tell us all you have in your thought, for you know we love you and think only of your highest welfare."

Then Tom, who had been so full of enthusiasm since his Christmas time visit with his friend Dick, found it very hard, and wondered why his voice trembled as he began. He was sitting in his favorite position at his mother's knee; she held his hand and felt it tremble.

"Well, it is this way," he said, "when I was with Dick last Christmas, his father—I wish you could meet his father and mother; they treated me as though I was their own, and often expressed a wish that they could meet you both—had received a letter from an old school friend who, at that time, was camping in some place in the Rocky Mountains. He, with two other men, had heard of the discovery of some silver mines in that region, so packed up some grub—that is what they called it—and each with a roll of blankets and cooking utensils started out to find something for themselves. I believe the names of these men were Staley and Whitlock. They built about the first log cabin, just like our forefathers used to build, you know."

"But," said the father, "are you thinking of mining, my son?"

"No, father, though I would like to discover some good lead. I expect to put in practice what I have been learning in college—that which you have both worked so hard to give me—civil and mining engineering, and use my knowledge of mineralogy. Just think, mother dear, of one who has gained this knowledge, as I feel I have, for I did my best, for your sakes. How could you expect me to settle down in such an unprogressive country to follow in the footsteps of my revered ancestors?

Neither can I stand to see you slaving year after year on a worn-out old farm. You know, father, the reason you do not get the crops you did when a young man is because the land is worn out; and then there is little market for what you do raise, for everyone is raising the same things—all working in the ruts their forefathers dug. With all my heart I wish you both"—and here he held his mother's hand as though he feared to lose her—"could see the advisability of giving up this beautiful home and begin with me to build a home in this far West. I have sometimes wondered why I feel this way, so filled with the desire to break loose from old ways and old ties. Why, as I listened to this letter written to Dick's father by this man, my blood would get on fire, as it were, and I longed to start in quest of a country where everything is new, and every man a prince in his own right. But I have come to the conclusion this unseen power which is forcing me away from what I hold most dear is nothing but the same spirit which actuated our forefathers. The East reaching out to the West then; it is the same today, always reaching out for more freedom. The East is not willing to give us up, so there is opposition; but the spirit awakened cannot be utterly crushed, and gladly we leave home, friends, comforts of every sort, to follow where this spirit leads, from a land of unrest to a land of larger freedom and greater opportunity; and grateful am I for your help in fitting me so well to meet the need of the hour and to work out life's battle."

"Boy," said the father, with tears in his eyes, "I felt this spirit, as you call it, felt it as strongly as you do, but I crushed it, for I could see no way out; but, in God's name, don't let it be crushed in you. Mother, don't cry; we will go together if we go at all."

The boy felt, though he did not understand—how could he—the sacrifices they were making, but he buried his face in his mother's lap, while the father, with remembrance of days gone by, stood by his wife's side, smoothing her hair with trembling hands. The mother broke the silence with words the son never forgot, and in after years, when tempted to be discouraged in the struggle, he remembered, and went on with renewed strength.

"It's all right, Tom, my beloved. You lead with your fresh young life before you, and we will follow as closely as we can. You see, it is not only you, but your father, who is going to have the desire of his life. When do we go?"

"Not yet, dearest and bravest little mother. I will stay and work with father until the last of the month."

"God bless you, my son," said the father. "You are a good boy, but let us go to bed now: we all need rest."

Mother took the lighted candle to her boy's bedroom, fixed the pillows as only a mother can—she is so used to it, you know. Then, with a long, mother-love kiss, she left him.

CHAPTER II

THE DECISION MADE

"Good morning, father," said Tom, as he bounded through the kitchen door to overtake his father on his way to the cowyard with milk pails in his hand. "Let me take them."

His father eyed him with satisfaction. His boy looked very manly in his working clothes, and the ring of his voice was clear and strong.

"What a beautiful morning! Should have been down sooner, but had to stop and admire the sunrise. I tell you, father, the farm beats the city in these things; even if the city man gets up early, he's so hemmed in he does not get much of the beauty you see every day."

When they were ready for breakfast, the mother and children were waiting to greet them.

"Good morning, mother! How are you this glorious morning?"

"All well, my son," she answered; although she smiled, Tom saw she looked like one who had not slept much, but he said nothing then. After breakfast, as Tom was leaving for the barn, he noticed Mary was eyeing him wistfully.

"What is it, Mary?" he said.

"Could you mend my doll now?"

"Not now, little sister; wait until evening. You see, father needs me in the field this morning."

"All right, Tom," and away she skipped, with Tige at her heels.

"My! you look dandy in your new suit of clothes," said Kate. "I'm glad you are here, Tom; father needs your help; he never has time to rest until he goes to bed."

"Yes, Sis," said Tom, "I've thought of him and mother very often and longed for the time for me to be here."

"And yet, you talk of leaving us?"

"Wouldn't you like to go, Kate? Go where we all would have better advantages—out West?"

"Out West! Why Tom, what in the world are you talking about? Aunt Hetty thinks it dreadful for people to do anything but that which everybody else does. What would she say, I wonder? I'm all the time shocking her as it is. Tell me more about it tonight."

School was out in the country, so mother and daughter worked together. While they were washing the dishes, Kate asked abruptly, "Mother, what does Tom mean about this going out West? I thought he was going to settle down and live at home."

"Well, my daughter, we had a long talk with him on the subject last night, and after he explained it somewhat your father and I agreed with him, that it would be better. So we are thinking it over very seriously, but we won't talk about it now, dear." The catch in her voice caused the girl to understand a little what it might mean to mother.

Kate was her mother's helper, thoughtless sometimes through her love for fun. As she said, she often shocked Aunt Hetty, for "girls never did such things when she was young," that seemed so natural for Kate. But mother could always depend upon Kate, and now she knew she would not fail her.

The day, with its work and pleasure, soon came to a close, and none more glad than Tom to rest.

"This life on the farm is a strenuous one, is it not, Bob?"

"You bet it is," said his brother, "but you are a tenderfoot yet; you will get used to it."

Just then Tom caught sight of a very mournful appearing little girl standing in the open door. "Hello, Mary. Brought the doll for repairs?"

"Yes!" she said, the sunshine coming back to her face.

"All right, let's go into the workshop. Rather a serious break for one of her age, but then, I guess it's all right now. I almost forgot something I have in the bottom of my trunk! Guess what it is!"

Mary's face flushed, for she had been wondering what Tom would bring her from the big city, but she did not dare express her heart's desire.

"Let us go and see, little sister," and away they went upstairs to Tom's room, and soon the little mother-heart was enjoying the bliss of a new doll.

"Oh, Tom, I do love you so!" she said, her eyes shining like stars as away she flew to show her mother.

"Father," said Tom, as he stepped to his side, "don't you think it would be better to have Kate and Bob sit up a while tonight? They should understand this proposition. We will need their interest and co-operation."

"Yes, Tom," said his father, "that is a good idea. We will." So Mary went to bed alone to dream of her treasure.

When the little family were seated around the grate-fire, father spoke first.

"Well, my boy, what have you to tell us tonight about this new country? We all want to hear."

"In the first place," said Tom, "I will read this letter Mr. Wilson gave me to read you; it is from this old school friend of his. Here it is, dated

" 'November, 1875.

" 'Dear Friend Wilson:

" 'You may be surprised to hear from me, but the long talks you and I used to have out of school hours have often come back to me. You remember how we used to plan for the future, and how I said I should never be content in the city, but felt the longing to go out into the wilderness and fight as our forefathers did for a home. You laughed and said, "I believe you will, and when you do, let me know how you get along; I may want to join you." So, old comrade, I am writing to tell you I am in the wilderness, sure enough; but don't picture broad prairies and lakes, but let me tell you how Staley. Whitlock and I were in a company prospecting for silver in the Rocky Mountains, north of Silverton.

and, after much hard climbing, we crossed the range to as picturesque a little spot as is to be found in America. It is shaped like a bowl, surrounded by high mountains reaching to and above timber line. The only way to see out is to look up. The sun is a most lazy fellow—always late getting up in the morning, and goes to rest soon after four o'clock at this time of the year. I wish I was good at the descriptive, but you know I never was. Do you remember the time Ralph got married and I was sent to report? When asked what color the bride's dress was, I didn't want to show my ignorance, so said it was red. You remember how they went for me. The walls are perpendicular in many places, broken and rough in others, some parts bare, but wherever foothold can be obtained, the hardy spruce trees grow. One never tires of looking at the mountains, though at present we do not spend much time admiring the scenery, for we came for something more substantial.

"'We have been most fortunate, so far. Just located a good silver mine. We have some other claims which show good indications. The mountains are so steep it is pretty hard getting around. A few other men have been here, having as good luck as we, but most of them have gone out for the winter. We have built us a cabin and expect to stay right here.

"'Now I come to the main reason for writing you. In the spring the camp will need an assayer and a surveyor the first thing, for there will be much work in those lines. I remembered you worked with ores and metals while at school, and wondered if you could not come out to this grand country and take up this line of work. And possibly you or your son know of some young man who has prepared himself for the work of survey. But I must close, for my candle has almost burned out. Let me know what you think about it. You will have to address to Lake City. No postoffice here yet.

" 'Yours for old times,

" 'SMITH.

" 'P. S.—Am sending this by one of the boys, who is going out.' "

There was silence for a moment after the reading of the letter, broken by Bob, who had been listening with both ears and eyes wide open. "I wish I could go."

"You, my boy?" said the father, smiling.

"Yes, these men are regular Robinson Crusoes, discovering what has been hidden all these centuries."

"But, sonny," said Kate, pulling his ear, "how would you like to be shut up in such a place all winter?"

"Go on, my boy; I see you have something else. Any more letters?"

"No, father, but you remember when I wrote you Christmas I spoke of meeting two strange men who had been out West and brought a letter, which proved to be this very letter I have been reading to you, from Mr. Wilson's friend. These men were invited to stay and rest, so we learned a great deal about this new country. I was much interested in these men from the first. They seemed different from any I had ever seen; their faces were tanned. They wore odd-looking clothes, leggings up to their knees. But it was not their clothes that struck me so much as the air of independence and ability to overcome obstacles. They had met the wilderness and mastered it. I felt like a child watching and admiring some strange guests. In the first place, they apologized for coming at such a time, but a friend of Mr. Wilson's had intrusted them with a letter, and, as they were so near, thought best to deliver it in person. You may be sure it did not take long for them to be seated by the big fireplace, and soon they began to tell of this wonderful mountain country. Mr. Wilson asked many questions, after reading the letter. One was:

" 'You spoke of the mines; is there anything else to be found there? Is there no land to cultivate? Where would these men get their supplies?'

"We boys listened for their reply, just as Kate and Bob are now.

" 'Yes, sir,' one said. 'To the north of the place of which we have been speaking is the Ute Indian reservation, distant about twelve miles, including large areas of fine tillable land, with the best climate in the world, sunshine every day in the year. Only a matter of a little time when the march of progress will compel the Indians to go. When that time comes, there will be all this land thrown open for settlement, and those who live near and are on the watch will have the first chance. My partner and I have made up our minds to return in the spring, work on our claims, and build two cabins, and the next summer take our families out and stay there. doing anything we may find till this land is opened up, then take up one hundred and sixty acres each and have a home that will be a home some day.'

"I asked the question which came from my heart. 'If a young man was going out there, how would he set about it?' He looked at me keenly, and answering, said:

"'In the first place, he would have to make up his mind it was no kid-glove affair, but a continuous conflict with the rudest forces of nature, requiring the same determination to win as when you go into a football game. Purchase your ticket to the end of the railroad. Arriving there, buy a pony and one or more burros, according to your need, fully equipped for the road. You will need them to carry your instruments, blankets, supplies, cooking utensils, and tools, and you will find the animals very useful in carrying on your work after you get there. Don't overlook rifle and revolver, with an ample supply of ammunition. They will furnish you with many a good meal. Lay in a stock of supplies and tools, inquire the way, and light out.'

"I was so taken up with what they were saying I was glad when I looked up and saw that Dick was busy, as I should have been, with pencil and paper, noting down these important items.

"Mr. Wilson said, 'Gentlemen, I will have a few moments' talk with my wife before you go, so if you will excuse me for a little while, these boys will keep you busy.'

"I do not know how long he was gone, for we talked about many things that will be of great use to us."

"What were the names of these men, Tom?" asked his mother, who was busy sewing, as well as listening.

"One was Edwin Gray. He was the dark looking one. The other, I believe, was John Eaton. He was tall, and smiled with his eyes, which were blue. When Mr. Wilson came back he handed Mr. Gray a note, saying, 'You give this to my friend Smith; he might not get a letter any sooner if I sent it by mail. In it I have written, after a talk with my wife and daughter'—we all looked up, for the tone of his voice seemed changed. It sounded as of one who had decided, no matter what the consequence might be—'that I will come and bring all the help I can, including, I believe, a surveyor,' as he looked at me, smiling. The men went away, leaving us with plenty to think about. We talked until late that night, with the result you can easily guess."

"Out with it, my boy," spoke up the father, who saw with his keen eye Tom was hesitating.

"Well, father, and mother," she, he noticed, had ceased sewing and was holding her breath for the answer, "we decided it would be best to strike out while the iron was hot, and if you are willing—I believe you will be—Mr. Wilson and Dick will be here to spend a day or two the last of this month; they want to meet you. Then I will be ready to start with them. In the meantime, I want to help you with the farm work all I can."

"Then what?" asked his mother, for again he stopped.

"Dear father and mother, it seems to take so much for granted, but we planned, if you saw it as best, we would go, spend the summer of 1876 looking around, earning what we can, building two cabins—one for our family, one for Mr. Wilson's—and come back in the fall, spend the winter here, in the spring you either sell or lease the farm, and we all go out together—Mr. Wilson's family and ours. They have to pass near here anyway, so one of these days they will come in a covered wagon, with an extra horse or two, and we'll be ready to travel in like fashion."

"You bet!" said Bob, as he turned a somersault off the sofa onto the carpet.

"But," said Kate, "a covered wagon, as you call it, won't carry much furniture."

"It's time to go to bed," said father; "we have heard enough for one evening. But, Tom, my boy! I am proud of you, and if mother is willing, we will fall right in with your plans; they appeal to me as good."

Tom went to his mother, his heart full, for his father's words meant so much. "Now, little mother, do not climb the stairs, but kiss me goodnight here, and remember I want you to sleep tonight. There is a higher power that is leading us in this."

"Yes, my son, I know it. During the night there came to me these words: 'He leadeth me, oh blessed thought!' and such a sense of peace came over me. I knew then it was all right. Tears may come, but always remember, in my heart I am happy and satisfied. Goodnight, and may God bless you."

CHAPTER III

STARTLING DEVELOPMENTS

Those were busy days which followed. Father and son felt that every bit of land must be utilized to bring forth means for this great change in their lives, but busy as they were in the field and home, the parents did not fail to notice Tom was not his happy self. When they came across him suddenly, they found him deep in thought, with a look on his young face that told its story of anxiety.

"You don't think he wants to give up the thought of going West, do you?" asked mother, as she and father were sitting alone one evening. Tom and Kate had gone for a walk.

"No," said father, "Tom is not a boy to begin a thing and then back out. How he persevered in his studies when many a boy would have become discouraged."

"Yes," smiled mother, "he would not be like you if he gave up easily."

The next morning, after Tom had gone to the barn to harness the horses, father, mother and Kate were standing near the door watching the boy at his work. Kate spoke up quickly, saying: "Tom told me last night how he lay awake nights, trying to think of some way to get the money to take this trip. He did not want to worry you with it, but, as he said, not only is there the expense of the trip, but he will have to have a complete set of surveying instruments. He was telling me how you both had worked to raise money for his schooling, that his one ambition was to pay you back as soon as possible, and now comes this extra expense, but try as he would he could not see any way out. I couldn't do much, even in the way of talking, but he said it did him good to talk it over with me. I won't let him know it, but for the first time in my life I lay awake thinking, too."

"Bless the boy!" said the father. "It will be a pity if we can't help him one more year. I will have a talk with him when we get to the field." Mother smiled; she knew father would see a way out.

But, to all appearances, when the men came in to dinner, the "way out," as mother put it, had not been found, for both seemed tired and preoccupied. After dinner was over, and Tom was resting on the porch sofa, mother went to him, as mothers have a way of doing, for a quiet talk. She drew her rocker to his side, and, holding his hand, which was not as white and soft as when he came, asked, "Didn't father make it plain to you how everything could be arranged?"

"Mother!"—but the struggle of the past week was too much, and sobs instead of words came. Father started to come on the porch, but drew back; this was a case when only mother was equal to the need. Oh, mother love, nearest akin to the divine! Blessed is the one who has such love to give, and blessed is the one who receives. After a few moments, when all the worry and the discouragement had been dispelled by tears and love, the boy spoke.

"It's all right now, mother! I do not see why I did not come to you first, but surely there will be a way opened, so I will not have to make you suffer longer for me. You have given the best of your lives, you and father, for me so far."

"Dear boy, the same Hand that is leading us in this change will provide the means. I feel it so strong, sweetheart."

"Oh, mother! your words put new life in me; it will come!" and the face of the boy shone with the old happy light.

"What is it?" asked father, who knew the victory was won and wanted to share in its glory.

"It's all right, father," said Tom; "it's just as mother said, the same Hand which is leading us out will provide the way. I believe you will not have to slave for me either."

"Bless you, boy! I never have slaved when working for you. I guess we had better go to our work."

They both kissed mother goodbye, and she, one of the happiest women on earth. Who would not be?

That evening, as they were resting, a neighbor brought a letter from the postoffice as he was passing, which proved to be from Aunt Hetty. She said she was getting homesick, coming home Saturday; would someone meet her at the station?

When Saturday came, Bob was given the pleasure of cleaning the buggy and going to meet Aunt Hetty. If anyone had noticed very closely, they would have seen a very knowing and mischievous look on Bob's face. For a boy of thirteen, Bob's sense of humor was well developed. The hearty peals of laughter as they went along were enjoyed, though not understood, by the horse, which was accustomed to Bob's ways. After a few minutes of waiting, the train came in sight, with Aunt Hetty at a window, waving her handkerchief at sight of Bob. She loved Bob, though he did enjoy teasing her. Soon they were settled in the buggy, and the horse, so used to the road, needed little attention.

"Aunt Hetty," said Bob, with a very grave face, though his eyes were dancing, "it's a pity you went away and left us alone."

"Why, child, why? What's the matter?"

"Everything," and he gave his attention for a moment to the horse.

"Tell me, Bob! Is anyone sick?"

"No, I guess not, but everything is upside down, and we are all going out West, and live in a one-room log cabin, and ride burros, and carry guns, and tell the Indians they must go—skip—and get out of the ruts our forefathers dug."

"What in the world, child, do you mean?" And she put her hand gently on the boy's forehead.

"I'm all right, Aunt Hetty, but I've not told you half what we are going to do. It's great! I have been wondering for some time how you would take it, and how you would look riding on a donkey!"

Bob laughed so heartily even Aunt Hetty was obliged to smile.

"Yes, indeed," said Bob, "and we will go bear hunting, for if we don't hunt the bear he will hunt us; and we are going to kill jack rabbits and live on sagebrush and cactus. I heard father and Tom talking."

"Tom!"

"Yes, he's a big man now—big as father—and when he felt bad because he didn't have the money to buy instruments with—"

"What instruments, Bob?"

"I don't know. Mother said that 'the same Hand that was leading us out would provide the means'—money she meant—'to take them there,' and Tom was happy, and father was happy, and we were so glad you were coming home to start, too."

"Well, I guess it's time I came home. None of the neighbors know of this, do they?"

"Not yet, we've been too busy, but they will know soon, and we will all go together."

It was well for Aunt Hetty's peace of mind that home was in sight, and Tige, the first to welcome, came bounding down the driveway.

"The farm is here, anyway," groaned poor Aunt Hetty.

"Yes," said Bob, "but father and Tom say it's no good; all worn out; hardly worth the taxes."

"Well, well! I will see what they mean before I sleep tonight. Heaven grant I shall sleep again."

"Aunt Hetty, see my doll!" cried Mary, as she held her face up for a kiss.

Her aunt kissed the child, but from the outstretched hands of Kate and the mother she drew back, and, with eyeglasses askew, she demanded the meaning of the story Bob had told about riding burros, chasing Indians, and throwing the beautiful home away, and living in a one-room log cabin.

"Dear Aunt Hetty," said the mother, who, seeing the news out, tried to rise to the occasion. "Bob must have been up to his tricks, teasing you again. Come in, and after supper, when you are rested, we will explain what seems so confusing now."

Then, turning to speak to Kate, she found that young lady had gone to assist Bob in caring for the horse. The mother was worried lest Aunt Hetty should hear the peals of laughter which came from the stable, for Bob was going over the whole story to Kate, who was lying on the hay convulsed with mirth. She, too, had wondered how the lady would take it, for she was very set and satisfied with what her family had done for four generations back.

There was a decided coolness in the atmosphere at the supper table. Mother had managed to give father an inkling of conditions, while Kate had waylaid Tom with Bob's story of it all. Bob was the only one at the table who felt at ease. He was happy, and looked at each one as though he did not understand the cause of this constraint. Aunt Hetty went to her room and waited, with ever-increasing indignation, for the evening's talk. It must be confessed the whole family dreaded the ordeal, for they were all a little afraid of Aunt Hetty. The father's thought went back to when he, a young man, having heard of the "new West," the same longing which had taken possession of Tom for a freer life and greater opportunity, had stirred in him, and in a moment of longing made the mistake of confiding his dreams to his sister Hetty, five years younger than himself. It was well he did remember, the bitterness of it all, when his spirit was crushed by the opposition that was brought to bear, for today, in his new-born sense of freedom, he felt nothing could move him again. His wife was watching him, and understood; she saw the hard look she remembered he wore when first she met him.

Looking over at Tom, she saw the resolute look without the hardness, and was glad. When the evening work was hurriedly finished, mother climbed the stairs to tell Aunt Hetty they were all ready for a little talk. In silence they went down to the cool sitting room, where all were seated—all but Mary, who was blissfully sleeping, with her loved doll in her arms.

"Hetty," said Mr. Barton, his voice gentle, but firm, "we are glad you are with us again; glad we can have this quiet hour to talk over the great change that has taken place in our plans since you left. It must be a surprise to you; it was to us. You know, as well as we, the hard time we have in making a living on the farm. You know I have worked early and late, but the fact is, which you may not know, the land cannot yield as it did one hundred years ago; it is really worn out. I have seen it for years, but saw no way out of it, but Tom, bless him!" and the man looked around at his son for strength to go on, "brought news of this opening on the western slope of Colorado. He read to us a letter sent to his friends, the Wilsons, whom Tom visited last Christmas, you remember." Aunt Hetty turned at this and glanced at Tom; she had found the starting point of all the trouble.

"In this letter he speaks of the need of a surveyor at once, and asked Mr. Wilson and his son Dick to come ready to begin work as assayers, and, if possible, to bring a young man fully equipped with a surveying outfit, for work was waiting; rich mines were being discovered already. So Tom, whose school work has been in that line, is the man for it."

"But why in the world are you going to give up your home here just because the boy can get work there?" asked the angry Hetty.

"But, sister! I was going to tell you. There are hundreds of thousands of acres of fine land which has never been plowed just outside this mining region, about twelve miles, I think it is, not yet open for settlement—may not be for several years. It is the 'Ute Indian Reservation' at present."

"Well, when do you start? You can't expect me to give in to such nonsense. What would people say?"

"Hetty," said her brother, and mother held her

breath, for he had never spoken to her in that tone. "Hetty, do you remember twenty-five years ago, when I came to you with a brother's confidence and told you of my hopes and desires, my longing to go out West and make my way? I was young, so young I did not believe there could be the strong opposition to new ways and new ideas there proved to be. You know, you cannot have forgotten, how all hope or desire was crushed out of me. I gave up and took what was given me, made the best I could with this farm. Wife knows how hard it's been. But I've done my best, and now the way is opening for something better, and we are going, and want you to go with us."

"But, how are you going to get the money? It takes money to travel."

"That is a question we cannot answer," said the brother, "but the way will be opened; I feel it. Tom goes with these friends the last of this month, to look around, earn what money he can, build us a four-roomed cabin for the present, come home for the winter, and in the year 1877—God willing—we will all go. I shall try to lease the farm—selling is out of the question—and begin life anew."

Aunt Hetty tried to grasp the situation, but it was too much; she could only fall back on the ruling thought of her narrow life, "what will the people say?"

"I know what they will say, Aunt Hetty," said Bob. "They will say, I wish we were going, too!"

The ice was broken and beginning to melt; Aunt

Hetty wanted to do what was right, and in a softer mood she bade them goodnight.

Things went on in the usual way, and very busy thèy all were, Aunt Hetty helping in the housework, leaving mother more time to sew. A few days after the aunt's return a neighbor, passing, handed Bob the mail he had brought for them.

"Why!" said he, "here is a letter for Tom from the Wilsons. I'll run to the field and give it to him." Away he flew, the bearer of news, but what? It took but a moment for Tom to read Mr. Wilson's short letter, but he could not understand it. It read as follows:

"Dear Tom: I send the enclosed letter. It is fine, and I am sure you will accept it. We will be there to visit you the 25th, and expect you to be ready to start with us the 27th, for time is short, my boy, for all we have to do.

"Your friend,

JOHN WILSON.

"P. S.—Dick says, hurry up."

Tom found there was another letter from Mr. Smith, which, when he had read, he waved in the air.

"Come, Bob! you blessed bearer of good news, let's go to father." The father saw them coming and waited. Was the prayer answered?

"Father, father! Read that!" The father read, though his eyes seemed suddenly to become dim, and he looked away to the distant hills. "That's good, my boy," he said. "Go and show it to your mother."

Tom started to go, but turned back, and with all the affection a son can have for his father beaming in his face he held out his hand. The father clasped it and said, "I am so glad, Tom, for your sake, that it came this way."

The second letter read:

"Dear Friend Wilson:

"I have a chance to send you a letter in the morning, so will write a few lines and tell you how I am longing to see you.

"I received your letter in which you say a young man just from college is fully equipped for the work as surveyor.

"Now, I want him to come. From your description of him, he is just the one we need, so make sure of him. You see, I have lots of work that needs to be done at once. You write him that I have sent the money in advance for the work he is to do for me; it will likely come in handy, for he will have to get a set of surveying instruments—better get the best; it will pay—then all his traveling expenses. If what I send is not enough, I will rely on old-time friendship and ask you to supply the rest. I will pay you when you get here.

"I have my family here now, so a warm meal and a good bed will be ready for you all. We appreciate such things out here.

"Your old-time friend,

"SMITH."

Tom went to his mother's room, where he found her busy sewing. "Read that, mother dear." Then he drew a low chair in front of her so he could see the happiness steal over her face. There are many who enjoy watching a bright sunset. There are some who, like Tom, have enjoyed the rare privilege of seeing a loved mother's face light up with joy—there is nothing sweeter on earth.

"I knew it, my son. I knew it before the letter came. And just to think! you will really be using your own money."

Aunt Hetty was quite overcome by the unexpected way in which the money came. She soon became interested and helped by wise suggestions, as though to atone for the wrong in the past.

CHAPTER IV

GOODBYES ARE SAID

In the country where the Bartons had lived all their lives, and their ancestors for several generations, a change so radical could not but cause some comment. The people were not only interested in the welfare of this family, but the news they heard startled them as from a deep sleep. The question came to some as they worked in the field, "Is there no other way but this continual grind year after year?" and as they looked away to the distant hills, they sighed, and wished they, too, could see a way out to try newer paths. A few began to cast about to see if there was not a possible chance for them to follow the example set, which showed they were waking up, were feeling that mighty force that has moved and will move the human heart for better things.

The news of Tom's going sped rapidly, and many of the neighbors came in the evenings to talk over this move, so new to them all.

Some, like Aunt Hetty, were slow to believe there was anything better than the old way, but the new thoughts and viewpoints presented by Tom and his father to these gatherings of men and boys were like the pebble thrown into the lake, which starts ripples that reach to the farthest shore, and their lives received an impulse which lifted their ideals, making it possible for greater accomplishments in the future. One neighbor, a strong, jovial man, DeLong by name, after listening to Mr. Barton tell the story of his own longing when a young man, said, with great emphasis:

"I just believe that is what's the matter with my boys, Jake and Harry. I have scolded and coaxed them by turns, and been at my wit's end to interest them in the farm work, but I am thoroughly discouraged. I was always content with things as they were, myself, and don't see any reason for a change, but if this is what they want—well, it would hurt, but they had better try their wings; they might get them singed, but that would do them good."

"Do you mean it, father?" asked Jake, who had listened dumbfounded to his father's remarks; "do you mean you are willing we should go?"

"Yes, Jake," and turning to Harry, who stood with eyes alight, causing a lump to come in the father's throat—he had never seen them shine as they did tonight. "You want to go, too, Harry?"

"Yes, father, and, forgive me, I was thinking I would have to run away, for go I must. I was thinking of mother."

"Wait until next year, boys. Let me get used to it a little before you go."

This father, so quickly moved to laughter or tears, met with a surprise next morning when, coming downstairs to begin another hard day's work, he called to his wife, who was busy preparing the morning meal: "You wake the boys, mother. I called, but received no reply."

"I should say not! They have been out for half an hour. Is there a circus in town?" But he was gone, meeting the boys with the pails full of milk.

"We beat you this time, father," said Harry, and the boys laughed at father's amazement.

"I fed the horses," spoke up Jake.

"Then I guess I will go back to breakfast," said Mr. DeLong, not knowing what to make of the change. Then suddenly a light began to dawn as he remembered the events of the evening before. That summer proved to the parents the wisdom of giving to the boys the opportunity to spread their wings.

On the morning of the 25th came the meeting of the two families whose interests in the future would be so closely connected. Mr. Wilson found Tom's home life all that he had been led to expect, and a warm attachment sprang up, which lasted through life. Tom proudly showed his instruments, the best to be found in the city, procured the week before, with other necessary equipment, while Bob stood by excited and observant. Aunt Hetty was fully converted to Tom's way of looking at things, and wondered why she had been so disturbed.

When the family was seated around the table for the last meal before the parting, little Mary made a suggestion. "Tom," said she, her face flushing, "don't you want to take Tige along to scare the bears?"

"Why, little sister, can you spare him?"

"Yes, if he is with you. You know I love you, Tom."

Though they all laughed, for it was either laugh or cry, the idea seemed a good one to both families, so Tige was loved and petted for a few minutes and given an extra meal.

We will not linger on the moments of parting, the few moments of silence with mother alone in her bedroom—we have all been through it, we who have helped to "blaze the trail." Even at that moment when the last goodbye is said, hope, as an angel, stands pointing to the hour of meeting again.

Father brought the spring wagon—the carriage was not large enough—and, with Bob to keep father company as he came back, and Tige, who was delighted to be allowed to follow, the little company started, Tom looking back and waving his hat as long as the dear ones were in sight. When they reached the station they found a number of the neighbors waiting to bid them goodbye. Jake and Harry were there, who, wringing Tom's hand, said, "Look out for a job for us; we will be there next year."

Several of the farmers brought their wives and children to see Tom off. There was one mother with her daughter who remained in their carriage. They knew Tom would come to them. The real parting had been the night before, but they had promised to see him at the station. "Here are some cookies I made for you, Tom," said the mother.

"Goodbye, Mollie; I'll be back. Remember what

you promised!" said Tom, as he held a hand that trembled. But the cry "all aboard" that always comes too soon on such occasions rang out, and Bob grabbed Tom's hand and said: "Goodbye, old man; I'll go with you next time." One moment, in which Tom whispered, "I'll make good, father!" and the train was soon out of sight, with its human freight rushing on to meet the realization of its hopes or fears.

CHAPTER V

THE JOURNEY

A little over a week had passed at the Barton home when Bob, who found time to go to the village postoffice himself, came home waving a letter, and a shout, "a letter from Tom!" reached the ears of his father in the field—he might have been watching; fathers have that way as well as mothers, some times. It took but a few minutes for father, mother and all to gather, to listen to Kate read the letter, as follows:

"Canon City, Colorado, July 2, 1876.

"Dear Home Folks:

"Here we are, all ready to start in the morning, early. I wish you could see us; we hardly know ourselves. I am sure Mr. Wilson and Dick look fine; they both laughed when I came out all dressed up—heavy shoes, with leggings, blue overalls, dark woolen shirt, drab canvas coat, with belt of cartridges and revolver around the waist. You need not worry, mother; the revolver will be used only to get game on our journey. Fresh meat will taste good cooked over our camp fire, we are told. We are fortunate in meeting two men, Ed and Sam Johnson, who are starting on their return to Ouray, having been there last season, and we will all go together. They were a help to us in getting our supplies, as they knew just where we should go to get the best. We bought three ponies and five burros. The burros will carry our baggage, except the blankets, which will be strapped on each man's pony behind the saddle. It will be better than a circus, Kate, to see us start. I do not feel a bit sleepy to-night. I tell you I am glad these other men are going along.

"This is rather a small town, but the people seem as refined as the people at home. You know we used to think no one except Indians and what they called cowboys lived here. I saw the state penitentiary last evening; it is on the edge of town. This afternoon, a tall, slender man, the editor of the 'Canon City Times,' was out looking for news. He seemed much interested when I told him where we were going and said he was thinking a great deal of going there himself. I told him I hoped to see him there. He thanked me, and, lifting his hat, said, 'Adios.'

"Dear mother, your love seems around and about me all the time. Father, we passed through so many kinds of country—some like ours, with sloping hills and green grass everywhere; then again, nothing but wide expanse of prairie, with no trees in sight, no grass, but here at the end of the railroad there are hills of bare rock, and just beyond them the massive mountains rise, and they say the sun shines three hundred and sixty-five days in the year. The air is light and invigorating—no wonder the people seem so wide awake.

"I must close and go to bed. Give my love to

Aunt Hetty, and tell little Mary she shall ride a burro some day, and that we are all so glad Tige is with us, though he does look a little homesick tonight.

"I will write again when we get to our journey's end. Love to everybody. TOM."

Before the sun was up, this company of five men, with their horses, and burros snugly packed, with Tige following close to Tom, began the journey so full of interest to them all. Many, many times during the next ten days, our friends had cause to be thankful they were blessed with the company of men who knew the road and the desirable camping places. They soon learned to build camp fires, set the coffee pot where it would not upset, stir the biscuit with a spoon, then bake in a "Dutch oven" with live coals under and on top. They lost their eastern appetites and dainty ways, and enjoyed this outdoor life, this roughing it, and found coffee drunk from a tin cup tasted better than from the finest china Then the biscuit, though sprinkled with ashes and without butter, beat even the bread mother made. The salt-side, fried to a crisp, made even Tige lick his chops, it smelled so good; and the gravy, made by stirring flour into the hot grease, tasted better than any butter. Oh! but it was fine, and whether it was breakfast or supper, their appetites were hearty.

At night, after a long day's ride, the animals cared for and the evening meal over, they were loath to leave the camp fire, for the stillness of the night.

the light atmosphere, the strangeness of it all, caused them to linger, especially Dick, whose love for all this outdoor beauty and grandeur was great. But when the blankets were spread for the night and the cry gone forth from those who had been over the road before, "everybody to bed, another long ride tomorrow," almost as their heads touched the hastily improvised pillows they were fast asleep, dreaming, if they dreamed at all, of home and dear ones, who, every night before retiring, would go to the door or window looking westward and pray God to care for and watch over these loved ones. Who dare say that these prayers were not heard and answered?

Morning found them rested and ready for another day's ride. This is the way one would tell it—one who has never known the exquisite experience of waking up in the early morning before sunrise on a summer day in the Rocky Mountains—to wake just in time to see the stars pull down the blinds at the first faint streak of light from the rising sun, to feel the freshness of pure air, laden with the aroma of brush and flowers; to hear the glad twitter and then the joyful outburst of song from the birds; to sense this joy of freedom in one's own heart; to look up with thanksgiving with no thought of having to be thankful; to feel so akin to nature, so at one with all its beauty and wildness, you have the feeling of being in a new world. Old thoughts and aims seem to disappear, or are so changed they seem new. Is it not an experience like this, rather than the new country, that changes the man or boy, for changed they are? Never again can they go back satisfied to merely live as their fathers have done before them, satisfied with the old ideas and old ways. They catch the spirit of the mountains, which ever points upward and onward, and they who hear and follow never regret the roughness of the road. These men felt all this as they traveled day after day on their journey westward, felt it, but as yet did not understand the change taking place in their thought. They did not talk much; the language of the past did not fit. A new country requires a new setting for expression. Right here is the secret the East has not learned, and never can, only as it passes through like experiences, why a man seems so different after being out West.

They had been out several days on their journey when they came, toward evening, to Cochetopa Pass, over the Continental Divide. Tom and Dick having become experts in preparing the meals, this work was left wholly to them. Tige, after a chase which well nigh wore him out, came back to the camp with a good-sized cotton-tail, which he proudly laid at Tom's feet. "Good for you, Tige," said Tom; "we will have something nice for supper," and Tige lay down to rest with one eye open, watching the cooks at their work. A little later, if our friends had been watching the Johnson boys they would have noticed they were more on the alert than usual, and went off together some distance, looking here and there as though trying to find something, looking around at the easterners and then smiling at each other. They seemed anxious for bedtime to come, though not making as much preparation for rest as had been their wont.

Mr. Wilson, before retiring, said to Tom, "Have you noticed how restless Tige is tonight?"

"Oh," said Tom, "he has rabbit on the brain."

"That may be the reason with him, but I never had such a time with the horses; they, too, seem restless. The men didn't say anything, so I guess it is all right."

Soon everything was quiet. Three of the men quickly fell asleep, for the ride that day had been hard, though they had not made as much headway as usual. Tige, lying close by Tom, growled as though having bad dreams, when the report of two guns caused the sleeping men to awake and stagger to their feet, too dazed to act. The dog, too frightened to even bark, whined at his master's feet, but a laugh from Sam and his brother brought them to their senses. "We caught him!" There, sure enuogh, lay a bear, whose tracks the men had seen early in the evening. Tom and Dick looked around apprehensively, making sure of their revolvers, for the darkness might be hiding a dozen others, but the matter-of-fact way the Johnson boys went to work, first dragging the carcass farther away from the camp, for the horses did not seem to know a dead bear from a live one, and were still wanting to break loose, quieted their fears, and a happy group they were when at the early meal the next morning they had bear meat instead of the usual salt-side for breakfast.

"Boys," said Mr. Wilson, "before starting out today we want to thank you for what you did last night, and we want you to show us the bear tracks. We have never had the pleasure of seeing any." So, after thoroughly examining what, to them, was a great curiosity, Dick said, "Tom, I guess we will be on the lookout for bear tracks after this."

That night they overtook a couple of freighters on their way to Ouray, taking provisions to the little camp. These men gladly accepted the fresh bear meat, and returned the compliment by bringing out a box of fruit they had stowed away in their wagon, which the party greatly enjoyed.

It did not take long for the two young men to tell, with wide-open eyes, of the killing of the bear.

"You just wait till tonight; we will tell you something bigger," laughed one of the freighters, Dick Collins by name.

When the evening work was done, the horses feeding on the fresh grass, the dog lying at Tom's feet, tired but happy, the stars shining overhead, a cool breeze blowing just enough to cause the camp fire to burn brightly, these men, with their rough clothes and tanned faces, with the enjoyment one always feels when talking to appreciative listeners, told of their experiences in the past year.

"But, to bed, you youngsters!" Sam said, as he covered the smouldering coals for the night; but, for the first time, Dick and Tom could not sleep.

With eyes as bright as stars, they thought of what they would do if they had the chance, and what letters they would write home when they reached their journey's end.

The next evening, about sundown, they crossed on to the Indian Reservation. The Johnsons were amused at their companions' uneasiness, shown by their taking every precaution in regard to their firearms, so much so, they felt a few words of advice were needed.

"Gentlemen," said Ed, "you don't need to fear the Indians; you have Uncle Sam back of you, but if you raised a hand at them you would have the whole tribe after you. They are friendly, and, in their way, kind. We must be friendly toward them, but don't let them for a moment see that you are afraid."

Next morning, as they were eating breakfast, two big Indians rode up, smiling and looking longingly at the food. Sam took a big biscuit, and, laying a slice of bacon on it, handed it to one of them. Mr. Wilson quickly reached over and gave likewise to the other. They expressed their pleasure by gestures, showing their finely formed teeth as they smiled. They lingered until the little company started on the day's journey, riding a few minutes with them, then muttering adios, left them, much to the relief of the newcomers.

Dick's eyes began to feast on the beauty of the valley as he silently rode beside his father. These men would often travel for hours without speaking;

the sense of sight seemed to obliterate the need of speech. Tige, fallen into the steady gait of the horses, seemed to be taking life very seriously. If he longed for a change, he never let it be known, but was always cheerful and ready. It was enough he was with his master, who sometimes would walk and let the dog sit on the horse for a rest.

The burro says very little, and faithfully plods along with its load, but when it does speak it seems to unburden itself at one effort. Its bray is one long, deep, mournful supplication.

A change came over the men. They began to feel a sense of ownership in the broad acres of fine tillable land they were traveling over. They remembered what they had read concerning this beautiful valley, and some time, before many years, they expected to have homes here—homes for mother and sweetheart. They forgot the weariness of the past nine days, their forms became more erect, their heads were lifted up, the feeling of a prince coming into his rights seemed to fill them, and when they spoke, although their voices were low because of the intensity of their feeling, there was the ring of the conqueror in their tones. It was inspiring to enter into this sense of ownership, to be in league, as it were, with nature in its bounty and wealth, worth all the privations of the past and future—another of the secrets the East has yet to feel. Dick pulled his father's sleeve as they rode slowly on—they felt no hurry now. "Father, let's build our house so we get the full view of these snow-covered mountains."

"Yes, my boy," said his father, his heart almost too full for speech; "yes, I was just thinking how your mother would enjoy that; your sister, too."

Tom looked up as father and son talked, and for the first time a sense of loneliness came over him, and he hastily brushed away the tears which came. He, too, felt the desire to talk it over with father at this time. "Tige, old fellow," he said, "are you homesick, too?" Tige wagged his tail a little, but it was not a joyful wag, and Tom knew it. "It's all right, Tige; they will come next year."

Just then Sam beckoned to them to stop, saying as they came up, "This will be a fine place to camp, right here by the river; plenty of wood and good fishing. We shall reach our journey's end tomorrow evening, before sundown." "Fishing!" exclaimed both boys in one breath, "but where will we get fishing tackle?" "We have all that is needed," said Sam, smiling. "You see, we have been over this road before." "Good for you," joined in Mr. Wilson, with much feeling. "The boys and I have been thankful every day since we fell in with you."

"That's all right," said Sam, "and I think, if you don't mind, we will let the boys go at once to try their luck, while we look after the animals and firewood. We are likely to have company this evening."

"Company?" exclaimed Dick, unconsciously feeling for his revolver. The men laughed at his warlike attitude.

"I would not be surprised," said Ed, "if at least

half a dozen of the nation's pets came to pay their respects tonight, but treat them as old-time friends and we will have nothing to fear. We are as much of a curiosity to them as they are to us."

The boys were more than willing to leave the evening preparations to their elders. Just as the men were wondering what luck the boys were having, they saw them coming, each with a good-sized string of trout, each boy happy, as the successful fisherman always is. The supper was fit for a king, Tom declared, while Tige, who had been in the river for a bath, lay by the fire to dry, with an eye on the "grub."

After supper, Sam and Ed seemed possessed with the desire to hurry with the work, though Mr. Wilson and the boys would have enjoyed watching the scenery better. Just as they were about ready to sit down, after replenishing the camp fire, without a sound, eight or ten fine looking, stalwart Indians came into view, smiling and gesticulating.

One, rather a short, heavy-set man, proved to be their chief, Ouray by name. These friends from the East did not realize they were in the presence of one of earth's noblemen, with many of the finest traits of character to be found anywhere. He was educated in a Spanish school, his word was law among his tribe, his face beaming with friendliness, a tried friend of the white man. He could talk broken English. The rest could understand what our friends said, but failed to make themselves understood, which amused the visitors very much. They would laugh and seemed to enjoy the white man's failure to understand. Sam and his brother passed around the sack of tobacco they had brought along for the purpose. All the Indians, except their chief, who neither smoked nor drank, enjoyed the hospitality. An hour passed, with but little conversation because of the impediment in the way, but who can say there was not a sense of oneness between them? A little of the oneness on the white man's part arising, no doubt, from his outdoor life of the past week or two.

Finally they all arose to take their leave as silently as they came.

"Well," said Tom, after they were gone, "that's something big to write about to the home folks, don't you think so, Dick?"

"I only hope they will believe us," replied Dick, "but we have passed through so much since we left home I am in a chronic state of amazement myself, so will not be a bit surprised if they think some things impossible."

The next morning, before the fire was started, they were surprised by the appearance of two of the visitors of the night before, one carrying a good-sized piece of venison, which he handed to Mr. Wilson, pointing back to the only house in the valley, indicating it came from Chief Ouray. No doubt was left in the minds of the Indians but that their gift was appreciated. A happy crowd they were as they set out on their last day's ride.

After riding an hour or two Ed turned on his

horse and stopped, signaling the others to do likewise. "Just see," said he; "talk of your broad acres back East; did you ever see anything to beat this?"

Outstretched before them was a valley nearly two miles wide, extending northward about thirty miles and gradually widening in the distance to perhaps ten miles, the whole apparently as level as a prairie, thinly covered with sagebrush, hedged in on either side by low mountain ranges, these affording the finest pasture in the world. Then, turning south, he pointed without a word to the distant mountains, with their mantle of snow. It was too much for artistic Dick, and off came his hat in deference to the magnificence of the view spread out on all sides of him. The artist's soul responded to the work of the Master Builder. "There," said Ed, "is the source of the water supply for this land." Quietly they resumed their journey until they came to the mouth of the Dallas, where they camped for dinner, their last meal before reaching their journey's end.

"It looks, too," said Mr. Wilson, "as though we were coming to the end of the world; there seems to be no outlet through these mountains."

Further they crossed the reservation line. Right in front of them on either side of the river were the outlined spurs of the higher mountains, enclosing the Hot Springs Park, where were a number of ranches already taken up and partially cultivated. Passing on for about six miles, the mountains gradually growing higher and drawing closer together.

closing up to a narrow canon the remainder of the way, about four miles. Wagons had gone through, and burro trains; there was nothing to be called a road, and often it was necessary to follow the bed of the river. On these horsemen rode, the Johnsons leading, the small burro train following, Mr. Wilson and the boys bringing up the rear. The thought of these tenderfeet was, what are we coming to? Their loved ones seemed very far away, but just then they came to an unexpected opening, like as a mother's arms opening to receive them, and, yes, they were there at last, in the vestibule of the mountains.

"Stop a minute," said Dick to Sam, and Sam, though not an artist, understood somewhat how the lad felt, and waited.

"Tom! Tom!" he said, and his voice trembled, "what a picture! Can an artist ever do it justice? And the journey—worth a man's life."

Then, turning to his father, he said, "Father, we are glad we came!"

"Yes, yes, my son; it's worth it all, it's worth it all."

In a few moments Mr. Smith, who had just returned from his work, met them with outstretched hands, and, leading them to the cabin door, called to his wife, a quiet, motherly woman, who made them welcome. A good supper, prepared by a woman's hands, was very acceptable to these eastern men.

CHAPTER VI

OURAY

A writer, a few years later, thus pays tribute to Ouray, "The Gem of the Rockies":

"Let us imagine ourselves entering the town of Ouray from the south. We have crossed the range of mountains separating it from Silverton, traversed the wondrous chasms, whose mighty walls tower heavenward for thousands of feet, stood on the brink of awful gorges and steep precipices, noted the mountain streams as they gushed out of solid rock far up above us, then dash down some terrific gorge to become mere spray before striking the massive rocks beneath. We have gazed far upward at the distant snow-clad peaks of the rugged giants of nature as they pierced the clouds and passed upward beyond our sight, and we now look downward upon the little village of Ouray, cradled in a lovely valley, surrounded by high, rugged mountains. Health and prosperity seem to have made themselves the presiding deities of the place, and we gratefully decide that we have arrived at a place where it were well to let the busy world pass on and away, while we rest in this paradise. And while we bask in the sunshine, gaze at the mountain peaks, view its caves and canons, breathe the fragrance of its flowers, or listen to its murmuring streams, we unite many a time in thanks to the kindly fate that led our footsteps to this garden of the gods, to this mecca of human pilgrimage.

"Endowed as Ouray is by nature with a health-giving climate, blessed with inexhaustible wealth and scenery surpassed nowhere on the globe, it is

LOOKING UP THE UNCOMPAHGRE FROM THE BRIDGE NEAR OURAY.

destined to forge ahead in population and wealth, in education and refinement, and in everything that contributes to the happiness of mankind. The town is about one and one-half miles in length, while its width is about one-half a mile. Southward we find Hayden and Hardin peaks, between which the restless Uncompahgre river finds its way. On the west are grouped a series of ledges surmounted by greater and more rugged heights; down between these and Mt. Hayden rushes Canon Creek to join the Uncompahgre. A little to the north, Oak Creek, leaping from crag to crag, loses itself at last in the onflowing river, while White House Mountain, covered with perennial snow, looks coldly down in silent approval. The amphitheater closes in the town on the east; from its walls Cascade Falls start from a dizzy height and are dashed into fragments when they reach the valley far below. There are many waterfalls, canons, caves and picturesque spots in and around Ouray which are a source of endless delight to the lover of nature.

"In writing of the surroundings of Ouray one should not fail to mention the Alpine flowers which lend to the peaks their wildest, sweetest charm. No language can express the beauty of the flowers which bloom all along the way, lifting their bright faces to the traveler at almost every step, nestling among the rocks wherever a resting place can be found, and uplifting their tender petals beside the snow itself.

"With all its sources of beauty and wealth, Ouray has justly earned its title of 'The Gem of the Rockies.'

"WILHELMINA."

BOX CANON, IN WINTER. OURAY, COLO.

CHAPTER VII

PLENTY OF WORK

The evening of their arrival several men, dressed in the garb of the frontier, came to the door to welcome the strangers, for the whole town knew the friends Smith expected had arrived.

"Come in! come in!" said Smith, "and get acquainted. We are pretty well fixed now. Mr. Wilson here, and his son Dick, expect to open an assay office at once, while this young man, Barton—Tom Barton—by name, is anxious to begin the work of surveying."

After a good night's rest, the men took a short stroll before breakfast, finding it difficult to find ground level enough to walk on. They found the air was very cool, being at an elevation of over seven thousand feet, and almost surrounded by snow-capped peaks. The sun traveled long before it cast its bright rays in the little park, which was hemmed in by high mountains. The streets were in a way laid out, enough trees cut down and brush cleared for wagons to pass.

After breakfast, Mr. Smith said: "Well, boys—we are all boys here—I have had my eye on a little cabin which has just been put up; it's not very large, but I guess it will do for the present. You three can bach together. You have your roll of bedding and cooking utensils—you are very fortunate, and then," with a smile, "you have learned to cook. I often think what a good preparation for the life here is the experience of the journey you have just taken. Just think how helpless a man would be if taken from his home in the East and dropped down here."

"I never thought of that," said Mr. Wilson, "but it surely has been a profitable lesson—or, rather, a series of lessons—eh, Tom?" And they all laughed at what seemed at the time no laughing matter.

They found the little cabin small but comfortable, their ideas of comfort having been greatly modified since leaving home. They were soon busy arranging their little office, kitchen and bedroom. It took some fine engineering, as Tom said, to make one room serve for every purpose, while Tige, who was in everybody's way, seemed well satisfied with his new quarters.

By noon the cabin was in apple-pie order, the sign, "Assay Office," hanging in the breeze, as also the sign, "Surveyor." Mr. Smith came over according to promise to talk things over with Tom. He liked the strong, manly fellow, and felt that each would be a help to the other.

"All ready, my boy, to begin work?" "Yes, sir," said Tom, "and I want to thank you in person for the kind offer you made me, sending the money in advance of my work for you. It was a great help, for I had not time to earn it myself, and I could not bear the thought of my parents being burdened with it."

"That's all right, my boy," said Smith. "I knew

how it must be with a boy just home from school. And now, to business. You have everything to work with in your line?"

"Everything," said Tom, proudly, "and I want to begin today."

"All right, I like your spirit; come. We will go and look things over. By the way, a man is going over to Lake City tomorrow and can take any mail you have ready."

That night, after supper, the last tin pan washed and put away, quite a number of the boys in camp came to call on the assayers and surveyor. They came not only for a social talk, but for business, with their pockets filled with what to the untrained eye were nothing but rocks. Some of the boys succeeded in veiling the intensity of their hopes, while others made no attempt to hide the joy of having made a big strike, each showing the other what they had found. When they had left, the newcomers had quite a little work to do, and more promised.

"Now," said Tom, "no going to bed yet. Smith told me a man is leaving for Lake City tomorrow; that we can send out letters by him." Weary as these men were, they sat down on their bedding to write home, only short letters, but oh! how full of love and cheer. Tom wrote:

"Dear Loved Ones at Home: Here we are safe and sound in the most beautiful place I have ever seen. Have no time to describe now, only a few minutes to write. We are well and happy. Mr.

Wilson and Dick, as well as myself, have all the work we can do for some time; more in sight.

"A crowd of the campers was here in our cabin this evening to get acquainted and bring work for us. I am busy already with Mr. Smith, whom I find a very fine man to work for.

"Mr. Wilson and Dick say, 'Tell them we are glad we came, and glad they are coming soon, and send our regards.' Will write more next time. This is a great life we are living now. With love to you all, TOM."

The days that followed were busy days, everyone was busy, every moment precious, there was so much to be done in a short time. The months go rapidly in a new camp where time means so much. New discoveries were being made every day, keeping the camp in a state of excitement. Tom settled down next evening, though there were others in the office talking to the assayer, to write a long letter home, which ran as follows:

"Dear Home Folks:

"I am well and hope you all are. You want to hear about my trip? I would not be able to tell it in a year, it is so big, this journey from the East to the West; you will enjoy it more if you wait until I come home, then during the long winter evenings, when the fire is blazing in the grate, we will live it all over together; it will be fine. I believe one of the secrets of the West, which makes life worth living, is that we have to live in the present; a dreamer who lives in the future has no business here; in fact, such a one must either wake up or clear out. The very atmosphere seems charged with the intense activity shown by the people. I am beginning to feel it myself.

"You would laugh, Kate, if you could peep in here. We have a door to our cabin, because it is an office, I guess; one little bit of a window—three panes of glass strung in a line. This one room—office and kitchen in the daytime, bedroom at night. Tige shares my bed when he is not out hunting. We are all three busy, and work in sight for the rest of the summer; men coming in every day or night with more work. Mr. Smith very kindly offered to let me work half of the time for others, for there is great need of work in my line being done at once.

"During last winter, two men, George and Ed Wright by name, came over from Silverton on snow-shoes and staked off a claim, 'The Wheel of Fortune,' which promises as well as any location in the country. The first discovery here was 'The Trout and Fisherman,' by Staley and Whitlock. The story, as told to us, was that they were fishing one morning before breakfast and noticed the signs which ran into the stream. They did not wait to eat breakfast before making the location. A man by the name of Begole, one of those quiet men one likes to have around, discovered the 'Cedar' and 'Clipper' lodes first, but did not locate them until after the 'Trout and Fisherman' were discovered. And I could go on, but you would not be as interested in this as we are.

"I must tell you, though, we rode over the land which will be ours before a great while. I wish you could see it; but you will. It is so fine, and the snow-covered mountains are in full view; just think of that, dear mother. We will have our house facing the mountains. Then the river, the Uncompahgre River, will sound like home.

"While in camp the last night of our journey, a number—I forget how many—of these big red Indians came to call on us. We had just finished our evening's work and were sitting by the camp fire when, without a sound, these men, only half dressed, came and sat down by the fire. We could not understand a word they said, except the chief, who spoke broken English. I tell you, Kate, I felt the chills run down my back, but the Johnson boys had told us we must not let them see we were afraid, and be friendly with them, but I couldn't help thinking how Bob's eyes would stick out, and Aunt Hetty's nose go up, if they were with us. I had to laugh at the thought. I stopped, for the chief looked up at me rather sharp, I thought, so, like the little boy we read about when we went to school, Kate, I tried not to think anything bad. The next morning, before breakfast, two of them brought us a chunk of venison. That reminded me of you, dear mother, sending something nice to a new neighbor.

"And, father, as we were traveling over the land which will soon be open for us all, I saw Dick and his father talking—planning where they would build their house, and tears came. I could not help it; I wanted to be talking with my father, too. Tige felt as bad as I did, tried to wag his tail, but gave it up and whined. And then again, father—bother the light, is it going out?—when we came into this beautiful park, at the end of our journey, Dick and his father grasped each other by the hand, too full for words, while I stood by, lonesome, and wanted to see your face light up as did Mr. Wilson's.

"I must close, with a homesick feeling for you all. TOM."

"P. S.—Tell dear little Mary I love her, bless her! But I am glad I came, glad to feel the thrill of this stirring activity. The roads are fearful; we were glad we came horseback, but a man, Otto Mears by name, is busy, though not making much headway as yet in overcoming this obstacle.

"TOM."

CHAPTER VIII

OTTO MEARS, THE ROAD BUILDER

Honor to whom honor is due.

In the opening of a new country, wagon roads are indispensable, and more especially in such a rough and rugged one as this. When the mineral wealth of these mountains was discovered by the pushing prospectors, with their earthly all on a burro's back, the nearest town of any size was Saguache, and between the new discoveries and this place there was no road. Roads there must be, burro transportation being too slow, and Otto Mears and Enos Hotchkiss undertook to build a toll road to Lake City, the principal town of the region. The need was urgent, and no pretense of building a finished road was made. After locating the route, the immediate object being to make a road or trail over which it was possible for a wagon to travel, to be finished later as circumstances would permit. This was pushed through as rapidly as possible, and naturally those who were among the first to pass over it were not particularly loud in their praises—the tenor of remarks being in the other direction.

Illustrating this phase of the matter, a story is told of how Mr. Mears one day while passing over the road in a buggy met a couple of unfortunates with their loads fast in one of the mud-holes with which the road was abundantly supplied. Accosting them in his usual cheery manner, he asked what the trouble was, and received in reply such an impassioned description of the character of a man that would collect toll for passing over such a road, and what ought to be done with him, that he immediately fell in with their views. Soon he was asked if he had seen this man Mears, who was reported somewhere ahead on the road. He replied he had seen him about ten miles back, and they would soon meet him. With this assurance, and a cordial wish for their success, he drove on, leaving the poor fellows in their wrath as well as in the mud.

Again, one day, he was riding over the road in one of Barlow & Sanderson's coaches, and, happening to be the only passenger, the driver thought he would give him the full benefit of his own road. So he lashed his horses and took especial care to hit every stump and rock in the road, and gave his passenger a thorough shaking up. Arriving at the station where they were to change horses, Otto crawled out, yawned and stretched himself, and said, most innocently, "Oh, but I had such a beautiful sleep."

No sooner had the road been made fairly passable than there arose the necessity and demand for a branch road from Indian Creek to Ouray, and Mears tackled this. Then the San Miguel section came in with the same urgent need, and he built the road down Leopard Creek and up the San Miguel. Later still, he built the road over Marshall Pass, shortening the distance to the railroad by many miles. We believe he built every wagon road leading into the country.

In the building of these roads Mr. Mears contributed a great stimulus to the development of this country; in fact, we believe his work did more toward that end than that of any other individual. Probably no man who passed over these roads in the early days but paid his respects to Otto Mears, mentally or orally, often not in any complimentary language, but not one of them survives today, we believe, but would render to him the full measure which is his due. That he was supposed to have made money out of these ventures is not to his discredit, but goes to show his foresight and sagacity. He saw the need, and supplied it, and in so doing became a public benefactor, while thousands of others waited for something to turn up.

CHAPTER IX

A DISCOVERY

A few days after they were well settled down to work Mr. Smith wished Tom to take his instruments to a small gulch near town, where there was some work to be done.

"I can't go with you, Tom," said Smith; "see if Dick can, and when you have done that we will call it a day's work. You might like to do a little looking around yourself."

Mr. Wilson was glad to spare Dick for such an outing, and a very pleasant sight it was to see these two young men walking together in perfect confidence.

"Tom," said Dick, as they began to climb the gulch, "do you have any idea what I am going through? My fingers fairly itch, and I find myself unconsciously reaching out for my brush; I am fairly intoxicated with all this beauty. While I am helping father with the ore, in my mind I am busy sorting my paints. Why, Tom!" and his voice broke, "this beauty seems to be inside instead of outside of me, and the desire to express it on canvas is so intense I feel I cannot live if I am kept back much longer. I know I did not come here to paint pictures, but God has made things so beautiful."

"Dick," answered Tom, and his voice broke, too, "forgive me; how you must have suffered. I did not know; how could I? You must have the chance. Can you wait until tomorrow?"

"Yes! Yes!" said Dick. "I feel better already. This outburst has done me good."

Soon they were busy with their surveying. After a hasty lunch they were at it again. Dick was his natural self. They laughed and sang the old school songs. How many, many years it seemed since they left school. Finally they gave their college yell. They never knew how many were startled and fe for their revolvers, thinking it was the Indian war whoop.

"Only half past two, Dick," said Tom, "and our work is finished. Now let us do a little 'looking around,' as the boys say, and if we find something good today, we share it equally, shall we?"

"Yes, Tom," said Dick, and the two boys clasped hands. Jesting and fun were set aside. It was not intense greed for gold that actuated them, but the natural desire to do their best in discovering the wealth these mighty mountains were holding for them. Just like the great truths of God, the wealth of the mountains have always been with us, but only by seeking do we find what they have in store. The boys were well equipped through the knowledge gained at school for just such work, and they kn how to apply that knowledge. Putting out of though for the time the beauty of the scenery, they studied the formation of the mountains, then the rock itself. Instead of looking down at first, as one would naturally do, they took a long survey of the hills as a whole, then with a signal from one to the other the boys parted, one going lower down, and the other higher. An hour passed, and still they worked, boys no longer, but men earnestly bringing all the understanding they possessed to bear on their work. All at once a shout from Tom brought Dick scram-

BOX CANON, LOOKING IN. OURAY, COLO.

bling down to find Tom on his knees nervously pushing away the soil from some queer looking rocks.

"See there, Dick."

Dick gave a long whistle, then clapping Tom on the shoulder said: "Good for you, it's a great find. We had better keep still until we get father."

"Suppose you go and bring him. We must finish this up before dark," and Tom's voice was low and shaky.

"All right," and Dick put two or three bits of rock into his pocket.

Soon the father and son were back. "Why!" exclaimed Mr. Wilson, as he silently scanned the formation, "you have struck a rich vein, my boy, and I am glad for you," as he grasped Tom's hand.

"But," said Tom, his eyes shining, "this with all it may hold is Dick's and mine together, his as much as mine; that was the bargain, was it not, Dick?"

"I believe it was," said Dick, with husky voice.

"Then to work, boys. We have not much time, the sun is going down already." It took but a short time for the experts to set their stakes and locate their lode.

As though to celebrate the event, Tige, having been prospecting himself a bit, came bounding to them with a rabbit in his mouth. "Why, Tige, old fellow," said Tom, "did you want to be in on this, too? Well this is enough for one day, let's pack up the things and get home."

The news quickly spread, and the cabin was too

small to hold the men who came flocking in that evening to congratulate the boys. Smith and his wife came, overjoyed to think it was "these young boys" who had struck it.

"What are the boys doing?" asked Smith.

"Writing to their folks at home, of course," said his wife, with tears shining in her eyes.

And so they were. Here is Tom's letter:

"Dear Home Folks, One and All:

"We have struck it, Dick and I. A silver mine, mother dear. We shall not be rich immediately; at first we thought we would, and so glad I was you and father would not have to work any more. On examining the ore, one of the old miners who came in this evening said it was a good find, all right, but would be slow in giving up its treasures, and offered to lease it for one year, he taking what he found in payment for the work done. Mr. Wilson advised us to lease, and then the opening of the mine would be off our hands. So, dear mother. 'Our mine,' we will call it—never mind about a name —is going to help us in time. I must close, for in spite of all the excitement, I am sleepy. Tell Aunt Hetty she shall have a pony instead of a burro to ride.
TOM."

The next morning while Dick was gone after a pail of water, Tom told Mr. Wilson of Dick's artist longings.

"I never thought of that," said the father. "These mountains are enough to set any artist wild for his brushes." So after breakfast, when alone with his son, Mr. Wilson said: "Dick, my boy, I want you to begin to put on canvas, if you can, your first impression of this little park, of these grand old mountains."

"Oh, father," and the catch in Dick's voice showed the father how much it meant to him, "do you think you can spare me?"

"Dick," said his father, "money is not everything. This gift you have is worth more than money. I want you to take one afternoon a week for anything you want to do in that line."

"All right, father, I will see that our work does not suffer."

And so, in the stillness, broken only by an occasional blasting of rocks or the passing of a miner intent on his work, Dick would sit for hours once a week expressing on canvas his sense of the beauty around him, Box Cañon was a source of delight and later of profit to the boy.

CHAPTER X

HOW THE FIRST NEWSPAPER CAME TO OURAY

The boys and Mr. Wilson were rushed with work, and as a result of a long talk one evening, Tom wrote to his people this letter:

"Dear Home Folks:

"We have been talking it over, and it seems the best thing we can do is for Dick and I to stay here this winter. Yes, dear mother, I know it is a great disappointment. You see there is so much to be looked after and the work is crowding. Mr. Wilson will leave us in charge of everything and start for home in three days, then you and they will come next summer together. I am sorry. I have been looking forward to this homecoming. Never mind, dear ones, we shall meet next year. I do not feel like writing any more. TOM."

When this letter was received, there were many tears shed, even Aunt Hetty felt the disappointment keenly, but when Mr. Wilson stopped over one night on his way home, with the Bartons, and told them how well the boys were doing and how much better it was for them to remain at the camp, they felt better about it. The neighbors came to listen to Mr. Wilson's story of the trip and the finding of the mine. DeLong, with his two boys, were among the first. A change had come over this father. He had learned the lesson so many are slow in learning. that the children, as they grow into manhood or womanhood, have longings that should be respected. The awaking to consciousness of ability to be and do is individual. And wise the parent or guardian who steps aside, and with bated breath, as it were, keeps from interfering. If their work has been well done up to this point there will be no need of interfering any more than in regard to the development of the body. The moment DeLong saw his boys' need and bravely met it, that moment they and the father became comrades, each working for the good of the other.

Mr. Barton, in introducing the DeLongs to Mr. Wilson, said, "Here are two young men longing to go to this new country; do you think there is room and work for them?"

"Indeed there is," said Mr. Wilson, as he grasped their hands, "plenty of room and plenty of work. It is such as you, with your strength and good will that we need. When do you go?"

"Next summer," said Jake.

"All right, we will see that you get work."

Early in the evening little Mary went up to Mr. Wilson and laying her hand on his, asked, "How is Tige?" "He is doing fine, big and fat. He will be lots of company for the boys this winter."

"I'm so glad," said Mary, her eyes glowing with love for Tom and the dog.

After Mr. Wilson's departure the little family settled down for the winter, receiving letters from

Tom as he had opportunity to send them. A letter received from him in January, 1877, read as follows:

"Dear Folks:

"We are having a fine time, work and pleasure seem to go hand in hand. I will give you a few items. November 13, 1876, Ouray had its first wedding, Dr. R. L. Wood to Miss Josephine Hadley. We boys—there were quite a number—woke the echoes of these grand old mountains with the charivari we gave them. November 23 the first white child was born. He is the son of Captain Cutler and his name is Harry. We kept quiet that night, and a few days after the father let us boys, who were homesick, take a peep at the little mite with its chubby fists all doubled up ready to fight with the best of us. I thought of you, Bob. I remember how bad I felt when I saw you the first time. I couldn't get it into my head that you could ever grow big like other boys. You see I was mistaken.

"Then there is a kindly lady who came a short time ago, the wife of Captain Cline. We all call her Mother Cline, she is so kind and motherly. She has taken pity on Dick and I several times and given us a square meal. I tell you, mother dear, a meal prepared by a woman nowadays seems mighty good.

"There is another dear lady, her name is Mrs. I. Y. Munn, reminds Dick and I of the ladies we met while attending college. She has taken a fancy to my chum and I. She has two sons, Charley and

William, manly boys, near our age, a little older perhaps.

"Another lady we have met, a Mrs. Morris, who has the honor of being the first woman in Ouray, and is proud of the fact. A school has been started by a young lady by the name of King.

"Near our cabin is a man by the name of Theron Stevens, a very pleasant man to meet, runs a blacksmith shop. He often comes in the evenings to sit with us, tell stories and inquire about our mine. He says it's a good one, all right, and sometime we will be rich.

"Then there is another gentleman with whom we pass some pleasant hours, a Mr. Geo. A. Scott, who erected one of the first cabins in the town. I know, father, you will be glad to meet him. How proud I shall be next summer when I introduce my family to these friends.

"Then Kate, you should have been here on Christmas day of '76. A public dinner was given to all miners and everyone who was pleased to come. It was fine. The ladies served the dinner in style and, though it seems impossible, the reports say there were three hundred who partook of the splendid dinner, which was given in a butcher shop used by 'Shorty Davis.' At night we had a grand dance—not one of those society affairs where you cannot speak to a lady until properly introduced, but where everyone has a hearty clasp of the hand and an honest 'glad to see you' to give. Some men, Harry Adsit and others, who came over the range from Silverton to attend, had a hard trip on their way back, poor fellows; they were three days making it to Mineral, about ten miles. They came near perishing.

"I wonder if you, Aunt Hetty, would have danced with these roughly dressed men—most of them left their white shirts where they belonged, at home. The ladies looked very nice, although they were minus the accustomed long-trained and low-necked dresses.

"With love to all. TOM.

"P. S.—A story is told why the hill east of us is named 'Vinegar Hill.' Christmas of 1875 was duly observed by some of the boys, who gathered at Long and Cutler's cabin and enjoyed an excellent dinner. None of the fluids which are by some considered indispensable on such occasions could be had, consequently vinegar was used instead. And the boys then and there christened the place Vinegar Hill.

"But I must close. You see, we are among friends. Kiss dear little Mary for me. TOM."

The year 1877 was a memorable one for Ouray because of the rapid changes taking place. The East was waking up to the advantages of the West, and those who, having heard the call years before and came as far as they dared, quickly decided to push farther on.

The first municipal election was held April 2, 1877, and H. Reed, I. Lobach, Dr. Dobbins, J. F.

Dowling and T. W. Hammond were chosen trustees, Geo. A. Scott, town clerk.

Rev. C. L. Libby preached the first sermon in Ouray, in Jesse Benton's uncompleted saloon building; boards placed on beer kegs and liquor packages around the walls served as seats for the congregation.

In the same year the first printing outfit was brought into Ouray, the first newspaper in the Uncompahgre Valley, by Ripley Brothers, who had published the "Canon City Times" for several years, but had now decided to cast their lot with the interests of this new country. We will let them tell the story of how the first newspaper came on this side of the range.

A PIONEER NEWSPAPER

One morning early in May of the year 1877, a train of six wagons pulled out of Canon City, their objective point being Ouray, in the San Juan Mountains, a new mining camp just coming into prominence. The way led over some two hundred miles of mountain road—that is, some of it could be called road, but most of it was a libel on the word—across the Continental Divide and two other minor ranges. The wagons were loaded with the presses, type, and other appliances which go to make up a complete printing office; in fact, the entire plant of the Canon City Times, which had been published there for about five years.

The first portion of the journey, that is, as far as Saguache, was over passably good mountain roads, and good progress was made, but it did not take long after leaving Saguache (Si-watch) to convince us that we had scarcely got started. There was supposed to be a toll road between Saguache and Lake City—at least, at frequent intervals we were held up for toll—owned by Enos Hotchkiss and Otto Mears, which consisted principally of a wagon trail cut through the timber where necessary, elsewhere of swamps and mudholes which one dreaded to enter for fear of never getting out. There were grades up and down, which tended to make one's hair rise, and at frequent intervals there were mountain torrents to cross, some bridged, others unbridged, and as this was the season of high water, very often those streams were far from inviting. However, by helping each other, we got through the mudholes and up the grades, at length reaching the mouth of Indian Creek, where we were to leave the Lake City road.

Crossing the Lake Fork of the Gunnison on a substantial bridge, we made the ascent to the Blue Mesa by "doubling up" the recently completed grade, for which we had to pay another assessment on reaching the top. From here on the so-called road was so villainous that we reached the conclusion that so far we had traveled a pretty fair road. All the road there was being the wagon trail made by Uncle Sam's mule skinners and in moving the Indians from Los Pinos to the new Uncompahgre agency, and such other unfortunates as had to pass over it. Many who read this will know how careful these U. S. drivers are in selecting their routes. Up one hill and down another. If six mules are not enough, put on twelve, and call all hands to keep the wagon from upsetting when necessary. The ordinary wagon is not built on the army plan, as many a poor fellow learned in attempting to follow their tracks. The Big Blue and Little Blue hills were the terror of the road. You could get up these hills if you had teams enough to move your load; if not, you must unload to the capacity of your teams and make as many trips as necessary to get your load to the top. Likewise, you could get down, with decorum and good luck, by locking both hind wheels and chaining a good-sized tree to the hind axle to ease your descent. Past these in safety, you felt you were equal to anything, and, in truth, you have surmounted the greatest obstacles. From here on is comparatively easy going. Down the Stumpy and the Cimarron to the ford near where the present railroad bridge is built, and up Squaw Hill, another hard pull, and you look down into the Uncompahgre Valley.

While in Saguache it was our good fortune to meet Chief Ouray. After good naturedly inquiring where we were going and what we were loaded with, he strongly warned us to beware of the Cimarron fords, and said, "Keep well upstream; big hole down here." Obeying the advice so kindly given, we had no difficulty, but not long after a poor fellow who had not this information lost his entire outfit, and his life as well.

From the summit of Squaw Hill the road follows down Cedar Creek, which we crossed a hundred times, more or less. No bridges; you just went down into the creek and up the other side, if your team was equal to the strain. But there was "one more river to cross," and several times at that. Arriving at the Uncompahgre, just below the present Main street bridge, the river looked somewhat threatening, and as none of our party had been here before, a council was held. It was decided that one of the party mount a horse with the end of a long rope and ride across, the other end of the rope to be attached to the wagon if such precaution seemed necessary. But there was no necessity for such precaution, and all crossed without difficulty. Up the valley, following practically the present road, past Ouray's house and the agency at Colona, another question confronted us—whether to take the river road, with its numerous crossings, or to go over the Log Mesa. Climbing the long ascent and reaching the summit, we found it necessary to get down again, and had to resort to the same expedients as at the Blue.

Crossing Dallas Creek and the Uncompahgre Park, we entered the canon and made our way through the timber in the bottom, fording the river many times, and sometimes following the bed of the stream, until at last we made our way into the beautiful park where the camp is located. Carefully picking our way through the trees and stumps, which thickly studded the ground where the trees had been cut away, we received the glad hand of welcome from the good people of the town, who appreciated what the advent of a newspaper meant to them.

In due course, the several wagons of material were transferred to a log cabin, and presses, racks, type, etc., appropriately arranged for the work in hand, the preparation and publication of the first newspaper printed in the Uncompahgre Valley.

The first issue appeared on Saturday, June 16, 1877. It was named the Ouray Times, was owned and edited by Ripley Brothers (Henry and William), and gladly welcomed by the people.

A great day it was for Ouray when the first paper was printed. All day long men came to the office to see how things were progressing. The first copy, as was usual in such cases, was put up at auction and sold for ten dollars. This brought forth much joking and laughter. Others came in and, grabbing a paper, rushed out to show it to the others. The paper was made as much of as the advent of the first baby, and well it might, for its travail in getting there had been long and hard.

That evening, while the editor was writing a letter home, Dick and Tom stepped into the office. "Hello," said Dick; "I believe I have met you before, Mr. Editor," and held out his hand. "Do you remember? Last July, near the Soda Springs at Canon City; we were leaving the next day for this place. When we told you where we were going you made the remark that you were thinking some of going there yourself."

"Oh, yes!" said the young editor, "I do remember. Glad to see you again. When do your folks come?"

"Next week," said Tom, with a catch in his voice.

"Good for you," said the editor, who was so quick to sense the situation. "And yours, Dick?"

"They both come together. Father went out last fall to bring them in; he knows the way, which will be a great advantage," said Dick.

"Have you a family, Mr. Editor?" asked Tom.

"Yes, a wife and two babies; they will come in the fall."

After they had left the office, Dick said, "Tom, a bright idea came to me a few minutes ago. The folks are going to send word by someone who may be coming in horseback where they will be two or three days before they get here. Let's close up shop, and, with Tige, go to meet them."

"Good," said Tom, "we will. I want to say, like the little girl who was shown over the farm for the first time, O! O! O! Don't we wish our mine was in full blast? Wouldn't Aunt Hetty be pleased?"

"Say, Tom," said Dick, "I have been looking around lately for a husband for that aunt of yours."

"Why, Dick!" said Tom, laughingly, "what is the matter with you? This light air seems too much for you."

"No, chummy, it's the light heart; just think what we will have soon."

"Yes," said Tom, breaking down, "home, mother, father, and all the rest. I can hardly sleep at night, and when I do I dream about it. I am too wide-awake tonight to sleep; let's talk about it."

They sat out in the starlight under one of the spruce trees which so thickly studded Ohlwiler's Park and talked of the homecoming, of what their loved ones would think of the log cabins they had built, the bedsteads built to the wall, made of small poles—one for Bob and another for little Mary and Kate; one made of rough boards for father and mother, no springs to be had for love or money, but the slats were well covered with branches of young spruce. Dick's bedsteads were made in the same way. They had made tables, chairs, and benches out of the rough lumber, not many, for lumber was almost as precious as gold, and only a little had as yet been brought into town. Little blocks of wood with three nails driven in the center for candlesticks, three for each house. Stoves, they had left for older heads to think about, but in the main room of each house was a big fireplace, with kindling already laid for a bright fire to welcome the weary homecomers. Together they went, each with a candle in his hand, to look over their cabins, as though they had not been there a dozen times that day. Proud they felt of their work, and well they might be. The whole town knew of this homecoming, and one lady had brought some white muslin curtains for the little front window, an another brought a little hanging plant to hang above the window in Tom's cabin, and someone else brought the same for Dick's. Tige went from room to room and back to the boys, uncomfortable and restless, for he could not understand.

"Well," said Tom, "we have done our best; I'm sure they will appreciate it all."

"Yes," answered Dick, "I can see, after their long, tiresome journey, how comfortable this will seem to them."

CHAPTER XI

THE PARENTS' HOMECOMING

As the boys were eating their supper one evening, a horseman rode up with the word that their folks expected to reach Ouray by the 21st.

"Hurrah!" cried Tom, jumping up and down in his joy. The next morning one might have seen these boys, with blankets strapped on their ponies, their eyes shining with pleasure, leaving town with their faces toward the north. People meeting them as they passed smiled, and felt their hearts grow lighter at sight of those happy faces. When nearing the Indian Agency, the boys met two men on horseback, and of them they learned that a company answering to the description given had just stopped by the river the other side of the agency. Thanking the men, the boys rushed on. In half an hour or less they could distinguish the little company. Tige, with more than his eyes to lead him, was the first to recognize the little party. With a quick bark, which told the whole story, he bounded to meet those he loved. Who can estimate the value of the love and devotion of a dog? The company were just arranging for the night when Tige rushed into camp. From one to the other, and back again, he went, until, worn out, he lay down at Mary's feet.

Words are too feeble to express the feelings of the weary ones.

Mr. Barton and Dick's father strained their eyes and ears, for well they knew the boys could not be far away. Just then Bob saw them turning a corner, coming as fast as their tired horses would let them, swinging their caps in the air and giving one of their college yells. Oh! the joy of such a meeting! But old-timers have all been through it. Thank God, it is not only the privations, the loneliness, the struggles, but the union of loved ones again we all have shared together.

There was so much to tell when the two united families, with Jake and Harry DeLong, whose faces shone with satisfaction, were gathered around the camp fire after the evening meal. Tom looked with surprise at Aunt Hetty, who seemed to have grown ten years younger since he saw her. She was sunburned, yet did not seem to mind it. Her laugh was heard as often as Kate's, and she seemed to have lost her fear of what others might say, and the narrow look on life had been broadened, by closer contact with nature. Kate, in her young womanhood, seemed full of the spirit of the mountains. Tom saw a change here, too, not the change he noticed in the aunt, but something that fills a young man with reverence for all womankind. The changes and struggles of the past year had changed her from a thoughtless girl into a thoughtful, earnest young woman. Little Mary was more lovely than ever. Bob was very quiet, but Tom knew, from past experience, quietness with Bob was only a calm before the storm. The father? Yes, there was a change with him that caused a lump in Tom's throat. He felt rather than saw, the old habitual quiet submission to the inevitable was gone. He presented the appearance of a man rejoicing in longed-for freedom, and often he noticed his father seemed to forget the presence of those around him as he glanced up at the mountains and across the valley, looking as though he realized fruition.

In Tom's eyes, his mother alone was unchanged, for love is unchangeable. Though she was tired and travel-stained, she seemed so clothed with the beautiful garments of love and peace Tom felt even more her sheltering mother-love. But this son, in after years learned, of them all, the mother had changed the most. The change began when she first knew, from her husband's talk with their boy, how the desire to leave the old for the new had been crushed. All the love of wife and mother rose up to bring about, if possible, her husband's life's desire. Hence, her answer to her son that evening when they talked of coming West: "It's all right, Tom, my beloved; you lead with your fresh young life before you. You see, it is not only you, but your father, who is going to have the desire of his life." From that moment this woman's thought had been changed from a quiet acceptance of things to an intense longing to leave no stone unturned that might bring about this change for her husband. After the first struggle and victory, she went about gayly, as when a bride, preparing for the journey. The neighbors wondered, but could not understand.

So the journey had been a happy one, and all sense of privation overcome before it was met.

Dick's heart was full and overflowing with gladness. He did not stop to notice as closely as Tom had been doing; it was enough that his parents and sister were with him again. His father seemed happy as ever, but he noticed his mother was very quiet, and complained of weariness, but when walking near the river alone with her, she said, "Dick, I am trying to keep it from your father, but I don't enjoy this wild life; I long even now to turn back." A cloud came over Dick's face. He thought of the log cabin he had prepared for them; it did not seem, looking at it with his mother's eyes, as nice as it did the day before.

"I am sorry, mother, for it will be hard for you. Why did not you tell father how you felt before you started? He would likely not have come at all."

"That's it, Dick. I knew he would not, and so I thought I must keep still."

"Well, mother, we must make the best of it now, for father's sake. How does Ruth feel about it?"

"Oh, she is young, and young people enjoy a change. I cannot understand how Mrs. Barton can be so happy."

Just then Mr. Barton came up to Dick and said: "Dick, have you any idea where Bob is? We have called and called and got no answer; we are all getting anxious."

Dick did not know, but while straining his eyes to see, for it was getting quite dark, he saw some distance away what seemed to be something moving toward them. He drew Mr. Barton's attention to the fact, when all at once they saw five or six forms steering directly toward them. He quickly told the ladies, company was coming. Aunt Hetty and Kate began at once to give their hair a few touches and pats, gazing at themselves in an imaginary looking-glass. Mr. Wilson smiled as he rose to meet the newcomers, for well he knew who they must be, but was a little surprised when he saw their leader. This was Bob, his eyes snapping with delight at the shock he was going to give Aunt Hetty. Bob had been told there was nothing to fear from the Utes, and when the bright idea flashed into his mind he went to a little company he saw sitting around their camp fire, and coaxed them by gestures to come and call on his people. So they came, nothing loath, three Indians with two squaws, each with a papoose strapped to her back. Quick as thought, Dick's artist-eye took it all in, a description of which he wrote to a friend, as follows:

"I wish you could have seen it. Some time I hope to picture it on canvas. The night was dark, though still; the sky full of clouds which partially hid the moon, making it look as though it had a nightcap on and was smiling at us. Right near were the horses, munching their feed, the wagons partly uncovered, as they were being prepared for the night; the fire, hastily piled high with dry brush, casting its bright light far and near, by its very brightness causing the shadows to seem more forbidding; the dog, Tige, standing by Mrs. Barton, with his eyes watchful and his jaws set, ready to be friendly or hostile. Our little company gazed almost paralyzed for the moment at the strange appearance of their visitors, who were smiling and gesticulating, their copper-colored bodies fairly shining in the firelight."

Bob knew Aunt Hetty was not only shocked, but horrified. Mrs. Wilson was disgusted, and even Mrs. Barton was glad her husband and son were near. Mr. Wilson and the young men stepped forward and welcomed the guests, telling them to be seated. The men sat down, but the squaws preferred standing. Mrs. Barton, Kate and Ruth, with little Mary, stood by them, praising the little fat papooses, whose black, beadlike eyes were bright and shining. Those mothers smiled proudly, as any other mothers, at the evident admiration of their babies—mother-love is the same the world over. Aunt Hetty and Mrs. Wilson kept their seats. Bob was happy in spite of his aunt's threatening looks. The visitors remained but a little while. After they had gone, Bob, with Tige, was starting to leave, but his father called out, "See here, Bob, you have done enough for tonight. You had better go to bed." Bob knew when to obey.

As the party started on its way early in the morning, even Mrs. Wilson smiled and seemed to enjoy the pure air and pleasant company. She, like her son, inherited much of the artist temperament, and the beauty of the surroundings appealed strongly to her. Toward evening, just as the sun was about to bid them goodnight, they entered the little town of Ouray. No one spoke. Tom and Dick watched with interest the look of surprise and pleasure both mothers expressed. A glance at his father caused Tom to look another way. On the face of his father was the expression of one who had at last reached home. Very slowly they wound their way through the little village, Jake and Harry riding the horses the boys had used, Tom riding in the wagon with his father, Dick in the other with his parents. As they were passing, several of the townspeople stopped them to extend the hand of welcome, causing the newcomers to feel they were among friends. Then, just as the mountain peaks were all aglow with the parting radiance of the setting sun, they reached Ohlwiler's Park, where two new log cabins stood. Instructions and matches had been given Bob and Kate, who jumped down and entered both cabins, lighting the fires, so that when the parents entered a cheery fire welcomed them.

"Why! why!" cried Mrs. Wilson, as her son led her in, "how beautiful." Poor Dick! Tears came into his eyes, but his mother never knew it was the sudden change from fear to joy which caused them. Yes, it was as Mr. Smith had said, the experiences of the journey were a good preparation for the privations of pioneer life in the home.

"I wish," said Dick, "I could have gotten some springs for your bed."

"Never mind, Dick," answered his mother, "we brought a feather bed."

"I am so glad," said the boy, a heavy load rolling off his heart. Turning to his sister, who was looking at the queer little candlesticks, he said, "What do you think about it, Ruth?"

"Oh, I think it's fine, Dick," she said. "This looks like a play-house to me. You remember how you and I used to play housekeeping?" "Yes," said Dick, "I thought of it when Tom and I were fixing this. How do you like Tom's people?"

"They are a lovely family. I hear he has a girl back home."

At the Barton cabin they were busy, too. Tom found that mother had a feather bed for Kate, as well as for herself. "That's good, mother dear; some time we will have springs. How do you like Kate's and Bob's bedsteads?"

"All right for the present, Tom. We will play that we are camping out this year—bless you, dear boy!—how glad I am to be under the same roof with you once more." Two happy families they were, and the whole town rejoiced over this addition to their number.

The next day Tom took his father and the younger members of each family, with Jake and Harry, to see the mine, which was a disappointment to the girls. "It is nothing but a hole in the ground," they told Dick.

"That's all right," he answered, "but you wait and see what comes out some day."

Bob and his father asked many questions of the men who were working in the mine. From them they learned the mine was "all right when a certain amount of work was done. You see, we are willing to work it for what we get out of it this year." "Say, boys," said the foreman, to Jake and Harry, who were looking on very wistfully, "Got any work in view?"

"Not yet," said Jake; "do you know of any?"

"Well, I need more help, and need it bad. Have you ever done any of this kind of work?"

"No, but we can soon learn, can't we, Harry?"

"You bet!" said the brother.

"All right," replied the foreman; "when can you come?"

"We are here already, Boss."

"You'll do," laughed the man.

So when the party returned they left the DeLong boys busy at work, their smiling faces telling how happy they were.

CHAPTER XII

DAYS OF DOING WITHOUT

These two families, like all pioneers, found there were many things they would have to do without—they were not to be found in town. They learned to do without, and it was surprising how many things were not really necessary. The girls even took pride in showing the boys what a nice dish they could prepare with "almost nothing." It was surely a great change for the Barton family, who, having lived on a farm all their lives, now had to do without eggs, milk and often butter. Seldom did they see a potato, but there was plenty of salt-side and gravy. Yes, and coffee and beans, but they were awake enough to the life about them to see the amusing side.

"Oh, we'll get acclimated, mother," said Tom, one morning when so many needs failed to be met. Not for herself did she mind, but for the little family. "You see, we have to get accustomed not only to the climate, but to the doing without."

Not only one or two families were "doing without," but everyone who came. It seemed to be in the air, and people in a way enjoyed it, and in later years vied with each other in telling the biggest privation stories.

There was quite a stir in the little camp that summer. Every day, either over the trails from Lake City or Silverton, or by the wagon road through the reservation, people were coming; buildings were going up as fast as lumber could be obtained; pack trains going to the mines loaded with supplies and returning with ore; everybody happy and prosperous.

PORTLAND CREEK CANON, UPPER FALLS, OURAY, COLO.

One evening early in October, Tom and Dick stepped into the newspaper office. The editor welcomed them with a smiling face. "Howdy," he said, "glad to see you."

"Why, what's the matter?" asked Dick. "Struck a gold mine?"

"My family will be here tomorrow," he said.

Dick gave a long whistle, while Tom grasped his hand. "Good for you," he said; "now you will begin to live."

"Yes," said the young editor, "this 'baching' is not living, it is merely existing." The story of the young wife's journey can best be told in her own words:

"All my life seemed to have been spent in coming West. Eleven years were spent in a village in England, when my parents decided to come to America. I brought with me the sweet memories of buttercups and daisies, beautiful groves and well-kept gardens; trees a century old; hunting the dear English violet at the foot of the hawthorn hedge in early spring; taking walks with my mother, who was to me the most beautiful lady in the world, up the lane and through the fields, living in a world where everyone seemed to be good and loving. Another eleven years passed, and I found myself bidding goodbye to this mother, who was weeping, for it seemed to her she was losing me forever, Ouray seemed at that time so far away. I remember as though it were only yesterday what a beautiful morning it was. I was too young then to under stand why anyone should shed a tear. I was so happy with the thought of soon being with my husband, it mattered not how rough or long the road. So, with my two babies, Fred and George, one in my lap, the other sitting by Uncle Tom, we started in a covered wagon with all the household goods we could store in such a small space. When we first commenced packing, the law of 'doing without' stepped in; no matter how much it was rebelled against, it stood its ground. The ride during the day was pleasant, but when the shadows of evening began to fall a sense of loneliness was felt. It was a new experience, sleeping in a wagon, Uncle Tom, with his roll of blankets, underneath. But when daylight awakened us we felt fresh and rested for another day's ride.

"One night we reached a house where people lived; the sight of people and flowers in the window seemed very good once more. While sitting in the dining room I was startled by the appearance of one of the women. She was tall and slender. her hair was white, her face very pale; she uttered not a word; when spoken to she did not answer. In the morning she was not to be seen, but I have often wondered what hard, strange experiences this lady must have gone through.

"As we were riding along that day, we met two men who felt proud over the capture of a good-sized mountain lion. When I saw the lion stretched on in the wagon the hills seemed full of them. But we never saw anything larger than a rabbit during the whole journey. That night we drove down into a narrow gulch, and, the horses seeming too tired to climb the hill, Uncle Tom decided it would be a good place to camp for the night. He unhitched the horses, while I and the babies sat down on the rocks, and he took the horses up the hill just behind us. He was gone quite a while and it was getting too dark to see anything distinctly. We kept looking behind us to see Tom come the way he went, when all at once I saw down the gulch in front of us, something moving our way. Its shape was fearful; still it kept coming nearer and nearer, straight toward us. I looked up the road Tom had taken, but what could I do? There I was standing with my fifteen-months-old baby in my arms, the other child clinging to my dress, almost as frightened as I. So, with a prayer to One who had never failed me, I stood ready to face the fearful thing. I knew not what it was until it was within ten feet of me, then it fell to the ground and Uncle Tom stood revealed. It was a big bundle of wood and brush he had picked up for our fire that night. I never said a word, but sat down, feeling very weak. I did not feel able to bear the laugh he would have over my scare.

"One morning we were climbing Squaw Hill; there were big boulders in the road, and the driver, in trying to miss one, failed to see another just in line for the hind wheel, and over we went, bedding and furniture on top of me and the children. When Uncle Tom jerked the canvas away, I saw he was very much frightened, so hastened to assure him that the children were not hurt, and I only had a sprained wrist. There was the task of unloading and reloading the wagon, so Tom decided to take the children and I up the hill first. When on top of Squaw Hill he made a fire and put the coffee pot on so there would be a warm drink when he came back. He put all the water he had brought in the coffee pot, for we could get no more until night. When the poor man came again with the loaded wagon the pot had upset and there was no coffee until night. We did not come to a suitable place to camp until dark, and it was raining hard. Uncle Tom made the children and I stay in the wagon while he fried flapjacks in the rain. For years I had lived on graham bread, but those sticky, half-cooked pancakes surely tasted good and never troubled me a bit. This dear old Uncle Tom confessed to me the next morning that he believed all the trouble of the day before was caused by his getting 'hot as blazes' with the horses early in the morning.

"The next day, after traveling a short distance, we met some colored soldiers swearing dreadfully. The moment they saw a woman they ceased swearing and doffed their hats. The question came as we rode along with little else to do but think, why cannot a man or boy be his best at all times, when women are not, as well as when they are, present?

"After awhile we passed the only house on the reservation, the home of Chief Ouray. He was outside, not looking as fine as when in Canon City, three years before, dressed in the gayly-colored garb of the chief; he entered my mother's house without knocking. I had just been combing my hair and it was hanging down loosely. He stepped behind me, and, taking all my hair in his right hand, turned to my mother with a smile on his face and said, 'Pretty! your papoose?' I felt the cold chills running down my back as I recalled Indian stories I had read. Now, as we passed by, I saw that he wore only common clothes, and looked very serious. Dear chief, he had much to try him, as I learned afterward.

"I whiled away the time telling the children tomorrow we would see papa. They never tired of listening to me talk of him. The next day, after a ride of fourteen days, we reached the pretty little town of Ouray. It mattered not how rough the cabin fitted up for us, it was home—the children with their father, the wife with her husband. The fire blazing in the big fireplace shedding a bright glow over the rough walls, and resting on the faces of the united family. Heaven seemed not far away."

As these experiences were told a little later around the supper table in the Barton home, Mr. Barton remarked, "I would not miss one experience we went through. They all seem to fit in so naturally as a part of this western life. I enjoy it all." His sense of enjoyment was to be sorely tried in the days to come.

The winter of '77 and '78 was a hard one, made so in part by the winter storms coming on earlier and more severe than usual. Some had been fortunate in getting in their winter's supplies, but the freighters, who, not being able to make the trip as quickly as expected, were overtaken by one of the worst storms of the season. Though doing their best, braving the storm when others would have given up, they finally were forced to leave their wagon-loads of provisions in the Blue Canon and come to town as best they could empty-handed, leaving the merchants with very little to meet the needs of the community. It was a never-to-be-forgotten winter, full of pathos. Winters before had been hard, but supplies had been sufficient, and very few women and children in camp. It was a time when old differences were forgotten, when the people's hearts were knit together, never to be separated. Soon after the New Year, sickness came to add to their discomfort. Tears come unbidden as the writer tells her own experience, tears of gratitude and love to those who earned the blessing, "In as much as ye did it unto the least." I remember I was down and dear Mrs. Crane and Mrs. Corbett called to see what they could do. Mrs. Crane bent over me and asked what I would like to eat. My reply was, "Some bread made by a woman." But it was too late when they came back that evening loaded down with good things; I can only tell what I was told or saw later. Forty nights willing watchers came to sit up and care for me, men and women. It was hard to keep it up, for during that time two others needed like attention; the whole community turned nurses; we were one big family; everyone wanted to do something. When the word was given out by Dr. Russell that I could eat fish, six men started out to fish that bright, but cold, March day. They failed to catch any fish, but one brought in a lone snipe, so I had snipe on toast. One woman, a foreigner, came over with an egg, the only one laid that winter. Mrs. Corbett brought the last cup of sugar she had in the house, not knowing when they would get any more. Mrs. Munn's son would come so loaded down with good things for me to eat and drink he had to kick at the door, his hands too full to knock. The Reverend Hoge had no flowers to bring, so he brought a little plant, its leaves so beautifully green. which my husband brought to my bedside, so I could touch the leaves and listen to the sermon they preached to my happy heart, for I was happy. Who could help being, with so much kindness shown? If I fail to give the names of others, it is not because my gratitude does not flow out to them.

One morning it was thought right for the children to be brought home. They had been lovingly cared for by Mrs. Cozens. I longed to see them once more. Thoughts of them had helped keep me from "crossing the range" by a shorter route than when we came to Ouray. I remember my husband coming in with George in his arms, while Fred ran on ahead "to see mamma!" The older boy stood by me with tears of joy in his eyes, while the younger crept quickly into bed by my side, where he knew he belonged. Some of the most beautiful pictures on earth are not those put on canvas.

As I was gaining in health and strength I found, while I was living on the very best, others were living on salt-side, with very little else. The time came when coal oil was three dollars a gallon, and the supply almost gone. Later, someone brought in a little graham flour and was paid fifteen dollars for a fifty-pound sack, we being allowed a sack because we had children. During the winter, when want stared them in the face, it was learned that the supplies brought in for one of the larger mines arrived too late to be sent up to the mine and were stored in town. The people tried to buy these supplies, but the manager refused to sell, with the result that the men broke open the storehouse and distributed the food among the people.

CHAPTER XIII

A Pleasure Trip

Mr. Wilson's home was far from happy. Mrs. Wilson, like the Israelites of old, was longing for the comforts of eastern life. When washing the dishes her tears would fall into the dishwater; when she sat by the river, as she often did for hours at a time, she envied the water its chance to go toward the ocean. She could see nothing but privation, nothing but a foolish idea on the part of her husband, this coming out West. The East had been plenty good enough for her. She turned the cooking over to Ruth; the "doing without" so many things in cooking annoyed her.

Mr. Wilson wondered if after all he had not made a mistake in coming, but the question at that time was not satisfactorily answered. What filled him with wonder was the contrast of the Barton family. The more they were compelled to "do without" the happier they seemed, not that it was looked upon as a joke by any means, but something we call real love and thoughtfulness of others seemed to govern. If there was no sugar for the coffee they were glad they had the coffee; if no butter, they declared they got a better taste of the bread without; if they became weary of salt-side, they laughingly said it made fine gravy. Even Aunt Hetty was a marvel to her brother, who did not yet understand how deep had been her repentance for the wrong done him in days gone by. Mrs. Barton, as she gave up all thought of herself for the sake of her husband's happiness, not only learned the secret of real happiness, but learned why this western life gave so keen a sense of freedom; she learned it was the getting back to the springtime of life, back to the reason why the birds always sing, why the cattle sniff the fresh air, why all nature rejoices together, and the tiniest blade of grass comes peeping up through the heavy sod. The stirring activities of nature and the stirring activities of life in the West have much in common. Happy is that one who turns from the hard side of pioneer life and feels the worn-out clothes of conventionality and century-old notions falling from him; not beginning life afresh, but learning the secret of real living; to feel akin to the birds and flowers, and trees, and—yes, the storms: with an appetite for food, not the way it is cooked; longing for a bed to rest upon at night, rather than of what the bed might consist; the thought broadening toward all mankind in seeing each, not as he seems but as he really is; to feel that open-heartedness that never stops to ask if there is enough for me and mine, but throws wide open the door to the weary stranger who comes at nightfall, giving the best, even if that best be but dry bread and coffee, with blankets unrolled on the floor. The opportunities of a new camp in the West are first given out by the hand of nature; happy are they who clasp and love that hand.

In the fall of 1878 it seemed best for the editor's

wife to spend the winter with her mother at Canon City. A few months later her husband followed her; but this trip can better be told in his own words:

A PLEASURE TRIP

On Monday morning, January 13th, 1879, a man with more courage than sense set out on foot from Ouray to make his way to Canon City. The reason for this rash act was his wife needed him, and the failure to receive promptly transportation over the buckboard line to Indian Creek. The ground was well covered with snow, the weather cold, and at least two men had lost their lives that winter through a similar venture.

The first day brought us to the Indian agency, where we were hospitably entertained over night by Chief Clerk Raymond. The next day, following a well-beaten wagon road across Dry Cedar, the old cut-off, we found we had taken the wrong road, the travel having been changed to the old road, and by so doing missed the buckboard, whose driver had orders to pick us up. Just at nightfall, after a weary tramp, we came to the old road, and were well pleased to find there two freighters, camped for the night, who kindly shared, as would anybody in those days, their "bed and board" with us. Most acceptable was their hospitality, for there was no place of shelter nearer than Cimarron, and we never could have made that. Bidding our hospitable friends goodbye the next morning, we made our way to the stopping place and stage station kept by

MULE TRAIN ON ITS WAY TO NELLIE MINE, NEAR TELLURIDE, COLO.

Capt. and "Mother" Cline, who made us captive for the night, and next morning placed us in the buckboard for Indian Creek, where, after a night's rest, we resumed our tramp the next morning and afterwards arranged with a freighter to take us to Saguache (Si-watch).

One of the never-to-be-forgotten features of the journey out is the night ride in an open buckboard from Saguache to Clearo. Starting from Saguache at six o'clock in the evening, out into the San Luis valley we rode. The stars shone brightly, and in their dim, uncertain light, the Sangre de Cristo range, appearing but a low range of foot hills into which we seemed certain to enter in a very short time, kept continually ahead and just to our right. Where the mountains were probably ten miles distant they appeared at most not more than half a mile. The ride was anything but pleasant. Under the most favorable circumstances a fifty-mile ride in a buckboard is not a pleasure to be longed for, but on a cold January night it is far from being desirable.

Reaching Bales' station, the stopping place of the stages between Canon and Leadville, at half past four in the morning, we found our old friend, Harry Kellogg, just about awakening the stage passengers who were to resume their journey at six o'clock. Two full stage loads there were making a raid on the breakfast table that morning, the larger number being on their way to the great carbonate camp. Boarding the stage, one of the Barlow & Sanderson six-horse affairs, the last stage of the journey was begun, and though preferable to the buckboard experience, was far from being a pleasure ride. Sixty miles in one of these coaches is somewhat of a "pleasure exertion." Night found us at our journey's end and glad enough to be with the loved ones.

When coming back in May they met Mrs. Wilson and Ruth near the Powderhorn, on their way East for a change. Each had much to tell the others. One bit of news given by Ruth was that Aunt Hetty had a beau.

"Yes, indeed," said Ruth, "and a time Aunt Hetty has, too, when Bob is around. He does so enjoy teasing his aunt. One night," and Ruth began to laugh at the remembrance, "Aunt and her beau were sitting on the sofa Tom made for his sister. They were busy talking, as lovers will, when a violent sneeze came from under the sofa. It took but a moment for the gentleman to drag poor Bob out. 'Plague take the dust,' said Bob, 'I was having such fun.' But Aunt Hetty was indignant, and led the dusty boy to his father, her eyes flashing fire. The father assumed a stern look and sent Bob to bed. As soon as Aunt Hetty and the boy were gone there was a good deal of silent laughter on the part of Kate and her parents. Why, I never saw such a boy; he keeps us all on the watch. But my, how he is growing, and he is doing so well in his school work."

Mrs. Wilson was losing her careworn expression; she was going back to the old home, the old life, and expected to fall back into the old ways, but she had yet to find, unconsciously to herself, she had grown out of many of them.

The spring of 1879 had opened early—none too early for the eager workers. Long trains of patient burros could be seen winding their way over the trails, loaded with supplies. As the mines developed the town prospered, since the mines were the life of the town.

The Barton family were happy, Tom and his father busy. They had been obliged to abandon work on the mine because of lack of funds, though all seemed to have confidence it would yet prove a good thing. A debt the father had incurred four years before, unknown to Tom until now, was being slowly paid off. The children were delighted to know school would soon be closed for the summer, there was so much of work and pleasure for all. Mr. Wilson and Dick were keeping house alone, with the kindly help of Mrs. Barton occasionally. In September there were hints of unrest among the Indians, queer stories being told. The town people were feeling anxious; they did not like the looks of things. Mr. Barton and his wife had a long talk over the advisability of her and the children going out for the winter or until the Indian question was settled. With tears in his eyes—for he had heard the talk in town—he begged her to go. Mrs. Barton said, "No, dear; we will stay with you, and meet everything together." Later, when talking it over with Kate, Hetty and Bob, they all declared they had no wish to leave their home.

TIMBER FOR THE NELLIE MINE.

"John said," and Aunt Hetty blushed, "we are just as safe here; Chief Ouray is able to control his people."

"Yes, John is all right," said Bob, "although he doesn't seem to think much of me; I don't see why. The fun, to my notion, is just beginning."

"What fun?" asked Aunt Hetty, getting very sensitive on one subject.

"Now don't fly off," said Bob, laughing. "I meant the trouble with the Indians. John is not the only person in the world. But say, mother, Aunt Hetty and Kate have been practicing with a gun for the last three months. Oh, I saw them, and knew what they were about; you can't fool me. Say, mother, when Aunt Hetty first tried her hand, she didn't know that I was watching; she turned her head clear around when she fired, didn't she, Kate?" and Kate was obliged to admit that it was true.

"No, mother," said Tom, who had just come in, "it's no use; we are not going to be separated again; we stand or fall together. I have written to Mollie I shall not go out to see her this fall, as I expected. I am needed here," and he gave his mother a kiss.

That evening they had cause to be glad their decision had been taken, the question of their going or staying settled.

5

CHAPTER XIV

"INDIAN TROUBLES"

The beginning of events which came so swiftly is portrayed in the following:

THE WHITE RIVER INDIAN TROUBLE

On October 3, 1879, the people of Ouray were thrown into a fever of excitement by the arrival of a special carrier with the following message from Governor Pitkin:

"Captain George J. Richards,
"Lake City, Colorado.

"White River Utes are on the warpath; have attacked the U. S. troops on reservation, killing Thornburgh and all officers but one. My impression is that the Uncompahgre Utes are peaceable, but the frontier settlers are so exposed that I desire you to send a courier immediately to Ouray and the Park to notify the people to keep close watch on the Indians, and to reorganize militia in Ouray. If there is any outbreak, then take your company to central point most exposed, get reliable information from Ouray and proceed with caution. Keep me advised. (Signed)
"FREDERICK W. PITKIN."

Messengers were immediately sent in all directions, and every effort made to prepare for the worst. The two companies of militia were reorganized, and every man was ready to respond to the call. Rifles and twenty rounds of ammunition were issued to each member of the militia. As it happened, there was no immediate danger, but so long as the attitude of Chief Ouray, who was believed to be friendly, was unknown, there was much uneasiness.

Dr. J. H. Lacy, physician at the agency, came up and made the following statement from the information brought to Chief Ouray by special couriers:

"The troops, which were proceeding to the White River agency, under command of Col. Thornburgh, were met about fifteen miles from the agency by a party of Utes, on October 1st, and a parley ensued. Thornburgh spoke in a rather peremptory manner to the Utes, and as he spoke fingered a rifle which lay before him on the saddle. Suddenly, no warning being given him, he was shot just below the eye. A general fight ensued, which resulted in the killing of some Utes and all the U. S. officers save one, who, with the remnant of the soldiers, was surrounded by the Indians and cut off from water. At the time the last runner came in to Ouray, three men were still alive. Simultaneously an attack was made on the agency. Agent Meeker, and every employee at the agency were killed, but the fate of the three women who were there was still in doubt. Immediately upon reaching the agency, Major W. M. Stanley, the agent, sent Joseph Brady to the scene of trouble accompanied by a bodyguard of fifteen Utes sent by Ouray, the chief sending a positive command to the hostile Utes to cease fighting. The chief also called in all of the hunting parties, which were out, in order to keep anyone who might be so inclined to join the White Rivers. The Southern Utes sent a runner to Ouray with the assurance that the White Rivers would have neither aid nor encouragement from them."

Gov. Pitkin sent out from Denver a special train with arms and ammunition, Gen. David Cook accompanying them, intrusted with discretionary powers. The Downer Guards were ordered from Saguache to Lake City, making two companies that could be placed in Ouray in twelve hours, while all other militia was gotten in readiness to move in short order. One thousand men could have responded if called for. Every precautionary measure was taken.

When Brady returned, he reported the soldiers all safe, as well as the women and children, who had been taken captive. A pack train arrived at Ouray from Lake City loaded with arms and ammunition, but fortunately there was no further use for them, there being no further hostilities.

The government marched a body of soldiers, under General Merritt, into the reservation beyond the White River agency, and then ordered them back again, without firing a single shot.

These were trying times for the people of Ouray; their only hope seemed to rest in their confidence in Chief Ouray, who was for peace. There was a meeting called and the situation discussed. One decision reached was that in case of any trouble in the night the people were to be warned by the beating of the gong (the fire alarm for the city, a large circular saw whose sound sent terror wherever it went). The next night when all who could were fast asleep, the whole town was startled by the sound of the gong, causing many a one to spring up in bed, fearing the worst. Someone, more thoughtless than kind, wanted to have a little fun, so in passing gave the gong a whack.

THE RESCUE OF THE MEEKER WOMEN

The success of the brave men who went to the rescue of the White River captives is told by one of the participants as found in the following, appearing in the Ouray Times of October 25, 1879. It was the first account of the rescue published, and was prepared by a representative of the paper who accompanied the rescue party:

"Last Saturday Gen. Charles Adams and Count Doenhall, of the German legation at Washington, arrived at Las Pinos Agency, having been specially commissioned by Secretary Schurz to proceed to the camp of Douglas and treat with him for the restoration of their friends, the women and children. Capt. M. W. Cline accompanied them, having been selected to go with the party on account of his skill as a frontiersman and thorough knowledge of the Indian character. Little time was lost in preparation, and at eight o'clock that night the party started for the house of Chief Ouray, whence the start was to be made on the next morning, having been increased by Major Geo. D. Sherman and the Times representative. Twelve chiefs and head men were selected by Chief Ouray to accompany the party, including Sapinero, Shaveno and Colorow. Sunday morning the start was made, a buckboard for the comfort of the ladies, and a provision wagon being taken along. The route taken was the Ute wagon road built by the army of Johnson in 1859, as far as thirty miles beyond the Gunnison river, where the vehicles were left and the rest of the journey, about sixty miles, made on horseback. At the Gunnison two Utes were sent ahead by Sapinero to inform Douglas of the approach of the Government representatives, and their arrival gave Douglas twelve hours to prepare. Tuesday morning at eleven o'clock the party emerged from a winding trail through the trees upon a level plain, and there in plain view were four tepees, in groups of two each, not more than a mile away. Gen. Adams led the way to the farthest group first, and arriving there accosted a squaw standing in the entrance of one, asking if the white squaws were there. A shake of the head was the reply. The question was repeated, the same reply given, and the General turned to ride to the other tent when Capt. Cline exclaimed, 'Hold on, General, I see one of them.' 'Good,' said General Adams, 'keep your eye on her.' He rode to the other tent, found it empty, and came back to the first. The lady whom Capt. Cline found in spite of the efforts of the squaw to conceal her by standing in the door, then came out and greeted the party.

saying she was Miss Josephine Meeker, and that her mother, Mrs. Price, and one child were at the other tents, she having the other child with her. After some conversation Gen. Adams told Miss Meeker he would soon be back, and led off to the other group of tepees. One was open and empty, the other was entirely closed save a small opening, and before that the party halted and dismounted, when a parley ensued between Sapinero and the occupants of the tent in the Ute tongue, Sapinero speaking in an angry and indignant tone, and the other speakers, who turned out to be Capt. Billy and Capt. Ware, seemed to be sulky. Douglas was absent at his camp, this being the camp of Johnson, but had been sent for and was momentarily expected. Nothing could be done until his arrival, so the only thing to do was to wait with patience. After perhaps an hour of this suspense, Douglas rode up, accompanied by three of his head men, and shook hands cordially with General Adams. Then there was a consultation between Douglas, two of his head men, and Shavano, after which Douglas went up to General Adams, who was waiting quietly, drew in the sand a diagram of the White River country, and began to explain that his Utes were retreating and the soldiers advancing, adding that he did not wish for fighting. The general replied by saying he had been sent from Washington to recover the women, that the government wanted the women restored, and did not want to fight. Douglas then made a proposition to General Adams that if he would go to White River and persuade the soldiers to cease fighting and retire, the women would be given up. To this the general assented, with the amendment that the women should be given up first, and he would start to see the soldiers. Douglas demurred to this at first, but the general was firm, and he finally consented. Upon the general asking Douglas to accompany him, he received a very decided 'no' from the chief. Douglas then arose from the ground where he had been sitting during the conference, and started for the tent which had been filled with the Utes, asking General Adams to come in. Then followed a council, which continued five hours. Fiery, as we suppose from the frequent applause, eloquent speeches made by Douglas, Johnson, Ware and others, they speaking in Ute, an Uncompahgre Ute interpreting in Spanish to General Adams, he replying in the same language, and his answers being in turn translated to the Utes. Sapinero sat in the council, but took no part in it. Shaveno utterly refused to give in, saying, 'Too much talk.'

"During the progress of the talk, a good chance was presented to observe the camp and its surroundings. Upon a sort of stand between the two tents hung a non-commissioned officer's sash and a cavalry sabre, seven army saddles were lying on the ground, mules and horses with the U. S. brand were grazing on the mesa, and army blankets and overcoats were lying on the ground all about. Presently the long pipe was passed around and General Adams came out of the tent, announcing that the council had terminated favorably, and that they were about to send for the ladies. It was a moment of breathless suspense. In a few moments Mrs. Meeker, a lady of about sixty-five years, came up the bank from the brush where she had been concealed, followed by Mrs. Price, a young and rather pretty woman, and a squaw carrying the little boy in a blanket on her back. Before the appearance of the party, we afterwards learned, these ladies had been hurried off to that hiding place and only the unlooked-for movement of General Adams in riding first to the farthest tent prevented the Indians from hiding Miss Meeker. From their place of concealment the ladies could see but not hear all that was going on, and their terrible suspense may be imagined. 'Oh! but we are so glad to see you,' they said when we came up. 'For nearly four weeks we have not seen a white face, and we sat down and looked at you with the most intense delight. Are you going to take us home—and when will we start?" Captain Cline was in his element immediately, took the little boy in his arms, began to pet him, and at once won the heart of the mother. The ladies spoke very freely of their sufferings and told of the hardships they had undergone, some of them so terrible that it hardly seemed that a woman could survive. Midnight rides without saddles, all-day rides without food or water, were common experiences to them."

The following account of the murders at the agency and the subsequent proceedings of the Indians is collected and arranged from the reports of the three ladies, with each of whom the "Times" had an interview:

On Sunday night, the 29th of September, the Utes at White River had a grand war dance, fiery speeches being made by Douglas and others. The dance lasted until well into the night. The next morning, Monday, the 30th, the fight with the troops occurred. Just as dinner was prepared at the agency a runner came past going at full speed to the Ute camp, a short distance from the agency. The occurrence was noted at the time by the ladies, and a remark made to the effect that a fight between the Indians and troops had occurred and this runner was from the scene of action. Dinner was eaten and the employes returned to their work, two being engaged in getting out rations for the next day, issue day, and the rest being engaged in roofing a house. The ladies were in the dining room, clearing away the dishes, when the attack on the employes commenced. The Indians first captured all their guns, except that of Mr. Price, which happened to be in the milk room, and then proceeded to fire at the men.

The chief, Douglas, who has been trying to make it appear that he had nothing to do with the fight and murders, is shown up in very black colors by these ladies.

Douglas it was, they declare, who led the party which murdered Meeker and the employes, but Jackson fought the troops. Douglas was always severe and cruel to them. Douglas had a large part of the captured agency goods. Captain Billy had a camp near that of Johnson. The squaw of Johnson treated the ladies, whenever she could, with great kindness, and, upon the departure of the party, this woman, who was absent at the time we left Johnson's camp, rode forty miles to overtake us and bid the ladies goodbye. Since the evening of the massacre they had been moved about from camp to camp, never staying long at one camp. Their tents had been pitched but a short time in this place when we found them.

Within an hour after the council was over General Adams and Count Doenhoff, accompanied by Sapinero and Shavano, started for the camp of Douglas, where they were to spend the night and push on in the morning to White River. The remainder of the party remained at Johnson's camp that night.

The next morning preparations were made for the homeward start, and then Johnson and his men began to make difficulty. The Utes who were to guide us were not to be found, it was impossible to buy any provisions, and the party finally got off by Captain Cline telling Johnson that he didn't care whether any Ute went along or not, he was familiar with the trail. The object of all this was to detain the party until news came from White River as to the result of General Adams' journey—if unfavorable, the women would still have been detained as hostages. After traveling about ten miles, another desperate effort was made to detain the party by sending Indians after us who pointed out another trail which they said was the right one, and the one they were then on was the wrong one. Captain Cline was here again equal to the emergency, and kept on the same trail, which proved to be the right one. These persistent efforts of the Utes to mislead the party were alarming, and after consultation with the ladies, who courageously said they could stand the ride, it was determined to push on to the wagon that night, instead of camping on the Grand River as was the first intention. Throughout the night, until about twelve o'clock, the ride was kept up, when the party went into camp—to find perhaps ten Utes busy pillaging the wagons of their provisions. They were told by Captain Cline that the thefts would be reported to Chief Ouray, and, either from revenge, or else carrying out the previous plan of delaying the party, the next morning before daybreak all the Utes save Colorow and one other left, driving the best pair of horses before them for about fifteen miles. Colorow sent out the other Ute as soon as the loss was discovered in search, and he returned at twelve o'clock with the lost animals. Notwithstanding this delay, the Gunnison was reached that night, Thursday, and the next night found the ladies safe within the house of Chief Ouray. He was extremely glad to see them, feeling no doubt that it was through his influence this happy ending was brought about, and a short time after our arrival invited us in to a supper that could hardly be surpassed anywhere. Inspector Pollock, Ralph Meeker, Mr. Caldwell and Dr. Lacy went down from the agency last night to see the ladies. Mr. Meeker's joy at beholding his mother and sister alive and in good health was intense, as might be imagined, and they no doubt felt that they were once more among friends. When the Times' representative left for Ouray, Inspector Pollock was preparing to take the testimony of the ladies in relation to the White River affair to be forwarded to the Interior Department.

Today, October 24th, they were taken by Captain Cline as far as his house on the Cimarron, and will proceed in a few days to Denver and Greeley.

Immediately the safety of the captive women was assured a commission was appointed to treat with the Indians, with the result as given below:

TREATING WITH THE INDIANS

In late October or early November of 1879, General Chas. Adams, General Hatch and Chief Ouray were appointed a commission to treat with the Utes over the White River massacre.

On November 8th, Adams arrived at the agency and went to Ouray's house for a preliminary talk.

On the 14th, General Hatch, Lieutenant Valois. Judge Advocate; Official Stenographer Harry Caldwell, and two clerks, arrived at the agency.

During the meeting of the commission, which, of course, resulted in nothing, Ouray lost the confidence of his associates through his actions, which they did not comprehend. In due time he made what was described as a most eloquent and impassioned speech, in which he made revelations which were a surprise to them, and revealed the cause of his peculiar actions. For the first time they learned

BELATED FREIGHT TEAMS COME TO OURAY WITH PROVISIONS FOR THE WINTER OF 1879.

that he had been in constant fear that at any moment the commission might be attacked, and a scene rivaling White River result. For the first time they learned that the guards posted around the agency day and night were not merely for display, and that Ouray's noticeable restlessness for days past was not without cause. The White River Utes did not propose to give up any of their men, and they came there ready to fight. Ouray had a body of fifty Uncompahgre Utes, under Sapinero, stationed near the agency, ready for defense in case of an outbreak. "Now," said Ouray, "there is no more danger," and for the first time he could speak freely to his brethren. The old chief then went on to state his position of danger and difficulty, what trouble and anxiety he had suffered constantly since the beginning of the White River troubles, his efforts to effect the release of the captives and his joy when he saw them free. He had no longer any desire to be head chief, he said. "I would rather stay on my farm and watch the seed I plant come to maturity than to rule the Ute nation." This speech, so startling in its revelations, fully restored the shattered confidence.

Saturday, December 6th, was the most exciting and eventful day in the commission's long parley. Ouray, accompanied by Jack, Colorow, and other White River and Uncompahgre Utes, reached the agency at one o'clock, and the commission went into session. Upon benches around the room sat the Utes, Sapinero, Shavino, and Waas, Ouray's three head men, being among them, the chief himself having a chair placed for him between the whites and the Indians. The weapons worn by both Indians and whites, though supposed to be concealed, told unmistakably what might occur, as both parties were loaded down. General Hatch opened the session by stating the demands of the government, and reading the names of the Indians wanted, including Douglas, Johnson, Persune, and nine others, and asked if they were willing to give them up. Parleying ensued, without a direct answer, when Adams arose and made a talk to the Indians, concluding with, "We have done all we can, and now your future good or bad treatment rests with you." Adams walked out of the council room and the Indians began to fidget and whisper among themselves, Ouray saying not a word. Sapinero pulled out the long pipe and passed it to Colorow, who filled it, and passed it along. Each Ute drew his knife and laid it on the floor in front of him.

After waiting some time, General Hatch, generally considered a very patient man, lost his temper, and, pale with anger, rose to his feet and roared out, rather than spoke: "I am tired of this nonsense; I have waited for your answer long enough, and now I want to know directly, without further evasion, will you, or will you not, give up the men whose names are on this paper? I came here to help you to save those of you who deserve it from the fate of those who are guilty, and now, what have you done? You come here day after day lying.

Today you have done no better. Now what will you do? I want neither lies nor evasions."

For an instant there was no answer. Then Colorow took up his knife and threw it violently on the floor, and there was a dead pause. This was his vote for war. As the ringing of the blade resounded through the room the hand of each man, both white and red, fell upon the hand of his revolver. The silence was awful. Each white had singled out his man among the Indians, ready at the next hostile motion to open fire in defense. What a situation! Is it peace or war? Finally Ouray broke the oppressive silence, and at his first words two or three Utes arose and left the room, going among the Indians outside who had been waiting for a signal of some kind, as could be seen by their actions. These immediately mounted their horses and rode away.

"We are willing," said Ouray, "to send for these men on one condition, and that only, that they be tried in Washington, and not in Colorado or New Mexico. If you will agree to that, I will send for them, and those whom you want shall go to Washington, and the Great Father shall see that they have justice."

Being told that it would take about five days to get these Indians, General Hatch consented to have them sent for, and Jack and Colorow started for their camp. The council had no further interest for the Indians and they left the room. Then Ouray addressed the commission, General Adams having returned, and said: "You are my enemies, and I can expect no justice from you. We have, up to this time, received none, and we can expect none in the future. Adams is a Colorado man, and the Colorado people are our enemies. You," pointing to General Hatch and Townsend, "are New Mexico men, and are also our enemies. And you," to Lieutenant Valois, "hate us all. Therefore, I want none of the people from either of your states to try my people."

Later, a telegram was received from Secretary Schurz granting the Indians the privilege of trial outside of Colorado and designating Fort Leavenworth, Kansas, as the place. December 12th, the commission dissolved for the time, Adams going to his home in Manitou, Hatch remaining for a time.

December 28, 1879, after a tiresome siege of forty-four days, the commission left the agency, accompanied by twelve Indians, not one of whom was ever punished.

CHIEF OURAY'S AUTOGRAPH.

HONOR DUE

We are told by good authority that many a kindness shown, many a firm stand for the good of the whites, by Chief Ouray, was brought about by his wife, Chipeta, who was always the friend of the white man.

And, in looking backward today, let the heart of every pioneer, old and young, be filled with gratitude to this grand old chief, Ouray, and his faithful wife, Chipeta; but for them, many of us would not be here.

Even today, we are told, when the subject of the White River massacre is brought up before Chipeta the tears roll down her face.

CHAPTER XV

COASTING DOWN VINEGAR HILL

Although the work of treating with the Indians was not yet complete, the undaunted spirit of the mountains enabled the people of Ouray to celebrate Thanksgiving of 1879 with the same sense of gratitude with which the first Thanksgiving was inaugurated, though few ventured out to the services on account of the storm—the worst of the season.

The people were rejoicing over the fact that the Indian Bureau had "concluded that perhaps it would be best for all concerned to have the Utes removed to some other locality."

Little did the people realize how much the safety of home and loved ones depended at that time on Chief Ouray's nobility of character, his firmness to stand by what he saw as right and just, and his love for the whites. Also, for the patience and tact of General Chas. Adams, General Hatch, and others in the conference held at the agency.

The holidays came with their thoughts of cheer and Christmas doings. New Year's most of the ladies kept open house. One evening Tom and Dick were busy doing a little carpenter work, then, a little later, went over to their neighbor's blacksmith shop, the result being two good sleds, with which they surprised their friends. Dick asked Kate for the pleasure of her company up Vinegar Hill for a coast, and Tom took Mary, who had grown quite robust since coming to Ouray, dolls now occupying only a portion of her time and thought; her merry laugh often rang out and the lonely miner passing to or from work was cheered as he listened. After enjoying the fun of coasting for about an hour that evening, Tom suggested to his sister they go home and try to get mother to take a ride.

"Why, the idea!" said mother, laughing.

"Yes, but mother, I wish you would try it," said Tom. "I'll take care of you." So mother, with a smiling face, went, father and Mary going to see the fun. Aunt Hetty and John had gone for a moonlight walk. Together they climbed Vinegar Hill, as Mary said, "having the most fun."

"Why," said mother, as she sat down on the sled, "there don't seem to be room for two."

"It's all right, mother dear; all you have to do is to hold on." Poor mother! She was shaking with fear, but would not let on, for she wanted to please her boy. Away they flew, and a little of the old-time pleasure came back to her. To the surprise of the husband, she was ready to try it again, while Kate and Dick, delighted to see mother out, gave up their sled to father and Mary. It was amusing to see how awkwardly father went at it.

"I could better use a plow," said he to Dick, who was explaining how to steer. But father was not to be outdone by anyone, and, as the trick of it came back to him, away they went, coming to the stopping place almost as soon as mother and Tom.

"Just one more ride," said mother, as they came

puffing up the hill, which was very steep, just the place for a good start.

"Allow me the pleasure," said her husband, bowing in old-time gallantry.

"Thank you, sir," said the wife, with the demureness of a girl. Father did not have to be shown this time; he would show them he was just as capable as the boys.

He forgot the long years that lay between, and thought of the first time they went coasting together down the hills and over the tops of the fences in the little eastern village, when they, too, were boy and girl together. A stolen kiss on the way, as is often the case, caused the sled to tip too far on one side, and both fell with a thump on the ice. An exclamation from a lady, "Why! if it is not my brother and his wife," and Aunt Hetty and her lover came rushing to help them. Father was almost provoked to think Hetty should witness this mishap, but joined in the laugh at his expense, saying with much firmness, "It's your turn now, John; we will see who comes out best." Poor Hetty was more frightened than Mrs. Barton had been, but with a hasty look around to assure herself the neighbors were not looking, she took her seat on the sled, all eyes of the laughing group watching John, but John was fully able to take care of his part as they started away, Dick and Kate following after.

"Let's go home, father," said mother; "Bob will soon be home and will wonder where we have gone. Come, little daughter."

When they reached home, Bob had just come in, and when told by Mary where they had been, said, "Well! well! mother, I am surprised; I heard such giggling as I passed near there I thought it was some school girls and boys having some fun. As Aunt Hetty used to say, I wonder if the neighbors saw you."

Yes, the neighbors did see the sport that clear, moonlight night. It was wonderful how quickly the rage spread. In two or three nights almost the whole town was out, and several had what they were pleased to call bobsleds. They held about a dozen people at once. One young man made a bobsled, and, wanting to have a little sport, would invite a certain preacher to ride. We soon noticed when this gentleman was on the sled misfortunes always befell us, and we landed in a snowbank. When it snowed during the night the men formed a broom brigade and swept the snow off the track for the evening's fun. Women would forget they could not walk uphill and go laughing back to the starting point as easily as when they were girls. It was a pleasant sight, and one to be remembered in after years.

One evening a concert was being given in one of the churches, and a gentleman was rendering an exquisite solo, when, the church doors being open, a big-eared burro, with intention kindly, pushed its head into the room and gave one of those unearthly, supplicating brays that only a solemn-faced burro can give. The gentleman attempted to finish, but the situation was too much for the audience, who burst out in a roar of laughter.

The spring of 1880 found the people happy and ready for the spring work. In March, hay was

BURROS STANDING READY TO BE LOADED FOR THE MINES IN THE SPRING, 1880.

seventy-five dollars per ton, and hard to get at that, emphasizing strongly the need of more land to cultivate.

It had become an assured fact that the opening of the reservation was only a matter of unwinding much red tape, and people began to flock in, ready for the exodus. August 26th people were startled by the report that Chief Ouray was dead. Always the friend of the whites, the troubles of the last year or two fell heavily upon him. The reservation to which he has gone will never be taken from him.

We copy from the Ouray Times:

CHIEF OURAY DEAD

Los Pinos Agency, Colo.,
August 26, 1880.

Editor Times:

The sad news of Chief Ouray's death has just reached here by an Indian runner, who came through with a communication from the commission to that effect.

GEO. D. SHERMAN,
Agent, Associated Press.

CHAPTER XVI

PLANTING THE FLAG ON UNCOMPAHGRE PEAK

Aunt Hetty and John were quietly married in September, 1880, renting a one-roomed cabin for the time being. John found plenty to do, and all their little savings were put in the bank, against the time when they would take up a ranch in the valley.

Kate and Dick, too, decided that coasting together on life's journey would be pleasant, the marriage day to be when the land was opened, the trip from Ouray to select and settle on the new ranch to be their wedding journey, their new life to be entered upon with new surroundings. Again Dick was busy every spare moment making bedstead, chairs and table out of lumber, but the lumber was planed and painted now, while Kate was happy preparing the little things that go to make a home, even a log cabin, homelike and inviting.

In October, about a year and a half after Mrs. Wilson and her daughter went back to their eastern friends, Mr. Wilson received a letter which read as follows:

"My Dear Husband and Son:

"We start for home tomorrow. I cannot bear the thought of another long winter away from you both. I would rather live on a dry crust, and be with my loved ones. I find things do not seem so good as I expected them to be when I came back.

The change must be in me, for those about me seem as content as ever. Ruth and I were talking it over the other night and came to the conclusion that the open-heartedness, the broader mindedness, of the West, has lifted our thoughts above the old routine of thinking and doing. We surely are not satisfied as we once thought we were.

"A family, with whom we have been in communication, is coming, and Ruth and I are getting ready to come with them. Since we have come to this decision, I seem to be a new woman. I am so happy, and look longingly forward to being with you again, sitting by that big fireplace in the evening. Dear husband, you cannot understand, perhaps, what it means to me to feel this great change, for I tried so hard to be happy and contented for your sake, but I could not, but this separation, and the anxiety for your safety last fall and winter, opened my eyes to see how very selfish I was, thinking only of my own comfort. To be with you, to do the little things that tend for your comfort, will be indeed a joy. I understand Mrs. Barton's source of happiness today. I did not when with her. I even remember I never thanked those ladies for putting up that little white curtain and bringing the little plant to cheer me up, but I am thankful now.

"Yours, with tender love,

"MOTHER."

Words cannot express the joy this letter brought to both father and son. They were too full for utterance. Dick wrung his father's hand and went out under the starlit sky. He thought he was happy when Kate promised to be his, but tonight a holier sense of peace and joy came. He uncovered his head and breathed a prayer of gratitude, a wordless prayer, which is always heard. Then he went to the Barton home. They were sitting around the fire, for the evenings were getting very chilly. Bob had just gone to the office for the mail. Tom and Kate welcomed their visitor, but Mrs. Barton was first to notice something unusual had come to Dick.

"Why, Dick! what is it, my boy?" The sympathetic tone of her voice was too much, and he burst into tears. Kate sprang to his side. Taking her hand in his he told them the news: "Mother writes she would rather have but a dry crust to eat than be separated from us any longer. She is longing for the log cabin, and starts on her journey—she and Ruth—tomorrow."

Mr. Barton grasped Dick's hand. "Bless you! my boy, I'm glad for you and your father." Mrs. Barton smiled through her tears, while Tom and Kate said not a word; this was too much for them, they could not understand it.

"Who are the people they are coming with?" asked Mrs. Barton.

"I do not know," said Dick. "They did not say; some neighbor, I expect."

After Kate and Dick had gone for a walk, Tom said, "I guess I will go to bed. Goodnight, folks."

A few moments later, mother rapped gently at

her boy's bedroom door. "Come in, mother; I knew that rap came from you." After closing the door, the mother sat down by Tom, who was sitting on the rough little sofa he had made for himself.

"What's the matter, Tom?"

"Oh," said Tom, "nothing much."

"Yes, it is, Tom; I have seen it for some time."

"Well, mother, it's this way. I see Aunt Hetty and John so happy, and now Dick and Kate, while I am seemingly as far off as ever. I do not see how I can spare the time to go out to see Mollie this winter; there is so much to do and so little time to do it. And then, yesterday I received such a queer, off-hand note—I cannot call it a letter—from Mollie. She said not to write for two weeks, as she was going away and wouldn't get her mail. I don't understand it. I know she loves me as I do her."

"Never mind," said mother. "It will come out all right, I am sure. We will soon see a way out for you to leave for two or three months anyway. It would do you so much good." Just then the outside door shut with a bang, and they knew Bob had come.

"Any mail for us, Bob?" asked his mother.

"No," said Bob, "just a paper for father." Tom sighed, his mother turned and kissed him and said: "Cheer up, my boy. The same Hand is leading now as ever; better come with me and hear what news Bob has; it's most too early to go to bed." So, hand in hand, they went, and Tom's heart was much lighter for a little talk with mother.

"Any news, Bob?" asked father.

"Not much," said Bob, whose eyes seemed unusually bright that evening. "Two more covered wagons came in tonight with people intending to be on hand the moment the reservation is opened. I must get to my books."

Entering Tom's room, he shut and locked the door very quietly, taking a letter from his pocket. After reading, he went dancing around the room on tiptoe, ending with a somersault on Tom's neat bed. Then, doubling himself up, he laughed until his face became as red as a beet. The letter read as follows:

"Dear Bob: I have a secret I want kept, and I believe a boy can keep a secret so much better than can a girl. I give it to you. It is this, but, honor bright now, no one is to know. It must be a complete surprise. Father and mother have made up their minds to 'go West.' Father has been thinking about it for some time, and as the time draws near for the opening of the reservation we are coming. We start tomorrow. Yes, I'm coming, too! Won't it be a surprise for Tom? Won't it be fun? Well, since you know, I will ask a favor for father and mother, that you look around for a two-roomed cabin for us. It will only be for a few months you know, and if there is a big fireplace like that in your home, we shall be glad. Mum's the word.

"MOLLIE."

"You bet!" said Bob. "Of course I'm the only one in the family can keep a secret. I can imagine what a change would take place with Tom if he read this letter. He has been looking very glum lately."

Carefully he put the letter away in his pocket, and, putting on an extra long face—always a sign of mischief in the Barton family when seen on Bob—he took his books and sat down by the sitting-room table with his back as much as possible to his mother and Tom.

Bob expected to graduate in the spring. He never felt the longing for a college education, as his brother had done, so his father knew the schooling he had received in Ouray, which was of the best, was enough for any ordinary line of work. Bob was a fine, manly boy of nineteen, a dear, home-loving boy, full of fun as a nut is of meat.

A few days later, as Mrs. Barton and Kate were busy washing the dishes, the mother asked, "Have you noticed Bob lately? There's something up, but what, I can't conceive. He seems to be holding something that is a little too big for him. I went into the boys' bedroom yesterday in a hurry and there was Bob laughing with all his might, reading a letter, which he crammed into his pocket as soon as I went in. He seemed very much embarrassed, and began to pick up his books."

"There is something on foot, you may depend," said Kate. "We must be prepared. I wonder if some girl wrote him a note. I believe that is it!"

"I don't know," said the mother, a sharp pang striking her heart. "He's not old enough for that."

"Not old enough! Why, mother! Bob is almost nineteen."

"Is it possible?" gasped the mother. "I thought I had him for a long time yet."

"Now mumsy, dear," said Kate, putting her arms around her mother, "put that thought completely out of your mind; it doesn't belong there; you, who have so bravely put aside self for others. You are not losing one of us, but you are gaining a lot. Just think, you have, or soon will have, three sons instead of two; three daughters, instead of only one. You will have more, instead of less, love, for the more we children love our wife or husband the more we shall appreciate and love you. I worked that out long ago," giving her mother a hearty kiss.

"Thank you, Kate, for reminding me. I had only just come to this part of my life's experience, and not as yet worked it out, but you have made it very clear. If I take my son-in-law into my heart I shall keep my daughter, for the daughter will stay where her husband is. Again, I thank you, Kate: I have grown much during this talk."

"Why, Bob! what are you doing with that cat?" exclaimed Mrs. Barton, as Bob came rushing pell mell through the kitchen.

"Why, you see," said Bob, laughing more heartily than the case demanded, "the cat looked so sleepy I felt it a kindness to wake her up."

Bob began to feel very important, a man of affairs, he said to himself as he found and rented the two-room cabin, putting the key in his pocket.

"Yes," said the landlord in response to the inquiry, "there is a number one fireplace in it."

Bob had been informed of the homecoming of Mrs. Wilson and Ruth and entered heartily into the preparations going on in the Wilson home, so heartily Dick wondered what the boy was up to, never dreaming of the poor boy's great need of something to use up the increasing exuberance of his feelings. One evening, Kate and Bob were alone for a little while, and Kate noticed Bob was very restless, so she let curiosity get the best of her and said:

"Bob, what is the matter with you, anyway? You have acted, for some time, as though you had something on your mind. Now, what is it, Bobsy?"

"If you must know," said Bob flushing, "I have."

"What is it?" persisted his sister.

"It's a secret. There, I hope you are satisfied," and, with a sob, Bob grabbed up his cap and left her. The laugh that started with this piece of news was strangled by a lump in Kate's throat.

"Poor boy!" she said, "it surely must go hard with him, but I wonder what it can be," as she confided the matter to her parents a little later.

"I think," said the father, "it would be more kind if we helped him to keep it by not paying any attention to him," and Mr. Barton laughingly added, "I know by experience what it is to have a secret, eh, mother? You remember how we tried to keep it to ourselves when we were first engaged. I wanted to shout it to the stars on my way home that night," and again he laughed to himself.

"But," said mother, "you don't think Bob—"

"No, no! mother," said Kate, "I'm sure he would not keep that from me."

The next evening, as the family were sitting down to supper, a covered wagon, with a cow and yearling heifer tied to the back of the wagon, and the driver all smiles, came slowly towards the Wilson cottage. "There they come!" cried Bob, as he sprang out, upsetting his chair in his haste. Yes, sure enough! there was Mrs. Wilson and Ruth clinging to Mr. Wilson and Dick. The driver strongly resembled someone they knew.

"But," said father, "who are those with them?. There are two ladies, and just look at Bob! He seems to know them!"

"I didn't tell! I didn't tell! Did I?" cried Bob.

Tom, who had just come up, stood as one in a dream, but Mollie, the first to speak, said, "Why, Tom; it's me!" Then, waking up, forgetting who might be looking on, he took her in his arms and held her there, until his mother said, "Say, Tom! the rest of us want a little of Mollie."

Bob was nearly beside himself, a little boy yet. "That was the secret, Kate! Don't you wonder I kept it?"

"Yes," said Kate, hugging him, "I do wonder; I'm sure I could not."

"No," said Bob, laughing, "that was why she told me. A boy, you know, can keep a secret better than a girl; Mollie said so."

"And where is our house?" said Mollie. "We want to take our team there."

"Your house?" asked Tom, wonderingly.

"Yes, indeed, she gave instructions to me to rent a cabin with a big fireplace in it for them," said Bob, who felt too big for anything. "I will lead; everybody follow." During the excitement, Bob had rushed over and lighted the brush and wood he had piled high in the big fireplace, so when the little party came in the cheering rays of warmth and firelight greeted them.

"Oh, father!" said Mollie, "this is fine!" and her mother, weary with the journey, sat down, fitting into the little home as though she had always been there.

"But Mollie," said Mrs. Barton, "if you had let us know we could have fixed it up for you."

"I wanted the fun of surprising you all," said the happy girl.

"You surely did," said Mrs. Barton, smiling.

Very soon they all returned to the Barton home for supper. That night the stars looked down on a very happy group of people. "Dear Bob," said Tom, as they were preparing for bed, "you and I are going to be closer chums than ever, but I don't see how you kept it."

"I don't either," said Bob, as he turned over in bed and gave a sigh of relief.

The next day, Mr. Brown, Mollie's father, called Tom's attention to what their wagon was loaded with—sacks of seed wheat and oats and two sacks of alfalfa seed. "Two sacks of wheat and one o alfalfa seed are Mollie's," he said, smiling.

"Good for you. We have never thought of that it gives me an idea."

That evening, as they were eating supper, Tom

SOMEBODY'S BOYS HAVING A LITTLE FUN BEFORE THE BURRO TRAINS LEAVE FOR CAMP.

suggested the plan which had come into his mind. "Jake and Harry DeLong are going out this winter to visit their parents before the land is thrown open. Do you not think, father, it would be a good plan for them to bring a load of seed in with them?"

"Why, yes; I had not thought of that; it's a good idea."

So when the DeLongs dropped in, as they often did, for the Bartons' home seemed to be their home, too, Mr. Barton opened up the matter by asking the boys when they were going out.

"In a month from now. We came to see if you could spare us your pony, Tom."

"Sure," said Tom, "mine is at your service, and I know Dick can spare his."

"We were talking as you came in," said Mr. Barton, "of the advisability of you boys bringing a wagonload of seed wheat, oats and alfalfa when you come back."

"Why, yes," said Jake. "We had not thought of that. We shall need a team anyway. We better come back early, while the roads are frozen."

When Tom came home that night, after a long talk with Mollie, and later with Dick and Kate, he announced there would be a double wedding when flitting time came.

Mr. Wilson seemed ten years younger since he received that letter from Mrs. Wilson. He could scarcely believe it possible for such a change to take place in his home. Mrs. Wilson was happy, everything seemed beautiful. Privations only drew them closer together. "And just think!" she said to Mrs. Barton, "I'm soon to have two daughters instead of one."

"Yes, dear," said Mrs. Barton, "and Dick is one in a thousand I would have chosen for my son."

Mollie's parents had lived all their lives on a farm and cared little for town life. The DeLong boys went out for the winter. Their father never regretted his willingness to let the boys try their wings. He saw when he went over the farm with them their interest in whatever pertained to farming was greater than ever, and the long winter evenings were spent in talking over the farm work they were soon to take up.

When the time came for Jake and Harry to start for the mountains, they bought a good work team and wagon. The father was in his element, happy as a boy, as he helped load up the wagon with the best he had raised himself. Mother was not to be outdone. There were comforts and sure-enough feather pillows, one for each boy, and some pretty tinware for use on the new farm. Yes, and a few flower seeds, gathered from mother's own garden. "They will seem like old friends when they look up at you," she said. The time for leaving finally came, and the boys realized more than ever the blessing of love father and mother had given them, while the parents felt their loss even more keenly than when the boys started on their first trip.

About three weeks later, in the spring of 1881, as the DeLong boys drove up to the Barton cabin, there were shouts of joy, for the boys had been greatly missed. "Come over to our house," cried Dick; "the grain is to be stored in my bedroom." So this homecoming was a foretaste of many more in years to come. This little company were all living in the future. Everything they did was for the homes they were going to make.

Time passed quickly. The Fourth of July came, with its usual preparations for a good time, with the town flag flying to the breeze, but word came that President Garfield had been assassinated, which cast a gloom on all, and the flag was lowered to half-mast.

Near noon, as the writer looked up toward the Uncompahgre Peak, she noticed a heavy, dark cloud hanging in that direction.

Will, the brother-in-law, remarked, "they are having a thunder storm up there," not knowing the experience his own brother, Henry, was passing through at that moment.

The story can best be told in the brother's own words:

The month of June, 1881, found a company of prospectors camped up on the head waters of the Cimarron River, near the base of the Uncompahgre Peak, at that time supposed to be the highest mountain summit within the state. It rises to an elevation of 14,289 feet above sea level, its northern face, for 1,500 or 2,000 feet nearer the summit, being practically perpendicular, giving foundation to the widely accepted belief that the summit was inaccessible. This group of mountaineers would not accept this idea, and had the audacity to plan for and announce a Fourth of July celebration to be held on the summit of the peak. A general invitation was extended to the surrounding country.

It was now up to these men to make good. A garrison flag was ordered, and on the morning of the 3rd one of the party went to Lake City to get the flag, while a number of others, with a mule team, started to make the ascent and get a suitable pole to the summit for the flag-raising. This was accomplished without notable difficulty, from the south side of the peak, the party camping for the night on the mountain side.

As the morning of the Fourth dawned, people began arriving from Lake City, Capital, and surrounding camps until there were thirty or forty assembled on the summit, a comparatively smooth tract sloping gently toward the south. The messenger arrived with the flag and brought the astounding news of the assassination of President Garfield. which had the effect of dampening the ardor of the company. The flag, however, suitably draped in mourning, was flung to the breeze half-mast, probably flying at the greatest altitude of any United States flag in the world.

Arriving at the summit of the peak, one was bewildered by the magnificent panorama spread out at his feet. Few, if any, points in the country can afford a view its equal, either in beauty or grandeur. To the southward, perhaps thirty miles distant, and sweeping away to the east to where it was lost in the Saguache range, was the Continental Divide, the Cochetopa range, from whose slopes start rivers which find their way to the gulfs of Mexico and California. Following the range to the east and north, getting constantly farther away, the horizon line takes in the Saguache range and the Elk mountains, till in the north there is but an indistinct grouping of mountains perhaps one hundred miles away. The same to the northwest, where the panorama stretches away into Utah. To the west, ranging a little to the south, is an irregular line of lofty peaks, perhaps unequaled in the same distance anywhere: Whitterhorn, 14,020; Matterhorn, 13,589; Engineer, 13,190; Sneffles, 14,185; Whitehouse, 13,469; Wilson, 14,250; with peaks innumerable reaching about 12,000 feet in a distance of perhaps twenty-five miles. All the country to the north and the northwest as far as the eye can reach, and farther, was the home of the Ute Indian, and woe to the white man who attempted to make his home in the vast territory, for it was not only jealously guarded by the Indians themselves, but Uncle Sam also had soldiers stationed in the Uncompahgre valley to see that the reservation was not intruded upon.

But to get back to our waiting company on the peak. About noon, as preparations were being made for the formal celebration, fragmentary clouds began to drift up the face of the mountain and disperse in mist about the summit, the breeze bearing up the flag finely until suddenly a gust from the opposite direction threatened to carry the flag, pole and all, over the cliff, the mound of stone in which it was planted not being sufficient to stand the pressure. Willing hands sprang to the rescue, but before the flag was released a report like that of a rifle was heard, followed almost immediately by a second. The first thought of all was that some of the boys had fired pistols, but a second glance dispelled that notion, for Joe Singleton was prostrate on the ground, unconscious. No further evidence was needed to show that an uninvited and unwelcome guest was participating in the ceremonies. Being a few feet distant, otherwise engaged, the first report attracted my attention, and looking at the group wrestling with the flag, I saw, simultaneous with the last report, what appeared to be a ball of blue fire exploding about the heads of the group. In common with many others of the company, I distinctly felt this shock. Singular as it may seem, these two explosions were all that occurred at that time. A groan from Singleton was a source of joy to the company, for the impression was that he had been killed by the shock. He quickly revived and was borne on the shoulders of men down the trail as rapidly as circumstances would permit. Fortunately there were no serious results, for Joe was himself again in a few days.

Of course, the celebration was forgotten, and all made tracks down the mountain, but none who were there will ever forget their participation in this, probably the highest Fourth of July celebration ever held.

CHAPTER XVII

MOVING ON TO THE RESERVATION

Late in August, 1881, one might have seen six horsemen leaving Ouray for the valley below. They went at a good pace until they neared the military post, when they slowed down, as though admiring the scenery. They were our friends, Mr. Barton, Mr. Wilson, Tom, Dick, and Bob, with Mollie's father, Mr. Brown. They were looking over the land, deciding where they would locate. Finally they all separated, each following his own sense of what he really wanted.

Bob felt in the way; he was not of age, so could not take up land at present, but as he rode alone he turned his horse down the river for a drink, where he noticed how thick the timber was in the bottom and how little there was anywhere else. After some study on the subject he smiled. Soon the men were all together again, wending their way home.

That evening they all gathered around the Barton fireside to talk things over, each telling what he had found and where he would locate if he had the chance. After each had expressed himself, Bob asked the question, "How about water for your land?"

"Water? Why, we were looking for land, Bob," replied his father.

"Yes, father, but land out here is no good without water."

"That's a fact," spoke up Mr. Wilson; "here we easterners forgot the land is seldom watered without irrigation."

"Why, Bob!" chimed in Kate, "how did you happen to think of it?"

"I did not happen to think about it. I have learned a whole lot by keeping my ears as well as my eyes open. I've been listening to the men in Kimball's hardware store talk at night and give their experiences, just like they do at prayer meeting, only they don't wait to be asked. One man told of the time he had in learning how to handle this adobe soil," and Bob went on to tell what he could remember.

"Well, well!" said Mr. Brown, "Bob is proving the best farmer of us all. I think we had better write for an up-to-date farm paper, printed somewhere in Colorado, that will likely deal with adobe soil."

"There's something else I saw, too."

"What was it?" laughed his father.

"When you all left me I went down by the river, and seeing how thick the trees were I couldn't help thinking a few acres of timber would be fine. Of course, cottonwood is not worth much, but for the first two years it would come in very handy for cabins and chicken coops and firewood."

"To be sure," said Jake, who with his brother had just dropped in. "I shall try to get near the river; father advised us to. And another thing Harry and I have thought of is that we, this little company, had better get land near together so we can help each other, and maybe get a ditch of our own."

"Yes, that's a good idea," said Mr. Brown. After much talk they parted for the night.

"Bob," said his father, "I'm glad you have been using your ears to such advantage. I wish you could take up some land, too, but if you stay by me—I shall need you—I will see that you get your farm by and by."

"That's all right," returned Bob, who was glad moving time was drawing near.

One evening a little later as the Bartons were sitting down to supper, Bob said, "I hear the sister of the editor's wife came in today with some people who intend to stay awhile. I saw her. She is very pretty, such a fair complexion, and cheeks as red as roses. She was laughingly telling someone how an Indian tried to buy her. He offered one pony, then two, and finally three, and was much disappointed to learn she was not for sale."

"How old is she?" asked Kate.

"A little older than Mary, I should judge," said Tom, "and her name is Hannah."

On the 28th day of August, 1881, the Utes took up their line of march for the new reservation. It was a very interesting sight. Soldiers were stationed here and there to protect both the Utes and the whites. There were several hundred Indians with their squaws, the papooses strapped on their mothers' backs, enjoying the ride more perhaps than white children would have done. They were brought up never to complain, and to take life as it came. Then the flocks of goats and herds of cattle. "The finest bunch of cattle," Mr. Nutt remarked, that he had ever seen. "All one breed, black and white—looked as though the stock came from the old country," he said. This company could not travel very rapidly. Word came to the Bartons, by friends who were interested, that the reservation would only be thrown open as far as the Post the first day of the exodus.

That same evening our friends celebrated the weddings of Tom and Mollie, Dick and Kate, and early the next morning, before day had fairly dawned, all preparations having been made the previous day, like the Israelites of old, with supplies to last a week, they locked their cabin doors for the first time, and started on a life as new to the parents as to the children, a life rich in experiences. Mr. Wilson and Tom placed a notice on their office door informing the public they would be back in a week.

The men of the party, not including the DeLong boys, who had started on ahead, rode horseback, leaving the women to follow with the wagons. The burros tied behind the wagons were loaded with tents and other things. This being the day after the departure of the Indians, the coast was clear for a number of miles. As the ladies, weary with their long ride, passed the Post, they were much relieved to see Bob tearing toward them.

"Hurrah, we have one place all fixed. Father says for you to come there. Hurry up your teams and follow me. When I show you where to stop I shall leave you, maybe till dark, but you are safe. You may have to wait on yourselves tonight, sweet maidens," he said to the girls. "You must get your own wood, make your own fire, and carry water from the river, just like the squaws did. Your husbands may not get in till after dark" And away he flew, for Bob so loved the last word. In half an hour they saw Bob waiting until they were near enough to see him motion where they were to go, then away he went to be with his father and Tom.

They soon saw one of the stakes with a white rag flying in the breeze. It was well most of these ladies had been brought up on a farm, for they knew what to do and how to do it. They unhitched the horses and led them to water, the river being close by, then tied them to trees to nibble the little grass that grew near. They carried water for the burros, but did not dare to untie them; they were not used to handling burros. They brought water for cooking and wood to build a fire. This was fun for the girls, while the mothers busied themselves preparing supper. It was, as Bob had said, dark before the men came back, and then it was only to hurriedly fix a tent for the ladies and drink a cup of coffee; then, taking the burros with them, they bade their wives good night, assuring them they were perfectly safe with Bob to look after them, for each man must stay on his own place that night.

"Oh, John!" said Aunt Hetty, "let me go with you."

"Why," said he, "you would have to sleep out under the stars."

"I don't care, I'm going." When John saw how much she desired it, he lifted her up behind him and went away in the darkness. The wives knew the land their husbands and sons had taken would have to be closely guarded, even perhaps with a shotgun.

"Oh, Bob!" said his mother, "how glad we are you can be with us," and the mother, as she looked up into her boy's eyes, felt, rather than saw, her Bob was a man now. She had lost her boy. They settled down for the night, but not to sleep. The excitement was not conducive to slumber. Their thoughts were for the loved ones alone under the stars more than for themselves.

Daylight came, and with it everything looked natural again. Bob had a big fire burning as mother came out, then as quickly as possible a can of coffee was boiling and some lunch prepared, which Bob carried to each of the men who was "holding down" a ranch for himself and loved ones. How Bob enjoyed it! He declared it was better than having a ranch of his own.

He brought back word that if the ladies wished, Bob could remain on the ranch and they could go and call on their neighbors. With much laughter they accepted the queer invitation, after the dishes were all washed.

"I wish Tige was here," said Mary.

"Yes, dear," returned her mother; "we will bring him when we bring the cow a little later."

"You won't have to go far," said Bob, as he gave them directions, "we have been very fortunate in getting near together, all except Jake and Harry; we have not heard from them yet."

"Why, Bob," cried Kate, as they were about to start, "what is that you have on?" for Bob had forgotten and taken off his overcoat, displaying what he had been carefully hiding from the women folks —a revolver and belt of cartridges.

"Oh!" confessed Bob, flushing, "I thought I would be ready for a jackrabbit when I met him." He did not fool his mother nor Mrs. Wilson; the girls were too young to look under the surface of things, and hoped a rabbit would make him a call while they were gone. What fun they had, meeting the weary watchers of the night! But there was little time for play. After a short consultation it was decided that each family should pitch their tent and start housekeeping, each on their own ranch.

"Of course," spoke up Mollie, "that's what we have been working for all summer." Then the fun began. No birds in their love mating outdid this little company, for all wanted to talk at once. The ladies stayed until every tent was up, "no help in the least, but only in the way," Tom laughingly remarked. Then they hastened back to the wagons, which had been packed with this very moment in view. So Mr. Brown's wagon contained nothing but what was needed on their ranch and Tom's. With the help of Bob they hitched the horses and emptied the Bartons' household goods on the ground, and, leaving Bob alone, went from one ranch to another, distributing to each his belongings.

"Well, mother," said Mr. Barton, a little later, "I guess we can go home now."

"Yes," she answered, with a catch in her voice, as she looked over at Tom, who stepped to her side.

"It's all right, mother; I'm your boy, just the same, and will be all through life. We are only following in the footsteps of you and father, and we want your blessing right now, don't we, Mollie?" She had come up and was standing by her husband's side.

"Yes, we do, and a warm place I shall have in your hearts, too, for where Tom is there you will find me."

"God bless you and your home and all that comes to you," said the father. With tears and kisses they parted.

"Now, mother," said Mr. Barton, as they rode back to the new home, "don't cry; the boy has done well. Mollie is——"

"Yes, yes, I know," said the wife, and she broke down entirely, "but I lost Bob, too, last night. I didn't sleep a bit, it came so sudden."

"Lost Bob?" her husband gasped, "what do you mean?"

"This experience we are passing through has changed the boy into a man. I saw it last night, and you will find that I am right." The cry had done Mrs. Barton good; it was just what she needed. Oh, these tears that are allowed to flow freely, how quickly the sunshine of peace and love shines out! It is the repressed tears that harm. In a few minutes love and hope had triumphed, and the face the wife turned to her husband was radiant with tenderness.

"Well!" said Bob, as they drove up, "everybody happy?"

"Yes, Bob, everybody," said his father, as he grasped the boy's hand.

"We sure are having strenuous times, and I'm enjoying it, but we had better get to work. What's to be done first, father?"

"Well, the first thing is to find out what we have to do with. I'm pleased with our piece of ground; what do you think, Bob?"

"I can hardly say, yet; I have been chasing over so many stakes I cannot as yet tell which is which. Leave the horses harnessed, father, and when we get straightened out we will ride over our place, better to realize what we have."

"A good plan, my boy; just what mother and I want to do. I wonder how the DeLong boys came out. I begin to feel anxious about them. I hope they are not having any trouble."

"I will hunt them up," said Bob, "after we come back." So they went over their ranch of 160 acres; it did not take long, but it seemed good to be on their own place once more.

It took Bob but a short time to reach the DeLong boys.

"What's the matter?" asked Bob. "We got anxious about you." He saw something was wrong.

"Haven't slept a wink," said Jake, "since we came. Two men, the worse for liquor, were determined to swipe our places; we didn't dare to come over for fear they might be waiting to jump them."

"We have a fine place, don't you think?" asked Harry.

"You bet!" said Bob, as he surveyed the level land reaching down to the river, "it's even better than ours."

"Could you stop just a little bit until we get some wood?" asked Jake.

"Sure," said Bob, "only wait until I run over and tell the folks; they will think they have lost me, too." When he told his parents how he found them, Mrs. Barton hastened to prepare something for them to eat, while Mr. Barton said, "I will go over and have a talk with them. Where's the axe, Bob? Here it is. You take the other, and bring some wood up while I'm gone."

Jake and Harry were very glad to see Mr. Barton. Everything was so new and strange. Molehills seemed like mountains to them, but they were pleased with their places. Mr. Barton expressed his pleasure in their success, "but you must have something up on your places, then there will be no trouble. Suppose Bob and I help you put up a log hut on each ranch, then you can leave them part of the time to help us."

"All right, we'll be glad to help you," said the boys.

"Well, eat your lunch, and let's begin. When you go down to the river call Bob. After you get a round or two of your building up, no one will molest you." By night two cabins, each 10x12, were ready for the roofs, and before breakfast the next morning they were covered, not with shingles, but with poles laid close together and covered with dirt to the depth of six or eight inches.

After breakfast they were ready to help Mr. Barton put up his log cabin. By night they had the walls up; the next day the house was finished. A curtain Mrs. Barton had prepared was strung across one end of the room, making two little bedrooms; clothes and other things were put in sacks and hung on nails driven into the walls. The week was a short but busy one. Mr. Brown found a part of his place joined Tom's. As Tom would have to be away much of the time with his surveying, it was thought best to put the buildings for the present on this part of the ranches, one almost joining the other, for Mollie would then not have to be alone. A one-room cabin on each place, built hastily of cottonwoods, with dirt floors and roofs, a good-sized fireplace, and one little window.

"The cabin is plenty large enough," laughed Mollie, "for what we have to put in it." Glad Tom was going away for a little while, so she could surprise him when he came back, for, womanlike, she had been busy making the little things which would go so far toward making this one-room log cabin inviting.

Mr. Wilson's place was not far away. He, too, with the help of others, put up two small rooms, a fireplace in one. Mrs. Wilson declared she and Ruth could stay alone, since Mr. Wilson would have to keep his assay office work going, for money would be greatly needed.

Dick's place did not join any of the others, but he was in calling distance of his mother's cabin. So for the present he built his cabin as near as possible to hers. Everything was put up only temporarily—something better by and by. Aunt Hetty and John were a little further off, but Aunt Hetty did not mind it. She was "a good walker," she said.

At the end of the week, in which both men and women worked from daylight until dark, Mr. Wilson, Tom and Mary left for Ouray, Mary to attend school and keep house for Mr. Wilson and her brother. They took with them a team, Tom expecting to return in about a week with more household goods and Mrs. Brown's cow and the heifer belonging to Mollie.

The little company now found time to look

around and see who were their neighbors. Mr. J. C. Frees, passing by, told of his experiences.

He, with Mr. Willerup and R. H. Roberts, had obtained a permit to go on the reservation a short time before to cut hay, one permit for three. Mr. Roberts wandered away from the others and the soldiers caught him. "Oh," he said, "I have a permit." "Show it," they demanded, but Mr. Willerup had the permit in his pocket and was out of sight. The soldiers took Mr. Roberts to the guardhouse. Becoming satisfied that his story was straight, the next morning they turned him loose.

Laughingly he told how Chief Billy came to his tent and wanted to swap guns, Mr. Frees having one the Indian liked better than his own. Billy wanted ten dollars to boot. No. Five, then. No, but the gentleman remarked, "I picked up a dirty cotton shirt I had thrown away and said, 'Here, you can have this to boot,' and sure enough that satisfied the Indian trader."

Then he told how reluctant the Indians had been to leave. There was nothing to keep them, but, like children, they wanted to take their own time. Some would take their ponies to the blacksmith shop. "Pony feet sick, need shoe."

"No, no!" said the blacksmith, "I do no more shoeing; vamoose."

Four days they dallied, and who knows the real reason? Should not the children of nature love and understand nature the most? The white man stands in the presence of the grandeur of the mountains awestruck—then finally words flow forth so beautiful and expressive we are delighted and exclaim, "How he loves these mountains!"

The Indian, born and bred in these mountains, living so close to nature its secrets are a part of his life, feels far more—yes, and loves more, but has not the gift of expressing this love in words. May not this be the real reason—their love for this land which had been their land?

CHAPTER XVIII

A Powwow

A few days later Tom came back with the cow and a load of groceries and household belongings, which were greatly appreciated. Tige, too, who was getting more sedate in his bearing, showed that his love for his friends was as great as ever. Tom was amused at the sudden appearance from every cabin of those he loved, all come to meet him. No soldier returning from war was ever met with greater pleasure. Mollie climbed up into the wagon. She was a warm lover of outdoor life, well fitted for the life she was just entering, and it was well she was. Tom was surprised enough to fully satisfy Mollie when he saw the change a few simple things can make in a room. A square of rag carpet her mother had woven lay upon the dirt floor near the fireplace, a part of the log walls were covered with white cheesecloth, and pinned on that were pretty pictures and verses she had cut from magazines, a bright cloth covered the trunk, a white spread the bed, a tiny curtain hung above not across the window, and Mollie, wearing a white apron, to Tom made a pretty picture.

After a lunch prepared by Mollie's own hands, Kate, coming to the door, said:

"Oh, Tom, come and see how pretty our house looks inside."

"All right, Sis," said Tom, and with Mollie they

went. Kate, proud as a happy young wife could be, explained the arrangement of her cabin: This part was the kitchen, and this, right where the table stands, was the dining room, while there, waving her hand towards the bed, with its white spread, is the bedroom—three rooms in one.

"It's very nice," said Tom, "and some time you girls will have something better, but I doubt if either one of you will be more happy than you are today," and he stooped and kissed the comrade of days gone by. "But come, young ladies, let's go and pay Aunt Hetty a visit." Long before they reached the cabin Aunt Hetty heard them coming and stood by the door smiling. She felt herself growing younger, for, as John said to her when she hesitated to say "yes" when he asked for her company all through the years to come, "love never grows old; you will always be young to me."

"Good evening, young folks," she said, "where's Dick?"

"Oh, he'll be here soon. He, like a dutiful son, is milking the cow for his new mother."

"Why!" said Tom, as he entered his aunt's cabin, "how cozy you are!"

"John thinks it is, too," said Aunt Hetty. "He said last night as we sat by the fire, this room reminded him of what, as a boy, he believed heaven to be—a place where one loves to stay."

"Aunt Hetty," said Tom, "you and John come over to father's this evening. We and all the rest of this blessed family are going to have a 'powwow,' as the Indians say, to talk over what seems best to be done right away."

That evening the entire company gathered around the bright fireside and discussed their mutual interests. The ladies, though their thoughts would wander to other things, listened attentively to plans for the fall work.

"Ladies," said Mr. Barton, "we wished you all to be here tonight because we men believe the best results are attained when the women as well as the men intelligently understand all the affairs of the farm, not that I believe in woman working as a farm hand—she has enough to do in the home—but a man does enjoy talking over his work and plans with his wife. I do; and these young men here had better keep on the way they have begun, for I notice Dick and Kate have much to talk about as they walk over their ranch, and as for Tom and Mollie, they can't think of anything else."

"After a talk with me," said Aunt Hetty, "John says he feels equal to almost anything."

"John's all right," said Bob, "but, gentlemen, has it occurred to you the ideas you have just advanced are discouraging to Jake, Harry and myself? You make us feel very much like the man at sea in a small boat trying to steer with one oar."

"Well, my boy," said his father, joining in the laugh at Bob's words, "that's about how it is, but we don't want you to be in a hurry. You have your mother, and Jake and Harry have us all, to be interested in their work. But let us get down to business."

"I am going to build a shed and corral for the horses and cow in the river bottom," said Mr. Brown. "They will then be near the water and grass."

"I will suggest something mother and I have been talking over," said Mr. Barton, "but it will depend on Jake and Harry to say if it's good," and he smiled at the DeLong boys, who showed their surprise. "It is this, though we must not be too hasty in our decision. It's out of the question to cultivate all of this land the coming year, for not only would we have to dig a good-sized ditch, but think of the fencing. Now, gentlemen and ladies, what do you think of us all, for the coming year, working Jake's and Harry's land to the very best of our ability. Help them make a good fence around it, all hands work together making a ditch for that piece of ground, instead of each working on his own and getting very little done. What do you think, Jake?"

"I don't see," said Jake, flushing, "how I'm to pay you for your work."

"The crop, my boy, will pay for it; we all have shares in the crop. You will have two or three hundred acres that can be utilized. This won't hinder us from doing a little on our own places if we have time. What do you think of this plan, Mr. Brown?"

"I don't know; I shall have to think it over," said Mr. Brown, with a shade of disappointment in his voice. "It's new to me."

"That's right," said Mr. Barton, "we will all

want to think it over, you DeLong boys more than we. Let us all meet at Mr. Brown's tomorrow night. You bring your proposition, boys, and we will be ready to present ours, in case we want to go on with this suggestion, which is at present only a suggestion." With cheerful goodnights the company separated.

During the next day there was much discussion of the proposition as Dick and Tom, Bob and his father, sat outside Mr. Brown's cabin.

"This is the way it looks to me," said Mr. Barton. "Since Jake and Harry's land is above ours, and the ditch we will have to make for their land we would really have to dig for ourselves, there will be no labor lost. One big ditch for us all would be better than four or five smaller ditches, each caring for his own."

"Yes," said Mr. Brown, "but how about the crop? It seems we are all going to help the DeLongs make a fine thing of their land while ours is still unimproved. I don't like that."

"Now see here, Mr. Brown," spoke up Dick, "I see what Mr. Barton is thinking of. We men join together in putting one piece of land in good shape, rather than each working individually. Is not that so, Mr. Barton?"

"Yes, that is the idea," said Mr. Barton, "for I am sure you will all see we have a big proposition before us, each getting out a ditch, fencing his land, putting in his crop, this first year. This plan is only for this one year, you know, but about the crop, whatever is raised on the DeLong place all share equally, all bear the expense equally, put in the same amount of work."

"Oh," said Mr. Brown, "so there would be some time for each to work on his own ranch?"

"Sure," replied Tom, "don't you see? Suppose we have to work on the average nine hours a day, the rest of the time we can use as we wish. I see plainly we shall each have to keep strict account of our time."

"Well," said Mr. Brown, "I begin to see daylight. There must be over two hundred acres which can be tilled, don't you think?"

"Yes," said Tom, "I was over there and surveyed it in my mind. There must be two hundred and forty. Now, divided by eight, this would amount to thirty acres each, a nice start for the first year. Why, the more I think of it the better the proposition looks to me."

"Yes, yes," said Mr. Brown, "I'm in for it, and everything looks brighter to me, for my raw ranch, with all the work needed before spring has, I must confess, kept me awake nights, but don't tell that to my women folks."

The matter was left until evening, when early the whole company gathered around Mrs. Brown's pleasant fireside, the ladies bringing their sewing with them. "I can think better when I'm sewing," said Mrs. Barton.

"Now, Jake and Harry, you have thought this thing over, what conclusions have you come to?"

"We," said Jake, "believe it would work out good not only for us but for you. Have you any suggestions to offer about the fencing?"

"No," said Mr. Brown, "only we are willing to help put it up."

"Well, friends," and Jake looked around rather embarrassed with so many eyes turned on him, "Harry and I have been talking it over and will now offer our proposition, which you may accept or reject as seems best. We have it written out, not only to better express ourselves, but if it is accepted, for reference later. Harry, you read it."

"This is the way we feel about it," said Harry, bowing, while the little company smiled. "We, the DeLong boys, propose, if you join hands with us in fixing our ditch, we will give, when the time comes, an equal amount of work on your ditch, as many days' work as you put on our fencing we will give in helping you with yours, which, to our way of thinking would be nothing but right. Then whatever is raised during this one year will be divided equally. Is that clear?"

"Very," said Mr. Barton.

"Then there is something else. I've been told to sow alfalfa seed with the grain. The next year we get a good crop of hay, and have the ground seeded for several years. This year we are working together, you would not get anything from that; we boys would be that much ahead. So we agree if you will help fence this alfalfa we will share equally in the work and hay until you have plenty of your own."

"Why, boys," said John, "that is too much."

"It's what we want to do," said Jake.

"I move we give a vote of thanks to Mr. DeLong and his brother," said Mollie. Kate quickly seconded.

"Well," said Mr. Barton, smiling, "if there are no objections to the motion, and from the smile on every face there is not, it stands approved, but I want personally to thank you boys for joining so heartily in the plan."

"In the first place," said Tom, "I want to speak of what has come to me. I thought Mr. Wilson and I would be out of this, since we are away so much, but the thought has just come to me. You must count us in; Mr. Wilson and I will find two men to take our places here during the summer."

"Good," said Mrs. Wilson, "Ruth and I were feeling left out on this proposition."

"You should not," said Jake gently.

"Tomorrow we had better begin on the ditch," said Dick. "Time is short for that kind of work. Someone else begin fencing, for Jake and Harry should begin plowing at once."

"Then," said Mr. Barton, "Tom will have to stay long enough to survey the ditch."

They broke up at once to get what rest they could, happy to have definite work ahead of them again. All hands were out next morning to take part in locating the ditch which was to be so important a part of their possessions.

CHAPTER XIX

The Water Question

Again the hearts of the company were happy, even joyous. They were working, co-operating, with nature. While the work of the women was just as important, only in a little different line. If the interests are the same it matters not what line of work, they are both one. If husbands and wives realized this more, if the word "our" was used more often, how much of sorrow might be spared.

When the young men came down to take the places of Mr. Wilson and Tom, Mrs. Wilson asked the privilege of boarding them, "for it seems," she said, "Ruth and I have nothing to do in this busy family." The young men ate at Mrs. Wilson's and slept at the DeLongs'.

A great change was coming over the new ranch. The ground, though dry, was in shape for plowing, the fence nearing completion, the ditch progressing. Mr. Wilson had made a short visit and was well pleased with the progress made.

One evening two men on their way through the valley asked for lodging for the night. Bob gave up his bed in the tent, saying he could sleep on the sofa in his mother's kitchen. That evening after supper, the company gathered at the Barton home to listen to these men. They seemed to be very intelligent and well posted regarding the conditions and needs of the valley, and were introduced to one and another of our friends as they came in. When they were all seated, Mr. Barton said:

"Friends, we have two gentlemen with us who, I believe, can give us some insight into conditions we know very little about. We Easterners are out West, but we find there is much to learn. We will begin by asking a question: What is the prospect of this land being taken up quickly and permanently? Are there any drawbacks?"

One of the gentlemen answered, "Yes, my friends, there are drawbacks, one of which—the most serious—is lack of water. All this fine land is useless without water, and it is lacking today. We are very much interested in the way you people are working; it is the only way to save your homes."

Here the company looked up at Mr. Barton and smiled, while he looked over at his wife with much feeling.

"You are going to pull through because you are working together. We surely congratulate you. It will be years before these ranches that are now being taken up can be well supplied with water. With some poor fellows there are miles of ditch to be dug before the land can be utilized. It has made us heartsick as we came upon people who a month ago expected to soon have a home, but learning the conditions as they are today are all broken up. They had sold their homes at a sacrifice to come here, men ready and glad to work, but what's the use? There's no water."

The little company, as they sat listening to this

man, became silent. He saw the effect it was having on them. He had seen it before.

"Now, my friends, the way for some who live near the river is to get together as you have done and form a small company, all working together in getting out a ditch. When you make your ditch, make it large enough, even larger than you think necessary; you will never regret it."

"Thank you," said Mr. Barton. "Is there any other way to get water than the one you have mentioned?"

"Yes," said the gentleman. "My friend and I are sent out by a company who are thinking of putting in considerable money and taking out a ditch costing thousands of dollars. We put in the ditch and the farmers pay for the water they need. We are sent to look over the land and judge of the advisability of making the attempt."

"We surely hope you can," said Mr. Brown, "but it will take years for you to accomplish such an undertaking."

"Yes, friends, it will, but it's the only salvation for this valley."

"I must confess," said Mr. Barton, "the water question never came to me. Land was the one thing. Do you think it possible for this valley ever to be thoroughly cultivated? Would it not have been better for the Indians to have remained?"

"Why!" said Dick, all the sunshine gone from his face, "even if we have plenty of water from the river, what would be the use of raising anything?

We could not sell it. No railroad would come for the few ranches near the river." Kate reached for his hand. She found it cold, and tried to warm it.

"I do not think," said Tom, and there was a strong ring in his voice that startled the hearers, "we should allow ourselves to be discouraged, but, as mother has said from the very first, the same Hand that brought us will lead us out of the difficulty." Mother looked up quickly at Tom, and he saw the tears she had kept from falling were shining like dewdrops.

"Well, my boy," said the gentleman, who until then had not spoken, "if you have something like this to lean upon, you have much to be thankful for. Some have not. And you, my kind friends," said he, as he looked around over the little company, "have indeed much to rejoice over. You have youth and hope and, I know, love, one for the other. You have parents, and you," he said, looking up to the older ones, "have children. You will win out, for you have the very foundation of success with you. I believe we will retire, as we have traveled far."

After they had gone, the little company sat for some time without speaking, and some rose to leave. But Mr. Barton quietly said, "Sit down, please; it is not late; I want to say a few words." And he replenished the fire, which had died away. "My friends," said he, "I believe it would be well to take a backward glance for a moment. It may encourage us. For myself I will say, when a young man I had been reading much about our forefathers who, having become restless under the conditions they found themselves in—it could not have been wholly a religious restraint they felt—class distinctions were very strong, and today we may easily see how a man with all the feelings of a man rising up in him should chafe under these distinctions. To be born poor was in a measure always to remain poor. The sense of equality, where one was just as good as another, provided he was honest and upright, was little thought of or brought out. As I said, I had been reading much on this line. Then as I went about my work I began to see, although our conditions were vastly improved here in America, we had perhaps unconsciously fallen into ruts both in thinking and in doing. Conventionality was very strong. My sister here," and he gave her an affectionate glance, "seemed controlled by the fear of 'what people would say,' so accustomed were we to following our ancestors, but since coming out into this country she never expresses such a narrow thought. So, friends, while pondering over these things I was led to read glowing accounts of what then was termed the 'Far West,' which then included everything west of the Missouri river. The more I thought about it, the stronger the desire grew to leave the old for the new life which offered greater opportunities, but opposition was so brought to bear because of ignorance on the subject that my longings were crushed for the time and I took rather than earned what was given me. The time came when Tom felt the fire or spirit, as he called it, of this western country urging him to give up the East, with its settled ways of doing and thinking, and beginning his life work in a land of freer thought and greater opportunity. The same desires again sprang up in me; they had only been crushed, not killed. Because of all this we are here today. Shall we, at the first sight of obstacles, be cast down? Rather, let us with the same spirit which animated our forefathers, rise up and overcome. I am glad we were born in the East, for I see now the West, with its great storehouses of wealth, needs the East, with its legacy of strength, to overcome. And what have we to overcome but the forces of nature? Nature is lavish with her gifts. We have the best climate, for the sun shines almost every day in the year; we have no extremes of heat or cold; and land—the best in the country; water is abundant—yes, Dick, you shake your head, but it is, more than we in this part of the valley need, but our overcoming lies in the direction of bringing this water where we can utilize it. At first, while these gentlemen were talking, I felt cast down, dumbfounded, but all at once light came and the reasonableness of our having to meet this very question came to me, and the plan these men so kindly explained to us is the only way out. A few like we, working together, or, as others seem to be doing, a whole neighborhood joining together and putting in a ditch, though I see it will mean much of time and some money. But for the larger part, and really most of this land, thousands of dollars must be expended before the water can be distributed, for a very small part of the country lies near the river.

"Friends, excuse me for taking up so much time, but this came so suddenly to me I could not keep it. We have started in the right way, and as these gentlemen have said, are going to win. Let us meet here tomorrow evening, and then each will have a chance to talk."

The men in their tent, when they heard the happy goodnights said and the laughter of the young people, wondered and were glad.

CHAPTER XX

JAKE MEETS THE ONE GIRL

The next day was a busy one, but in spite of the work a peace and gentleness was felt; the talk of the evening before rested as a benediction. As soon as they were seated the next evening in Mrs. Barton's cabin, Dick said:

"Kate has an idea which is new to me and may prove a good one for us all."

"What is it?" asked Tom.

"That we put in two or three acres of garden stuff on this land we are going to cultivate."

"That will be more than we can use," said Mr. Barton.

"Yes, but father!" cried Kate, who could keep still no longer, "I worked it all out in the night. Don't you remember how scarce vegetables were in Ouray? Not near enough to supply the market! Why can we not all join in raising at least three acres of garden stuff? The one best adapted to the work take the produce to Ouray and dispose of it. We women can help in caring for the garden."

"A good plan," said Mr. Brown. "What do you think of this, Jake and Harry?"

"I believe it will prove good, all right, but Harry and I know very little about gardening."

"John knows a whole lot about such things!" spoke up Aunt Hetty, excitedly. "John's father made a business of gardening near New York."

"That surely is fine," joined in Mrs. Barton. Let us turn the superintendency of the garden over to John and Aunt Hetty." All the company agreed.

"Now," said Mrs. Wilson, who evidently had something on her mind. "I rise to suggest we raise three acres of potatoes."

"But," said Mr. Brown, "in this way there will be little land for grain," for Mr. Brown saw no real profit but in hay or grain.

"I've been reading," went on Mrs. Wilson, "in this farm paper we are taking that this soil is very good for potatoes."

"All right, let's try our luck on three acres of potatoes," said Tom.

"It appears to me," said Bob, "that the ladies have all the bright ideas tonight."

"That's all right," returned Mr. Barton, "but perhaps, Bob, you have an idea to give us."

"I've been reading up, too, and a few loads of manure would be fine for that dear little garden."

"Yes," said John, "but that is out of the question; there is none to be secured. We must remember this is a new country."

"What will you bet," asked Bob, his eyes twinkling, "that I cannot get a load of the finest kind in less than two hours?"

"Now, Bob, don't keep us all in suspense," said Kate. "Where can we get it?"

"I used my eyes. When near the fort I noticed a good many horses were kept there, and in reasoning it out in my mind I came to the conclusion they would likely have plenty of that article, and be glad to get rid of it."

"Good for you, Bob!" said his mother, smiling.

"I give up," said John, "and will go and help get a few loads when the time comes."

A rap at the door startled the little company. Mr. Barton went to the door and found two horsemen.

"Hello," said one of them. "My name is Long; this gentleman's name is Sherman; our home is in the Park. I believe I have met your son, Tom," he said, smiling, as they were introduced to the company. "We were passing by and thought we would drop in a little while."

"Won't you stay all night?" asked Mrs. Barton, who had taken on the spirit of the hospitality so strong in the West.

"No, thank you, Mrs. Barton. Our women folk would be uneasy if we did not return tonight. They have been so accustomed to worrying nights the last year or two on account of the Indians being so restless, we hate to cause them any anxiety."

"You have a cozy place here," said Mr. Sherman, as he looked over the group.

"Yes," said Mr. Barton, "we enjoy it. We were gathered together tonight to talk over our work and plans for the coming year."

"Will you have water enough," quickly asked Mr. Long, "for all your land?"

"No, not until we have a ditch. Then we hope to get all we need from the river." Then Mr. Barton explained what their plans were in regard to only cultivating the DeLong places for the coming year.

"That's a good proposition," said Mr. Long. "One ranch well cultivated is worth a dozen only half cared for. Going to take out a ditch together?"

"Yes," said Jake. "What do you think of this water question? It is new to us."

"It's a tough question," explained Mr. Long. "That is, you who are just taking up land will find it so. I know of several men who have taken up land and are getting together to get out a ditch, each man doing his part, you know, but it's slow work. We people in the park have seen all the time what you fellows would be up against when you got this land. It's all right if you can afford to wait, for we see a great future for this valley if you pioneers can hold on, if you have grit enough. I met those men who stopped with you last night. They told me they represent a company who see the need of today, and show they believe in the future of this valley as well as we, for they propose to spend a large amount of money before they have a chance to receive any returns. That, of itself, is encouraging."

"So it is," said Mr. Brown. "I never thought of it in that light. We are of the number who intend to hold on, are we not, mother?"

"Yes," said Mrs. Brown, blushing at having to speak before such a crowd.

"Well, we must be going," joined in Mr. Sherman. "If there is anything you need that we have

THE STAGE JUST IN. SNOW VERY DEEP. OURAY, COLORADO, 1881.

don't be backward about asking for it. The women folk have been hinting pretty strongly for us to bring them down to see you people. Some Sunday we will come for dinner," and with a hearty shake of the hand they left, leaving the little group brighter for their good fellowship.

A month later our little company was agreeably surprised to see two wagonloads of people drive up. Mrs. Barton stepped to the door and recognized their former visitors, Mr. Long and Mr. Sherman.

"Here we are," said Mr. Long. "We have come to eat dinner with you. This is my wife and two daughters."

"And here," said Mr. Sherman, "is my wife and children," the children a boy about five and a girl about seven.

"Come in, come in!" said Mr. Barton, who had just come from a walk with Tom. "We are glad to see you."

The ladies came in, each with a basket of eatables. "We knew you would not be prepared for such a crowd," the ladies explained.

After dinner an invitation was given to the DeLongs and the rest of the friends to meet the visitors at the Barton cabin, and a jolly time they had. One of Mr. Long's daughters, a girl about seventeen, Myrtle by name, proposed they have a song. All joined in with hearty good will, one song following another, until Mr. Sherman said, "One more, and then we must start home. Let's sing 'My Country, 'Tis of Thee'."

The party broke up with a warm invitation for the little settlement, as Mr. Sherman called it, to come and visit them.

"My! but that was fine," said Mrs. Barton, "to have people feel so free to come, to take it for granted they would be welcome."

"Jake seemed to take quite a fancy to the oldest girl, Myrtle. I would like to joke him," said Bob.

"Don't you do it," said his mother. "It's too serious a thing; I don't think Jake could stand very much of that."

Bob endeavored to obey, though, as he told his mother the next evening, it went hard.

Winter passed rapidly and spring came with its encouraging voices. Hope and courage rose high, for these people were so in touch with nature they felt its stirring impulse. The winter evenings had been spent in planning their work to the best advantage, so spring found them prepared.

"Why, Jake!" said Bob, who had gone over on an errand after the evening meal was over, "what are you doing?" for Jake was busy digging a little space near the cabin door.

"I'm going to plant some flower seeds my mother gathered from her own garden." A catch in his voice caused Bob to keep back the light words that almost came. "She gave them to me the day we left and said they would seem like old friends. They sure will remind us of her."

"Indeed they will," said Harry, who came out just then.

"But," said Bob, "how will you get the water to them?"

"I shall carry it from the ditch—will be glad to, for a sight of something that reminds me of home." It came to Bob then as it never had before what a lonely life these boys were leading, notwithstanding this little company's affection for them.

"I wish your mother was here, boys. I never realized how much you must miss her, and your father, too. It's no fun cooking and washing dishes all alone. I wish you would give me a few of those seeds; mother might like some, and say, boys," said Bob, with a catch in his voice, as the thought of these boys' loss came over him, "I want to share my mother with you. Talk to her just as you would to your own mother."

"Thank you," said Harry, and the boys shook Bob's hand in a way he understood. That night, when wiping the dishes for mother, he told her all about it, "and mother, put these seeds they gave me in the best part of the garden where they will be sure to get plenty of water and attention. I've no faith in anything doing well that is dependent on sprinkling. These boys must have their flowers. Let's see, how soon will Mary be coming home?"

"School will be out next month," answered mother, smiling, for she had missed her little girl, who had not been home since Christmas, though the whole family had been up to visit her late in the winter, taking their beds with them.

Tom's work at Ouray was not rushing. He often

ON THE WAY TO THE HILLS.

came down to work on his ranch and that of his father, making it look as though they meant business, although nothing could be raised, as the ditch did not reach either. In due time Mollie's heifer had a calf, which they kept. When the company went to the Park to return the visit made them, Mr. Barton asked the gentlemen many questions about how to irrigate. Mr. Long finally said: "I'll tell you what I will do. Let me know when you are ready to run your furrows, and I will take a day off and bring my family down to visit your women folks, while I show you a thing or two."

It was well they did, for irrigation was new to them, and the help they received from this kindly neighbor meant the saving of half the crop, for there is much to learn about irrigating to advantage. Not long after the water was turned on one could see the tiny shoots springing up in the garden. responding so quickly to love and care, and even before the people in the park, our company sent vegetables to Ouray, which were greatly appreciated. John and his wife peddling them from house to house, Aunt Hetty enjoying it with no thought of what people might say. A trip was made each week. They had great cause to be thankful for the income the garden brought them, besides having a plenty of vegetables for themselves. The potatoes gave evidence of producing a good crop. The grain was looking fine.

One evening Mrs. Barton took a walk over to Jake's place, taking with her something inviting for the boys to eat. They were both sitting outside, resting after the day's work.

"Why," said she, "what's the matter with your flowers? They don't seem to do well."

"No," answered Jake, "I've carried water all spring, but they get dry so quickly. They started all right, expecting the same treatment, I guess, they would have got back home, but they got plumb discouraged; they should be blooming now."

"Let's go down into the garden. You have not been there for some time, have you?"

"No, we have been too busy attending to the grain." They went to the garden, and were kept busy admiring the vegetables, when all at once they came to a little bed of flowers all in full bloom.

"Oh, mother, mother!" said Jake, as he knelt down and hid his sunburnt face among them, the flowers sprinkled by water not brought from the river. Harry stood by, his eyes, too, filled with tears. "It looks like home," said he.

"Yes," said Jake, patting the flowers with his rough hands as gently as a woman, "they surely do. We have you to thank for them, dear Mrs. Barton."

"No," said she, "it is Bob. You remember he asked you for a few of your seeds; he feared they might not do well, he told me, away from the ditch, so asked me to put these here for you."

"He surely was kind," and Jake gently gathered a few of the flowers and handing them to Mrs. Barton, said, "Give them to Bob. Tell him we thank him."

The mother gave the flowers to Bob, and after giving the message said, "You have no idea how much those flowers mean to these boys. We must see they go home this winter."

"You bet we will," said Bob, and Mary, who was home now, said, "I know a little how they feel. I never let on, but my! I was homesick many a time in Ouray," and Mary gave her mother a very loving kiss.

CHAPTER XXI

HOLDING DOWN A RANCH

Our people often had callers during the summer, not always the most desirable—men who were out for adventure—the scum of the cities, not intending to make homes, attracted by stories told concerning the mines; but those men soon learned it was not wise to go too far in their lawlessness, for there were men everywhere who would not stand for it, and in a moment of provocation would quickly start to string a man of this kind up to a tree. This condition of things did not last long. Stories often came to these people about the lawlessness around a village named Montrose, nine miles below the Post, thirteen saloons justifying the report.

News came of the near approach of the railroad, which reached Montrose October 1st, 1882, causing the hearts of the homeseekers to rejoice.

Jake and Harry decided, after much persuasion of their friends, to go back home for the winter, the friends promising to look after everything, when a letter came which caused the boys to hurry over to the Bartons as soon as supper was over. "Mother and father are coming! Be here in a few days!"

"Good for you," said Mr. Barton, and Mrs. Barton added, "Yes, and good for them; it will do them good."

"Yes," said Harry, "they say in their letter the crops are all cared for and they want to see us, and hearing the railroad came within a few miles of our place, decided to come."

"Well, well!" said Tom, for he was home for a few days, "we have no time to spare. All hands to-morrow sharp—a room must be added to Jake's cabin."

"Yes, Tom," said Bob, and away he went to tell the news. As soon as the necessary work was done on the farms all hands went to work. By night the 12 by 14 cabin was ready for the roof, a fireplace at one end, leaving the door and window, with the chinking, to be done on the morrow. After the cabin was all finished, Mrs. Wilson brought over four sheets, two for the bed and two for the wall around the bed. Mary found some pictures to pin on the sheets, making the room look, as she said, "very cozy." Mrs. Brown gave up her square of carpet for the present, and Mrs. Barton two chairs. and Tom his bed: together they loaned whatever they needed for the comfort of the visitors. Jake and Harry were in a state of excitement between thankfulness to the friends for their kindness and the joy of seeing their parents again. They said they could not stand much more. Four days after the letter was received a team drove up from the town of Montrose, stopping at the Barton place to inquire where Mr. Jake DeLong's ranch was. "Why, Mrs. DeLong!" laughed Mrs. Barton, "how glad we are to see you, and Mr. DeLong, happy as ever?"

"Getting there," said he, with a warm grasp of the hand, "and Mary, how you have grown!"

"Why, Mollie Brown!" exclaimed Mrs. DeLong, as that young lady came to the door, but Bob, coming in a moment before, called out, "It's Mrs. Tom Barton, if you please," and everyone laughed.

"Well, well," said Mr. DeLong, with his genial smile, "Bob has not changed one bit, only grown larger and better looking."

"He can go with you," said his mother, "and show you the way. It looks like it was going to rain and the men are hurrying to get the potatoes gathered."

It was too early for the men to be in from their work, but the door was open, and Bob led them in, hastily lighting the brush in the fireplace. Stepping to the door a few minutes later, Mr. DeLong called to his wife, who was busy putting her things away, "There they come, bless 'em," and the mother, through her tears, exclaimed, "What a beautiful picture!"

A cool breeze was blowing, the bright yellow cottonwood leaves flying in every direction to make some longed-for visits to friends who, too, were on the move; then, casting their eyes to the hills, saw them covered with the bright hues of autumn; then, directly south, they saw what was new to them—the snow-capped mountains. Above it all were the clouds; to the east they were dark and threatening, while toward the south they were broken by rifts of blue sky. To the west the sun was doing its best to show its face, but failing, threw back, as in token of good will, every tint of the rainbow; then, to these parents the most precious of all, they saw their boys, their faces all wreathed in smiles, with their potato forks on their shoulders, running to meet them. The boys saw nothing of the scenery, although they might have felt it, but the sight they so longed to see was with them, their mother standing in the open doorway, smiling her loving welcome, the father with tears and smiles chasing each other over his happy face. One is led to feel that the joy of meeting far outweighs the sense of separation. The whole settlement came over to welcome the parents that evening, the ladies bringing ample lunch along. What a happy evening they spent, rejoicing in the happiness of this united family.

"I must say," said Mr. DeLong, "our boys are surely among friends."

"Indeed we are," said Jake.

"Well," said Mr. Barton, "you have just come in time to help us harvest our potatoes. We have something in that line which will open your eyes; they have mine. And people say that if the water had not run so low that they would be twice as large."

The company left at an early hour, knowing full well how weary the travelers must be. The next day was a jolly one, in spite of hard work. Mr. DeLong was in a state of amazement at the size and number of the potatoes. "Why, man!" he said to his old-time neighbor, "if you had written me how it is, I should never have believed you. We never raised such spuds back East." Yes, it was a happy surprise for them all.

One day Mr. Long stopped on his way to Montrose, and when shown what a fine crop of potatoes the boys had, he said, with very little show of interest, "Yes, they have done fairly well. You'll do better next year. There is lots to learn about raising potatoes, and then the water played out on you."

"You don't mean to say you can beat this?" asked Mr. DeLong.

"Sure I can," laughingly answered Mr. Long, as he bade them goodby.

The DeLongs were well pleased with their sons' prospects, and thanked the friends over and over for their kindness to the boys. "It's all right," said Mr. Barton, "they would do just the same for us. I'm glad they are not going out this winter; we need their help on the ditch. We hope to get it over two more ranches this winter."

"Which two will you take this next year?" asked Mr. DeLong. He was curious to know, for this working together was new to him.

"We have not decided yet," answered Mr. Barton, and hastily changed the subject. "You see, we are taking the time now to get cedar posts for the fence; we can get all we want in the hills."

The three weeks passed by very quickly, and the day came for the parents to start on their homeward journey, the boys taking them in the wagon as far as the railroad, and these boys came back with renewed courage to work out life's problems.

November winds have come, with their songs of rejoicing, though some believe them mournful, the trees in the river bottom, shorn of all their summer beauty, mutely proclaiming, "We still live!" Our friends were busy as bees gathering what little garden stuff was left into the cellars, for each house had a cellar, and it is well they had, for in spite of selling such quantities during the summer on their trips to Ouray, there is plenty for all, the coming winter.

One evening, after the first light snow, the winds having gone to sleep, the stars shining bright, the new moon just passed by, a tiny cry rang out on the stillness of the night. Another pioneer had started on his journey—it was a boy—to explore a country very new and wonderful to him. This country so new to him seemed filled with love and tenderness, many willing hands waiting to do his bidding, and Mollie, realizing a sense of heaven as she lay with her baby in her arms. And Tom, the happiness too big for words, with a tenderer love for his mother than he had ever felt before. It was queer, but everyone in that little company seemed to have taken on a sense of tenderness towards eac' other because of the presence of the little stranger.

As winter advanced the Bartons had many callers, men sometimes bringing their families with them, who told the pitiful story of having parted with all they had to come to this country, expecting, because of wild reports, plenty the moment they took up land, and, like our little company, never thinking of the water question. To these people, with fine tracts of land, but far from the river, realizing it might be two or three years before a ditch could be built to benefit them, the question came, what should they do? Leave their ranch with the chance of losing even that, and try to find work elsewhere? But where? All over the valley were the same conditions to be found—men growing heart-sick and wives utterly discouraged. Then there were others, who, with a little to live on, worked away, preparing their places for the time when the water would be coaxed to turn from its usual course to flow in man-made channels; for come it must. The need was urgent, and the call was being heard. Men with money at their command came, looking over the country, studying the needs and possibilities of the valley—men quick to perceive the rich reward for him who dared to make the attempt to overcome the obstacles in the way.

Reports came of men making the attempt to what they called jump a ranch, where some poor man, gone perhaps to earn a few dollars, came back to find men, usually more than one, on his ranch, with ready revolvers, refusing to give up the ranch, standing on the statement, "possession was nine points in the law." What could a man do, heart-sick and discouraged anyway, but yield? One man they were told was prevailed upon to give up three different places. Report came to Montrose that an attempt was to be made to jump the Parker Lupher ranch. His wife gives her own experience in the following sketch:

"Montrose was a pretty rough town when we

came riding in on the railroad just completed this far, in the year 1882. Only fourteen women were here at that time, and every last one would have preferred to have been somewhere else—it was so wild—so much shooting. One night Parker loaned his gun to a man to stand guard all night outside our house; he never saw the gun again.

"I remember one man, a big, fat fellow, who jumped two lots and built a shack on them. He was so big he had an idea he could do as he pleased and no one would dare molest him. But one night the vigilance committee called on him and with some sleight-of-hand performance threw a rope around his neck and led him down to the bridge, but after considerable discussion they agreed to let him go if he would leave town immediately and never come back, and he was glad enough to go.

"One day word came, just as Parker was leaving to go to his mine at Red Mountain, just beyond Ouray, that someone was going to jump our claim, a ranch near the Post. That was to be our home, and I was not going to sit still and see it taken from us, so I volunteered to go and hold it down. I was not as big as I am now, but I had the courage which belongs to the young, and there were the children to think of. With some misgivings, Parker found a woman to go and keep me company. Much of my time on the ranch was spent in pulling cactus thorns out of my feet, the shack being built in a cactus bed and by a village of prairie dogs. One night these prairie dogs migrated, every one of them. They went in single file. I saw them myself, calling and barking as they went to the arroyo. They never came back.

"The next day I saw five or six cowboys. I had read such awful stories about the cowboys I was more frightened than if they had been Indians. The woman that stayed with me slept all night while I watched. I don't know to this day what I was watching for, but I watched. I was even more afraid of the soldiers—never did trust them as long as they were here.

"One day I was looking for my husband home, and felt pretty proud of my work in holding down a ranch for him and the children. But he did not come, so I took up my accustomed watching, while the other woman and the children were fast asleep. All at once my heart seemed to jump into my throat. I heard footsteps near the house, and, having no gun, knew I must play a bluff for all it was worth. Just then a man's face came to the window and a disguised voice asked, 'Can't you let a fellow in?' Shaking with fear, but determined to protect myself and home, I said, 'No, and if you don't move off pretty quick I'll shoot you.' The man at the window saw he had made a mistake and began to laugh; then I found it was my husband playing a joke on me. I was so frightened that if a gun had been in my hand I surely would have shot him.

"No attempt was made to take our ranch away, and as far as any cause for fear of cowboys, we found them friendly, always ready to do a neighbor a kindness."

CHAPTER XXII

A FRIEND INDEED

One morning in December the Barton family were seated around the breakfast table. It was too cold to work outdoors very early, so they took time for a little chat about things that interested them, when Bob, looking across the fields, remarked, "There is the Jones kid coming horseback as if in a hurry." The door was opened before the boy had time to knock.

"Why, Jimmie, good morning!" said Mr. Barton, who saw at a glance something was wrong. "How's your folks?"

For a moment the boy was silent—the warm room and the warmer sympathy shown were too much for him; finally he blurted out, "Pa said tell you we had a baby at our house, and ma's sick, and we have nothing to eat," and the child burst out crying, trembling all over.

"Bob," said his mother, with a sob in her voice, "hitch up the horses for your father and me; Mary, give that boy his breakfast." Mr. Barton waited for his orders. "Father," said the wife, "here is a sack; go to the cellar and fill it with vegetables." Then hastily she prepared the little things only a woman can think of in a case like this. "Mary, take this flour sack and fill it with bread—a good thing we baked yesterday—and get father's overcoat out."

So quickly did they work that in less than twenty minutes Jimmie, warm and well filled, was sitting between his two friends as they rode rapidly away over the frozen ground, his horse tied behind the wagon.

Mr. Jones saw them coming, and came to the door, a little girl five years old crowding her father aside to get a better view herself, smiling in her happy babyhood. The father, with his hair uncombed, his eyes red, with a look of shame on his face for being unable to meet the needs of his family, could not bring out the words he wanted to speak. Oh, ye wives, who are tempted to censure the man who loves you! may you live long enough to understand the sufferings of a husband who seems worsted in the battle, he, so full of hope and courage when you started on life's journey together, believing himself capable of making a home with all its comforts for you, to come to a strait like this. Blessed is the woman, and blessed the man, when the wife feels, if she really cannot understand, what it must be to a man at such a time.

"Good morning, dear," said Mrs. Barton, as she knelt by the bedside, putting her strong arms around the frail little woman, kissing her and loving her as though she was her own daughter, "everything's coming out all right. I'm sure it will. It's always darkest just before the dawn. Many a time it has seemed dark to me, but light always comes; it will to you, dear heart." With loving words like these a change came over the woman, and though the tears rolled down her face, they were not rebellious tears, for peace, the angel whose presence we sometimes fail to recognize, was creeping into her heart.

"Dear Mrs. Barton, you have helped me so much; don't you want to see the baby?"

"Not yet, you must be looked after first." Soon a warm breakfast was prepared for the whole family, the mother looking sweet with clean clothes and smoothed hair, a halo of joy about her—the mystery of mother love. Even the father, buoyed up by the neighborliness and good will shown by Mr. Barton and his wife, seemed like a different man. What a change a little kindness can bring about. Why do we stint ourselves in these things?

"It's all right," said Mr. Barton, in reply to Mr. Jones' words of thanks. "Consider these things our Christmas present, just come a little ahead to avoid the rush, you know. And soon we shall need help on the ranch; you might as well help us till something else comes your way, but we will go now. By the way, if Mary comes over tomorrow to spend the day, could you go with Bob to get us a load of cedar posts? We need a little help right now."

"Yes, indeed," said the man, "shall be glad to."

So these neighbors, when they went home, found their own hearts light and happy. Mrs. Barton had something on her mind, for as soon as dinner was over she, with Mary, went over to Mollie's home, where she found that happy young mother singing to her baby, who was, as Mollie declared, "the picture of his father."

"Yes, indeed," said this young mother, "baby's growing so he is getting too big already for some of his clothes, so just take them." Then Mrs. Barton went to Mrs. Wilson's, and, stating the needs, there was soon another bundle for Mary to take with her the next day when she went to stay with Mrs. Jones. And a little money found its way to Mr. Jones' pocket after the day's hauling with Bob. This was far from being the only case of need.

Mr. Brown and his wife, returning home from a visit to the grocery store in Montrose, a little later, overtook a man who, when invited to ride, accepted the invitation with thanks. Mr. Brown, being a sociable man, began to inquire about this man's home, and found the same story of hard times; said he had just been to the store to ask credit, but, as he owed a little bill with no prospect of being able to pay, was refused. "I'm going back home now," he said, "empty-handed to my wife. It hurts." And the gray-haired man's lips quivered. Finding this man lived farther up the valley, Mr. Brown, after a few whispered words with his wife, turned to the man and said, "If you don't mind accepting a few things as a Christmas gift, we will stop at our house. I am sure we have more vegetables than we need, and we will take you home. It's early yet." Again this western large-heartedness prevailed, and another family was tided over a hard place, for it was not just vegetables, but other little things Mrs. Brown knew would come in handy, and better than all, a lifetime friendship was formed which brought about its attending blessings.

Mr. Wilson was home. No work of any consequence for him at that time in Ouray, he was getting more and more dissatisfied with that way of living, and, to the joy of his wife and daughter, decided to sell out his interests up there and stay on the farm. "Begin to live," he said. Tom was home, too, for it was the time of year when little could be done in his line of work. He had hoped to get work on the government land survey of the valley, but had decided to stay on the ranch and make a home.

Christmas came, with its message of peace and good will. A happy company they were, for Christmas was celebrated by all meeting together at Mrs. Brown's, Mollie's baby the guest of honor, to whom all brought their gifts of love and admiration; even Bob had to give a smile, and admitted to Mary, "it was a mighty cute youngster." Aunt Hetty was made supremely happy by the baby being named after her husband, "a case of big John and little John," she said.

New Year's eve the little company gathered at Mrs. Wilson's to celebrate Mr. and Mrs. Barton's twenty-fifth wedding anniversary, and also to decide what two other ranches should be cultivated the coming year. After a hearty supper, Mr. Barton said, "Friends, we will now talk over the coming year's work."

"Mr. Barton," spoke up Jake, "we would like

to offer our ranches again for the coming year, and we to help you in working two more ranches, which you are now going to decide upon, I believe."

"This is very kind of you," replied Mr. Wilson. "We surely would like to do so since we have decided to keep on the way we began."

"Now," said Mr. Barton, who was not smiling as much as usual, "we want to consider this question of what ranches we will cultivate this coming year. We are glad, as Mr. Wilson says, for the kind offer of the DeLong ranches another year; now, which shall it be? I know you have all been thinking over the subject; it really should be the two nearest the ditch; that should govern us all the way through; are you willing it shall?" he asked.

After a moment it was suggested that a vote be taken on such an important question, and it was agreed to take the advice given, taking the two nearest the main ditch.

"All right, friends," said Mr. Barton, smiling again, pleased to see the kindly feeling shown. "Mr. Wilson and I were over the ground and found the land next available belonged to Mr. Brown and Tom."

"Good for you, Tom!" said Dick, his face showing his good will.

"And, good for you, Mr. and Mrs. Brown," said Mrs. Barton, her voice showing her sense of relief.

"Well," said Mr. Brown, "I might as well confess, there is no use in trying to hide it, there has been a mighty strong hankering to get my place in shape, but I was not going to let on, for the way we are working together is fine—it beats anything I ever heard of—and I will work just as hard as anyone to help fix up the last ranch."

"It's all right," said Mr. Barton. "We all have had a touch of wanting to see our own fixed up. Now we want to see where we stand and begin the year afresh. According to our books, we find the DeLong boys have paid to each of us in cedar posts for the time we put on their fence, and the amount of work we put on their ditch they will put on ours, so that leaves us square with them."

"Now," said Mr. Brown, who was all smiles, "I propose that Tom and I make the same proposition to the rest of you that the DeLong boys made about the alfalfa; we will put in the same amount that they did, you all joining in putting in the fence."

"Gentlemen and ladies," said Harry, who was growing into a very handsome young man, and not so diffident as when they left home, "I propose the alfalfa question be settled once for all. Every ranch have put in the same amount of alfalfa, and until the last ranch is in cultivation, with its second crop coming on, we all share equally in the crop raised." The clapping of hands showed their approval.

"Another thing I want to say," said Mr. Brown, whose soul was now in the work. "I want five acres of potatoes raised on my place this coming year; I believe they beat the grain in this country."

"Good for you!" said John, "and I would like to care for five acres of garden this year."

"You had better," said Jake smiling, "take the three acres of ground on my place; it is in good shape and you—"

"I want to have a hand in this," said Tom. "I wish you would take two or three of mine, John, for your garden."

"All right," laughed Aunt Hetty, "we—I—"

"Well, what is it, Hetty?" asked her husband, his voice always tender when addressing her. "Why, we are going to try a few strawberries, you know."

"Yes, I believe it would be a good plan to experiment with a few; suppose we put two hundred plants on each ranch, as fast as we cultivate them," suggested John.

"Yes," said Mollie, "all share alike until the last ranch is in bearing."

"Good," said Mr. Barton, "better and better."

"We women folks can care for the berries," explained Ruth.

"And now, friends," said Mr. Wilson, "we men propose to give the ladies a New Year's present by all hands taking our teams to Montrose and buying enough lumber to put floors in our cabins."

"Then we will have to scrub," exclaimed Kate.

The next evening, when the men came home, the ladies, who had gathered at Mrs. Barton's to wait their coming, came running out to feast their eyes on the fresh lumber which each had longed for, but never once expressed in words.

"Why, Tom!" said Mollie, "what is that bundle on top of the load?"

"In that bundle, fair ladies," said he, "you will find a little window for each of our front doors to shed more light on your dear faces." Again the men felt well repaid for their thoughtfulness.

Jake and Harry wished they, too, were in it. Mrs. Barton made them feel they were by saying, "Jake and Harry, we shall need your help in laying these floors."

What a happy crowd they were, with no remembrance of bygone complainings to mar their happiness.

CHAPTER XXIII

A House Party Brings Startling Results

The next evening, Aunt Hetty came over to the Bartons' on what to her seemed very important business. The family were just seated at the evening meal.

"Good evening, Hetty," said Mr. Barton; "won't you sit down and eat some supper with us?"

"No, thank you," she answered, "but while you are eating I want to tell you, John thinks we had better put the floors down in the other cabins first, and leave yours till last, if you don't mind, and the day yours is put down, you could put most of your things in the tent, and, why not, while your house is empty, have a big party? Invite our friends in Ouray and the Park, and some around here?"

"Good for you and John!" said Bob. "I always said John was all right. This room is big enough to hold a hundred."

Aunt Hetty beamed on Bob, Mary was all smiles, and so were the father and mother.

"Well, sister," said Mr. Barton, "you surely have suggested the right thing; it will be fine."

"I shall enjoy it so much," said Mrs. Barton; "it will seem like old times, when we had husking bees, before father and I were married."

"We will never have husking bees here," spoke

up Bob, who was hurrying to finish his supper. "I was talking with some men the other day who seemed to know; the nights are too cool to raise corn, that is, very extensively."

"I would rather have the cool nights, with the breeze from those snow-capped mountains, than all the corn I ever raised back East," said father.

"Wait, Aunt Hetty," said Bob, pushing back his chair; "I will go with you, to tell the rest of the company."

"Hetty," said Mrs. Barton, "I wish you would suggest that Dick have his floor put in first."

"Yes, a good idea," said her sister, "and I am perfectly willing to wait a month for mine. I am so happy with John, this 'doing without' don't seem to matter, and John says I'm such a help to him." She looked up at her brother while speaking and saw the affectionate glance he gave her; a lump came in her throat and she did what she never remembered doing since a young girl—went deliberately and put her arms around him and kissed him.

"Now, father, what are you getting so red for?" laughed teasing Bob, who was just as pleased as anyone.

"Let's be going," said his aunt; "John will be lonesome." Away they went, Bob very much in love with his aunt, and she—why the stars never seemed to shine so bright and life to hold so much of good. Mary was busy clearing the table, mother went to her husband, for she knew that he had been greatly touched.

"I never could have believed that she would blossom out like this," said he.

"It's love, my dear," said his wife. "We are all like the flowers which bud and blossom only in the sunshine. It's love that brings everything good to the surface."

"Let's surprise Tom and Dick by writing to Ed and Sam Johnson to be here."

"Yes," said Mr. Barton, "and those two men who brought the letter to Mr. Wilson that Christmas day seven years ago—Mr. Grey and Mr. Eaton; I believe they are on the mesa somewhere. A letter addressed to Montrose will reach them. Then there is Mr. Smith and his family, Mr. Long and Mr. Sherman, yes, and Mr. Jones' family, and that old gentleman the Browns were speaking of, the one who could not get credit in Montrose; Mr. Woods and his wife; we will have a house full, all right."

"Yes," said Mrs. Barton, all aglow, "let's write to our grand old bachelor, Mr. Newhall. He will bring his violin—you remember he often came to see us in Ouray, and he called his violin his wife, because he loved it so."

While they were busy talking, the news had gone from cabin to cabin, everyone delighted with the thought, and Aunt Hetty went home to John, her heart fairly jubilant because he, her John! had proposed this which everyone so heartily approved.

Next morning, after the chores were done, Jake and Harry came over with saws and hammers. "Which house first?" asked Harry, as they stopped at Mrs. Barton's.

"Have you not heard the news?" said she. "We are going to have a party."

"A party!" said Jake. "Are we invited?"

"Of course you are," said Mary, just coming in with an armful of wood. "It's you boys and we who are going to give the party. It's this way: mother is too slow," glancing up at her mother, who smilingly let the daughter have the pleasure of telling the boys the news. "John proposed that we have a party here when the floor is put down, and invite our friends in the Park, and some up at Ouray, and some around here; won't that be good?"

"You bet!" said Harry.

"And, Jake," said Mr. Barton, coming in just then with his saw and hammer, "I wish when you go to the Longs' on your weekly visit—now don't blush, it's no secret—you would ask them and Mr. Sherman to bring their families, and anyone else you think of. We will have a big—what is the word that man used the other day?"

"Oh, yes," answered Harry, laughing. "We will have a big 'blowout.' "

And soon the sound of hammers and saws was heard.

The ninth of January, being Mr. Barton's birthday, they decided that should be the time for the party. Everyone was heard from and the invitations accepted, save Mr. Newhall, who, the postmaster wrote on the returned letter, had left Ouray a few months before. The evening of the party came, the friends from Ouray getting in near dusk,

STARTING FOR THE HOUSE PARTY.

tired and hungry. A warm supper was waiting for them at the home of Mrs. Wilson, where the Bartons also ate, Bob remaining at home to look after the fire and the early guests.

"How are you getting along?" asked Mr. Smith, as they sat around the supper table.

"Fine!" replied Mr. Wilson, "and how is it with you and Mrs. Smith? You both look well and happy. Do you remember the Christmas we spent at Grandfather Wilson's when you and I were boys? How we took our sure-enough sleighs, with the bells jingling, you and I, and gathered up our girls for a ride to the next village to the Christmas tree; how the boys, knowing we would be coming, made a big snow man, put a pipe in his mouth and a lighted lantern on his arm by the roadside? The result was, we had two badly frightened horses and the boys lost their fun, as they saw our horses tear down the road."

"Did you get hurt?" asked Mary, to whom the story was new.

"No," said Mr. Wilson, "the horses quieted down after awhile, but we went five miles out of our way rather than pass that snow man again, but we heard later the boys were so scared they pulled the snow man down before they left."

"But, father!" said Mrs. Wilson, "wait till we get together before you tell any more yarns."

"How old is your little daughter, and what is her name?" asked Mrs. Barton of the editor's wife.

"Five months; her name is Mary," replied the

little mother, her heart full of joy because she had a daughter as well as three hearty boys.

Just then Bob rushed in. "Hurry up! folks, the room is getting full already; I want these chairs."

"We will be over in a few minutes," said Mrs. Wilson, while the men each took what chairs they could carry with them. They found the big table in the corner already filled with good things to eat, for this rough western life, with its spirit of hospitality, was caught by these pioneers and shown in their every act, desire to give rather than receive, and yet, the spirit of receiving, too, was everywhere. The true spirit of giving and the true spirit of receiving are very closely related—another secret the East, as well as the West, is fast learning.

"Well, well!" said Mr. Wilson, as Mr. Gray and Mr. Eaton came to meet him. "How glad we are to meet you."

"We sure were glad to come," said Mr. Eaton. "Let me introduce my family, Mrs. Eaton and our daughter, Helen," a bright, sweet-looking girl, who, like her father, smiled with her eyes.

"And here is my wife and our two sons, Alfred and Grant," said Mr. Gray. "You see, I have plenty of help on my farm."

"You surely have," laughed Mr. Wilson, as he grasped the hands of the two young men. Alfred was like his father—short and rather slender—while Grant was more like his mother—tall and stout—who, when he laughed, shook all over.

"Here are Mr. Jones and his family!" said Mrs.

Barton, and she hastened to greet their neighbors and see that the wife had a comfortable chair. "I wanted so to come, I didn't get one bit cold," she said, as she looked up in Mrs. Barton's face with eyes full of love. Work was coming to Mr. Jones now, the outlook was brighter.

Very soon Mr. Woods and his wife came—the gentleman Mr. and Mrs. Brown overtook on their way home from Montrose two weeks before. Mrs. Woods, a gray-haired lady, with all the sweet refinement of the East, won the heart of Mrs. Barton at once, for though her heart was wrapped up in the West this sense of refinement seemed as pleasing to her as the perfume of the violet to the English man or woman. Mr. and Mrs. Brown were surprised to see the change in Mr. Woods. Tonight he was among friends, and the crushed spirit was gone. Although his clothes were rather shabby, they could not hide the true nobility of the man. He smiled at everyone, and naturally everyone smiled at him, and loved him.

The editor was welcomed by all, for they knew him and his family in the days of privations in Ouray.

Just then Mr. Sherman, with his family, and Mr. Long, with his wife and younger daughter, drove up. "Why," said Mrs. Barton, "where is Myrtle?" "Oh," chimed in the younger sister, "Jake came for her an hour before we left; aren't they here yet?"

"Never mind them," said Aunt Hetty, who had

just come in, "they are all right. But here they come now, and it appears to me they look very happy over something. My! but don't Jake look fine? Good evening, Jake," cried the lady. "How kind of you to help Mr. Long out by bringing one of his daughters here tonight."

"Why, yes," said Mr. Long, soberly, "if Jake had not come I should have been compelled to bring the wagon instead of the buggy." Poor Jake, he wondered if everyone had as hard a time as he, but everyone was kind and began to talk of other things.

"I propose," said Bob, whose eyes were very bright that night, "we do as they did in Ouray the first two or three winters. Men would gather in some store and tell stories. Let us all tell stories of what we have gone through, or experiences some of our friends have had."

Just then the tramp of horses outside caused Mr. Barton to step to the door. "Hello," said a rather rough voice, "any show to stay all night? Me and my partner have our blankets."

"If you have your blankets, come right in; we will see that you have something to eat." The men felt rather abashed at seeing such a crowd, but they were about exhausted from cold and hunger, and gladly accepted the places made for them by the fire.

"Have you ridden very far?" asked Mr. Brown, of one who gave his name as Tom Thornton. "Yes, since daylight, looking after some cattle which have strayed. My partner's name is Baker, Joe Baker;

we are in the cattle business, have been for some time."

"Friends," said Mr. Barton, "these gentlemen must be half starved, been riding all day. I propose we have our supper before we begin to tell stories, and then perhaps they can tell us some cowboy experiences."

"Good!" said Dick, "we are glad you came. You see, we are having a party in honor of Mr. Barton's birthday." What a change came over the ladies, who had been quietly listening to the gentlemen talk. They all jumped up and began preparations for supper.

"Come, John," said Aunt Hetty, "we will have the coffee here boiling hot in fifteen minutes," and away they hurried, for everything was in readiness, while the others began to undo the parcels and empty the baskets of their precious contents, everyone talking and laughing. The two men by the fire, half dazed by the warmth and kindness shown, looked on in wonder. The scene took them back to their childhood days, and yet the spirit of freedom and neighborliness was not new to them—these rough men who lived together in the open—it was a part of their life.

The meat was sliced, the cake and bread cut, all ready to pass around as John and his wife came in with two big steaming pots of hot coffee. In a moment the men by the fire were eating and drinking, the ladies insisting the gentlemen should eat first, but Mrs. Barton, seeing the disappointment on Jake's face, said, "Let all the young people eat now." Bob went straight to Mr. Eaton's daughter, Helen—he always knew what he wanted—and asked for the privilege of her company; his mother saw it, and more, but it did not hurt as it once had done. Harry was content to sit by Dick and Kate, while Grant, laughing all over, sat down by Ruth and Mary. John ran back for the third pot of coffee. The men by the fire began to smile and join in the conversation with Mr. Wilson and Mr. Brown, who sat near them.

"Now, mother dear," said Mollie, as the company began to refuse another piece of cake, "it's your turn." So baby John was given to his father, and the girls very demurely waited on the older ones. Swiftly things were put in order amid jest and laughter, and beds made in one corner for the younger children, who were getting sleepy. When this was done and quiet reigned, Mr. Barton said:

"Friends, I want to say how much we enjoy having you all with us tonight, and glad we are to have these strangers, too. Let us now begin our evening's amusement by each telling some experience, either of his own or of someone else they know. Mr. Wilson, you give us the first one."

"Well, ladies and gentlemen, I will tell one I heard told in my office in Ouray, by Mr. W. Rathmell.

"He said: A crew of men, of which I was a member, was hired to work for a lessee on the Chicago Mine of Imogene Basin. Our accommodations were meager, but such as the employer in those days could furnish; we lived in tents until developments would warrant the building of a bunk and boarding house. The work was some distance above timberline, with no one to be seen but an occasional prospector and very rugged scenery. With these conditions we wanted to put in all of the time working, including Sundays, but our employer, a very devout Christian, could not see the matter that way and refused to let us work on the Sabbath. He was a tenderfoot from Massachusetts, a man of wonderful endurance and a worker. It was not at all uncommon for him, on week days, to work three or four hours after the day's work had ended for the hired men. One Sunday he told the boys that he was a member of a Salem, Massachusetts, choir for twenty years, and during all of the time carried the part of bass. The boys pricked up their ears at this and forthwith cast about among themselves for someone to lead some good old revival song so as to verify or disapprove the statement of the choir singer. Finally, one of the boys consented to sing, and the song selected was, 'How Tedious and Tasteless the Hour.' We sang with a will, and, to our delight, our employer joined in with a bass that for volume, melody and expression would do credit to any choir. After the song, our employer was out of breath and just puffed for wind. We tried in every way to get him to sing again, but of no avail. He declared that singing at that altitude was too hard. After coaxing him for awhile, one of the boys said, reproachfully, 'You can work without looking up for ten, twelve or fifteen hours, but when it comes to praising the Lord, you cannot stand fifteen minutes of it.' "

"Now, Mr. Long."

"I can tell an amusing story, as told by James W. Stell, showing what we men, without our women folks, have had to do. It was in the fall of 1882. He says: I was trapping for beaver on Tongue and Surface Creeks, when, going through the brush, I tore the only pair of pants I had all to shreds. There I was, a hundred miles from Gunnison, the nearest place where I could get another pair. There was a store down the Gunnison, where Delta is now, so I went down there to get me a pair of overalls or pants, but found, on getting there, that they had nothing but flour, bacon and tobacco. I was sure up against it. I remembered having some canvas to put over my packs, so, as necessity is the mother of invention, I ripped my old pants up for a pattern and cut my new pants out with a butcher knife. I had no thread or needles, but that didn't bother me. I took a piece of oak wood and made an awl. Then cut out some buckskin strings and started to sew. It was a slow job. The first mistake I made was to make the two legs of the pants for the same leg, so had to rip one apart and start all over again. After making more mistakes, and working harder than I ever had in my life, by night, I had them finished. They were fine, not very stylish, but did not tear as I went through the brush. I caught one hundred beavers that fall and sold the hides to Harry Tevis, who tended the tollgate above Ouray."

"Pretty good story," said Mr. Barton, laughing. "What strikes me is, a man with such ingenuity could not help but make a success of anything that he might undertake."

"Mrs. Woods, won't you tell us something?"

"Once upon a time," Mrs. Woods began, "a man and his wife had everything heart could wish—children, home and friends, money came from different sources, they did not have to think for tomorrow. But one day both children were taken from them by a flood. Being crushed, business was neglected for a time, and those trusted proved unworthy. Almost everything lost, their home, too, had to go. These people were past middle age. One evening the husband came home after a weary search for work, heartsick and discouraged. He was surprised to find his wife cheerful and even smiling; he wondered why. After the supper work was done and they were seated by the fire, the wife said: 'James, here are some papers which came in the mail; I wish you would read them. They remind me of my girlhood days, when I lived on a farm, with all outdoors to call my own. There is something awakened in me that I cannot explain or understand. Since reading these papers I feel nothing would be so comforting, so satisfying, as to have some land where you and I could live alone—where we might forget much we have passed through, make new friends, grow up with new surroundings.'

BEAVER TRAPPER'S WORK.

"This man was surprised at such suggestions from one who had seemed satisfied with city life, with all its round of pleasures. He read the papers carefully, and then both sat watching the fire. Finally the husband said, 'I will think about it, Sara.'

"The next day he went again among his fellow men, seeking work where he had been wont to give work. It might have been fancy, but everyone seemed different; there was not the same hearty greeting, the old-time fellowship seemed lacking. When he came home that night his wife saw the effort made to hide the sense of discouragement. A warm supper was waiting. She had been reading those papers again, and her day-dream began to seem real. The papers lay convenient for him to take up as he sat by the fire after supper, and again he read them through, but said nothing, his wife busy mending clothes that once would have been cast aside. The next day he came home earlier than usual, a look in his eyes the wife had not seen for many a day. He walked more upright, as though conscious of the power to do for himself, not depending on what others could do for him. He was met by his wife with the old question, 'Get some work?' 'Yes, Sara, but wait till after supper.'

"They talked of everything but the subject nearest their hearts. Soon the evening work was finished, and, picking up the papers which again lay near him, he said: 'Wife, I've been thinking of what you said and what I've been reading in these papers describing the conditions out West, in the

Uncompahgre Valley, where there is land for the taking, the air fresh from the snow-capped mountains the year round, the telling of the great opportunities for those seeking homes. Like yourself, my thoughts have gone back to the time when, as a boy, I worked in grandfather's fields, and wished father would leave the dingy office in the city and live on a farm, but when I spoke to him of this he smiled sadly—I see now, but I did not understand then—and said, "Your mother and sisters would not enjoy it, my son." I was allowed to work in my grandfather's fields all summer, and earn and receive wages. How I enjoyed it, Sara; I learned a good many things, for I asked questions, the answers to which come back now, though forgotten all these years. I seem to smell the fragrant hay and taste the fresh buttermilk.'

" 'Yes,' said the wife, 'and how sweet the night's rest after a day's work in the field.'

" 'Yes, wife, and, sweeter than all, being your own boss, as grandfather said. You want to go and try it?' he asked, and she, with a catch in her voice, said, 'I do.'

"So they gathered the little they had left and came, happy as two children out of school, but it cost more than they expected to get settled, and a little money they were looking for from the city failed to come in time, and they found by experience what it was to not have enough to eat, but friends were raised up in this land of open heartedness who tided them over that never-to-be-forgotten time, and hope again rose up and pointed to ways and means for the future.

"Friends, we are glad we came, for we are the ones I have been telling you about. Life is becoming more worth while as we work so close to nature. We find no artifice there, and the people we meet seem one big family; what interests one seems to interest all. Only yesterday a little money came which we had long given up as lost. We both enjoy being with you tonight."

The little gathering smiled back at her as she pulled her chair closer to her husband, who took her hand in his.

"The editor's wife surely can tell us something."

"I remember," she said, "we had been in Ouray for about two years; it was in the summertime, the doors and windows were open, a man with a train of burros was coming down Vinegar Hill. He was swearing dreadfully. I shut the doors and windows, but heard as plainly as before. So I rushed outdoors, standing where the man could not help seeing me. He never swore again, although I was a stranger to him, while I was in hearing, and yet the burros went along just as well. The driver of a burro train will tell you he has to swear, for the burro is so used to it he don't know what to do if you don't." A flush came over the faces of the men by the fire, but they said nothing.

"Now, Mr. Editor, it's your turn."

"I'm no good at telling stories, but remember when I was out with a couple of others hunting.

We had not rifles for all, so the Colt's forty-four was given to me and I was sent around to drive the deer in the direction the others had gone. I had not gone far, when, a short distance ahead, I saw a bear running away from me, apparently. Sending a shot after him, he turned and came directly towards me. I turned likewise and started for home, but fortunately for me bruin's den was between me and him, and he, too, seemed to think there was no place like home, and turned in. Looking about to see how much he was gaining on me, there was no bear in sight, so my courage rose and I turned back, going cautiously until reaching a large rock, under which the bear had made its winter quarters. He had evidently just started out for his morning walk and I interrupted his going. The entrance to his den was on his side and in he had gone, not knowing what awaited him. On my side the opening was smaller, fortunately, so Mr. Bear could not get out, but through that hole I poured shot after shot until he rolled down in the bottom of the den. Following up the other boys, who had a fine fat buck, I told them what I had done and they laughed at me. Sticking to my story, they finally concluded there must be something to it, and went with me the next morning to find things as I had said."

"I believe Mr. Baker could tell one," said Mr. Barton, smiling.

"Well, friends," said Mr. Baker, "I remember some time ago, we boys were riding in the hills rounding up the stock. There were five of us. We had stood together in many a scrape, but the one I am about to relate stands out more clearly than any others at the present moment. We had a neighbor, one of the meanest fellows you would meet in many a long day. We knew that he had stolen some of our stock, but we couldn't prove it. We had held back many times because he had a wife, one of the best women that ever lived—do anything for a man when he was down. We remembered the time when Dick Jones got sick up there in the hills, how she nursed him and cared for him as though he was her brother, and no matter how much she had to do, with her five children to work for, she always found time to lend a helping hand to us boys.

"But it was more than human nature could stand. When we found two of our best heifers gone, we agreed to take him, so we watched a night or two. He seemed to have become suspicious, and kept out of the way. The third night two of us went to their kitchen door, thinking to find him at home. His wife came to the door, and she smiled a welcome which made us completely forget what we were going to give as an excuse for coming in case he was not there. She gave us no time to talk, but bustled about to make room for us near the fire. They had just commenced their supper, she and the children, and nothing would satisfy her but we must eat, too. She hurriedly set plates for us and poured out the coffee, and so we ate, though every mouthful seemed to choke us. We noticed there was not much on the table to eat, but she was too much of a lady to apologize. We felt too ashamed to look her straight in the eye. If she noticed anything wrong, she never let on, but inquired after the rest of our crowd. But when she had poured out my second cup of coffee and I looked up quickly into her eyes, I saw they were full of tears. I gulped down that hot coffee without putting the sugar in it, and scalded my mouth without knowing it.

"Muttering something about being in a hurry, we left that little cabin, with its warmth and kindness, that mother with her five children; one, the youngest, was a girl with the loveliest blue eyes and golden hair—reminded me of my sister. We never said a word until we got to our shack, where the other boys were waiting to hear what we had found. Their hands felt for their revolvers as we entered, each with his eyes alert.

" 'Well,' Tom asked, as we stood silent.

" 'Boys,' I said, 'we can't touch the husband of that woman, the father of those children.'

"Then we told of the reception we met, and in a whisper I told of the tears I saw, that she did not mean I should see. That settled it with the boys. 'But,' said one, 'we must do something.' So we agreed to find him, tell him what we had intended doing, and why we let him go.

"The next night we waylaid him. The moon had just arisen and made the shadows seem even darker, so when we who had been in hiding sprang out, he could not tell but what there were fifty of us.

"We took him into our cabin and, relieving him

of his gun, we went over the whole charge against him. He knew without being told what the penalty was for such work. I never saw a man wilt as he did. After a little while, when we thought it had made enough of an impression on him, we told him why we were going to let him go free. Then he broke down completely, and vowed he would treat us as white as we had treated him. And he did—made as good a neighbor as one would wish.

"But when he left the cabin we had to give vent to our pent-up feelings in some way, so he had not gone more than a dozen yards before we stepped to the door and fired our guns in the air. Maybe he wasn't scared. Thought we had changed our minds. Months after, when talking with his wife, she spoke of the great change that had come over her husband. He used to be so gruff in his ways with her and the children, but now he seemed to think nothing too good for them. I said nothing, for I saw she did not know about what occurred that night at the shack. I was glad she didn't, and very well pleased that we had given the man another chance."

"That's good," said Mrs. Wood.

"Now, Ed, we want one from either you or Sam. You see, friends, Ed and Sam were our companions on the way out to Ouray," said Tom, "and the way they told yarns to us tenderfeet! Just to scare us, I know now."

"I remember," said Ed, "a story Jesse and Roy Bell told upon themselves. They were some younger than they are now, ten and twelve years old when this occurred. It was part of their work to take the horses out to pasture after the day's work was done. One evening they were a little later than usual, and when they had left the horses in the pasture and started down the trail it was getting quite dark. They had gone but a short distance when they heard a noise in the bushes behind them as of some animal coming toward them. They looked at each other and thought 'bear,' and away they started on the run, fear giving wings to their feet as they heard the stride and tramp of at least one bear following their trail. The faster they ran the faster their pursuer followed, and the shorter came their breath, until they were compelled to give up the mad flight. Roy, who was in the rear, thought he would at least find out what it was following them, turned about, and had scarcely done so, before some black object rushed squarely into his arms, which, upon closer acquaintance, proved to be a black burro colt. Evidently the burro had either been frightened by some animal and sought them for protection, or had become separated from its fellows and wanted company."

"Now," said Mr. Barton, "we will have a change of program. Mr. Sherman has brought his violin. Let the young folks have one hour for a dance, then we will all get to bed." Mr. Woods and his wife said it was time they were home, and bade them goodnight. Mr. Jones and his family had already gone. A jolly time they had, even John and Aunt Hetty joining in. When the hour was up, Mr. Barton said, "Let us have one song, with the violin accompanying, 'My Country, 'Tis of Thee,' and then everybody to bed." Out into the stillness of the night rang the grand old song, as dear and grand as when first written.

Just as he was leaving Harry asked the cowboys to stop at his cabin on their way home, as he wished to have a talk with them, and they said they would.

The two families from the Park went home, but those from Ouray and the mesa remained all night, the ladies and children cared for in the other cabins, while the men slept on the new floor at the Bartons. A fire was kept by watchful Bob, who was glad of something to do, for he could not sleep. He had met the girl he wanted at last—but could he win her?

The next morning, after a good breakfast, the two cowboys thanked their friends for their kindness, handing Mr. Barton a bill.

"What is this for?" said he.

"For our food and shelter."

"Why," said their host, "you were welcome to that; we were glad you came."

"We would rather pay, but thanks to you all. Should you ever, any of you, come up in the hills, drop in to see us." The men left with the feeling there were some pretty good people in the world.

As the company lingered around the blazing fire, their horses having been fed an hour before, Mr. Barton said, "Mr. Eaton, you and Mr. Gray have taken up ranches on the mesa, have you not?"

"Yes, we have, the finest places in the country,

we think. There is no water yet, but from what we hear a big ditch will be put in within a year; we feel it is worth waiting for. Our soil is red and inclined to be sandy, the finest kind for fruit. We will put in orchards as soon as water is in sight. It's queer how the soil is divided up; on the east side of the river it is adobe, while on the west side it is this red, sandy soil."

"Sam, where have you and your brother located?" asked Tom, who still cherished a strong liking for these men, the comrades of their first journey out west.

"Way down below Montrose, about twelve miles. We have good places, too."

"Any water?" asked Mr. Wilson.

"Yes, we have the river the same as you, and the water on the mesa land we fully expect this next year, too."

"Say, Bob," said Mr. Gray, "why don't you take up some land? You are of age now. I know of a fine piece I would like myself if I had not already taken some. Can't you come and look it over—go with us now?" Bob looked up at his father.

"Why," said his father, a pang striking his heart, "go, my boy; we are not very busy just now," and so it came about that a buggy borrowed from Jake enabled Bob to have the pleasure he so longed for—a ride alone with Helen. It was taking him away from his father and mother, bringing about a change that occurs so often when the young begin to make nests for themselves.

CHAPTER XXIV

HARRY TURNS COWBOY

When Bob came back his parents felt he had been gone a year, so great had been the change in their lives. They had faced the inevitable. And Bob? He felt the change even before he met his loved ones. He loved them just the same—even more, but there was a difference. That night he had a long talk with his father and mother, just like Tom when he came home from college—the same old story so familiar to all—a new life, but one each must live for himself.

"It's all right, my boy," said his father, "we knew this must come some time. I believe it comes suddenly to us all. Yesterday we felt you were our very own; today we feel, mother and I, we have in a way lost you."

"But, Bob," said his mother, "father and I only had each other when we were married. Today we are getting back to that time. It's all right, dear, you have been such a comfort to us all your life, and will continue to be. We want you to be happy—that will be enough—and with all our hearts," her lips quivered. "We know all is well."

"Dear mother! pray as you never have prayed before that I win her," and Bob—fun-loving, happy Bob—broke down and cried. It was the best thing he could have done for his mother. In a moment mother-love was tenderly wiping away the tears, reminding him that the same Hand which had led so far would still lead, and how happy she would be to see him well settled in life with a home of his own.

"You will have to go soon to keep a place like that, won't you?" asked his father.

"I expect I will," said the boy. "I want you and Tom to go with me tomorrow, if you can, and lay it out."

"All right, Bob, better see Tom tonight. I will be ready."

The news spread among the little company, and they all came the next morning to see him off, with his father and brother, to take up the ranch which would now be his home. Many tears were shed; they had never realized how much Bob had been to them. They had taken him as they had taken the fresh air—as a matter of course. How they would miss him!

Kate called him to her, in her mother's cabin, alone a moment.

"Oh, Bob! I wish I could go with you. You and I have been together through so much."

"I wish you could, Kate, but I'm always going to be just Bob to you. Don't cry, and take good care of yourself," and he kissed the comrade of the days gone by. Aunt Hetty would not be comforted. She had loved him all his life, regardless of the teasing she had received.

"Say, Bob," said Jake, "tomorrow we will all go.

won't we boys?" looking around at the men standing by. "We will all go, except Dick, with you up to the hills and get spruce logs for your cabin. We have plenty of time the rest of this month."

"You bet we will!" spoke up Mr. Brown.

Goodbyes were said, his mother standing in her cabin door smiling until he was out of sight. Tom came back on his pony toward evening and told the eager listeners that Bob had a number one piece of ground, and that Mr. Gray would look after the place so Bob could go with them after logs. The next morning all the men, except Dick, with their teams and bedding, with food to last three days, started for the hills beyond the mesa, Bob going with them.

That night about nine o'clock another little homeseeker took up its abode for a while with Kate and Dick. It was a boy, and Mrs. Barton was comforted. "Let's name him Bob," said Kate to her husband, as she lay with her baby in her arms.

"Of course," said Dick, "his name is Bob—little Bob."

When the men came back with their first load of logs, Grant Gray came rushing out to meet them with the news that Bob's sister, Kate, had a boy and he was named Bob.

"The dickens!" said Bob, but his eyes sparkled all the same.

"I will sleep in your tent again tonight, Bob," offered Grant, "if you would like to go home with the rest of the men."

"Thank you; I am sure I would."

A happy crowd they were as they drove into the Barton yard that night.

After a warm supper, Bob went over to see the newcomer. It was Kate's baby, and Bob looked very tenderly at the wee boy, with its eyes blinking.

Again, with food for three days, a jovial crowd left for the hills. Bob was to have a good two-room house, each room 12x14. "Big enough," Mollie declared, "for this whole company to stay over night when we want to."

The second time the men were in the hills, busy with their log cutting, the two cowboys entertained by the Bartons came by. Hearty greetings were exchanged, and the boys invited to stay that night, which they were glad to do. They were still hunting the lost cattle.

"Things have been moving our way," said Harry, "since you were with us a week ago; Dick's wife has a boy, Bob has taken up a ranch on the mesa—we are out now getting logs for his two-roomed house."

"Why!" said Mr. Thornton, "you going to get married, Bob?"

"Not yet," said he, blushing.

"Well, well, we had better stop over a day and help; we happen to have our axes with us." A busy crowd they were, making the woods ring with the sound of axes and falling trees.

"We know," said Mr. Baker, " a fine patch of

corral poles, only about two miles from here. Harry, you might go with us and we will show you where they are." Harry went and learned more than where the poles were to be found, for he was very much interested in this stock business, it attracted him, but he kept still until his mind was made up.

The men were in good spirits this time as they unloaded their wagons at Bob's ranch. They had plenty of logs, and one more trip to the sawmill for lumber would finish that part of the work. Mr. Gray and Mr. Eaton drove up as they were unloading and suggested that they have a house-raising the next day, that they would be glad to help. "You see, gentlemen," said Mr. Gray, "if the walls are up there will be no need of anyone staying here, no one would attempt to jump the ranch."

"A good plan," said Mr. Brown; "let's do it."

Food for only one day was needed, and the men went, accompanied by Ruth and Mary, to look after the dinner and make suggestions about locating the doors and windows. Alfred and Grant were there, too, ready to help, so before night the walls were up. A few days' work by these willing hands and a two-room house, with board floors, two windows in each room, a big fireplace in the front room, stood completed.

"It's too good for me," said Bob, as he stood by his mother surveying the comfortable house, roaring fire sending its warmth in every direction.

"The best is none too good for you," said his mother. "You have always done your best for us."

"Dear mother! we are alone just now; give me your blessing."

"Dear boy, may the consciousness be yours that has been mine, that the one Hand is leading, the one Power is bringing you into the fruition of your hopes."

"Thank you, mother, this gives me strength and courage."

"Well, my boy," said his father, coming in just then, "there's plenty of lumber left to make bedsteads, tables and chairs; you will not be lonesome. but you better come home with us tonight. Harry wants to have a talk with us, I have no idea what about. I hope he is not getting dissatisfied; he has been pretty quiet lately."

"Yes," said his wife, "I have noticed something myself, but he is not dissatisfied, you can be sure. I have felt when he is around that he was seeing something that pleased him."

"You don't think it is a girl, do you, mother?" asked Bob, betraying his own inclinations.

"Oh, Bob!" The little mother gave a quick laugh which sounded sweet to her husband. "Hardly that, I think, but we will soon know."

When they reached home a surprise awaited them. Mr. Baker, one of the cowboys, had called and left a six-months-old heifer calf as a present for Bob, "as a starter," he said, on his new ranch. Bob was much pleased and touched by this kindness. "Yes," said Mary, "and he said he and Joe would never forget how you sat up and kept a fire that night they were here. And we have something else, too; see that, a quarter of beef and a saddle of venison for the whole crowd of us."

"Well, well!" said Mr. Barton, finding his tongue first, "we certainly do appreciate it."

"And Harry was here and said he found Kate was able and anxious to have this business meeting, he called it, at her home, and he wished everybody to be present, ladies and all."

After supper everyone was present at Kate's little cabin to hear what Harry had in mind. The present to Bob and the meat for them all had been discussed.

Harry said: "I'm glad, Bob, of this present to you. It leads up to the subject I want to talk to you about. Ever since the night Mr. Baker and Mr. Thornton were here, I've been studying the question of turning cowboy myself."

"You?" said Bob, and all the little company showed their surprise.

"Yes, and I have had a long talk with Jake to-day, and he seems willing."

"Can't help myself," said Jake, "he has made up his mind."

"It's this way," and Harry never seemed so manly as he did then, "we are all getting a little stock which should be taken to the hills during the summer, and as time goes on we shall be astonished how they will increase. There is money in this business, too, from what our cowboys have told me."

"Yes, but Harry," said Mr. Wilson, "it won't pay you to spend all your time with the few we have at present, will it?"

"Oh, no, but I have been thinking I can likely gather up quite a few from the neighbors; there is Mr. Jones, Mr. Wood, and one or two others."

"Oh, I see; in that way you might get quite a bunch, but how about the winter?" asked Mr. Brown, to whom this was all new.

"Perhaps I had better read a statement I have made out; it will clear matters up. Here it is: I, Harry DeLong, promise to take charge of all stock placed in my care for the next three years by this company, taking them to the hills early in the spring, and in the fall bringing them back to your ranches and caring for them myself during the winter. I agree to put my time in at this business, you agreeing to run my ranch as though I was doing it myself, this to be my pay for caring for your stock for three years."

"But how will we get feed for them all?" asked Dick.

"I have thought it all out," said Harry, smiling. "Here is the rest of the statement: Each family, as fast as the land is put in cultivation, put in a goodly amount of alfalfa; I shall have all mine put in alfalfa, except twenty-five acres for grain, and a little fruit for home use, the cattle to be put on your pasturage as well as mine. What do you think of it, friends?" said Harry as he put the paper in his pocket.

"I think it the finest thing we have started yet," said Tom. "While Harry has been reading, I have been figuring."

"So have I," said Mr. Wilson.

"But where would you get anything for yourself?" asked Mollie.

"Why, don't you see?" said her husband. "The way we are working, he gets his share in the ranch produce, the same as if he were there."

"Yes," said Harry, "and you get your share of what I make outside."

"Why, Harry!" smiled Mrs. Barton, "are you sure you want to do all this?"

"Yes, dear Mrs. Barton, it's a reasonably sane way of working, and Jake and I can never repay you people for letting us in with you the way you have; this sharing business is fine. Why, when Jake and I go among the people and see how each is struggling alone, and a poor out they make at it, too, we realize how much we have to be thankful for."

"But you boys are a great help to us, too," joined in Mrs. Wilson, as she glanced affectionately at them both.

"Friends," said Mr. Barton, and his voice was husky, "I believe we are blessed, as Harry says, more perhaps than we realize, in the way we have been led to work together. I am sure we all enjoy it, and I will put the motion. All in favor of Harry's proposal, say aye."

The ayes rang out over the room.

"Those opposed, say no." Just then Kate's baby gave a little cry.

"There seems to be a dissenting voice."

"Oh, no! Harry," laughed Kate, hugging the baby, "you woke him up saying aye."

"He was simply giving his approval," said Bob, "and I am mighty glad I have that calf for a starter in this venture."

"Oh, Dick!" whispered Kate, "I have an idea."

"Out with it," said her husband, smiling.

"We will give Brindle's last calf—it is most three months old—to little Bob and let him in on the deal!"

"Little John shall have our calf, which is seven months old," said Mollie, as she looked up excitedly into her husband's face.

"Sure we will, Mollie," said Tom.

Dick said, "Ask little Bob if he approves," as he peeped at the little mite in his mother's arms.

"There," said Kate, "he winked; that meant 'you bet!'" and they all laughed.

Just then there came a rap on the door. "Hello," said Dick, as Mr. Jones held out his hand, "come right in."

"I heard there was to be a gathering here tonight, so knew where to come. I can't stay but a few minutes, but wife suggested I come over and make a proposal, that as work is rather slack, we all hands, take our teams, get some spruce logs, and put up another room for Mr. and Mrs. Barton."

"Oh, Mr. Jones!" cried Mrs. Barton, her face flushing. "That would be too much."

"No, it's not," said John, who as yet had not spoken, "it's just the thing, and we thank your wife as much for the suggestion as you for your help; let us do it."

"When shall we start?" asked Mr. Jones.

"Day after tomorrow; that will give the ladies time to cook us something to eat," proposed Mr. Brown.

"Won't it be fine?" smiled Aunt Hetty.

"Indeed it will," said Mrs. Barton, "for then I will have more room for those who come to stay over night."

"Let us go home before anything else happens," said Mr. Wilson. "We have had enough good things for one night." Shaking hands with Harry, he said, "We are all well pleased with your plan."

"Hurrah! We have a sure enough cowboy in our company," cheered Ruth.

One trip was enough, with such a crowd, for a load of logs and lumber from the mill run by W. A. Eckerly. The putting up the room was play for the willing hands, Mrs. Jones and the children coming over for the day.

The winter passed quickly, Harry making all preparations for his new work. He found the neighbors, including Eaton and Gray, glad to have one they knew care for their stock. Harry saw to it every animal was carefully branded before leaving its owners.

One morning in the spring Harry started with his bunch, about twenty-five head all told, with Bob to help him the first day, up into the hills to live with his stock. He took plenty of reading matter for the evenings, but soon found he was ready for sleep as soon as supper was over. He built a little cabin, and found the experiences of the past, his trip out West, served him well now.

CHAPTER XXV

JAKE'S WEDDING AND SURPRISE

The farm work was progressing, Bob working with the folks at home, for which they would repay in helping him get his fence up during odd times. Jake missed his brother—eating alone was not pleasant, more and more his thoughts dwelt on the advisability of getting married. John and Hetty began their weekly visit to Ouray, the garden doing even better than the year before, the strawberry plants starting nicely. The whole valley assuming a more settled condition, those coming with the expectation of becoming suddenly rich gone to more inviting fields, those who remained convinced there was something worth while in the near future. Montrose was becoming a more inviting town, a better element ruling. The town was organized May 16, 1882, being then a part of Gunnison county. During the winter of 1882-1883, the legislature made Montrose county of what was then part of Gunnison county. The governor appointed O. D. Loutsenhizer, A. E. Buddecke, and S. H. Nye as the first county commissioners. These gentlemen met March 12, 1883, and organized by the election of A. E. Buddecke as chairman. They then recognized the bonds of Frank Mason as sheriff, Joe Selig as clerk, and George Simmonds as county judge, and the county of Montrose, so named by Joseph Selig, from the novel by Sir Walter Scott, was officially launched.

In this early period, no one had money, but all were full of hope.

The early history of the town of Montrose was one incident to all new towns at that time. Saloons, with all their attendant evils, one general outfitting store, one grocery store, blacksmith shop and post-office, and the usual amount of cheap restaurants made up the business part of the town. This was the distributing point for all the mountain country for passengers and freight. The largest dining room was the Quaintance tent, where one hundred mule drivers could seat themselves for corned beef and cabbage. The streets, when it rained, were harder to cross than an irrigated field. The first church services were held by Rev. L. Wright, in a saloon, temporarily closed. Dave Wood was the railroad. Nothing was too great for him to move with his famous sixteen gray mules, driven with a jerk line, the driver riding on the near wheeler. To give a more direct road to Telluride, Dave built the road across Horsefly. The Montrose Messenger, started in May, 1882, a weekly newspaper, was published in the town by Abe Roberts.

The city of Montrose is at an altitude of 5,801 feet above sea level. To the south are the ranges of the San Juan, Mount Sneffles and Uncompahgre Peak, as well as others, rising from the rocky mass to heights exceeding 14,000 feet, snow capped and treasure filled. To the west is the Uncompahgre Plateau, to the northwest the great valley, and to the northeast the rugged mountains of the Gunnison.

About the middle of June Jake called on Mrs. Barton at a time when she was alone, but when he entered the kitchen, to make sure, asked where Mary was.

"Gone to see Kate and the baby; my! but he is growing," said the happy grandmother. "Anything I can do for you, Jake?" asked Mrs. Barton, who could see something was troubling him.

"Yes, there is," but for once Jake felt his tongue was tied.

"How is Myrtle, Jake?"

"Oh," said the poor boy, falling into the kindly trap and forgetting the question, "we are going to be married the Fourth of July."

"I'm so glad, my boy," said Mrs. Barton, holding out her hand. "She will make you a good wife, and she knows what it is to have to rough it."

"Yes," said he, "but, Mrs. Barton, I don't want her to have to rough it any more; I want that all left out of her life."

"That's all right, Jake, for you to feel that way, but I do not think I am mistaken in the girl; I believe she would not be happy unless she believed she was helping you and sharing the roughness with you."

"You think so, dear Mrs. Barton?"

"I do. I tell you, the children brought out West when they were young, raised in the atmosphere of this new country, are richly endowed; they have taken in the spirit of these mountains. But, tell me, Jake, what are your arrangements?"

"That is what I came to speak about. I have such a longing that the wedding take place here, down in the little grove by the river, where I have spent so many happy hours with you people. If we had it there, and on that day, all our friends could be present, those in the Park, up on the mesa, and Mrs. Woods and the Jones family."

"Jake, it would be fine; why not?"

"I thought I better talk it over with you first, Mrs. Barton. Tonight I will speak to Myrtle and Mrs. Long. I hope they will be willing, and there is something else," and again he lost control of his tongue.

"Want me to help fix the house up?"

"Oh, Mrs. Barton! that is it; would you mind going with me, just as my own mother would, you know?" and tears came into his eyes. "I wish mother and father could come, but it is their busy time, but if you could go to Montrose and help me pick out a little furniture and such things. Then I want to get some cheese cloth and cover the front room walls."

"Why, to be sure, I would enjoy going with you, and Aunt Hetty and Mary can sew up the seams and we can help put the cloth on."

"Thank you, Mrs. Barton; I must be going, but if there is anything in the world I can do for you you will let me do it?"

"Yes, Jake, I will," and in the days to come years after, the promise was remembered.

"It's all right; it's going to be down by the

river! They are delighted!" said Jake, the next morning, as he stopped on his way to work.

"What is going to be down by the river, Jake?" asked Mary, who overheard his remarks to Mrs. Barton.

"You go on, Jake, I will tell Mary."

TIGE, OUT WITH HIS MISTRESS FOR THE DAY.

"I wish to goodness you would, and tell all the rest, too," and Jake whipped up his horses.

"What is it, mother?" asked Mary, who scented a secret. When mother told the news, Mary said, "Won't that be jolly? I must run and tell Kate."

"Better wait, daughter, till the breakfast dishes are washed; then you can tell the whole family."

It was a matter of rejoicing, although, as they said, "they had been expecting it," but to have it take place in their own little grove was fine.

Mrs. Barton went with Jake to Montrose, and they had no difficulty in getting what they needed. Although they acted as unconcerned as possible, the clerk smiled and asked Jake, when he was alone, "when it was going to be?" but Jake's tongue got tangled up and he did not answer.

Those were busy days for all. Bob went over to Jake's one evening and let him know how glad he was, and Jake asked him to be best man.

"All right, Jake, I'll be there." The eventful day dawned clear and bright. "Jake's to be married today," the birds seemed to sing. Although no ties of the flesh existed, there was felt by every one of the little company that kindly affection for Jake, who was always so ready to lend a helping hand. Harry came down the night before, bringing a tub full of flowers from the hills. Columbines (later made the state flower of Colorado) in all their beauty, and many other flowers he had gathered which grew in the hills in such profusion, a big bunch of ferns, gathered from the shadow of a great rock where the sun seldom shone, around which the big white and purple violets bloomed, and the grass was a lovely pale green, where the birds twittered and sang to their hearts' content, where clusters of aspens grew quivering with glee, never still, some bearing the marks of the sportsome bear, and down on one side a tiny stream of water trickling, coming from a little spring just above, where often Harry's cattle came to drink. He had carefully guarded these ferns, they were so fine and feathery; these he had brought to Mrs. Barton. Jake was too deeply touched to speak; he put his face close to the flowers, and held out his hand to Harry, whose thoughtfulness and love had brought them. The ladies were delighted, and spent the evening before, while Jake was away for the last time to visit the one who would so soon be his wife, in adorning the little cabin, which was snowy white inside, lined as it was with the white cheese cloth; a few pictures hung on the walls, with the flowers and ferns. The snowy bed, with its clean white spread and pillow cases; the bedstead, the cheapest kind, but that did not matter; the little rug by the bedside, all telling the sweet story of kindly affection. The cabin Jake had "bached" in was scrubbed, and in one corner was a little cookstove, so unlike what Jake had been putting up with—nothing too good for her, he had said many times. And Jake, as he took a last look before he closed the door and left for the Park that eventful day, said under his breath, "Oh, God! I wish father and mother could see it."

The wedding was to take place at four o'clock in the afternoon, so dinner was over and Jake had gone. Bob was down early, resplendent in a new suit of clothes to do honor to the occasion, and something else he had made up his mind to. He brought Helen, who was to be one of the bridesmaids. Everything was in readiness, chairs and benches were down in the little grove, the sun, as Ruth said, "had in due courtesy withdrawn from that part of the river," so it was cool and shady. The men had reluctantly donned their coats; Aunt Hetty had told John he could take his off after the ceremony. The friends from the mesa, and the Woods and Jones families were already down in the grove. They were expecting the company at any time from the Park, when Bob stepped to the door of his mother's cabin and saw a rig coming at full speed from the direction of Montrose. Our little party, who were all ready to go down to the grove, babies, little John and little Bob, laughing and crowing as though in full sympathy, stood wondering who it could be, for they knew the minister would come with the company from the Park, when all at once they came into full view, and Mrs. Barton exclaimed, "If it isn't Jake's father and mother!"

"Here we are, not too late I see," laughed Mr. DeLong, as he jumped out of the wagon and was about to help his smiling wife to alight.

"Wait, wait!" said Mr. Barton, "there is no time to say how glad we are to see you: they will soon be here; they have to pass by Jake's house to get to the grove. Have this gentleman drive you over there, and you both be standing outside as you did when you came before; Jake told me all about it. Quick, we will go down in the grove."

So it came to pass, as the company, with quite a number of old-time friends from the Park, came in sight of Jake's cabin, Jake saw what almost made his heart stop beating, so great was his joy and surprise. His mother standing in the open door, smiling, his father standing outside, his whole body shaking with laughter. There are some experiences which come into the lives of us all which seem profaned by words.

The everyday, common cottonwood trees which grow so quickly when transplanted have never been lauded for their beauty, but today that little shady grove seemed a paradise. The trees by which the bride and groom were to stand while the ceremony was taking place were trimmed with flowers and ferns Harry had brought. Greetings were not exchanged until after—only smiles showed the happiness each one felt. There, surrounded by loving friends, the sound of the water as it flowed by, the song of the meadow lark pouring forth its sweetness for very joy of living, in the distance the snow-covered mountains, all lent a charm never to be forgotten, as the few simple words were uttered that made Jake and Myrtle one—one in all that might come into their life, each living for the other.

Then, what a babble of tongues! Even Jake found talking easy.

"Our train was late," said Mr. DeLong, "but we got here in time. It was too much for mother and me; we just had to come. The neighbors were kind; they declared there was nothing for us to do but go; they would see to everything, and gave us ten days to get back in. Hello, Kate, is that your baby?"

"Sure," said Kate, with her old-time ringing laugh.

Harry was beaming; he felt he, too, was in it, with his mother and father there. A happy time they had talking and joking. The mothers went to Mr. Barton's cabin a little later, where the table was already set, only the teakettle needing a fire. After supper the company left, even Myrtle's father and mother, with their battle fought and won, going back happy in their daughter's happiness.

Harry's bunk room was hastily prepared for a bedroom for Mr. and Mrs. DeLong, while Harry slept in Mrs. Barton's kitchen. He stayed over another day to visit with his parents and tell them about the cattle. His report was surprising to his father, who had no idea there was so much in cattle when well cared for.

When Bob was leaving the evening of the wedding, he held his mother close in his arms as he kissed her goodbye. "It's all right, mother; she is mine. Tell father, but keep it awhile; we want to enjoy it alone for a time. Her people are willing. I am glad I live, more so than I can tell, dear mother."

CHAPTER XXVI

What Sweetened Aunt Hetty

"What a change for Jake to have a home with a little wife to welcome him," said John to Hetty the next day as they were sitting down to their supper. "I tell you, Hetty, I have had a tender feeling for him all this time, because I know by hard experiences what it is to live alone, with only bare walls to meet you when you get through with a hard day's work. Oh, little wife! you don't realize how much you have done for me, how much more life is worth living today. Why, when I am out, hard at work, my thought comes back to you and such a feeling of thankfulness comes over me that I have a home and a wife in that home planning for my comfort. I forget I am tired, and the first thing I know I am singing and loving the cabbage plants I am cultivating, and I give them an extra hoeing, for they seem at such a time to be alive, trying to do the very best they can, and I want to help them."

"Why, John!" said Hetty, blushing with the sweet satisfaction a wife has when her husband praises, "that is the longest speech I ever heard you make. What is the matter?" anxious to hear him talk some more.

"It's that wedding of Jake's, Hetty, stirred me up so. Let's go over this evening."

And so, a little later, as Jake and Myrtle, with the father and mother so happy in the joy of their children, were sitting outside watching the bright sunset extending far on the horizon, John and Hetty, with smiling faces, came to visit with them a little while.

"Glad to see you," said Jake, proud as a boy with his first pair of boots. "You came to visit me and my wife, did you? I tell you, John, I have more than I deserve."

"No, indeed!" declared Mrs. DeLong. "You always were ready to help others, even when a little boy."

"How is the crop, John?" asked Mr. DeLong. "Going to have some more fine potatoes like those I took home last fall to the neighbors? One man asked me if they had many of that size. 'Yes, sir!' I said, 'tons of them.' One neighbor asked me to sell him three or four for seed. I told him he was welcome to the potatoes, but I was afraid it was the climate and the sunshine more than the potatoes that made them grow to such a size."

"What do you think of our strawberries, Mr. DeLong?" asked Aunt Hetty.

"They look fine; I am glad you have started in that line, but what will you do with so many? Jake tells me each ranch is to have the same amount; you can't eat them all."

"Oh, no!" said John, "we expect to sell them; send them to the mountains, Ouray and different places. These mining camps are a great thing for us ranchers; almost like a gold mine. Everything of that kind they need, and will need, and, best of all, a ready cash market, too. I am glad we live as near as we do. Men come from away below Montrose, a pretty long trip for them, up to the hills. What do you think of Harry's turning cowboy, Mr. DeLong? Think he will make it pay?"

"Can't help it, I guess," said Harry's father, "from what he tells me. It is all new to me. I offered to put a little cash in to help him out, but he laughed and said, 'Keep your cash for railroad fare,' that he would show me when his three years were up whether there was money in it or not. He wanted me to go up with him; wish I could, but we will have to start back day after tomorrow."

"But we are glad we came," said Mrs. DeLong. "The trouble is, we begin to want to stay out West. There is something in this light air and bright sunshine very attractive."

"Well, we must be going," said John. "There is another hard day's work tomorrow. We get ready for our trip to Ouray the day before, so, goodnight."

"There is a man clear through, and his wife is just as good," said Jake. "I did not take to Aunt Hetty, as we all call her, when we lived back East. She was always wondering what the neighbors would say, and never would look at us boys. But this western life has done wonders for her: she makes me think of our strawberries—you see a bunch where the sun never reaches them, and they are small, pale and sour, but there is another bunch in the same soil, but out in the bright sunlight, the berries are large, bright, red and sweet."

"So you think it is this bright sunshine has sweetened Aunt Hetty," laughed Mr. DeLong.

"Yes, that, and something else very much like it," said Jake, smiling up at his young wife.

The next day Jake took his wife and parents up on the mesa to see Bob and his ranch. They found Bob busy.

"Well, boy, how are you?" asked Mr. DeLong.

"Fine, sir; how are you all?" He looked up at them, with his face beaming with happiness.

"What's up?" asked Jake.

"Up?" rejoined Bob, flushing and wishing for once he could turn pale.

"No use, Bob; you can't hide it," said his tormentor. "Glad for you, old man." No, happiness cannot be put under a bushel and hid; it will out. Happiness has a light all its own, and, like the sunshine, brightens and purifies.

"You have a good, substantial cabin," remarked Mrs. DeLong, anxious to change the subject for Bob's comfort.

"Yes, come in, come in!"

"And, how clean!" laughed Myrtle, as she glanced around the room.

"Yes, Mary and Ruth were over yesterday; they said you would likely be over; they seemed to think I was not a very good housekeeper."

"How many acres have you, Bob?" asked Mr. DeLong.

"One hundred and sixty acres; that is what the law allows; too much for one man to work alone.

I was talking to Mr. Eaton and Mr. Gray last evening and they seem to think that in time, after the land is proven up on, one will be able to sell part and do better work with less."

"I don't know about that," said the easterner. "I should think the more one has the better. Going to raise hay and grain?"

"Yes," said Bob, "a little, but, like others over here, I expect to plant an orchard as soon as the water gets here."

"When do you think the water will be here?" asked Mr. DeLong.

"We have it from a reliable source that the work will begin in earnest this fall."

"Then you have to wait another year?" said his questioner. "But from the looks of things, it will pay you. I like the looks of this land, level as a table, and what a fine view you have of the mountains. Don't you know, when we went back home last fall, after being out here, mother and I felt awfully cramped up on our ranch, although it is one of the best in the country. We seemed to miss something and wondered what it was; then mother said, 'Why, father! I know what is the matter; it's those snow-capped mountains the boys have we are missing.' Sure enough, that was it, and I felt like crying for joy when they first came in sight the other day."

That night there was another gathering at the Barton home, and a happy time it was.

"What do you think of our coming out West,

now, Mr. DeLong?" asked Mr. Barton, as they were seated outside, where the cool breeze reached them.

"I think it was a mighty fine thing. You are not going very fast; it's like laying a foundation so far, but the superstructure will be fine. After all your land is under cultivation, you will be comfortably fixed, with more coming in each year. I am sure glad you came, and that my boys are with you people. In another two years you will have it all under cultivation, won't you?"

"Yes," said Mr. Barton, "two years from this fall everything will be in good shape; our garden pays better than anything else, with the mines for a market."

"Well, say, neighbor, if you don't mind telling me, how did you get the idea of working together this way? I never heard of such a plan."

"Since you ask it, I must tell you. My wife suggested it; it took me a week to think it over, but the more I thought of it, the more I saw the advisability of the plan. It did not take the rest near as long to give up as it did me. I wanted to look after my own, and let each look after his. I would not change now for anything. But how do you like the appearance of our ditch? We are proud of it."

"You may well be, and as long as there is snow in the mountains you will have plenty of water."

"Yes, Mr. DeLong, it was Bob who got us in the notion of locating by the river. I told him it was land we were after, but that boy saw that which I did not."

"Bob is a very observing boy. I am glad he has a good place, and it won't hurt him to wait a little. As we were coming along, I overheard some men talking about the ditch. They said it would positively begin this fall. But say, folks, it is time we were going; it is getting late."

Jake and Myrtle parted with their parents the next day. Their visit had meant much to Jake. As they came back from the railroad station at Montrose, Jake and his wife, driving up to their little cabin, the world seemed very beautiful to them. No more did Jake have to eat alone, and it was astonishing how much more work he could accomplish.

Fall came, with the fruition of their summer's work. Water had been abundant for the four ranches, the potato crops even better than the year before. The first of November Harry proudly brought each owner his cattle, with some increase. The cattle of the little company were kept together, and fine pasturage it proved on the alfalfa owned by Jake and Harry. The alfalfa on Tom's and Mr. Brown's places had made a good start.

The company were feeling good over the prospect of water on Bob's place the last of the coming year; for over a month, work had been progressing. The ditch was located and filed upon by Joseph Selig, and was finally named, in days to come, The Montrose and Delta Canal. About the same time, the Uncompahgre Ditch and Land Company made

ONE OF THE LAKES ON GRAND MESA, NEAR DELTA.

filings for a ditch on practically the same line, by O. D. Loutsenhizer.

The people were jubilant; hope rose high; the outlook was very encouraging. Other ditches were being built, one, the Ironstone Ditch, having been completed the year before, covered California and Ash mesas.

It is useless for the writer to spend time locating each ditch in this beautiful valley of opportunities: the fact remains, the need was seen and nobly met.

Not only in the Uncompahgre Valley, but all over the western slope, towns were springing up, teeming with life and activity. Delta, a growing little town, situated about twenty-two miles below

Montrose, sprang into birth in the spring of 1883, nestling as in a mother's arms at the foot of Grand Mesa, northwest of town. On top of Grand Mesa are many small natural lakes, that abound with fish. As described by a local journalist: "Delta is situated in a basin, surrounded on three sides by high mountains, and open to the northwest. To the south is the Uncompahgre range, whose peaks are covered with snow the year round. The Elk range lies to the east, some forty miles distant. These two ranges are the highest and most rugged in Colorado." Fine ranches were already being taken up, the air of intense activity manifested everywhere.

CHAPTER XXVII

THE MARRIAGE OF THE EAST AND THE WEST

The end of the year was drawing near. Our little company met the middle of December to talk over the year's work.

The potato crop and garden proved a great success; the grain and alfalfa, too, were fine.

"Well, folks," said Mr. Barton, smiling, "the report, as Mr. Wilson and I have it, is better than we expected."

After the report was read, everyone was smiling.

"Let us plan for the coming year," said John.

"All right," said Mr. Barton, "we are all agreed, I believe, to be governed as we were last year."

"Sure!" they all declared.

"Then," said Mr. Barton, with a happy smile, "Mr. Wilson and I find the two nearest in line with our ditch are our friends, John and Dick."

Aunt Hetty's face was beaming, not that she wanted their ranch to be cultivated so much, but she wanted it for John's sake.

"I wish I were the last one," said John.

"You have nothing to say about it, sir," said Mr. Wilson, "and I am well pleased as it is; two more years of working together seems good to me."

"I move," said Jake, "that John put in three acres of garden on his place and two on Dick's, and use as much of mine as he has time; he will then be nearer home."

"And put on each ranch the same amount of strawberry plants," said Kate.

"And the same amount of alfalfa," joined in Mr. Barton. "Why, people, that will mean two hundred acres of alfalfa when we get through, each having twenty-five acres—enough to feed our cattle at present."

"I move," said Tom, "we put in ten acres of potatoes this year."

"All right," laughed Mr. Brown. "I believe it pays more than grain, and I want to say right here, for I feel so strong about it, lack of water is not all the trouble with the people out here. I was over to see Mr. Clark on some business; he took me over his place; he has plenty of water, even a better show than we, but he is working alone and a poor out he is making at it, too. I felt sorry for him. I told him what we were doing. 'Why!' said he, 'I never heard of such a thing, but it must be a good idea.' "

"How is the ditch coming on, Bob?" asked his father.

"It's getting along all right; be bound to get as far as our place before next fall," said Bob.

"Harry has been very quiet," said Mrs. Barton.

"I am used to it," said Harry, laughing. "I spend so many hours without speaking, except to the cattle and Tige, I enjoy hearing others talk.

Had a letter from father the other day. Let me read it: 'I'm doing lots of thinking these days; seems like everything goes by clock work. The sun rises and sets, rises and sets, always the same; so with the work; never any change; don't expect any change. But, with you, it is different; more life, more variety the whole year through. And then, the sun seems more and more on the sulk; never noticed it before; took it as a matter of course; it would not shine for days at a time. Our sun is just like a neighbor of mine—you go to her house one day and she is smiling and kinder cheerful; you go a few hours after and she is that gloomy one wants to get away quick and dread to go near next time. While with you, the sun, as someone said, "makes a business of shining," cheerful every day of the year, something to be depended on. And then, I notice mother has a habit of looking away off instead of down at things. I know, without her telling me, what she is thinking of. One day lately I was sitting by the fire; looking up I saw mother looking straight at me, never moving, and I asked her what she was looking at. "Oh!" she said, "I was looking at those snow-capped mountains." Blamed if I didn't get out of patience, her taking me for one of those mountains. Then when she talks, it is always Jake and Myrtle, Jake and Myrtle. Guess if we were there she would see me once in awhile. But the truth about it, boy, is that I am as bad as she in that line, but, as Mr. Barton has said, I don't see any way out at the present.'"

"We will have them here before a great while," said Hetty, smiling.

"Friends," said Bob, "why don't you who have the water begin to plant fruit trees?"

"Never thought of it," said Mr. Wilson.

"You see," said Bob, "it takes years for them to mature. The sooner they are planted the better. We on the mesa are learning all we can in that direction. It is only an experiment, but we believe this will be a good fruit country."

"I move we plant an acre of fruit trees on each farm, this spring," said Mr. Barton. "That will be enough to experiment with."

"Mr. and Mrs. Woods were over last evening," remarked Mrs. Brown. "They are happy over the fact that they have parted with half the land they had taken up. They could not sell the land, of course, as they had not proven up on it, but they were paid a nice little sum, enough to live on this summer, and they still have plenty of land for themselves."

"They look younger than when we first met them," said Mrs. Wilson.

"Yes, indeed, they do, and how they enjoy ranching," laughed Mrs. Brown. "They are planning now what they will do this coming year, and are rejoicing over a letter they received not long ago from their oldest son, who is thinking of coming out in the spring to look over the possibilities of this new town, Montrose. He is a dry goods merchant, is married, and has three children. It's the schooling he is afraid won't be good enough in a new country."

"I don't believe," spoke up Mr. Barton, quickly, "they need fear in that direction. People so wide awake in everything else are not apt to be indifferent on such a vital subject. I was surprised to find such a good school in Ouray."

"We don't need to be surprised," said Mr. Wilson. "We seem to forget the love of education and the desire for it was brought by these brave men from the East. And, since we seem to be inclined to be serious tonight, will say this proposition appeals to me somewhat like a marriage, as it were, the East and the West meeting, the East bringing its best and laying it at the feet of the West, and the West giving of its sense of freedom, of large heartedness and vitality to the East, each needing the other. We do not yet realize what the children may become from such a union."

"Mr. Wilson," said Mrs. Barton, grasping his hand, "I thank you for voicing the feelings and thought I have had for a long time. Then, just to think, we, you, and all who come, have a part in this development. I am glad I live today and wish for once that I was younger, but what we will not live to accomplish, our children will."

Kate's and Mollie's boys were getting restless, so each bade the other goodnight, each going home with the consciousness that life was worth living.

CHAPTER XXVIII

HARRY'S SECRET

The spring of 1884 opened, and with it a year full of great possibilities. The work on the canal was growing as rapidly as such a gigantic undertaking could. Theodore C. Henry, who had it in charge, was the first to see the possibilities of irrigation when applied to the soil of this state, and in this connection earned for himself the title of "Father of Colorado Irrigation."

Harry, gathering up his herd as the shepherd would his flock, went to the hills early, for the snow was gone and the grass springing up in every direction. It was amusing to see the older cattle as they started that morning; they seemed to know as well as Harry where they were going, and almost laughed in their knowing way as they remembered those cool days, the clear spring water, and the green grass they soon would have. They jogged along very contentedly, while Tige was almost beside himself with joy. Harry was well pleased with the outlook for the summer, the cattle were in good condition to start with.

Just as he was turning to cross a bridge leading to the hills he spied a white sunbonnet coming through the brush. He whistled a few notes, to which a sharp, clear whistle answered back.

"I saw you coming, Harry," said the girl, while he, all smiles, stood waiting. Again it was the old, yet ever-new, story, when the world seems to change from its roughness, its commonplaceness into everything that is beautiful. Tige seemed not to understand the situation and finally left them alone, for the cattle needed immediate attention.

It was such a beautiful day, the meadow larks were outdoing themselves in giving out the sweetest of all music, the bluebirds, though more quiet, were just as active, just as happy. The tiny blades of grass, the fresh new leaves on bush and tree were feeling the warmth of the bright sunshine, all nature seemed to be rejoicing together.

In the distance one could see the men at work on the ditch. Soon Harry was on his way, much to Tige's satisfaction.

Harry was very much occupied in thought and forgot to notice Tige for awhile, much to the dog's discouragement, and ever after when the dog missed something in his master he associated it with that white sunbonnet, and, strange enough, he did not miss it far.

At noon they stopped at Brown's spring for dinner. At night they reached Harry's cabin. Desolate, indeed, it looked, everything rust and damp, but it did not take long to build a big fire and cook supper. A draught from the spring tasted good, and Tige was made to feel his welcome then all right. A man needs a dog in such a place, needs its companionship. The cattle, showing almost the same intelligence as their caretaker, lay resting near, content with today's blessings.

Just as the first streak of daylight appeared, Tige, with his tail wagging joyfully, licked his master's hand and gave a quick bark, which awakened Harry from the sound sleep of youth and mountain air.

"Hello! Tige, old boy; it's you, is it? It's you and I, you and I. We are in for a whole summer together, ain't we, old fellow?" And he patted the dog's head, while Tige wagged his tail so fast one could scarcely see it.

The cattle began to open their eyes, yawn and get up, one at a time. Some of the calves content to watch with one eye on their elders, for they were still tired from the long journey of the day before. The birds overhead darting from one tree to another, gossiping over the change taken place during the night. The birds of the year before explaining to the disturbed newcomers that all was well. Some of the birds, more venturesome than others, flew down near the cattle and pecked the tender green grass, start to fly away, then stop for one more bite. They knew "they had wings," so there was nothing to fear. The squirrels began their morning gambol, running up and down the trees, chasing each other, giving a knowing squint at Tige as much as to say, "catch me if you can." The chipmunks, little fat things, peeping around the corner of Harry's cabin, gone in a flash if Harry stirred, but later becoming so tame they would eat out of his hand. Living near to nature's heart is the privilege of the cowboy.

To Harry, although he had been there the year before, everything seemed new, more beautiful. He noticed the "little things" around him, and was surprised to find so many claiming his attention. He noticed the sweet unfolding of the flowers, with their exquisite shadings; the fine tracery of the fern

THE EDITOR OF "THE OURAY TIMES" AND HIS FAMILY. 1884.
FACING EAST.

as it grew by the big rock, and, a little later, the spruce tree in its new growth of light green.

Harry often sang—he couldn't help it—sang just as the birds, from very joy. One day, after carefully examining his axe, he said to Tige, "Come on, old boy, let's begin to get ready."

Tige assented cheerfully, for what his master suggested was always good to him. They did not have to go far to find what they needed, and soon the sound of the axe was heard by the startled birds.

"Fine logs for a cabin, don't you think, Tige?" asked Harry as he sat resting and eating his lunch, after which he took out his pencil and began to figure how many logs it would take for a cabin twelve by fifteen.

Toward evening, about time to return home, Harry was surprised to see two cowboys riding through the woods toward him, and was greatly pleased when he discovered his old friends, Mr. Baker and Mr. Thornton.

"Hello, pard," said Baker. "We were at your cabin, but failed to find you."

"What you up to, Harry?" quizzed Thornton. "Your quarters getting too small?"

"Yes," said Harry, blushing.

"Oh, that is it, is it? She must be a peach to get you."

"She is all that," said Harry, suddenly growing dignified. The boys took the hint quick enough. "Come to the cabin and have supper with me."

"Guess we will."

When they reached the cabin, Harry found a fine chunk of beef lying on the table.

"That looks good; much obliged," and Harry showed his appreciation.

"That's all right; glad to bring it," said Thornton. "How are the home folks?"

"Doing fine," said Harry. "Did you know Jake was married?"

"Yes, glad for him. But say, how soon will you have these logs ready?"

"In about two weeks," and Harry's face flushed.

"I just wanted to know," replied Baker, as he jumped into the saddle at parting. "Then, two weeks from today, we will be back bright and early to help you put that cabin up."

"Thank you ever so much, boys," said the delighted Harry.

Harry worked faithfully the next two weeks and a big pile of logs were ready. He hitched his horse to each one and dragged them over to his building site, so when the boys came, one morning early, they made quick work of it; by night the walls were up, the logs hewed smooth on one side. The boys stayed all night and a jolly time they had, the hills resounding with their songs and laughter, but never once did they speak but with the deepest respect of her who might come to live in that little cabin, and Harry, with all his heart, was glad.

It was a great thing for the little company to have the cattle away and so well cared for, it lightened the work, but Harry, with his jovial laugh and pleasant ways, was missed.

Work went on rapidly, not only on the ranches, but on the canal, everyone seemed to be in earnest. The great need of the valley was being met, the people possessed with patience and perseverance often met at social gatherings, thereby strengthening each other.

Bob, being much with others up on the mesa, had many a story to tell his folks when he came home, stories of privation, of bitter "doing without," and yet, of the patient determination to win out. Schools were being started and taught under much disadvantage, the teacher often supplying food for the children, and many an hour spent in explaining not arithmetic, but the possibilities of good for the future in this valley, for the children needed the uplift as well as the parents. With this encouragement, the children helped relieve the hard strain at home. Wives who passively felt affection for their husbands grew more loving and thoughtful as they felt the pathos of the husband's struggle, and many a man wondered at his wife's smiling face, and took heart. The transformation was not all in the country, but in the lives, the hearts of the people. But, as one of earth's noblemen said a few years later, "If we as a people had known what we would have to go through, we would not have dared to have come." This same man, in after years, was proud he had had part in this experience.

CHAPTER XXIX

BOB'S WEDDING

Bob had a long talk with his mother one day, which strengthened him in doing what seemed right, waiting until the water was on his place before he asked Helen to leave her home for his. Not that it was really necessary, for they loved each other too much to care for that, but they also loved enough to wait. In some way the word got out, and it was surprising what an effect it had on the ditchmen—they almost forgot their weariness from the hard work in their desire to get it done, thinking of Bob and his girl, and often they caught a glimpse of Helen as she came down off the mesa with Bob to get a barrel of water from the river.

The little company of home folks were having a secret, in which Bob and his girl were not aware. A wedding present was being prepared by Dick, the artist, and his mother, Mrs. Wilson. It was surely a labor of love, for which the whole company, in a way, were giving, for Dick was released a good deal from farm work, so he, with the help of his mother, could bring out, as far as possible on canvas, his first impression when entering Ouray the first time, the beauty and grandeur of the "Gem of the Rockies." And then another, a vivid picture of the meeting of Dick's mother and sister when they came back to Ouray, accompanied by Mollie and her parents, the meeting of Tom and Mollie after their long separation, entitled, "Bob's Secret Revealed." The work was progressing finely. Many a glimpse our people enjoyed in Dick's studio, watchfully guarded from Bob. Enthusiasm ran high, for the pictures were indeed faithful and lifelike.

Jake's bright thought for the wedding, when confided to Mr. and Mrs. Barton, was heartily approved, though they objected to his bearing all the expense, but Jake said, "That is my pleasure, dear Mrs. Barton, and Bob is worth more than we can ever do for him."

Mr. Woods' son, with his family, came in the early summer, and, after visiting his parents a week or two, started, in a small way, a dry goods store in Montrose, his family staying for a short time at the "Old Lot Hotel," run by Mr. James A. Kyle and Colonel Peters. Although the growth of Montrose county had not been apparently rapid, the assessed valuation of taxable property in 1884 was $757,878.00.

The first census showed this to be the most healthy valley in the United States. The director of the census sent the report back for verification.

To the observing eye, it was an interesting sight when traveling over the country to see the universal need of water being met in a universal way. In every direction ditches were being dug, the whole country, as it were, being honeycombed with channels through which the supply would come, and some, it may be many, as they worked, realized they were working for the years to come, not just for the present, looked beyond the struggle to fruition.

The time came at last for Bob's wedding. What preparations had been going on! Everyone loved Bob, everyone interested in his welfare; even the birds seemed to understand, and practiced daily to give their sweetest music when the time came.

The highest tribute Bob gave his mother, and which she treasured most, were those words he gave her the night of his engagement: "I'm glad I live." In the joy of such a time the parents lost all sense of self, and rejoiced with their boy. Everyone was happy. It seemed more like a Christmas time, the many consultations held, the hasty glancing around before speaking to be sure Bob was not there to hear. But once they thought he was down by the river, and were talking very freely. Bob heard, but with his big brown eyes bulging with fun, he quietly passed out of the back door and they never knew, for Bob was one who "could keep a secret."

During the last two months, Bob's two-roomed log cabin had been comfortably furnished, partly with home-made furniture. Many little things the girls, Ruth and Mary, had prepared, which made the room look very pretty. The invitations were out, including all who were present at the house party the winter before, and a few new friends they had made lately, besides Helen's grandparents, who had come from the East to be present at the wedding of their favorite granddaughter, and see the country at the same time.

Presents kept coming in from the ditch men and neighbors. Often the present consisted of something to eat—a rabbit, vegetables. These were appreciated just the same.

The day before the wedding, Bob, with his father, had a walk over the ranches of this little company.

"I wish I could have stayed and helped you get your place in good shape, father," said Bob, with a cloud on his face. "It looks like I was going back on you."

"No, no! my boy," said his father, "it's all right; I am glad you are getting settled; it is what we want you to do. It was hard at first, but now we, mother and I, would not have it otherwise, and you will have a wife worthy of you, Bob, and I am glad. I tell you, boy, it is a big undertaking for any woman to join a man, to be his help, to meet every circumstance, no matter what, in life. To stand by him in the storms, as well as in the sunshine, and, Bob, I want to tell you," his voice broke and there was silence for a moment, "I tell you, in our darkest hours in the years that have passed, your mother's face was always the brightest, like a beacon light to a sea-tossed sailor. I knew why she so heartily took up the idea of coming out here, leaving her comfortable home back East. It was a noble woman's love for her husband, and, boy, may you never need to know what I went through during those hard times at Ouray. I felt, as I watched her loving bravery through it all, I was not worthy of such devotion, and would have given my right hand to see her back home. But today, Bob, we are glad we live, glad we came, for now our comforts are increasing and will increase, and I shudder to think of how it might be even today on the old farm, for I was fast losing my grip; I knew it, but I don't think mother did. I believe, boy, Helen will prove as good to you as your mother has to me. I ask no more than that for you, my son." And the two men clasped hands and looked steadily into each other's eyes for a moment.

This talk with his father was treasured by Bob as long as he lived.

That evening, before Bob left for the mesa, he whispered, "Go a little way with me, mother dear."

"Oh, yes! Bob, I was wishing there was a place where we two could be alone just once more."

So Bob, laughingly, bade the friends goodbye till morning, and no one asked to go along with mother and Bob. Father watched them go, she and her boy, and understood.

"It's all right, Bob," she said, after a few moments of silence. "I am glad for you; I only hope, dear, you will have as happy a home as father and I. Your father is, as my mother used to say, 'one in a thousand.' You have had a good example, Bob; he has ever been a sheltering rock from the storm for me. Every day I love and respect him for his pure, loving spirit, and always I feel like bowing in gratitude to the Hand that led us out to this country where he could have the desire of his life, for he is happy, but no more than he deserves. And you, my son, will, I am sure, make as good a husband, and Helen, I believe with all my heart, will prove a worthy wife for you."

"Yes, mother, I know she will. She is worth the long waiting, don't you think, mother?"

"Yes, dear. Now go on, tomorrow will soon be here. We will be over early. God bless you, dear boy. He has blessed you."

"Goodnight, my mother," and Bob sprang on his horse, lifting his hat as deferentially as though to a queen.

Mother did not have to go far alone. Father was near to see her home, and as they walked arm in arm back to the little cabin, their thoughts turned to the long ago when they, too, were starting life's journey together, and each felt tonight they were happier after all those years than in that long ago. Oh! the wonder of it all; it is beyond the human to understand.

Morning came, with one of its sunshiny days. Mother and part of the company went over to Bob's early to prepare everything. The wedding was to take place at eight that evening. A mysterious bundle went over about the time Bob would leave, and the contents hung on the wall.

After the wedding supper it was arranged for everyone to escort the newly married couple to their home and visit there awhile. So, with much laughter and fun, they walked—it was not far—the bride and groom, surrounded by their friends, when, to the surprise of only two, the Montrose band began to play the wedding march, following the little party, and as they entered the little home, just on the threshold, the band began to play, soft and low, "Home, Sweet Home."

"Oh, mother!" Bob said. "Is this music your work?"

"No, dear; it's Jake's. Is it not fine?"

Bob turned to that young man and said, "Jake, you are a brick!"

But still another surprise awaited Bob. As his eye caught sight of the pictures, he stood for a moment spellbound, then, turning to Dick, he grasped his hand.

"Dick, old fellow, I know this is yours. I am bankrupt for words to thank you." But a sob, more eloquent than words, came from Bob's heart.

Just then the band struck up, "My Country, 'Tis of Thee," and as though it were all arranged, everyone joined in that immortal song. The band boys, after a few words of congratulation, bade them goodnight.

Harry was there, and, with him, a sweet-faced girl, who, though a stranger, won the hearts of all but one, who felt a great loss had come to her even at this happy hour.

Very soon the friends bade Bob and his bride goodnight and they were left alone to begin a journey which depended so on themselves for its brightness.

CHAPTER XXX

THE DEMONSTRATION MADE

The year 1885 found the little company busy cultivating and putting in good shape the Wilson and Barton ranches. Work was progressing in fine shape.

Fall came, an important time for all. Harry came home with the cattle as the November winds began to blow; his three-year contract was up. Proudly he brought his fine bunch of cattle in for inspection and approval, the increase had been good and all were in fine shape.

The first of December a business meeting was called, all the little company present, each happy, but serious.

"Friends," said Mr. Barton, and his voice trembled, "I am glad to see you all here. We have been greatly blessed in our work together. It has been a pleasure to me, to my wife, and, I am sure, to us all, to have worked together in this way. The last four years have been happy ones for us, as well as beneficial. When we first started, we had no thought except for the one year, but finding how well it proved for all concerned we kept on. Now, at the close of the four years, we find the eight ranches all under cultivation, with a ditch big enough for them all, of which we are proud. Each ranch has a strawberry bed and one acre of fruit trees, a small garden patch in good shape, and we all have board floors to our cabins. I believe, for all concerned, the time has come for each to work alone; we all have our own notions of what we want to do. Are you all agreed?"

"I want, for myself and wife," said Mr. Brown, bowing to the little company, "to thank you people for your kindness and good will in the past four years. It was so new to me, this working together, and I was slow to take it up. But when once I saw the point, I grabbed it, and must say I hate to make any change, but I see, as Mr. Barton says, the time has come to separate and look only after our own."

"Yes," said Mr. Wilson, "I believe the time has come for the change, but as wife and I have talked it over, though we may not work together, we will still have a warm interest in each other. This working together, as we have, has, for me and I believe for us all, broadened our thought toward the whole world. One can get very narrow-minded when thinking only of his own interests. Our work for the last four years will remain a beautiful memory all our lives."

"I want to say a word," said John, his kind face beaming. "My wife and I cannot find words to express our thanks for the happy time we have enjoyed with you people. We wonder why there are not many working this way. If there were more of this working together, there would not be the need of that blighting cloud we call a 'mortgage.' It is fearful the hold that this has taken with our people. It robs one of all the joy of living, to think at any time another man has the power to close down on you and take your hard-earned home from you. Why, some men, good men, who would not do a dishonorable thing for the world, have told us, wife and I, on our journeys back and forth with our vegetables, they take the mortgage to bed with them, just can't let go. They declare with clenched fists if they ever get from under that load they will never go in debt again. But it is the getting from under it, they say. And their wives, as they see their husbands struggle, wish they had learned to 'do without' many of the comforts they were enjoying at such a fearful price."

"Yes," said Mrs. Barton, "this doing without till better times is not half as bad as one would think."

"No, indeed," spoke up Aunt Hetty, quickly; "what makes it hard is getting in the way I used to be, forever fearing what the neighbors would say. I would not go back to that time for anything. What does it matter, anyway, what others say, if we are doing the best we can, I would like to know?" And Aunt Hetty looked around indignantly at the smiling faces.

"Dear Hetty," said her brother, "you and I have come up out of a great deal since we came to this land of broad-mindedness. But Harry, how have you gotten along with the cattle according to your idea? You understand it more than we do."

"I am well pleased with conditions. The cattle

are in good shape, we have all been well supplied with fresh meat, a few have been sold, bringing in a little cash, and what is left is a good start for another year's trial. I ask the job of looking after your cattle for the next three years, knowing there is money in this business for us all, and will say right here, I am perfectly willing to take my pay out of the increase; it will simplify matters for us all." This matter was arranged to the satisfaction of all. "And now, friends," said Harry, and for a moment losing his tongue, "I would like to let you, dear friends, know, for you are all interested—I am going to be married in two weeks. Yes," said he, warming up to the subject, "to the sweetest little girl in the world. Her folks have a store down at Delta."

"What is her name?" asked Mr. Barton, smiling.

"Ada," said Harry. "I know you will all like her."

"I am sure we will," said Mr. Barton, laughing, amused at Harry's boyishness, which they all loved.

"Yes," he went on, knowing he was with friends, "I shall go down there to be married, then come up here for the winter. I have already built a good-sized cabin up in the hills; the cowboys came and helped put it up."

"Well, well!" laughed Tom, "you have it all fixed, haven't you?"

"Yes, as I was saying," said Harry, "I have in mind a man to whom I will rent my ranch this summer, reserving the right to pasture my stock on the alfalfa next winter, and enough ground, with my cabin for what I may need. I am going to put up a good-sized cabin like Jake's on the place; that will be good enough, Ada says, till we get rich from our cattle."

The men looked at each other, seemingly all having the same thought.

"Good for you, Harry, my boy," said Mr. Barton. "You must let us men help you build that cabin. Let us go the first of the week, boys, and get the logs, spruce logs, just like Bob's."

"Why, Mr. Barton!" said Harry, his face very red, "it would be mighty fine of you."

"Yes, yes!" said Mr. Brown, blowing his nose pretty hard, "we all want to do it."

Just then Mrs. Wilson turned around to speak to Ruth, but found her gone. "Why, where is Ruth?" she asked of Mrs. Barton.

Mrs. Barton quickly whispered, "She left a few minutes ago; I saw her go out." But she did not tell what her observing eye had seen.

The mother startled, a sense of fear coming over her, hurried home. She found Ruth lying on her bed weeping bitterly. She was not expecting her mother so soon, and when the loving mother arms enfolded her, she could not hide the secret she had long kept.

"Oh, mother! I loved him so!" she sobbed. The mother found no words for such a time, but held her close and wished she could bear the suffering for her.

The father, coming in, heard enough to understand, and had surmised it long before, and all the joy of the evening faded from his face.

"Let her sleep with you, tonight," he whispered.

All night they fought it out together, mother and daughter, the first sorrow they had ever known. The father laid as one stunned, his daughter was so dear to him. Life looked very dark. When the bright sunlight came through the window the next morning, as though doing its best to cheer them, an attempt was made to be cheerful, and life began as it were, anew—never could it be the same again.

CHAPTER XXXI

HARRY'S CHARIVARI

The first of the following week the men, including Mr. Barton, Mr. Brown, Harry and John, with Aunt Hetty and Mary to do the cooking, started to the hills, to be gone four days.

Aunt Hetty was delighted with the trip, but more so with the little cabin Harry had built for his bride, and soon had the cabin fixed up for camping. A gay time they all had. The night after their arrival, some of Harry's old friends came to see him, and were surprised to find ladies present. But there never yet was a cowboy who could not rise to the occasion when necessary. A jolly time they had that evening. Some of the boys, when they saw the need, went to their cabins and brought back some fine venison, for Harry was a favorite with them all. In some way, from the unsuspecting Harry, they found out the exact date of the homecoming. That was all they wanted, and many a laugh they had at Harry's expense.

At the end of four days, just at dusk, the logging party came home, loaded with the treasures from the hills, such as pine and spruce cones, and the tender branches from the spruce trees for decorating Harry's home, and the loveliest Christmas tree, for the whole party.

It took but a short time to put up Harry's cabin.

built just like Jake's. The roof, though, was of shingles, and it had a board floor. The women folks took charge of fixing it up, and ordered Harry to keep out of the way, Ruth bravely doing her part.

The days flew by. Harry left for Delta, expecting to be back in five days. His parents could not come this time; it was too cold. On the fifth day, Jake and Myrtle went with a two-seated rig to Montrose to meet the bride and groom. Our little company of friends, still one in their interest for each other, had a bright fire burning in the fireplace, sending a bright glow over everything. The room, trimmed with evergreens, was pretty, indeed. So thought Harry and his bride as they entered their home, where they found a warm supper awaiting them. The friends, a merry crowd, remained during the evening. The little new wife, sweet and lovable, won even the heart of Ruth, who could not hold it against her for having won one of the noblest men on earth.

When our good people had gone home, and, with a clear conscience, were all asleep, they were awakened by the most unearthly yells, as though a thousand Indians had been turned loose. It took but a moment for the men folks to sense the situation and quiet the fears of the women. Harry and his wife were getting a real charivari. The cowboys, dressed up in their wildest manner, bent on fun, had come as quietly as a band of Indians, the very suddenness of the attack striking terror to even Harry's heart, while Jake grabbed his gun before he realized what it all meant.

The yells, mingling with the ringing of a half-dozen cowbells, were enough, but when they began to pound on the door, although they knew what it meant, the noise of itself was unnerving. As quickly as possible, Harry opened the door, and with his girl-wife's hand in his, smilingly invited the crowd to enter. Nothing loath, they came, Harry doing his best to hold his own, but his little wife felt his arm tremble.

"Glad to see you, boys!" said Harry, laughing.

"You look like it!" said Thornton, and the whole bunch laughed, making them seem more human. Even Ada smiled and felt they were all right.

"Sorry, boys, I have no chairs, but sit down on the floor and make yourselves at home. I wish I had something for you. This had never entered my head, but my wife—gentlemen, I forgot to introduce her—will find you some cake the friends left us, and I, you know, can make good coffee."

With this invitation, the cowboys, nine in number, made themselves at home. Jake and Myrtle came in, determined not to be left out at such a time, and added to the merriment. What a jolly time they had. When kind-heartedness is at the bottom, fun is to be desired, and proves a blessing. We all need more of it.

CHAPTER XXXII

THE DELONGS COME OUT WEST

After the holidays were over, Mr. and Mrs. Wilson decided to make a short visit with old-time friends in Ouray, Ruth going with them. There being a vacancy in the school at that time, Ruth was urged to apply for the position, and was accepted. Her parents felt it was the best thing for their daughter. After finding a home for her with one who had been such a help to them in days gone by, they went back to a very lonely home.

A letter from Ruth to her parents a week or two later was received with much satisfaction. It read as follows:

"My Dear Father and Mother:

"I want to tell you I am glad I have this work; I believe it is what I have been longing for all the time. I enjoy bringing out in these young people the best that is in them. I enjoy seeing the great possibilities for good in each one, and working in the direction that will help them the most. I am beginning to realize how much I owe to you, dear father and mother, for your sweet, loving influence through my life. The long talks I have had with my landlady has helped me to see you and everything in a new light, and I am happier than I ever expected to be again. I am glad to have a room full of children to love and care for. I see happiness consists, not in being loved, but in loving.

"Your daughter,

"RUTH."

This letter was read and re-read many times by the father and mother, and the old-time peaceful happiness reigned.

It took the little company some time to readjust themselves to the new conditions, but by spring, each was settled in his own way of working, and it was surprising how natural it proved to be.

One morning the Barton family received a call from the Rev. A. D. Fairbanks and wife. Naturally, the conversation drifted to the old pioneer days, to the hardships each had to endure. The gentleman referred to the time when the doctor pronounced the trouble Mrs. Fairbanks had as incurable if she remained in the East. Swiftly the journey was taken to the western slope of Colorado for the benefit of its dry climate and higher altitude, where she regained her health—even preaching when her husband failed to "make good."

The gentleman told of an experience he had when calling at the home of O. M. Stephens, living on Garnet Mesa, near Delta. The good wife, who was out feeding her chickens, saw him approaching from a distance and immediately the cry of the helpless chicken arose. When he arrived she explained that she saw her preacher coming, and as that meant a chicken for dinner, she might as well take what she saw to be a good chance to get the game.

After the laugh at the story, a guest remarked, "I believe I could tell a joke on you, sir. Years ago you were going across the field to your sister's home with a gun on your shoulder. The wife of one of the neighbors saw you, and, remembering the awful stories she had heard about the cowboys, ran as fast as she could to her husband, who was working in the field.

"Oh, Bob!" she gasped, all out of breath from running and from fear, "do you see that dreadful cowboy coming?"

"Why, wife!" said Bob, "that is no cowboy; that is the preacher Fairbanks."

None joined in the laugh more heartily than the gentleman himself.

"Yes," said another, "never will I forget the time when we came to Montrose to live. You, dear Mrs. Fairbanks, worked three days preparing food for me and my family. We had five boys, with big appetites. It took you that long because the stove was so small and the wood was green. As it was raining, the water ran down around the stovepipe onto the stove, with it much of the mud that was on the roof. I remember I wondered why you did not clean that stove and pipe, but later, when it rained I saw the uselessness of trying to keep them clean. I remember when we were riding within half a mile of the place we had bought, our youngest boy, a child of four years, lifted up his voice and wept and would not be comforted. We laughingly said, to cheer ourselves up, he was the band. Many and many a time I, myself, felt tempted to weep, too, but the need of hope and courage was so great we tried to sing instead."

The year 1887 was an eventful one. A branch railroad was begun from Montrose, running up the Uncompahgre Valley to Dallas in Ouray County, in the spring. It was completed to Dallas August 31st, extended to Ouray, December 27th, of the same year.

On March 14th, the work of casing up the artesian well at Montrose was accepted, costing the town $731. The well was bored the previous year. The water was found heavily charged with sodium carbonate, calcium sulphate, and other mineral ingredients.

March 31st, just as they were laying the last planks of the floor of the arroyo bridge, east of Montrose, while yet in the act of nailing the last plank down, a cracking of timbers was heard, and, without other warning, the whole structure collapsed and fell in a pile at the bottom of the arroyo, carrying with it three workmen, who were not hurt.

May 19th, according to the "Messenger," Mr. J. T. Heath put out six hundred standard fruit trees, besides small fruits, he having faith in this as a fruit country.

"In 1884," says the "News Democrat," "all the flour used in western Colorado had to be brought across the range. This set the people in the lower country to thinking, and the result was a flouring mill which turned out as fine flour as the world could produce, although the production was limited to the amount of what was at that time grown in a new and unimproved country. At the time it was built it was said it would be years before the valleys of the Uncompahgre, Gunnison and Grand rivers would be able to supply it with grain. In the short space of three years the country has outgrown this mill, and it has been found necessary to build another at Montrose, and also one at Grand Junction. Colorado has a source of great wealth in her mines and stock ranges, but the day is not far distant when the grain produced will nearly, if not quite, equal that from her mines and cattle."

From the "Messenger" we read, "Even the children appreciate the glories of Montrose. Billy Block's little daughter, Lee, accompanied him on his trip to St. Louis. When they arrived at Montrose, the little one, who had never been out of the mountains before, remarked, 'Why, papa! it's all sky here.' "

At Montrose, the birthday of American Independence burst forth clear and beautiful, and was heralded by a national salute by Co. I, Montrose rifles. Frank C. Goudy was the orator of the day. The following is an extract from his speech:

"The West is full of meaning to all, especially to the young men. Here all is new; here every man is taken at his worth, measured by his merit; here the question is not what was your ancestor, but what are you? Vigor, brain and action are in demand. Communities are springing up. Vast territories being converted into homes. Already we are adding to the world's material supply. Daily we see the smoke curling up from the rude cabin of some new settler, attracted to our midst by advantages innumerable. The rude cabins of yesterday are today giving way to comfortable homes. The voices of strong, energetic men, of splendid women, lovely, active children (God bless the children) have driven back the echoes of the solitude of the West. Our marshals, faith, hope and industry, are leading us on to a great victory in our conquest of peace.

"In our march to success, we are not accompanied by the grand music of war, but around and about us we hear the hum and buzz of industry. We are not tearing down, but building up. We are advancing. We are growing. But a few years more and the scene will have changed. Labor, perseverance and western energy will soon have decked this magnificent valley with homes environed with all that goes to make the life of a farmer happy and contented; upon the picture there will be seen orchards and vineyards loaded with delicious fruits, cool, refreshing lawns and groves, fields of green and of golden grain yielding and producing bountiful harvests; cattle upon a thousand hills, and with all our prosperity will come schools and churches for the convenience of all, where intelligence, the great bulwark of our liberty, will be instilled into the minds of those who in turn will be clothed with the full and glorious privileges of American citizenship. With the wisdom and experience of the fathers, of all who have gone before, to guide our footsteps and to keep us from the breakers that have so often endangered the life of the republic, we will go on to greater and grander achievements, preserving and perpetuating to our children, and to the generations to come, the priceless boon and heritage of practical liberty, making this the greatest, grandest, best land beneath the sun, with liberty ever enlightening the world and flashing its rays of freedom on all lands, giving to the world an era of universal peace."

Mr. Barton and his family, including Bob and his wife, spent a part of the Fourth in Montrose.

Another son came to Mollie and Tom, and later a daughter to Dick and Kate. Harry and Ada went up to their home in the hills, and lived so near to nature they learned many of its secrets.

A letter addressed to Jake and Harry ran as follows:

"Dear Children:

"Mother and I have been doing a lot of thinking and talking the last year, and our minds are sure made up. Mother began to pack the minute we made our decision. We are coming to live in that country of sunshine and snow-capped mountains with you, my boys. What is the use, anyway, for us to be separated? Railroad fare is costly, too, so look out for us. We want a twenty-acre piece of ground, enough to keep me busy, and we want to run a dairy. Mother can make the best butter around here, and I can help her. We want to have a cabin, not too near you, Harry, but near enough so we can see each other every day. You raise the cows, and we make the butter. What do you boys think of that? We are coming anyway. We start in five days.

"MOTHER AND FATHER."

This letter was not a surprise, for the boys knew their parents' hearts were with them. Jake went to meet them at the appointed time, and it was amusing how important Mr. DeLong acted.

"Of course we have come; been hankering for the chance ever since you boys left home the first time, but did not see the way out till now."

The next day, Jake and his parents went up in the hills to Harry's place, taking plenty of bedding and grub along, Myrtle remaining at home.

Harry and his wife were finishing their supper when they heard the rumble of wagon wheels in the distance, and soon father and mother came in sight. What a happy meeting there under the spruce trees.

A sense of peace seemed to surround the little group as they sat around the blazing fire that evening, and talked over their plans for the future. The result was, a dozen cows were found with which Mr. DeLong started his work of "running a dairy," as he called it, his wife happy as a girl with her new work. A contract was made with a firm in

Ouray to take all the butter they could make, John and his wife taking it up with their garden produce, for they still kept up with the garden work, finding it paid them to hire someone to do the farm work.

Fall came and the little company returned from the hills, happy and contented with their work for that summer.

"We seem to be like Jacob, going back home with his herds," laughed Mrs. DeLong, as she, with Ada driving the team, Harry and his father, with the help of their dog, not Tige, much to that dog's grief, for he was getting too old and needed to rest, driving the cattle.

Bob was brimming over with enthusiasm, with his fruit trees in good shape and most of his land plowed for the coming year. Bob and Helen often came to visit his home folks, and the son was a strength to his father.

One day, just before Christmas, another little homesteader came and took up its abode, this time with Jake and Myrtle. There had been babies born before, but, to Jake it seemed, never one like this. He told everyone he met about that boy of his, and people forgot to look worried and smiled back at him.

The following spring, two men, miners in appearance, stopped at the Barton ranch and inquired for Tom Barton and Dick Wilson. The two men were in the field nearby, so Mrs. Barton called them. After being introduced, one of the men began asking questions about a mine near Ouray they were told belonged to the boys.

"Yes," said Tom, "that is our mine, all right."

"Why don't you work it?" asked one of the men.

"Been too busy running the ranch, and no money to spend for the mine for awhile," returned Dick.

"Gentlemen," said the older man, "we have been looking over your mine and would like to lease it for one year; if we make nothing out of it, it's our loss, but if we strike it rich, want three thousand dollars for the year's work; this is to be taken from the proceeds of the mine."

The lease was soon made, though Tom and Dick were not very hopeful of the outcome.

A break in the ditch at the most important time of the year caused Bob's bright hopes to fall. The fruit trees even were likely to be ruined. Bob and his wife drove over to his father's that evening. He was dazed at the sudden change.

"Don't you think, dear, the ditch will be fixed in time to save the crop?" asked his mother.

"It's too big a break, mother dear; they are doing the best they can; it will be two weeks at least, and maybe longer, and then the land is washed out so. Can you give me work, father?"

"Yes, my son, glad to."

What was true of Bob's place was even worse with others. Not only was the crop ruined, but the land was washed in bad shape. One lady heard the sound of running water long before it came in sight. She rushed out to save her chickens. Her husband had to carry her back to the house. The water was running everywhere, acting as though in glee over its escape from its enforced confines.

The people were not utterly cast down. Hope sprang up, and in some way or another there was always enough to eat, though hardly the kind they wanted sometimes. Wives and children, too, were doing their best to earn the money to keep them another year.

The ditch company saw the mistakes they had made and built stronger banks the second time. The pluck and perseverance of the people made the owners of the ditch try to do their best.

"I wish you had a ranch near the river, Bob," said his father, one evening after a hard day's work.

"I don't, father; I like it much better on the mesa; you do not have all the water you could use, and, from what I gather from those who seem to know, you will all be glad to get some, at least, from the canal."

"You think so, Bob?" said his father, who saw the water question was a serious one.

CHAPTER XXXIII

A BIG STRIKE

A year later a note was sent from the mine to the Barton home, which read as follows:

"Tom Barton and Dick Wilson:

"Come at once; bring your father with you, Dick. We think we have struck it big.

(Signed) "JACK."

The bearer was kept all night for the needed rest, and the next morning, before daylight, the men started for Ouray.

At the mine they found the miners in a state of great excitement. A crowd of town folks, old friends of our people, were there, pleased and glad for the boys they liked so much. Many a warm handclasp they received.

After Mr. Wilson had carefully examined the ore, and Tom and Dick had thoroughly examined the formation, the conclusion was reached they had, indeed, struck it rich.

"And mother will have a good house to live in at last," thought Tom.

"We were about discouraged," said the miner, "ready to give it up and call our year's work a fizzle, but that last blast did the job."

"We want you to keep on," said Mr. Wilson, after a brief talk with the boys, who were too excited to think for themselves.

"All right, boss," replied the man, "we are willing."

After a short business talk about future work, the men were left to go ahead. The horses, fed and rested for several hours, were ready for the night journey home, with their tired but hopeful riders.

A little reception was held at Mr. Barton's cabin the next morning, all the neighbors coming to hear the news and congratulate the boys on their good luck.

"Mother says she is going to stay right where she is till we get used to having a rich mine," said Tom to Mr. and Mrs. Woods, who had come over to rejoice with them.

"That is right, Tom," said Mr. Woods; "enjoy the old as long as you can; you will never be happier than you are today."

"Of that, I am sure," replied Mrs. Barton. "These years have been the happiest of my life. I shall lose much pleasure when it is not necessary to make an appetizing dish almost out of nothing." She looked up at Mrs. Woods with neighborly affection.

"Yes, dear, I have learned the pleasure you speak of, and have no desire to have it different."

Mrs. Woods' smile showed the sincerity of her words. "My husband is always praising my cooking."

Mr. Barton and Mr. Wilson had very little to say, but they enjoyed listening to the others talk.

"It seems to me," said Mrs. Wilson, "we have come up out of so much without the help of the mine, we have made the demonstration that one can succeed out West, can overcome the many obstacles which arise in a new country, and be happy. Why! money cannot buy one thing we have not already. Except," and a light shown in the mother's eyes, "Dick can now devote his time to art. How bravely he gave it up until the farms were cared for."

Ruth and Mary wandered to the chicken yard, where they could, girl-like, build air castles.

"I want to go back East," said Mary, "to our old home—I was so young when I left, you know—and see for myself how it compares with Colorado."

"It will do you good," said Ruth, quietly.

"What will you do, dear Ruth?" asked Mary, for there was much nowadays about her friend she did not understand.

"I have not thought much about it, as yet, but have longed for the opportunity to better myself for teaching. You know, that is my life work," and Ruth's face shone.

"Hello, you girls," called Tom, as he came near, leading his horse to water, "come down to the river with me. I've been up in the clouds till I need letting down a bit. Let us talk about mother's new home, such as we planned when we first came West. We didn't know what we had to go through first, did we?"

"No," replied Mary, "it was well we didn't, but, as father has often said, we are glad for every step of the way. Mother thinks we had better wait,

Tom, another year for the change you speak of, but there is one thing we must see to—us children—that father and mother have a long-needed rest."

"Sure," said Tom, "and that of itself will keep us busy, I imagine."

One day as John and Hetty were coming home from their weekly trip to Ouray, John said, "Hetty. I've been thinking a good deal about this strike of the boys. It may prove a good thing for them. and then again, it may not. If it had come a few years ago, I am sure they would never have been the men they are today, and would have missed a whole lot of pleasure. It's not what money we get, but what we make out of life, that counts, Hetty. I would rather be jogging along in this old wagon, with you, little wife, than to drive a four-horse rig in the big city."

"Yes," said Hetty, her voice very tender, "I am glad we have no mine to bother with. We made quite a little today, didn't we? How the people appreciate our vegetables and eggs."

Kate and Mollie, Dick and Tom, spent their evenings caring for the babies and making plans for the pretty cottages they would have soon. Youth and hope are great factors in life.

Bob, refusing the offered help from his brother, declared he wanted to show what he was capable of doing himself, his father proudly assenting.

Another year of peace passed by, the mine proving to be one of the best.

One morning, before the birds were awake, just

before the first streak of daylight appeared, a bright fire was burning in Harry's cabin, casting its rays here and there all over the room. Harry was going through the awful sense of helplessness that comes to a man at such a time, harder because he could do nothing.

When, all at once, as though the sun filled the room with its bright, warm rays, there was joy and heartfelt gratitude, and smiling faces—another wee cowboy had arrived and fatherhood shone all over Harry's face.

CHAPTER XXXIV

THE SMUGGLER-UNION FIRE AND LIBERTY BELL MINE SNOWSLIDE

From a copy of the "Telluride Journal" of November 28, 1901, kindly furnished us by Mr. Charles F. Painter, editor of that paper, we compile this account of the greatest casualty in the history of mining in the San Juan:

"About 7:30 of the morning of Wednesday, November 20, 1901, fire started in the tram house of the Smuggler-Union mine in Marshall Basin, near Telluride. The buildings were grouped about the mouth of the tunnel and the fire spread rapidly in spite of all that could be done. The workings of the mine, many miles in extent, acted as a flue, and the heat and smoke were drawn in, catching those men who had but just gone to work. As the situation was realized by those outside, Thorwald Torkelson, the shift boss, and Carey Barkly rushed into the tunnel to give the men warning to get out, closing the tunnel mouth door as they went in. Meeting a couple of trammers on the way out, they ordered them to unhitch and run for their lives. Unhooking their loads, each seized the tail of his animal and gave it a slap, starting for the entrance. The horse in the lead burst open the tunnel door and pulled his driver to safety right through the burning buildings. The other horse was overcome and fell dead before reaching the surface, but the driver finally found escape in another direction. To shut off the smoke and poisonous gases, the mouth of the tunnel was blown up, but, unfortunately, it was too late, the deadly work had been done. The brave men who entered the mine to give their fellows warning did well their work, but never came out alive, their dead bodies telling the tale of heroism. Some of the men escaped through other openings, but twenty-eight dead bodies told the awful story. All died of suffocation.

"Many stories could be told of individual heroism, but from the record it would appear that every man there was a hero. Such occasions as this bring out the best in every man. All honor to those brave men who fearlessly laid down their lives in the attempt to save others. All the heroes did not meet their death. There were many of them who did not hesitate to face any danger where there was a possible hope of rescuing a fellow being, bravery and self-sacrifice governing them all."

Again the tragedy of the mountains is brought out in the following:

THE LIBERTY BELL MINE SNOWSLIDE

From a copy of the "Telluride Journal," February 28, 1902:

"Another dire mining disaster has overtaken Telluride, second only in destruction to life and property to the fire at Smuggler last fall.

"At 7:30 this morning a tremendous snowslide

swept away the boarding house and bunk houses and the tramway station and ore loading house at the Liberty Bell mine.

"The accident, of course, broke the telephone circuit, and it was an hour before word reached town of the disaster, being brought down by one of the workmen who escaped. All the doctors available and many citizens at once started up the trail to lend such assistance as was in their power in digging out the buried and injured men, and it was well towards noon before any authentic information could be secured as to the extent of the awful disaster.

"The most lucid and connected account of the disaster is that given by L. M. Umsted. Mr. Umsted is employed, with a few mules, packing a short distance from a crusher to the train station. He had just come from breakfast and was in the stable saddling his animals, when he heard a terrific crashing and rattling. The stable grew suddenly as dark as night, and, stepping to the door, he opened it and found the outside totally dark and the air filled with flying snow. Thinking it was a terrific gust of wind, he slammed the stable door shut, and, waiting a few seconds, he peered through a crack, and as it grew light again he opened the door and saw the tram cable swinging about and buckets rolling down the hill. As the snow in the air settled, he stepped out a few feet, and, looking up towards the boarding house, could see no signs of these buildings. Then, looking down the hill, he saw boards and timbers sticking out of the snow and scattered about. He then started towards the boarding house and met his brother, Charlie Umsted, who told him what had happened. The number killed by the first slide is not ascertained.

"At 1:30, word came to town from the Liberty Bell office asking that bulletins be posted asking for all the help possible, as a second slide had come down, covering the rescue party. At 2:15, word came to town to send no more men up, that the storm was so severe that the work of rescue could only be carried on under extreme danger to the living, and that the men buried in the snow were all dead, beyond question.

"It is not known who nor how many were in the crowd of rescuers caught by the second slide. Men from the mine who came down since the second slide seem to think the dead will number a dozen or fifteen, and perhaps more.

A THIRD SLIDE COMES DOWN AND KILLS THREE

"After the rescuers quit work and started for town, a party was caught in a slide near the curve station on the tram, and three men were killed.

"Dr. J. Q. Allen was one of the rescue party and received injuries, but, turning to regain a hat which someone had lost, saved his life."

While recording the events of that day one is led to see that while the grandeur of the mountains uplifts and broadens one's thought, the tragedy of the mountains brings out in wondrous distinction man's love for his fellow men.

Photo by Geo. Pedley. Copyrighted.

AN ELECTRIC STORM AT NIGHT. JULY 8, 1902.

CHAPTER XXXV

A SURVEY OF CONDITIONS

Great changes had taken place in the last few years, towns were springing up in every direction, the water question was settled, in that it had proved to be a demonstrable fact that the water in the Uncompahgre, Gunnison, and other rivers were now being utilized through canals and their interlacing ditches. The ingenuity of the East, united with the perseverance of the West, had worked wonders toward mastering the many difficulties presented by nature.

The question of "overcoming" to the people who come out West is both individual and collective. The best water system in the world is not enough; the people must do their part, even to the youngest child, and, be it said with all reverence, the people rose up manfully to meet the need of the hour. They allowed themselves to be led on by hope and courage, and infinite patience. When, through the breaking of ditches, the expectations of one year were broken off, they looked forward to the next as making good. The struggle was not alone with the farmers. The towns pulsated with the prosperity or failure of the farms.

How different would have been the outcome of many an honest effort, many a noble struggle, if an offer of help in these financial straits had been seen in its true light, not as an angel of light, but as it really was, an angel of darkness—this opportunity to borrow.

Men came—honest men—with money to lend, lending it on such easy terms it seemed good to the needy ones, their very hopefulness making them an easy prey.

Soon a blight—greater than the blight of Egypt—covered the land. Its name is known as a "mortgage." This was an unknown quantity in the blessed West when this story began; the West, with its outstretched hands full of gifts, included not one mortgage. Have you ever thought of this, dear reader?

Harder times began, not because of greater privation, but because every cent they made went to pay the "interest on the mortgage." Happy were they who had escaped the inducements to borrow.

When bowed down with a mortgage, one forgets to look up to the blue sky, forgets the beauty of the flowers, forgets the grandeur of the mountains, and many a gentle, loving heart has been crushed to the grave because of its weight.

Some of these self-sacrificing, noble men and women lost their homes and had to begin all over again, but, having learned their lesson, steered clear of mortgages, and, in time, were rejoicing in a little home of their own, satisfied with what they could make, rather than reaching out for all they could get.

During these dark days, Tom and Dick were glad they had their mine, with its steady income.

Many an evening these boys spent with their parents devising ways and means to tide some of these tried ones over the hard places, often buying a small part of their ranch—for all had more than they needed—not that they wanted the land, but with the kindness of heart we find in so many, they strove to help in such a way that the receiver could keep his self-respect, which is as dear to many a man as his life.

CHAPTER XXXVI

AN AWAKENING

A year or so after the income from the silver mine was a settled fact, Tom suggested to Dick the advisability of dividing the ownership of the mine with their parents. To this Dick heartily agreed.

An invitation was given to both families to spend the evening at Tom's neat little cottage. After greetings had been exchanged, Tom rose to his feet —the better to express himself, he told his mother.

"Dick and I have invited you here tonight, dear people, to let you know what we want to do in regard to the mine—don't look anxious, Mr. Wilson, the mine is all right. We, Dick and I, have come to the conclusion we want you, our parents, to share equally with us in the mine, each of us to have one-fourth interest."

"No, no! my boy," said Mr. Barton, his lips quivering. "Keep it all yourselves; we have all we need, haven't we mother?" Mr. Barton looked up at his wife, as a child to its mother, for verification. "Why, boy—please excuse me, Mr. and Mrs. Wilson—Tom, you and mother helped me to the desire of my life, the freedom of this western life. It was all I craved. It's all I want today. Our ranch, with our cattle, brings in enough for us to live on, besides a few of the comforts of life. What more do we want?"

Mrs. Barton drew her chair nearer her husband's

side and laid her hand in his, she loved so to feel its warm clasp. "It's just as father says, Tom; we have enough," and the mother smiled, not at Tom, but up at her husband.

"Mr. and Mrs. Wilson, dear friends, we want to hear from you," said Tom.

"For myself," answered Mr. Wilson, his voice very husky, "I feel as our friends have expressed themselves; we have plenty to live on very comfortably."

"Yes, indeed," joined in Mrs. Wilson, "a great plenty."

"Friends," said Tom, and very manly and noble he looked to his mother, "I have been thinking a good deal on certain lines lately, and so has Dick. It has come very strongly to me in the last six months that to live just for ourselves, to be content with just enough for ourselves, is not carrying out the principles we have felt, or the lessons we have learned from these grand old mountains, whose outstretched arms give to all alike, no sense of 'me' or 'mine' there.

"At first, while getting our ranches in shape, we were obliged to center our interests more or less to that work, for it was a struggle, how much of a struggle no one will ever know, in spite of the united effort in working together as we have. But today it is different: the mountains have opened their heart of gold to us. You, mother, in days gone by taught me that when we feel the great heart of God we begin to take on His nature. So

I feel tonight, just as we see the heart of these mountains, so we have the privilege of taking of their nature, and, what is their nature? To give.

"Father," and Tom's voice broke, for tears were rolling down the father's face, "let us talk it out, for well I know you feel as I do, for you, more than us all, have drank in the lessons these mountains have been teaching, the lesson of living for others. What have we given to the mountains? Nothing. What have we received from them? Everything worth while. As a grand old judge said, when here, 'I love these mountains; everything good comes from the mountains.'

"We breathe the pure air of this country and our wings begin to grow. To merely live for ourselves seems so paltry, so small, we begin to look around to see what we, too, can do for others. All these years we have, many times, helped to relieve some struggling one; that is good; the mountains abound with springs and flowers to refresh and comfort the weary ones, but today there are greater needs."

"Greater, my son?" said the father, whose tears were dried.

"Yes, father, greater. It was good to tide over a rough place for another, but today the need is not to 'tide over,' but to construct so there be no need of tiding over. When a strong bridge is built, there is no need of a plank.

"Today there are schools to be built, a higher tone in society to be brought out, a need of ways and means for promoting the good of all, not only in the country, but in the towns which are springing up in every direction. A great responsibility rests upon us who have eyes to see and hearts to give. The interests of the whole western slope will be no bigger than the people who help bring them about.

"These are the reasons why we ask you to come in with us, so that we can more effectively work together for the good of this valley, this valley of opportunity."

Rising to his feet, Mr. Barton said, "Boy, my boy! God bless you! And you, too, Dick! With all my heart I will go in with you for others' sakes. And you, too, old and tried friends," turning to Mr. and Mrs. Wilson, who had risen with him, and together they clasped hands. "All right, boys, fix the papers to suit yourselves. I feel the spirit of these mountains are with us; they speak of peace and good will to all."

As they were wending their way home, not a word was spoken by the Bartons. Later, as they sat alone, for Mary had gone to spend the night with Ruth, Mr. Barton said, "Wife, I feel I am in a new world. I have gained something I felt these mountains held for me. I live today in a world of self-forgetfulness, living only for the interests of others."

"Bless you, dear," was all his wife could say, as she kissed the brow she loved so much.

CHAPTER XXXVII

RUTH

A change had come over our friends. Their horizon had broadened.

Not thinking how much will this year's crop bring in for us, but, rather, how much will it bring to help us with our work for others.

Strange as it may seem, the soil seemed to feel the spirit of giving and yielded of its richness more and more abundantly.

Every town in the valley seemed to feel the impulse of Tom's vision as though, as it were, the pebble of unselfishness had been cast into the sea of western life, touching every crevice from one end of the valley to the other—and bore fruit.

Brave men and women, but accustomed to think only of their own interest, awoke to the fact there was something more satisfying.

There were others who already had given much of their time and thought for the welfare of the community in which they lived. There were some, how many we cannot tell, who from the first "dug deep" for future as well as present needs and hailed with joy the change taking place.

Many a talk Mr. Barton and his son had with these capable and energetic ones to whom the people naturally turned to lead in town affairs, not pushing themselves forward, but quietly dropping suggestions when opportunity offered, and men awoke to the need and spirit of working only for the good and uplift of those around them.

Often Mrs. Barton and Kate, with Myra, the baby, accompanied their husbands on their trips, giving the women of the valley the needed encouragement in their different lines of work, and never a home did they visit but when they left the inmates felt a greater love for each other, a greater patience with the tasks set before them.

Late one spring, Ruth came home from school. To her parents she seemed changed in some indefinite way which they could not understand. The evening of her homecoming, as they sat in the twilight, the father said, "Well, daughter, still in love with teaching?"

"Yes, father, still in love with teaching, but," her face flushed, "I will tell you, dear father and mother, I still love teaching; I believe it is the grandest work in the world; gives one such an opportunity to help so many individually to lay the foundations for a useful life. I believe I have been very successful in that line, but for some years my thought has been changing in regard to many things. There was a time," and a catch in her voice reminded her listeners of a time they never could forget, "when I thought I never could change, but I have been watching you, father and mother, your lives together, growing more and more beautiful, leaning so on each other for companionship, until to me you seem to be as one. The question has come to me often, what am I missing? The last day at school has always been the hardest day of the year to me, after the last goodbye has been said and everyone has gone with hope and glad expectation for the future—their future, in which I have no part—such a sense of loneliness comes over me as I sit alone. I have kept this all to myself, for I did not want you to be troubled as you once were."

"Have you met one you could love, dear?" asked the mother, who could not wait.

"Yes, mother, I have. He is the principal of the school where I have been teaching. I know you will like him. He lost his wife many years ago. He has one child, a son, who graduated this year."

"What is his name?" asked her father.

"John Pierson. He is coming to see us next month," and a happy light shone in Ruth's face.

"I am glad for you, my daughter," said the father, as he held out his hand and kissed her. "We are getting along in years. It will be a satisfaction to know you are happy in some good man's affections."

"I know it, father; I feel I shall respect and love him more every day I live, and then, we think alike about so many things—have been all our lives, it seems. It is the companionship I prize so much."

"Bob and Helen are coming this evening," said the mother, as she clasped her daughter in her arms. "There is another happy pair; I hear them now," and, without waiting for them to knock, opened the door as Bob and his wife came up the steps.

"Good evening, Ruth, we are so glad to see

you!" and Bob's face beamed. "Why! you look ten years younger; what's up? What you blushing for? Tell me, Ruthy, you know I am the one to keep a secret."

"Oh, Bob! you still love to tease, but you don't need to hurt yourself this time trying to keep it, for it's so!"

"Glad of it, Ruth. Mother and I were talking about you this morning, that you were the last of the little crowd to get married. Had a letter from Mary yesterday; Grant took her back East to visit her childhood friends. She always said she wanted to see for herself. From her letters, she is already homesick for Colorado."

"The children," said Helen, "will surely lose a good teacher when you stop."

"There are others, dear," Ruth smilingly replied, "even many whom I have prepared to carry on this work."

Yes, it was true, Ruth had accomplished much, not only in teaching, but in preparing others to see the work from her viewpoint, to lift the young thought above the petty, trivial things to the noble, refining and uplifting; the worth of this far-reaching work who can estimate?

The news went around very quickly among Ruth's friends, but, as Kate said when Bob told her that very evening, "It's so natural it ceases to be a surprise."

Mr. Pierson came to make his promised visit. Ruth's parents saw at a glance their daughter had chosen wisely, and took him into their hearts, so keeping Ruth, who always stayed where he was.

Ruth soon found her work in educational lines increased instead of diminished; although she did not teach, she found herself busy every day inspiring her husband to do his best, and so it came to pass, as one school girl expressed herself to her schoolmates:

"Professor was good before he was married, but he is ever so much better now."

"Perhaps we are having two in one," said a young man standing near. "Professor's wife used to be my sister's teacher."

Yes, real marriage is unity of thought and life purpose.

CHAPTER XXXVIII

AN OLD-TIMERS' REUNION

One evening, as John and his wife, Hetty, were sitting by the blazing fire, for they still enjoyed the comfort of an open fireplace, Bob and Helen came, as they said, "to make a suggestion."

"What is it, Bob?" asked Aunt Hetty, who was always in a hurry to hear if it was something Bob was thinking about.

"What do you think of us getting up an 'Old-Timers' Reunion' for father and mother?"

"Just the thing, Bob!" and Hetty's eyes gleamed with pleasure, "don't you think so, John?"

"Yes," said John, "and let it be as near like the first party we had as possible, you and I making the coffee."

"Oh, John!" replied the little gray-haired wife, "you forget the years that have passed since then. We cannot have it just like the first one. Let me see, it's just twenty years ago, John. Oh, Bob! let's have it on brother's birthday, yes," and Hetty's thoughts took on a reminiscent mood. "What changes have taken place! Twenty years ago we were happy with mud roofs and dirt floors—happy as we are today. John, what a good time we have had, too, working together, you and I going on our trips to Ouray with our vegetables; we do not have to do it now. Then the children; there's big John, thank God, but no little John; there's big Bob, but no little Bob today. Kate's Bob and Tom's John are as fine young men as their fathers ever were—that's saying a good deal; then there's your children, Bob, the girl the picture of you, Helen, and the boy just like his father; then the change with Jake and Harry—not much like it was twenty years ago, with their young folks bubbling over with fun. Then, dear Mr. and Mrs. Woods, both have taken up their abode in the 'Mountain of God.'"

"Why, Hetty!" and John smiled at his wife's outburst, "that is the longest speech I ever heard you make. I see very plainly it won't be the same; it will be much better and require more room, but you and I, Hetty, will make the coffee."

"I shall never forget that party you speak of," said Helen, flushing, in spite of the years that lay between. "It was there I first met Bob. He told me afterwards the reason he kept the fire going for those men was because he could not sleep—thinking of me. I do not mind confessing tonight, I did not sleep either; I was thinking of Bob," and the love-light shone brightly as she turned her face towards her husband.

John replenished the fire, then asked, "What are your plans, Bob?" "Helen and I have talked it over, and if you think it advisable, invite everyone as far as possible who were with us twenty years ago—with all the children, of course. Some will have to stay all night, just as they did then, but there is plenty of room."

After talking it over with the rest of the friends, invitations were sent, and accepted by all.

On the ninth of January, 1905, early in the afternoon, Mr. and Mrs. Barton were happily surprised to see two carriages turning in at their gate, and an exclamation from Mr. Barton brought his wife to the door. "Why! Mr. and Mrs. Sherman; and Mr. and Mrs. Long! how glad we are to see you!" said Mr. Barton as he stepped out to shake hands. "Why, what have you there?"

"Oh, a little grub," answered Mr. Long, as he brought out a big basket. "We are going to stay to supper."

"We, too!" called out Mrs. Sherman, as her husband pulled out another basket. "Looks like old time, doesn't it?"

"Why! what is up?" demanded Mrs. Barton. "There are two more rigs coming, one from Montrose—if it is not the editor, that used to be, and his family; and the other—Mr. and Mrs. Smith from Ouray. Father! it's a surprise party, I do believe; see Bob peeping around the corner, laughing. Is this some of your work, Bob?"

"Yes, mother, we all have had a hand in it, just as we did twenty years ago. Father, I might as well tell you, it's an 'Old-Timers' Reunion' for you both."

"Bless you, my boy! It surely will be a pleasure to us all."

And so it was, to judge from the smiling, happy faces when all were assembled.

SOMEBODY'S GRANDCHILDREN.

Mr. Barton, with form erect and clasp of the hand as strong as ever; Mrs. Barton, sitting beside her husband and her lovable face wreathed in smiles, her hair beautiful in its whiteness.

Mr. and Mrs. Wilson, with the signet of peace on their faces, sat near their old-time friends.

Mrs. Wilson's experiences in the past had wrought out all the enduring qualities of a noble wife and mother. She was still a marvel to her husband.

Ruth, beautiful in her wifehood, her husband one of those men of whom the world is made better for his having lived.

Dick and Kate, strong in their love for the true and beautiful everywhere.

John, dear old John, who still blessed the day he first met Hetty, while to Hetty "Out West" meant all that was good—for it meant John to her.

Mr. and Mrs. Brown, happy in the love of Mollie and Tom, with the grandchildren to cheer them up.

Jake and Harry, with their wives and children, were there. Harry makes his home on the ranch now—"time too short," he says, "to live in an unsettled way; beside, the children needed the schooling." A trusted friend has charge of the cattle, which proved a paying investment for them all.

The boys' mother, Mrs. DeLong, was with them, and the most comfortable chair in the room was brought for her to sit in, for she, in a sweet, tender way, seemed to belong to them all, and they to her, and yet, this love and tenderness, though piled as high as the mountains, could not make up for the loss of the husband who has gone a little while ahead to greet her later on with even more of love than has ever been known here.

When the loved form and voice seemed to pass away, his kindly spirit of unselfishness and good will to everyone seemed still to be near. She looked up to the snow-capped mountains he loved so well; they seemed to speak of him. She listened to the song of the meadow lark; it reminded her of him. When the boys took her up in the hills for a few weeks, it did her good, for the trees, the birds, the ferns and flowers, the ripple of the water as it flowed from the spring, reminded her of her loved one, and when evening came, with the stars shining over head and the moonlight making its way in her little room, her prayers, as of old, seemed filled with love for him, as well as for God.

Bob, proud of his fruit farm on the mesa, his wife prouder of him because he had proved what he "could do for himself" without the aid Tom wished to give him when the ditch broke.

Mary, with her husband, Grant, returned from the East, glad to get back, as all people are who have once lived here.

Mr. Eaton, Mr. Gray, with their families all doing well, having found Spring Creek Mesa the finest place to raise all kinds of fruit.

Ed and Sam Jones, with their families up from

near Olathe, which had been the favored spot to them from the very first.

Mr. Baker and Mr. Thornton, both retired from the strenuous life of the cowboy, and settled down, with homes in the valley. These friends, with their children, gathered and recounted the experiences of the past with the attendant blessings of today.

After the bounteous supper had been passed around by the younger people and John had poured the last cup of coffee, the desire for a speech from Mr. Barton was strongly expressed.

After a moment's hesitancy, with a look of appeal to his wife, he rose and started to speak, but the words would not come. The silence was great; tears sprang to the eyes of the older ones.

Recovering himself, Mr. Barton said: "Friends, dear friends, comrades, many of you, of the days gone by, you know we are glad to see you; we thank you for the pleasure you have given us. My thought while sitting here went back to the time when wife and I first decided to come out West; it seemed a big undertaking, but time proved it bigger than we had any idea.

"We came, and, in spite of all we were called to pass through, we, from our hearts, and you, too, old-time friends, can say with us tonight, we are glad we came, glad for every experience we passed through.

"We are glad for the people all over this part of God's earth that they and we together have part in the building up of one of the richest and most beautiful countries in the United States.

"And now the project has started to bring more water, not over the mountains, but through the mountain. Soon, in the course of a few years, the Gunnison River will flow into the valley through a tunnel cut in the very heart of one of these mountains, to water the many acres yet untilled.

"It's for our children, and their children, to love and behold what this valley may become.

"But friends," and the voice of this grand old man trembled with feeling as he spoke, "I have spent much time traveling over the western slope of Colorado, have studied its possibilities for good, have studied its men and women, then my thought has gone back to the land of my birth. I see the East is still reaching out for the good the West has to give. The wise men of the East over nineteen hundred years ago brought gifts to the babe in the manger, knowing full well they would receive still greater. Just so, the East has brought much to the West, but far more has the West to give in return. In proportion, as we, as a people, partake of the grandeur, the greatness, the freedom, the stillness, the spirit of giving, the spirit of these mountains, then will come to pass—there will be no 'East and West,' both will be one in the handclasp of good will to all."

Mr. Barton sat down and his wife, from habit of many years, slipped her hand in his, a symbol of how they had walked together so many years.

"Oh, father!" said Bob, as he came and stood by his parents, "I'm proud of those words, proud of you. Mother, it's good to be alive."

They were happy moments for them all, the old pioneers and the young rejoicing together.

So, quickly the time came to say "Goodbye," but before they parted, Tom stood up to speak, and again silence prevailed.

"Friends," said Tom, "like father, my thoughts go back to the time when we decided to leave the old for the new.

"I shall never forget that night I learned a little what a mother's love was. I also gained an insight into what a wife's love for her husband will cause her to do for his sake—to gladly give up a comfortable home, old friends, and old associates, and turn her face smilingly towards an untried life in the West. Bravely meeting every privation, every untoward circumstance with a strong, unfailing reliance on the 'One Hand' to lead."

And Tom, as though in benediction from above, stooped down before them all and kissed his mother.

CHAPTER XXXIX

STORIES TOLD AROUND THE CAMP FIRE

One evening, as a company of old-timers were gathered around the camp fire, a reminiscent mood seemed to take possession—it might have been the company, or the surroundings, which brought it forth. We had been watching the fire which lighted up the surroundings, casting bright rays in some directions, gruesome ones in others.

The saucy moon playing hide-and-seek behind the tall, silent trees, the stars looking down with friendly faces, the tinkle of the water as it fell from the spring nearby on its slow but eager journey toward the ocean, the hoot, hoot, of the night owl, the sleepy twitter of a bird as it turned over in bed, the lone cry of the coyote, the lowing of a distant herd of cattle turned out to pasture for the summer in grass up to their knees, a tiny breeze kissing the topmost branches of the trees, the leaves, a happy crowd, clapping their hands and dancing at its gentle touch. Then the sweet scents coming from earth and flower, from bush and tree, all combined to awaken memories of other times in the long ago, and so, one by one, we began, after replenishing the fire, which had almost died away, so deep had we been in thought, to tell, each in his turn, some experience of the past.

Mr. Parker Lupher commenced by giving his experience in a snowslide.

He said: "In the late fall of 1892 it was necessary for me to go up to Red Mountain to work assessments on claims there. Taking a man with me, we reached the cabin, wading the latter end of the journey through two feet of snow. While working the assessment, on November 11th, it began to snow, and the next morning there was twelve inches of fresh snow. The storm raged for two days, the snow reaching the depth of five feet, and, while passing the time as best we could awaiting its abatement, a snowslide came down over the cabin, nearly carrying it from its foundation. The first intimation we had of the slide was the rushing noise and the shooting of sprays of fine snow through every little hole in the cabin like jets of steam. It was over in a moment, and we began the investigation of damages. There was a roaring fire in the stove, and as the two or three joints of stovepipe extending above the cabin roof had been carried away by the slide, the smoke began to pour into the room. We made an effort to open the door, which was no easy matter, the snow on the outside being so solidly packed against it. By a united and strenuous effort we soon succeeded in opening it, to face a solid wall of snow, with only a narrow streak of light at the top of the opening. There were three or four feet of snow on top of the cabin.

"We were now in no pleasant situation, though for the time being, perfectly safe and comfortable.

The storm still raged, and the snow kept piling up. What were we to do? To remain was but courting death, for every additional inch of snow but added to the probability of a fresh slide, which would almost certainly have wrecked the cabin; to attempt to wade out through the fresh snow meant still more certain destruction, as the track made through the snow was almost sure to start a slide. The situation was by no means a comforting one, and the problem resolved itself into how to get out. The only course that seemed open was to make snow-shoes and attempt to get out by their use, and as neither of us had had any experience with snow-shoes this was not especially inviting. There being no choice in the matter, we set to work and hewed out two pairs of shoes, and attempted the arduous task.

"It was only three miles to Ironton and safety, but such miles! To those accustomed to the use of shoes it would have been no task, but to us who had never used them before it was no easy matter. The cabin was left before daylight in the morning, and, by devious turnings and twistings and careful descents, our lives in danger every minute, we succeeded finally in reaching the light, warmth and shelter of a hospitable cabin in Ironton.

"It scarcely seems possible that it should have taken us all day to make that three miles, but it is an actual fact that the lights were burning in the cabins when we reached there, and glad enough we were to take off those snow-shoes and sit down to rest.

"Again, in 1895, this time in the spring, I took two men with me to do the assessment work on this same property. To get to the workings it was necessary to run twenty feet of open cut and twelve feet of tunnel through the snow. This was in April. When this work was about completed, I went to the cabin to prepare supper, and, having things well under way, looked out of the cabin door to see if the men were coming. Not seeing anyone, I sat down again and picked up a paper to while away the time until they should come. By and by I heard a shout, and, looking out, saw one man near the mouth of the tunnel, and in a moment more the other crawled out of a hole in the snow like a prairie dog. The men had just finished clearing out the old snow and were starting for the cabin when the elder heard the ominous roar of the slide, and, seizing his shovel and telling his comrade to do likewise, rushed back into the tunnel. They were no sooner well under cover than the slide ran over them, filling up all the work they had so far accomplished, and shutting them up in the tunnel. With their shovels they set to work to dig an incline through the impacted snow to the surface, throwing the snow back into the tunnel, and had just emerged when I responded to the call of the first man out. They were glad enough to get out and do justice to the supper prepared."

Then, Joseph R. Brown, one of those whole-souled men it does one good to meet, told the following:

"About the last of February, 1877, a party of five men, composed of John Benson, Jack Phillips, A. D. Crosswhite, J. Hale Brown, and myself, all old-time prospectors, left Rose's cabin at the head of Hensen Creek on snow-shoes to go to Mineral City to complete a contract on the mine there known as the 'Thunderbolt,' which belonged to William Boot and brother, who made their home in Denver.

"All of us five men carried a pack of fifty-five pounds on our backs in the way of provisions and bedding, as at that time there was only one man living in Mineral City, the city being deserted for the winter; his name was O. D. Loutsenhizer. There were no supplies of any kind, but those which you took with you on snow-shoes.

"Leaving Rose's cabin early in the morning, climbing to the top of what is known as American Flats, or Engineer Mountain, we were caught in a terrible storm. We were soon convinced we were lost, and, not able to find a place of shelter, we buried ourselves in the snow, as it was impossible to live in such a storm, and there waited developments. By the time the storm, which lasted three days, abated, all but one of us men were snow-blind. Led by this one, who was not much better, we traveled all day, to find when night came we had traveled in a circle.

"What were we to do? One suggested we keep shouting for help; some one might hear us. Sure enough, an old prospector by the name of Berry, who had a cabin near timberline on the Hensen

Creek side, having started for Ouray, heard our cries. With snow-shoes he soon found our trail. A time he had getting us to his cabin, where he cared for us until we were able to start once more on our journey.

"To show the depth of snow, when arriving at Mineral City there was but one fireplace chimney to be seen, all the others, ten in number, were completely covered with snow. This one was occupied by O. D. Loutsenhizer, and so kept open to some extent.

"These experiences, boys, will never be forgotten. If we had not been accustomed to the mountains and had some experience before, we would surely have perished.

"I remember another time," said Joe, who seemed to be in a reminiscent mood. "It was in March, 1878, the end of the winter never to be forgotten by the people of Ouray, when provisions ran short. I was asked to make the trip over the range to Lake City to carry some mail. One was a letter of importance to be delivered to Judge Bell in connection with the sale of the 'Mineral Farm,' which then belonged to Gus Begole and Mr. Eckels. There were about one hundred letters altogether, as at that time Ouray was still snowed in from the outside world and had no mail for about one hundred days.

"It was a tough proposition crossing the range at that time of year, but I was young and strong, and my brother was going with me.

"Our return trip was made in a hard snowstorm

ABOVE THE CLOUDS, NEAR THE SMUGGLER MINE.

on American Flats, and we took, by mistake, what is known as the 'Horse Thief Trail,' which proved to be one of the most dangerous trails in the Rocky Mountains. Very few traveled that route on account of one place where a misstep would cause one to fall hundreds of feet.

"We finally retraced our steps, and, after much difficulty, reached Ouray, where the shouts of welcome made us almost forget the hardships endured. and many a heart was made glad with letters received from home. Just think, boys! Over three months without any mail. At that particular place I spoke of on the Horse Thief Trail, I saw the most beautiful sight one day. It was bright and clear around me, but below me was a sea of clouds:

through the rifts of these I could see the lovely town of Ouray, hundreds of feet below. The trail was seldom used, except by mountain lions, foxes, and mountain sheep, which were quite numerous at that time."

"Now, E. D. Nichols, it's your turn, but wait till we pile on more brush."

As all were seated again, Mr. Nichols, one of those kind-hearted people one likes to have around, said: "It was in the year 1882 wife and I came to make our home in this valley. Not finding any claims vacant, I purchased a right from a man who had a cabin built on a good piece of land. I bought a 'squatter's right,' living on the land—actual possession, you know.

"The country being new, none of the land had been surveyed, so no fruit trees were planted until this was done. We had to utilize the native berries. Squawberries, or buffalo berries, and hawthorn berries were abundant, and, by making preserves from watermelons, muskmelons, tomatoes, and so on, we forgot we had a fruitless country.

"Beaver were very plentiful along the river at that time, and easily trapped. The first winter I lived here I made considerable money trapping beaver and selling the hides. Deer were also thick in those days, coming out of the woods at night and eating in our garden patches. One morning my wife saw fourteen deer in one bunch.

"In those days the first new potatoes brought

eight and ten cents a pound, and other vegetables accordingly.

"While everyone worked hard, they all took time for amusements, and literary meetings and dances were very frequent. The majority of the early settlers were young people, but a sprinkling of elderly people gave tone to the gatherings.

"Log cabins with roofs covered with dirt were all we had for a few years. One night a dance was given in the cabin owned by Ross Brothers. A heavy shower of rain came up and the dirt, being thin on the roof, let the water and mud come spattering down. The dancers hurried for dishpans to catch it, and went on with the dance, dodging the streams of water. As girls were scarce, sometimes a gentleman partner was designated as a lady by a handkerchief tied around his arm.

"The valley being mainly settled by bachelors, who were lonely, some amusing incidents occurred. One day we were watering our horses in the stream by one of the early settlers' cabins when he came to the door and yelled: 'Say, you fellows, you know some place vere I get good vomans? Ay got no time to take care of mah horses. Ay got to get married purty quick.'

"One German by the name of Shrader was building a cabin. One day when we were passing he sang out, 'Yas, I build dis house, den I get me a rocking chair, and if I don't find a vomans to sit in it, I sit in it myself.'"

"Had a good chance, too, I guess," laughed one of the crowd.

"Now, Uri, tell us some bear stories." So Uriah Hotchkiss, one of the most successful hunters in the West, who could keep you interested the whole evening and still have more hunting experiences to tell, began, while the men around the camp fire settled themselves into a more comfortable position to listen.

"I remember," said Uri, "the time my brother, Walter, and I were out hunting. The snow was very deep. We had been following bear tracks for about four miles, when all at once we saw Mr. Bear near his den. He was a monster. At our approach, he slipped under the rock. We banged away at the opening, but could see nothing of him. I said to Walter, 'I am going to crawl in the hole and kill that bear with my six-shooter.' Walter said, 'You are very foolish,' but I, determined not to be outdone by a bear, crawled in and shot the bear, which fell, as I supposed, dead. I then squeezed in behind to boost him out. Just then Bruin revived and started for me, but fell dead right there. I attempted to push him out, but found I could not move him, he was so big. I yelled as best I could, almost smothered as I was in that small den, the bear closing up the opening, to Walter to hand me a rope. I fastened the rope to the animal and Walter pulled, but made no impression. You see, boys, just inside the den was a hollow place like a saucer, worn by the bear. It had slipped in that and we could not move him. For the first time in my life I got scared. Walter then tied the rope to the horse, but he could do no better. Then I told him, as best I could, to tie the rope to two trees and make a windlass.

"Bruin came out, all right, and so did I."

"Tell us another!" said one of the listeners, and Uri, always ready, said: "When Fred Martin, Bert Morris' brother Willie, and myself were out hunting on the big Cimarron, we found a bear track and followed it for about twelve miles, to the bear's den.

"It was late in the evening. We held a council to decide what we should do. I wanted that bear; it might get away before morning. So, with my rifle in my hand, I looked in the den, and saw nothing but two bright, shiny eyes. I shot the animal, but only wounded him. Then he went for me. Quick as a flash, away I banged at him, and, as I supposed, killed him, as he fell back in the hole. I crawled in, with instructions to the boys to hold my feet, and if I kicked, to pull me out quick. I started to move the bear, when all at once it raised up and caught me on both sides of my head as though to kiss me. I kicked all right. You would yourselves, boys!" said Uri, casting a reproachful glance at the men, who were laughing. "The bear was too near dead to hold its own, so when the boys pulled me out, I held onto the bear, and he came out, too."

"Now it's your turn, comrade of the mountains," said Joe Brown, as he smiled up at O. Bever.

"I remember," said Mr. Bever, "as though it were yesterday, the time I was out on Last Dollar Mountain, northwest of Telluride. I went with a party of men, Mr. Hawkey, Mr. C. D. Lavender, Mr. Breckenridge and Mr. Wheeler, to capture, if possible, a mountain sheep, a large black buck. It would have made a fine specimen; we wanted it just for a curiosity, you know.

"We rode about nine miles, and when we had climbed near the top of Last Dollar Mountain—pretty rough climbing with snow up to your waist; ever tried it, boys?—we saw about seventeen sheep, all bunched together. Soon we saw another bunch. We were going single file, I in the lead. We were just about ready to fire when I came to a ridge where the snow was drifted. I kicked my toe in the drift, which exploded like a revolver, and the first thing I knew, down the mountain I was going, like the wind, four or five hundred yards, rolling like a barrel, not hurt, but all drawn up like a knot. I found myself underneath three feet of snow. I knew enough about snowslides to get out as soon as I could, for the snow gets crusted hard very quickly; then you can't get out.

"The slide shoved Mr. Breckenridge and Mr. Hawkey out to one side, after they had gone about one hundred yards down the hill. I lost all desire for sheep hunting, and so did the boys. I have traveled many a time over the mountains with a yoke of oxen, have run stage and freighted with Dave Wood—no small thing you may be sure—but never an experience like that ride down Last Dollar Mountain."

"Frank Ripley, it's your turn."

"I shall never forget," said Frank, who was always the life of the crowd wherever he went—kind-hearted and ready to help a neighbor at any time. "When I came back from Olathe on my way home to Wilson Mesa near Telluride. I was taking home a load of furniture. Another man—a stranger to me—was just behind with a load of vegetables which he was taking to Telluride. There had been a cloud-burst that afternoon and the hills were a sight—water running everywhere. I was jogging along as best I could, the horses very restless. All at once, above the noise of water running and the wind, I heard the man behind me yell, 'Run! Whip your horses!' I did not wait to ask him why, but gave the horses a lick which surprised them. By so doing, just missed a big boulder, which was rolling down the side of the hill at a fearful rate, and crossed the road where I was a moment before. After it had passed, I turned and looked my gratitude to the stranger, who had waited on the other side. I had not gone far when it began to hail. To protect the horses, I drove them under a big spruce tree, and again this stranger, seeing my danger, had left his team—there was no use yelling this time, for the noise was terrific, the running of water in the creek close by and down the hillside, the sliding of rocks and driftwood, the hail pelting as though in fury—the man—I wish I knew his name!

—sprang into the wagon and yelled, 'In God's name, get out of here!' We did, quicker than it takes to tell it, just in time to save ourselves from the shower of rocks and boulders rolling down the hillside, piled high where I and the horses had stood. The stranger's horses were not injured, though badly frightened, the wagon hemmed in on all sides with rocks and rubbish, we had a time getting them out. I tell you, boys, there is something about these hills and mountains that seems to bring out the best that there is in you. Just think! a stranger doing all that for me." "You would have done it for him," spoke up one of the boys. "I expect I would, Jack. What added to my anxiety was, I phoned to father (he and mother were up on Wilson mesa that summer) some hours before to meet me at Newmire with a fresh team of horses, as mine were getting pretty well played out. I knew he was out in all that storm alone. When I reached Newmire he was not there; I felt I could not stand much more; I called up mother; she knew there had been a cloudburst near where father must pass. When I asked, 'Has father started yet?' I felt, rather than heard, the sob in her voice, as she answered, 'He started nearly three hours ago.' The distance was only seven miles. 'All right,' I said, as carelessly as I could, 'I will go to meet him.' Just as I started, he came in sight. Glad? I guess I was. Father was wet, not a dry thread on him. I called up and told mother as quickly as I could. Father told me he had just reached Bear Creek when the storm began. I could see at a glance, in spite of the drenched clothes and the cold, father, being such a lover of nature, had really enjoyed it all. 'Yes, Frank,' he said, 'it was a sight I shall never forget. I heard the roar of the water in the creek, which was usually so low and quiet. In a moment it was dashing down in a perfect torrent; huge boulders and logs came down as though they were straws; it soon came over on the narrow road I was crossing. It were well I was horseback; a wagon would have been no use. and the rain? It came—I was going to say in bucketsful, but not quite. My shoes were soon full, the horses did not like it a bit, but I patted and talked to them as best I could, my teeth chattering. I had two or three narrow escapes, but am here all right, and the storm is over.' Of course, boys, we were obliged to leave the loaded wagon at Newmire, for the roads were washed out. We unhitched my horses and made our way through Bear Creek. I gained some idea of what father had passed through, all alone. Home seemed a good place to get to, and mother soon had us warm and dry, a good supper already prepared."

"Say, boy," said one of the old-timers to Johnny Lupher, who was listening, for these stories always interested him, "tell us how you began in the stock business."

"Not much to tell," said the young man. "I was busy looking after the horses one day, noon, I think, when a man by the name of Mostyn asked me to take a cow up to Ouray for him. I found father could spare me—it was early for the spring work—so I went. This way I became acquainted with the man, who, a little later, offered to pay me good wages if I would go and help him take care of his cattle. I went, caring for my father's cattle at the same time.

"It was the custom then to take the calves from the mother as soon as they were born. One day, Mr. Mostyn said to me, 'Johnny, there is a calf you better take to that cow of your father's; she has a calf about the age of this one. Take good care of it and you may keep it.'

"This started me to thinking. Why could I not have a herd of cattle as well as my boss? My thinking resulted in a bargain being made, in which we went on shares with the young calves, me to care for them and receive half of what was raised, every cow my father had helping me with the bawling calves. My mother laughingly said, 'I had three calves to their one.'

"After awhile, I became a partner in the firm with my boss, but, gentlemen, as you know, I had to attend strictly to business, foregoing the pleasures most young men enjoy, and snapping my fingers at privation some men could not endure."

"You surely made good, young man," said one of the gray-haired old-timers, as he turned to another and said, "Charley, it is your turn."

"There are no kinder hearted people in the world than you find in these out-of-the-way places," said Charley. "I remember," and his voice broke, warning the listeners of what was coming, "the time we moved, wife and I, up into the gulch. I tried to coax her to stay with her folks till afterwards, but she would not. These women are strange creatures; she said she wanted to be with me. We did not see another woman all that winter, but every night, as I went home from work, she would come to meet me, and we would laugh and talk of the things we both loved, until, sure as I live, before we reached the little cabin, I would forget I was tired and felt as rested and happy as though it were morning. Then, after supper, we would sit close together before the blazing fire with never a thought of care or sense of loneliness, when, near spring, just as the crocus was doing its best to cheer us up, the baby came.

"I tell you, friends, that log cabin seemed to be heaven, or Solomon's Temple filled with glory we read about, when I first realized the fact that I was a father, and that woman, who would not be left behind, was a mother. The baby was a girl—the prettiest thing I ever saw. Well, in a few days, something seemed wrong with the tot, and before we could even start for a doctor, she died.

"There we were, miles away from anyone except a bunch of cowboys, who were camped within a mile of us. One of them happened along that morning, and before the words were hardly out of my mouth he was gone to let the others know. The way that horse went was a caution. The whole camp came. Boys, I'll never forget it, though it is so many years ago, if every one of them did not have to take a look at her with the baby lying in her arms. They knew what was needed without a word from me, and soon they brought a little casket, covered inside and out with the only white shirt in that camp. Wife had not been able to cry until she saw that white cloth. Then the question was asked, 'What shall we do without a preacher?' Then one who, to all appearances, was the roughest of the crowd, with his big sombrero under his arm, said to wife, who was lying with her eyes closed, 'Where is your Bible, little mother?' She pulled it from under the pillow, and, handing it to him, whispered, 'The twenty-third psalm.' 'Won't you please find it for me?' he said, 'I lost the one mother gave me long ago.' I disliked to leave wife alone, but she would have me go, said she would not be alone—women are such strange creatures. This little company and I, just as the sun was getting low, when everything was touched with the brightness of the coming sunset—the birds, I remember, were singing their evening songs as tenderly and low as though they knew—we went to the prettiest little grove of aspen trees, a half mile away, and, before laying the little body away, the boy read the psalm as well as any preacher could have done, and when the grave was filled up, and covered with flowers and bits of spruce, these men some might call sinners sang, softly, as though afraid they might disturb the baby, that hymn, 'Nearer, My God, to Thee.' Then, with that fineness of feeling so noted in these men of the West, each shook hands with me and left me alone with the tiny grave and the flowers.

"When I went home, a strange peace came over me, and as I entered the cabin I saw wife, too, felt it, as though angels had been and ministered unto us."

A silence came over the little company as Charley finished his story. The fire had died down and someone suggested it was "time to turn in."

CHAPTER XL

REMINISCENCES

The following incidents are told by Hon. Frank C. Goudy:

The early San Juan and Gunnison bar included among its members some of the brightest lawyers and orators of the State of Colorado. Among them I might mention, Matt Taylor, Lafe Pence, Adair Wilson, John C. Bell, H. M. Hogg, William Story, A. M. Stevenson, D. T. Sapp, Theodore and Thornton Thomas, Thomas Brown, Henry L. Carr, Judge Sprigg Shackleford, L. F. Twitchell, Alexander Gullett, A. R. King, J. W. Bucklin, S. S. Sherman, Sam Wood, and many others who were actively engaged in the practice of the law in that section of the state.

Those stage-coach, non-railroad days were golden and glorious days, but they have passed forever.

I regret that I did not keep a diary of the many funny, as well as serious, incidents and situations that the earlier settlers experienced in their litigation. I arrived in Rico in June, 1880, after a fifteen days' trip from Colorado Springs, having walked most of the distance. Upon my arrival in Rico, I found myself half owner in two Winchester rifles, a small tent, some bedding, and other camp equipment. We had taken the rifles along in order to preserve the peace between the settlers and the Utes.

During the first day at Rico, my partner became blue, or homesick, and I bought him out, and then had left about eighty dollars in currency with which to equip my office and on which to live until I could get into the hoped-for practice. The only banker of the town was a Mr. Bissel, and I promptly deposited my money with him and then gave the hotel-keeper a check for a meal ticket, and the next day the landlord halted me as I started into the dining room and demanded twenty-five cents exchange on my check. I paid the twenty-five cents, and the following morning called upon the banker to ascertain why there was any exchange upon the check. Mr. Bissel rubbed his hands in good banking form and said: "I charge this on account of there being no roads into this town, and you know it is very expensive and quite dangerous to bring currency to Rico." I replied, in much heat: "Well, you didn't pay anything for, or take any chances, getting my eighty dollars into Rico." We finally compromised by my taking desk room in his bank. In my first case, I was employed to represent a freighter whose outfit had been attached on a writ issued by Justice of the Peace John Gault, whose side business was running a butcher shop. Upon arriving at Gault's office, which was a soap box set near his meat block, I found that the attorney for the plaintiff had obtained a writ without the formality of presenting and filing an affidavit and bond. Upon calling the court's attention to these omissions and advising him that he might get into trouble, he uttered a few Rico words and started out of the room with his meat cleaver to bring in the opposing lawyer. Upon appearing in court, plaintiff's lawyer tried to satisfy the justice that he had complied with the law by having the plaintiff stand up and swear that the defendant was indebted to plaintiff for work performed, and had presented another man who pledged himself to pay all costs if plaintiff should not be successful in his suit. Plaintiff's lawyer left town soon after saying he would not practice law in a state where the practice consisted of a lot of fool technicalities.

In the month of September, and after the rainy season had let up so that walking was good, I moved to Ouray, the county seat. The firm was then known as Rosser & Goudy, Rosser remaining at Rico and the writer representing the firm at Ouray, but it was not the volume of our business that caused the Rio Grande Southern Railroad and the telegraph and telephone lines to be built between Ouray and Rico. Shortly after arriving in Ouray, Judge T. A. McMorris of Colorado Springs, then serving as district judge of the seventh district for a short time, held a special term at Ouray, and, among other things, heard and determined a demurrer in a case in which the brilliant John Taylor appeared for one party and J. Patrick Cassidy and George P. Costigan for the other. While Taylor was presenting his argument, Cassidy became very nervous, and put in the time walking up and down a space outside the railing, waiting for his time to reply to Taylor. Becoming impatient, he exclaimed to the court: "The supreme court of Illinois settled that question long ago." Whereupon, Taylor, in his suave and elegant way, said: "Will the learned barrister disclose to the court, and to myself, the case and the report to which he refers?" Cassidy promptly replied: "It is the case of Jones vs. Smith, to be found in First Scamorhorn (meaning First Scammon) of the Illinois reports." This was too much, even for Judge McMorris, who, though a serious and sober-minded man, was compelled to adjourn court for the rest of that day, although it lacked an hour of adjourning time.

In March, 1881, Governor Pitkin appointed Columbus W. Burris judge of the new seventh district, and Judge Burris appointed me district attorney for the district. In the fall of 1883, M. B. Gerry was elected to succeed Judge Burris. During Judge Gerry's term, many amusing things happened in this court, although he was a very dignified man and always aimed to have his court run in a most orderly way. Judge Gerry held his first term of court at Lake City, his home town. Upon opening the court, he asked the assistance and indulgence of the members of the bar in making his term a success, and closed his remarks by announcing certain rules, among which was the rule forbidding smoking during court sessions. Just as he commenced calling the docket, he noticed a man by the name of Finley, who had been his long-time friend and one of his clients, smoking in the court room near the door. The judge ordered Mr. Finley arrested and brought before the bar. After he had sworn Mr. Finley, he asked him to state his name and place of residence. Finley looked at the judge in amazement, and the judge then repeated his question, but in a little more emphatic manner, whereupon Finley, not having heard the judge announce the new rule, and supposing that the judge was trying to make him the butt of a joke, said: "Oh, hell, Gerry, don't get gay." Whereupon court adjourned for the rest of the day.

Some two years afterward, Judge Gerry, while holding a session of court at Delta in a dingy court room, called up a cowboy whom he discovered smoking in the court, and, after lecturing him severely, said: "Don't you know, sir, that it is against the rules of this court to smoke while the court is in session?" The cowboy, who was a graduate of Harvard, answered, in a timid way: "Your Honor, I didn't know it; I was never in a court like this before." While the court did not adjourn on that occasion, it took some time to restore order so that the business could proceed.

H. M. Hogg, at one time district attorney of the seventh district, was noted as always ready with a witty reply when opposing counsel gave him an opening. At a term of court held in Montrose by Judge Gerry, District Attorney Hogg was vigorously cross-examining a witness for the defense and was standing in front of the witness and smiling at him in a way that disconcerted the witness, whereupon defendant's counsel objected on the ground that the district attorney had no right to confuse the witness by smiling in his face, whereupon Hogg promptly rejoined: "Your Honor, I withdraw the smile; I don't want it in the record."

At a term of court presided over by Judge Gerry at Gunnison, Alexander Gullett, representing the plaintiff in a civil case, was earnestly pressing for an early trial. Mr. Tom Brown, representing the defendant, was urging the court to let the case go over for the term. Finally, the judge ordered the case to come on for trial on the following day. Whereupon, Brown exclaimed, in great earnestness: "Your Honor, I can't go on trial tomorrow. The truth is, I haven't even had time to formulate the facts."

In a case pending in the district court at Gunnison, the defendant made a showing that plaintiff was so fixed financially that he could not pay costs, and secured a rule requiring a cost bond, or a showing of financial ability. The attorney for the plaintiff had his client make a showing by affidavit that he owned, unincumbered, fifteen unpatented mining claims, located in various parts of the county, of the value of at least eighty thousand dollars. Judge Gerry presiding, after duly considering the affidavit, held, that while the showing was insufficient to demonstrate the plaintiff's ability to pay costs, it would be held sufficient to justify an order allowing plaintiff to prosecute his action as a pauper and without costs, and the rule was discharged.

Immediately following the opening of the Ute reservation and the founding of Delta, an old frontier lawyer named Keithly was employed in a homicide case at Delta. He came to Gunnison when Judge Gerry was there holding court and verbally demanded of the judge a writ of habeas corpus for his client so he could get bail. The judge informed Keithly that it would be necessary to present a proper petition for the writ. Whereupon, Keithly went back to Delta and soon returned with a petition reading, in substance: "We, the undersigned citizens of Delta, petition the court to grant to Mr. Keithly for his client a writ of habeas corpus." This was signed by practically all of the Delta citizens.

We thought the incident very funny at the time, but, reflecting in these days upon this incident, we are now inclined to think that Keithly was in advance of his time, as our present tendency is to do everything by petition from the people.

Judge Burris and Judge Gerry have passed away, but both presided over many interesting trials, cases that could only arise under pioneer conditions.

Many amusing incidents took place during the early days when the lawyers and judges were compelled to travel from county seat to county seat, either on foot or on horseback, as the stage roads were not always in condition and there were no railroad lines constructed or in operation until a later period.

One of the most exciting incidents that ever took

place in the San Juan district was the bloodless duel between one of the leading editors of the district and one of the leading lawyers. The lawyer and editor had agreed to go out beyond the town limits and settle their differences by a pistol duel. Just after they started for the outskirts of the town, a happy thought struck the editor, when he said to the lawyer, "Here, Judge, it won't be fair to go down and have this duel without a witness. I see the sheriff standing on the opposite side of the street; suppose we have him go with us." It is needless to say that ended the duel.

A MAN AMONG MEN

By Olga C. Anderson

It was many, many years ago, in the spring of the year 1880. The first wee flowerlet had shown its dainty head after a long winter of snow and cold. The nearby mountainside still wore its coat of snow, no longer white, but a grimy gray.

Along the hillside road an old stage came lumbering along. It was well that it was the only vehicle in that part of the state, for the road was too narrow to allow passing.

The stage was crowded with men—uncouth and unlearned, perhaps, but well taught in the ways of life. Among the occupants was a young man not yet thirty. Broad-shouldered and with a determined look in his face, he showed that he, at least, was not afraid of the struggle that was before him.

Behind him lay years and years of toil, with no recompense.

At last his time had come, and he was entering the "Land of Hope." In the huge, grim mountains that were before him lay tons and tons of gold. Surely, his share would be allotted him.

Coming to a rude log structure standing alone against the horizon, the funny old driver stopped his horses, and the stage was emptied in a minute. Upon entering the house, the men found it to be the typical western "hotel" of that period. There was a large bar extending along one side of the room, at which cheap whisky, beer and wines were sold. Scattered about were rude chairs and benches, none of them made for comfort.

The bedrooms were mere coops, furnished with bunks and boxes. It was not a pleasant place to stay, but was the only place where lodging could be secured.

That night, when all were in bed, that young man sat looking out upon the valley. He was musing to himself, "This is the land of hope and success. I must succeed. What others are doing, I can do."

The valley was a beautiful one. It was framed on all sides by the huge, massive mountains, masterpieces of their kind. Away off in the distance could be seen the falls of the Bridal Veil and of the Ingram. At that early day there were no mills to take the water, nothing to mar the work of nature. To him it all seemed the work of his imagination—

never before had he seen such beauty. The night was clear and crisp, and every breath such as to give new life. Truly, it was a wonderful valley—this valley of the San Miguel, and the town later to be known as Telluride.

There were no good roads at that early date, only the beaten paths made by the prospectors. Next morning, with a couple of pack animals, the stranger made his way to the nearest mine. He had no trouble in getting employment, for men were scarce and the work hard. The room which was to be his was small and cold; a tiny bunk, a box, and an old-fashioned stove was all that it held. The barrenness alone made it desolate, but the man did not notice it lacked everything to make him comfortable. He was used to this; he had come to look upon hunger and cold as part of the necessities of life. At the age of nine his father had died and from that time he had provided for himself and helped his mother and sisters. He had worked for ten years earning money enough to come to America.

He had brought with him to the mine two books, a dictionary and a Bible, and from these he must study and learn. The hours that he must work were long—sixteen out of the twenty-four; another four he must study, and the remaining hours he slept.

For two years he kept up this routine, until he had mastered the English language. Many times he had been tempted to give it up, many times he even fell asleep from exhaustion while reading, but always he kept on. In him was born all the courage of his Viking ancestors, and a determination unconquerable, till, little by little, he accomplished his task.

I can honor my father no better than by saying. "Where others may have failed, he succeeded."

A story this father has often told comes to me about a snowslide in the San Miguel Mountains.

THE STORY

It was in cold, bleak December. Day after day the snow had fallen, and the four men living high up in the mountains had hard work keeping a path open from their wee cabin to the tunnel, in which they hoped to find gold. One morning the wind started to blow. As dusk cast its dark shadow over the mountain tops, it became more and more violent. It was not the wind, however, that frightened them. It was the likelihood that even now a snowslide might be creeping upon them. The night passed at last, and the wind lost its fury at the coming of the dawn. There never was a more beautiful morning. The wind had gone down, the sun shone brightly, and all around seemed a bed of diamonds. One could almost see the snow diminish inch by inch. Two of the men had gone into the mine to work, while the other two prepared the meals. Suddenly, away off in the distance, they heard a rumbling noise. The two men rushed to the door; they were too late. The snowslide was upon them. It took them down, down the mountainside, now buried deep in the snow, and now on top.

In some wonderful way, one of the men had drifted to the outer side of the slide. All at once he felt a violent jerk and then knew no more. An old tree had saved his life.

As it was nearing dark, the rescuers found him. And, after a long, hard fight, they succeeded in bringing him to consciousness again. This man was my father. Late that spring the body of the other man was found. For years his body has lain in the beautiful valley of the San Miguel, unclaimed and forgotten, save by one.

PIONEERING THE DESERT

By W. M. Ash

Three years at the carpenter trade in Denver, and six years' farming on the uplands of the St. Vrain, brought me up to the fateful summer of 1882.

It was while rusticating with friends and relatives in that lovely mountain resort known as Estes Park that I received word I was wanted to assist in making up a party to go to the Uncompahgre and locate land and water for a colony. The "urge" to "move on" took hold of me at once, and I lost no time in getting in touch with the promoter of the scheme. The late M. H. Coffin, one of the earliest settlers of the St. Vrain, a man of sterling character and a personal friend of mine, was backing the proposition. He had just returned from a tour of investigation of the promised land, and water, and the data he had gathered would make a large book. He was a veritable walking encyclopedia of useful knowledge on the subject. He and his companions had made the trip over the range in June by team and knew all the details. On his way back he had developed a complete program. Nothing could be thought of that he had not already considered.

Here was the greatest opportunity of a lifetime. An empire of marvelous resources untouched by man awaited our presence. The only thing in doubt was, could we get there soon enough to possess it? The D. & R. G. railroad was building right into this paradise and every scrap of land would be taken in short order. He had discovered a tract of table-land in a solid body containing 20,000 acres as level as a floor. A few miles of ditch with a small amount of labor would turn the Uncompahgre river upon this land. And now, since the law favored corporate ownership of water, we would be the corporation that would own the water that would own that land. He knew of 200 families ready and waiting to come out from Kansas at his word and settle on the land. We had danced to corporation music all our lives and now at last our turn had come to play. We would have our recompense.

There was no getting away from the enchanting picture. Every detail necessary to the program was provided for in the fertile brain of Professor Phelps. Hay? Yes, he had discovered a mountain mesa of hundreds of acres of the finest hay in the world, only 30 miles from the land in view. We would take a mowing machine and horse rake with us and make our hay the first thing. Owing to the demand for hay by the railroad graders it was selling at $75 a ton. We would make some money selling hay. Building material? Grand Mesa, only about ten miles distant, was covered with cabin logs, fence posts, and saw timber. Game? Why, deer and elk were as numerous in the mountain parks and valleys as cattle on the plains. And scenery? Nothing equal to the mountain skyline bordering this Uncompahgre valley. Here the professor went up in the air.

With such a vision ahead of us it was impossible to procrastinate. All arrangements were completed within a few days. With a brand-new wagon and my best team loaded with hay-making machinery, feed, flour and other necessities, and the professor outfitted with team, wagon, and camp equipment, we were soon en route for the promised land. It was, of course, an interesting trip, without serious mishap. We crossed the hills from Morrison to Turkey Creek, the South Platte, South Park, and over the range by Marshall Pass to Gunnison. This city then was a very busy place, owing to the advent of the two railroads at the same time. But we did not tarry. A few days later we doubled teams up the Crystal Creek mesa. This beautiful mountain tableland was the most enchanting spot on our entire trip. Here we got our first view of the

San Miguel mountains. The scene, in its local beauty and magnitude, was sublime. And here it was that we would make our hay. But not now. We must first go and "spy out the land" on which we were to settle, locate and incorporate the big canal that was to water the land. It had taken a hard day's work to get from Curecanti Creek to the top of this mesa, and it was dark when we went into camp. We reluctantly descended from this mountain paradise the following morning and camped for the night at a farmhouse on Crystal Creek. Here we decided to leave the wagon loaded with haymaking machinery, etc., and hurry on to our destination. Our next camp was at the town site of Hotchkiss. There were only a few settlers in this neighborhood. The only ones we remember were Hotchkiss, Frady, and Wilmot. Our next camp was on the Gunnison a few miles above Delta. There were no bridges over the river, nor roads to speak of. We passed through Delta the following morning and camped for noon on the banks of the turbulent Uncompahgre river. The railroad was just entering the valley. The roads and atmosphere above the roads was a streak of dust from Delta to Montrose. The big freighters were hauling supplies for the railroad graders. Delta had a few houses, mostly of cottonwood poles, logs, and adobe. The contrast between the Uncompahgre valley and the mountain mesa we had left behind us was very depressing. The water muddy with red adobe, the air full of dust, no sign of grass for our teams.

This must indeed be the heart of the "Great American Desert." It was very discouraging. We crossed the river, left the valley road and drove over the tableland that is now known as "Ash mesa." Sensing my feeling of depression, the professor became enthusiastic in his portrayal of the land and its surroundings. "Here it is; just cast your eye over it—ten miles to the west—ten miles to the south, and as level as a floor. A hundred thousand acres all by itself. A little world of our own. Look at that magnificent snowy range to the south. That high ridge there to the east, the Vernal mountains. These slopes to the west are the Uncompahgre Plateau. And right here to the north of us, standing up, is the Grand Mesa, a mile high. And to think of those poor fools squatting down in the alkali and sagebrush in the valley with this land right above them. My, there is a cool million in this for us."

Indeed it was a promising glimpse of a future paradise in the prospective. But not a sign of a drop of water, a spear of grass, or a stick of wood, was there on the land. No camping here. We hurried on and down off the upper end of the mesa and pitched our tent at the mouth of Spring Creek for the night.

With water and some scanty grass for our horses, and plenty of greasewood for our camp fire, we sat up late discussing our future plans. Our spirits were high. On the morrow we would locate the mammoth canal. What should we name it? How big? How much the capital stock? The professor was optimistic. "Let us say 50 feet wide, and a capital of $500,000."

We spent a good night, and the desert had a greener shade in the morning sun. A jack-rabbit appeared on the mesa-side above us. It was the biggest game we had seen in our four hundred miles of travel. The professor got down his "old Daniel," such as grandfather used to have, laid down on his back, rested the muzzle end on his feet, and took aim. The suspense was too long. The rabbit got the range first, the professor the laugh.

We now proceeded to lay out the proposed canal. Having located the headgate at the mouth of Spring Creek, we each got astride a horse and surveyed the line of ditch. By a very gradual and easy stretch of imagination we saw that a little climbing over a few ridges, or perhaps tunneling, would lead the Uncompahgre river into several large basins, which by damming the outlets, would form a chain of lakes leading to the head of the mesa we wished to water. Seeing was believing, and we saw it all with our naked eyes. It was splendid: we would make these lakes a summer picnic resort. This should be the beauty spot of the Western world. The name of our corporation should be "The Geneva Lake Irrigation and Canal Company." And it was so.

The next day we hurried to Montrose to complete the incorporation of the company. We made the acquaintance of Abe Roberts, who was just then starting publication of the Montrose Messenger. The professor explained our plans and gently took him in. We also met the members of the firm of Selig & Eckerly, with whom we did our legal business.

Now we are climbing back on that mountain hay field, and my, what a climb! Four horses to a wagon, and then a hard struggle. At last we are up and in camp. We build a tepee of poles and brush next an island grove near a crystal stream. This is our cook and dining room. A commodious tent and the two covered wagons complete our shelter. Life takes on a rosy hue. We place our horses on picket ropes. They graze for a week at a time on the one circle. No grain is required. They become hog fat. Ah, what a relief! Now we unload our machinery, rig up our mower and rake. It is in September, the weather is ideal. What a lovely world is this! Words are powerless. "Man hath no part in all this glorious scene." But where are the wild animals of the wilderness? We take our guns and make a stir.

"Shoot," says the professor. "There he goes, there!" A flash of deer horns flying through the quaking asp, that was all. What was the use? Better let the animals hunt us. We go to work. But another day I try again. I go alone, carefully, through the young grove of trees; am standing beneath the spreading bough of a spruce. A large buck arises from behind a log not fifty feet away. He stands as though riveted to the spot. I take deliberate aim. I have a splendid gun. Surely he is my meat. I fire and off he goes unharmed. How impossible! Is the gun at fault? I see a grouse as far away as the deer. One shot brings it down. Two more fly up in a tree. Each shot brings one down. I tell my story and the laugh is on me.

Now we are making hay. The professor drives the mower, I the rake. Soon we want our mail. We should have news from home. Our address is Gunnison, about fifty miles away. I take my best mare, a pair of blankets, no saddle, a little grub in a sack, and the Indian trail for a short cut down the hill. Three days on the road. Two nights sleeping on the ground by the side of my horse, studying astronomy. Then up the zigzag trail to camp. Now we stack our hay, bury our machinery in the hay, fence the stack, take on as much hay as we can carry in our wagon, break camp and go back to the mesa on the desert. Now for the transformation.

Cabin logs we must have. I start to the Grand Mesa alone with team. Arrive on top second day. Timber hard to get. Hunt for game half day. Not a thing in sight. Spend two nights on the mesa, one night each way in the Gunnison valley, and get to camp the fifth day with my load. Ninety miles for a dozen logs. Life is too short. Now I get word that my brother George is on the road from Longmont with his wife to join us. He has new team and outfit. We are out of hay. I will go and meet him, and bring back a load. I take tools to make a hayrack. Alone, I see with my own eyes. Our hay field is seventy-five instead of thirty miles away. And such rocky roads, especially the ford of the Gunnison. One hundred and fifty miles for a load of hay. No—a half load, I should say. I get up on the mountain at the old camp. How lonely! But oh, such spruce poles for my rack! And just look at the cabin timber!

I make my rack, leave the wagon, and with my horses go on to meet my brother. It will take both teams to get him up the mesa. I pass only a few miles beyond Curecanti Creek when he comes in sight. We camp at the creek over night, and reach the hay camp the next day, load our hay and the following day are off the mountain.

After three or four days we are safely back on the desert mesa. It is now well in October. We must build cabins and prepare for ditch work. There are many things to be done. Brother and I decide to go up to the head of Dry Creek for cabin logs. No roads. We arrive at edge of timber and camp in a cabin. A storm in the night, and a blizzard of snow the next day drives us back. The storm had blown the tent over, and Mrs. Ash was compelled to seek shelter elsewhere. To make matters worse we were out of money. We had been expecting the sale of our home property to invest here. Something soon must come.

The professor thinks it time to haul our hay. I am "a quitter." I give it up. He takes the job. Makes three trips, and is out of hay. In the meantime I hear of the Eckerly sawmill, and haul slabs while brother builds the first cabin on the land. I learn of a man who had hay at Cimarron to trade for a horse. I make the trip, but it is too far.

Luckily I find a man six miles away who makes the trade.

Now we must know about the ditch. We are done with castles in the air. No surveyor can be had. Necessity is the mother of invention. I study out an instrument that will do the work. We make a wooden pipe five feet long, bore a hole in the upper side of each end, and fit in the necks of two inverted bottles with the bottoms knocked off. This we mount on a tripod. We pour water in one bottle and it comes up to a level line in the other. Over this water line we sight the target. With this instrument we run a new line of ditch, place our stakes, and do some work. Later we incorporate under the name of "The Ironstone Ditch Company," with a capital of $8,000.

The professor returns with his last load of hay, and with him comes M. H. Coffin and several other Longmont people. They look over the big ditch route, and give it up. We ask them into The Ironstone. But the prospect does not look good. Mr. Coffin returns home. A few of the party remain and settle on the lower part of the mesa. Other people come and they start the Home Run Ditch.

Brother and wife being established in the little slab cabin, we go to work in earnest on the ditch. At last we have sold our home in Boulder county, at great sacrifice, and we ship in a carload of feed, flour, seed and so on. The freight bill exceeds the Longmont price of goods. We have a little money and many needs. Other cabins are built. The professor abandons his claim and settles near Delta, on Lower California mesa. New people are coming in slowly. Mr. Cushman settles on the mesa west of Dry Creek. Others follow him, and they call it Cushman, but changed the name later to California mesa.

The Uncompahgre valley land was all taken before we arrived. The country is still unsurveyed. The railroad was completed past Delta during September. The little station opposite our settlement is named Brown, the same being kept by H. H. Brown and his esteemed wife. The Church brothers, J. L. Foster, Reed, Lee, Schrader, Platt, W. F. Mueller, S. H. Nye, Young brothers, Gus Frost, Loper brothers and Elmer Nichols were all settlers in the valley in 1882.

In those days there were no classes in society. All were on a level. If a dance was held it was at a private house and the whole population for ten miles were there. The first school in our neighborhood was held in Chep Church's cabin in the winter of '83 and '84. It was taught by Charles Young. In the following spring a community schoolhouse was built by contributions. The story of the hardships incident to the development of "Ash Mesa" cannot be told in detail. Only the participants can fully realize what the early settlers had to contend with through all those experimental years. Everything was new and untried.

REMINISCENCES OF EARLY DAYS

By Mrs. Miner

It was the morning of the first day of September that we left the end of the railroad at South Arkansas, now Salida, to begin the ascent of the "backbone of the continent." That never-to-be-forgotten morning! What we saw when we awakened was so different from what we expected when we went to sleep the night before. Then the mountains looked an inky black, reflecting the color of the threatening sky, but now, in the morning sunlight, there were but two colors visible in all nature—a dazzling whiteness and a vivid blue, and the two colors met far, far above, where the mountain tops meet the sky. Coming from a climate where the mercury stood from 100 to 110 degrees in the shade, the change from a torrid to a frigid zone, apparently, was as delightful to every sense as agreeable to the eye. But we had gone but a mile or two up the mountainside before the sun began to disappear and the birds began to sing as cheerfully as in midsummer, and when we reached the summit of Marshall Pass we climbed out to pick violets, something we never expected to do in September. There, long before a railroad was built or snow sheds were necessary, we could look with nothing to obstruct our view for miles, and the sun, which had been hidden for several hours, now burst full upon us, bringing out the vivid green of the pines and aspens in beautiful contrast to the snow-clad mountains around.

Then, as we passed on toward the setting sun and

began to descend on the Pacific slope, we realized that we were leaving behind what had been ours for so many years, leaving a life we knew all about for one of which we knew but little, leaving a highly civilized country for one 180 miles from a railroad, for we were bound for the "Silver San Juan," that part of Colorado little known to the outside world, being bound around with the most inaccessible mountains to be found anywhere in the world, for here in the very southwest corner of the state are clustered together the loftiest, roughest, rockiest and most rugged mountains in Colorado. We were not only bound for the Silver San Juan, but for Ouray, "The Gem of the Rockies," and the little mining camp named after the chief of the Utes.

The climb on the east side that took seven hours to accomplish was easily done in two hours coming down on the west side; all that had to be done was to put on the brakes and let the horses go. At first we held our breath, expecting every moment to be thrown out at some sharp curve thousands of feet below, but after the first half hour it became so exhilarating and exciting that we wished it might last longer. Sargent's log cabin, where we spent the first night, marked the spot which is now a station by that name.

On Sunday morning, the sixth day of September, we left the agency for Ouray. When a few miles on the way we came across an Indian settlement and had the honor of shaking hands with Shavano, the new chief of the Utes.

Can we ever forget the first entrance into the canon of the Uncompahgre just before we reached the town of Ouray, and when we came out of the deep shadows into the open sunlight, which lighted up the scenery around the little town with a beauty and grandeur that can never be eclipsed anywhere on God's green earth? We wondered how so much grandeur, beauty and sublimity could be massed together in a space so small. The towering cliffs, lofty mountains, sloping foothills, covered with green pines and flecked here and there with autumn tints of brilliant orange and red, the innumerable cascades and water-falls, the piles upon piles of boulders larger than the largest buildings, brilliant flowers and birds met the eye and greeted the ear on every side. As we saw the sun drop behind the dome of White House mountain we watched the shadow of it creep higher and higher up the mountainside on the eastern boundary, till away up against the sky just one little point was left glowing with the brightest crimson.

When my friends bade me goodby in the far East they thought I was going quite out of the world. After I had been here a few weeks I wrote them that for the first time in my life I found myself in the world. We had been here but a week or so when a reception was given Gov. Pitkin in the only public hall we had at that time, a room over Pat Hess' saloon, then a wooden structure. It was there we were introduced to all the elite of the city. There we shook hands with more judges, colonels, cap-

A TRAPPER'S OUTFIT IN THE MOUNTAINS. CAMP NEAR HORSEFLY, COLO.

tains, lawyers and doctors than we supposed could be found in all Colorado and with people not only from every larger city and state in the United States, but people from Paris, London and from nearly every country on the civilized globe.

Those were the times when all were young and full of life and hope, for everyone came with the expectation of digging a fortune out of those mountains. We never thought of locking our doors or fastening windows. When the freight wagons failed to get through with supplies, neighbors divided up with each other. When the husbands failed to get home from outside or down from the mines the wives protected each other over night and learned to saw wood when the wood pile failed. There was little rivalry or jealousy, for all lived in log palaces alike, and now we feel like joining in the song, "Oh, for the Days Beyond Recall, Oh, for the Golden Days."

SUMMER ON HORSEFLY

In the spring of 1893 a family well known to the writer concluded to go into the dairy business. A few of the best cows were bought, the husband devoting his whole time to the making of butter and care of the stock. The buttermilk brought 40 cents a gallon, and the hotelkeepers were glad to get it at that price. During the winter the stock was warmly housed on their ranch near town.

In the early spring the family with their stock would migrate to the hills some twenty miles southwest of Montrose on Horsefly range. Here the cattle found abundance of the finest grass, pure water flowing from many a spring and plenty of shade.

The house was but a one-room log cabin with a large tent to sleep in and a small room adjoining for a milk room. But they had all outdoors—one of the loveliest parks to be found anywhere. No matter how often they had seen it, the moment they were up in the morning the door was thrown wide open for another glimpse of the beauty awaiting these lovers of nature.

As far as the eye could reach in the distance could be seen a little of the Grand Mesa, at the foot of which the little town of Delta nestles. To the right of them a low sloping hill, dotted with tall, straight, white-trunked aspen trees, their leaves never still, always on the quiver. There was the tall, dark green spruce tree with its sheltering branches, a cover from the storm as well as the heat. To the left and behind were higher hills, with trees of different kinds, little clusters of trees and bushes where one could sit all day and never feel the warmth of sunshine. Farther down to the left one could hear the tinkling of the water flowing from the cool, refreshing spring, and find the loveliest flowers. Everywhere, no matter in what direction one would look, could be seen the green grass. The sky seemed so far away, only a little peeping through the thick foliage above.

The stillness was broken only by the twitter of birds, or the gambol of squirrels, or the lowing of

CAMPING IN THE MOUNTAINS. PEACE AND QUIETNESS.

cows longing to be relieved of their heavy bags of milk and turned out to wander as they would through the grass up to their knees. Oh, but it was beautiful beyond expression!

This family would always take their little four-octave organ with them, and often the cowboy riding hastily by would be surprised to hear the sound of music.

One day these cowboys came to the milk room for a drink of buttermilk. After drinking all they wished, they offered a dollar in payment, but were told they were welcome to all they could drink. With hearty thanks they sprang onto their horses and rode away. The next evening one of these cowboys brought to this family a big chunk of fresh beef.

One morning while Frank, a lad about 15, the chief herder of the cows, was busy at his task, a big storm came up. He gathered the herd under the spruce trees for a shelter, but the storm was so terrific the cattle took fright and stampeded, as well they might with hail stones three and one-half inches around pelting them on the back.

The mother was very glad to see the boy come home. The father said: "Never mind, Frank, they will come home at noon now the storm is over." Yes, they came, for well they knew a trough of skimmed milk awaited them. How they enjoyed the drink! One fat young steer outran the rest every time and would never stop drinking until he was so full he would lay down and groan, while others drank so much they would puff and blow for half an hour. Many a time, when coming down for their noon drink, the bellowing of "Pocus," the bull, would cause the mother to rush to the window to see what was the trouble, to find Will or Bert holding onto Pocus' tail, the bull bellowing with fright or pain, rushing down the hill as fast as he and the children could run, the rest of the cattle following, both children and cattle—except Pocus—enjoying the fun.

Sometimes the whole family would go with the cattle, picnic near some spring and eat their dinner, then gather the loveliest flowers. The mother would find after she came home there had been fresh bear tracks where she had eaten her dinner. The boys and little daughter never let her know at the time, for bear tracks never looked funny to her.

Once, when returning home, they found visitors from town, and a good supper awaiting them. "We

PREPARING THE EVENING MEAL WHILE THE BOYS ARE AWAY HUNTING.

found everything we needed, so helped ourselves." This was the law all over the hills: "Help yourselves, but take nothing away." Many a man when coming home from work would find someone "helping himself," the stranger always being made to feel his welcome.

One day late in the afternoon they heard old Shep, the dog, barking furiously and the noise of at least twenty animals rushing through the timber, coming toward the house. It proved to be a large steer, crazed with fright of the dog, which was holding on part of the time to his tail. So crazed was he and thinking only of safety, he ran right into their little milk room. So small was the room, filled up as it was on one side with milk racks, there was only room enough for the steer to wedge itself in, the dog and family, an excited crowd, at its heels outside.

The room was too small for it to turn in the least, and to back out, with that dog now barking fiercely at its heels, was not to be thought of. The father called the dog off, much to the dog's disgust, and then, taking a long stick, poked at the steer as best he could through the side window, the mother and children seeking shelter. Finally, the poor animal, not hearing the dog, backed out. But such a milk room! Milk spilt in every direction, the racks broken down.

The trouble seemingly over, the father and son went to the corral to milk the cows, which were standing around as peacefully inclined as well behaved cows usually are, when all of a sudden, over the fence, which was very high, jumped this same steer with the dog trying to follow. The cows were completely demoralized and the pails of milk spilt. With a club the angry father went for the steer. What with the club and the dog, the steer rushed again for shelter. This time the mother, standing by the open door, saw the steer coming around the corner of the cabin just in time to close the door, or he would have bolted into the living room. He passed and went into the milk room again. The children rushed to the corral wild with excitement. and yelled, "The steer is in the milk room again!"

The father stopped milking a second time and laughed; it was getting funny. Not so thought the steer, which stood panting in the disordered milk room till after the milking was finished and the dog tied up. Then with a long stick the father persuaded the steer to come out. Starting in the right direction this time, the steer went with a rapid gait over the hill and never came back.

Those were happy and never-to-be-forgotten days, and often they have looked up to those hills and wished to be there again, with the flowers, the birds and the trees.

THE DISCOVERY OF AN IDEAL HOME

By Stephen Edward Keating

The first time I saw Sanbourne Park, 35 miles southwest of Montrose, like some scene vaguely recalled from memories of fairyland stories I had read in my youth, a strong wave of desire swept over me —the selfish desire to possess it all and to become a "fairy prince," such a one as I had dreamed of, and believed in, when as a child I read those ancient fables, for all the heroes in those brightly colored memory pictures were possessors of large and beautiful estates, and the castles in which they dwelt with their lovely ladies, the princesses, the magnificent, many-turreted, mysterious old piles of real masonry, with paneled walls, secret staircases and underground passages, and the stately banquet halls, sometimes filled with gay companies and flashing lights, and on other occasions with the silvery moonlight streaming in at the windows, and the ghosts of bygone ancestors assembled for their midnight revels. I had wooed and won my lovely lady, and was now in search of a beautiful home for her, and with my first glance at this apparently enchanted fairy-land, it seemed only natural that those pictures of long ago should come trooping in. But alas for the practicalness of modern man; as I gazed the picture changed, all the unreal and fantastic features vanished one by one, leaving only the realities and the wonderful possibilities. With the fairy picture went also the selfish desire to possess it all, and in its stead came the fervent wish to share this lovely park with all the world, glad to obtain for myself only a small portion of it. Here was all the environment for a life such as I had hoped to find, wild isolation, with plenty of hunting, fishing and outings, almost unlimited range for cattle, and coupled with this wild, free life were broad, fertile fields for the cultivation of grain and hay and a market close at hand. Only a few years ago this fine expanse of country was practically unknown, and, turning back the pages of Colorado history, one finds that here where we found the imposing old house of logs, a famous chief of the Ute tribe, together with his braves, were wont to pitch their tepees and lie in wait for the deer that came to drink from the clear cold spring a short distance away. This, we were told, was the favorite hunting ground of this noble tribe, and, as though wishing to add proof to the testimony, the forest near by has yielded up many arrow heads and spearpoints, which make valuable additions to our collection of Colorado souvenirs.

As I look out over the miles of beautiful landscape, with the fine ranches already dotting its surface, there comes to me the realization that only a short time must elapse before the march of civilization and progress will have discovered and utilized every portion of it, and even now in my fancy I can almost hear the merry jingle of school bell and feel the companionship of my lovely lady.

A TRIP TO SANBOURNE PARK

By Della Shotwell Keating

My husband took me down into Sanbourne Park from the upper country where we were camped, in fulfillment of a promise made to a friend that we would "look the park over" before making a decision in the purchase of a ranch, which was then our intention. In the summer of 1913, as is usually the case in Colorado, the weather was perfect, clear, cool and bracing, enabling us to travel many miles without feeling the slightest fatigue. We rode down through the quaking aspens, tall, stately white columns, growing less frequent and imposing as we came down from the higher country.

As we passed on down the trail, the soft summer wind blowing gently in our faces was laden with the balmy odor of pine and balsam growing far below, whose waving green and blue tops we could see even now in the distance. The columbines, Colorado's State flower, were in full bloom, peeping out from the cool, shady places, with purple and white faces

Summit of Lone Cone. Elevation over 12,000 feet. Monument of County Line between San Miguel and Dolores County.

of wondrous beauty. Thousands of flowers covered the sunny hillsides like a huge carpet flaunting its glorious and almost indescribable colorings to the dark, sober pines, and the gloomy canons down below. Out from the rocks scampered many kinds of small wild creatures, each one, it seemed, more beautiful than the other in their bright array of feathers or fur.

As we came on down the landscape seemed less rugged, and the grand old pines, the yellow variety, more frequent. Now and then beautiful little parks opened through the trees, with the hundreds of cattle grazing on the luscious mountain grasses which grew there. The trails had long since terminated in fine, well-traveled roads, and now the forests of pine grew more and more dense. Presently, just as we were becoming accustomed to the sameness of these plumed giants, a sudden turn in the road brought us out into full view of Sanbourne Park. It is not possible for me, with my limited vocabulary, to describe the wonderful beauties of the broad expanse of fertile land that stretched out before us for miles, flanked on all sides by a fringe of dark green pine, and in the distance, rearing their noble heads high in the afternoon sun, were the misty outlines of the La Sal mountains, across the border in Utah, and the Blues in Arizona. Looking again to the left of these, we behold part of the San Juan range of the grand old Rockies. Here after some study we recognized four of the most prominent peaks in the state —Mount Sneffles, Mount Wilson, the Dolores peaks and the Lone Cone, bearing on its lofty crest a mammoth W of purest white, formed there by rocky crevices filled with snow, which even the July sun had failed to efface, and, to me, symbolic of one whose dearly beloved presence in these environments seemed very near. All were silhouetted against a sky of deepest sapphire, such as it seemed to me was only seen in Colorado. Plainly outlined between these famous peaks were many other lesser ones, among which we could see the Little Cone and the Lizard Head, rising up and strangely alert and significant, as though guarding the portals of the wonderful park, this beauteous "land of promise." Far to the right of these mountains we could see the purple red haze which marked the location of the Red Canon, where, I was told, abounded all manner of game, such as deer, bear and cats of many varieties, making it one of the most famous hunting grounds in the state. After crossing a wide strip of Indian paintbrush, their brilliant petals looking as though they had just finished streaking in those gorgeous colorings of purple red mists, we looked down to another and smaller canon in whose depths rushed a swift stream filled with mountain trout. The steep sides running down to its clear, cold waters covered with a growth of bright green oak.

Last of all, after feasting our eyes on those marvelous gifts of natural scenery we turned to the stately old mansion of logs, standing like a sentinel, its many windows commanding superb views of the park, blazing in the setting sun, all its old-fashioned lines showing clearly against a background of pines centuries old, and somehow there came to me the conviction that this was—it must be—the home for which my restless nature had been searching for always. The home my husband had found for me.

LAKE SAN CHRISTOBAL

One beautiful morning, so early the birds and neighbors were fast asleep, a number of people, with repressed laughter and lowered voices, glided away in their autos from the pretty town of Montrose to Lake City, a distance of about seventy-five miles, their object a few weeks' outing, fishing and lots of fun—the capacity for fun they took with them.

They reached the end of their journey beside Lake San Christobal, which is situated about three miles from the once-thrifty and well-known town in pioneer days, Lake City, a beautiful place yet to the nature lover.

Our friends were glad to reach their destination and begin their camp life, so fascinating to everyone. While dinner was being prepared the men of the party put up their tent; the ladies sheltered in a large log cabin near by.

Even after the day's ride they were loath to leave the beauty, the quietness, of outdoors, the moonlight and the stars which sparkled as though glad to see such a happy crowd, but remembrance of plans laid for the morrow's pleasure, they retired. The men in the big tent found little to say to each other when alone—they had talked and laughed so much during the day they were glad to rest, and soon were fast asleep, unmindful of the activity of nature around them.

A light breeze was stirring, causing the leaves to clap their hands gently as though not to disturb the sleepers; in the distance the rumble of thunder and fitful flashes of lightning, the hoot-hoot of the funny night owl, the sharp bark of the coyote, and above all the pure sweet air of the mountains—no wonder the men awoke the next morning refreshed and glad they lived.

The ladies did not go to sleep so quickly, their sense of fun, like a spring on the mountainside, constantly bubbling over; quietness reigned for a moment, then an amusing remark made caused them all to shake with laughter. When quietness was restored and a few fortunate ones were fast asleep a strange noise was heard by the wakeful ones, who, with bated breath, would whisper, "What is that?"

Oh, it was fine sleeping in a strange old house minus the comforts they were accustomed to! The pure fresh air and the aroma of brush and tree could not reach them.

Morning found them glad and happy, not realizing how much sweeter their rest if they too had slept in a tent.

After breakfast they left camp with fishing tackle and lunch, not expecting to return until evening.

Yes, it was a day of enjoyment. The lake, one of the most beautiful in the world, three miles long

CAMPING NEAR LAKE SAN CHRISTOBAL.

and about one mile wide, but very treacherous; nothing that falls into it ever comes to the surface, because of the undercurrent and the quicksand.

Two of the ladies, wading in the water to get a better place to fish, found themselves being drawn under and with much difficulty were pulled out by the men who fortunately were near. No one knows how deep the lake is; it is called bottomless.

But in spite of this scare, they enjoyed the day and proudly brought back to camp a hundred trout —beauties they were, too—while the appetites of these people was great and their sense of fun keen.

During their stay Ed Sherman, one of Montrose's bright lawyers, after a visit to his father's mine, the Bourbon County Lode, lost his pocketbook. He walked back the next day, a distance of seventeen miles, hoping to find it on the way, but failed to do so.

Day after day they fished, the ladies sleeping so soundly at night the strange noises did not disturb them.

Once they caught two hundred fish—a big fish story to tell their friends when they came home. Would they be believed?

Once the writer's husband proudly brought home a bunch of trout. The inquisitive wife asked if he caught them. "There's the fish," was his answer, as though that was proof enough. But the most enjoyable outing will come to an end, and the friends came back to town refreshed and ready to take up life's duties, feeling the days in the mountains so close to nature well spent.

"Who owns most of the valleys, hills and woods,
The streams, the grazing flocks? 'Tis the same man
Who owns most of the sunsets, clouds and stars.
And who is he? 'Tis he who loves them most;
For only by the measure of his love
Can he discern their perfect loveliness,
And know the joys of their companionship."

—Hon. Clarence A. Buskirk,
Indianapolis (Ind.) News.

A SUMMER DAY'S OUTING

An inhabitant of the valley living on a ranch near town tells how the longing to get near the mountains, "out in the open," was gratified.

For weeks the children had been coaxing father to take a day off for a trip to the hills, and now, the busiest part of the season being over, it was found possible.

One morning, before the birds were fully awake, we started. The horses were rather sleepy, but so accustomed to obey they soon caught the spirit of the occasion, lifting their heads in the sprightly way horses have when feeling good. They almost smiled as they turned their heads to watch the family packing things snug and away from the heat or rain.

The "grub box" proved a source of satisfaction to the younger members of the family, who with their special chums were stowed in the back seat, while little daughter sat in the front to help father drive, and ask questions. How peaceful everything was, just as though not only the people but all nature was still asleep. No part of the day is so full of sweet suggestions as the early morning.

The blades of grass standing like sentinels guarding the white clover leaf, which closes itself when darkness comes, but this is learned only by the nature lover. Then the birds. We may think they fly right out of their nests and begin to sing at once, but no, they are as slow as you and I sometimes. They almost wake up, then nestle down with a chirrup or two for a little more sleep. When one would think them fast asleep their eyes fly open as bright as a babe's; then, just like a baby, they begin stretching, first one leg and then the other. All the time a sense of joy and gladness for being alive in such a beautiful world comes to them, and they begin tuning up for a song. It does not come all at once; a note or two, and then, as though surprised at themselves, they stop, think about it, then try it over again, perhaps a little more carefully, with better success, then, letting go of all thought of fear, burst forth with their morning song of gladness.

The water, running through the ditches as we passed along by well-kept farms, is clear at this time. It runs very slowly, a low, tender song it is singing, which tells of contentment to those who have ears to hear and hearts to receive. The ripple of the water as it passes by is but the combined chatter of drops of water as they talk over the experiences of the night, for the water has just come from the mountains; it has not always been confined in a ditch, but no sense of discontent creeps into its song of freedom.

The sun is up now, and here and there we see men feeding their horses or milking their cows, while the farmer's dog is leaping about with a desire to help, but hindering every time, while our horses, by the way they go, seem to say, "No work for us today; we are out for a good time."

The boys in the back seat are bubbling over with happiness, while little daughter gives a sigh of satisfaction as she looks up in her father's face, and he, understanding, smiles back; while mother, with heart and thought too full for expression, sits drinking in the peace, the beauty and love of it all.

Soon the boys asked mother if it was not nearly time to have "something to eat." Mother smiles in a way the boys understand, while father, looking up, nods at mother, the horses stopping as quickly as if they had been thinking so, too. Yes, it was a good place to stop, for there was a fine spring of water, and water would be scarce soon. What shouts of approval as mother brought out the good things to eat, and such appetites!

Strange as it may seem, the boys were the first to stop eating. There were other things more alluring; they could eat any time. The mother, looking around a moment later, said: "Where are the boys?" Father smiled and said: "The boys are all right; they are hunting for something." And sure enough, a woodchuck, taking its morning walk, fled panic-stricken at sight of dog and boys. There was a lively chase, but the woodchuck was too swift, and the boys, hearing their father call them, went back. While climbing into the wagon they told how they "almost" caught a woodchuck. Father smiled understandingly. They were still out of breath.

It was well the horses were rested and willing, for there was a long climb for them, and the journey fairly begun. With forethought gained by past experience the father had filled a can with water from the spring. There was a change now as we began to climb, leaving town, farms, and river with its cottonwoods, far behind.

At the first decided rise in our progress we came to the cedars. Rough, gnarly trees they are, with no attractions save to the thrifty farmer who comes here for his fence posts and the winter supply of wood.

A few miles further we leave the cedars for the pinon. These, too, have very little symmetry of form, having no water but that coming from the clouds. Here the boys spied the well-formed but green nuts of the pinon. With a shout to "wait a minute," they climbed down before the wagon stopped, so eager were they to gather the sweet little nuts encased in their hard shells. As the boys came back with their arms loaded with branches the mother exclaimed: "Why, boys, what's the matter with your hands?" "Oh," they replied, "that is nothing but pitch; it will wear off." "But your clothes, children!" "Why, mother," answered Will, "you forget these clothes came out of the rag bag." Then they all laughed, even mother.

It was not very long till we came to a stretch of rather open country, very rocky. Here and there, seldom very close together, stands the pine. We pause in the description of it; we always do. It has a strange effect on the imaginative mind; it never needs or calls forth the word beautiful—"The Pine!" is enough. There it stands, often alone as though it courted solitude, amid the most rocky and barren parts of the hills. If its outspreading arms are short there is no concealment; if it tells no secrets it certainly keeps none. The wind, whispering through the needle-like leaves, can be drear or pleasant, according to the minds which listen. My love goes out to thee, O Pine! for the lessons of steadfastness and bravery amid the storms which so often have passed over thee.

Then, as though nature loved contrast, the soil is covered with the greenest of tender grasses, and the tall, graceful quaking aspen, with its light green leaves dancing in the breeze, never still, its trunk so white and smooth one is reminded of a Southern plantation, where every building, great or small, is whitewashed. You will notice the closer these trees grow together the taller and straighter they are, not looking down at each other, but up at the blue sky.

Closely associated with the aspen is the red spruce. Here again words fail to express the feeling of satisfaction and delight which comes over one. Its arms are strong and outreaching enough to satisfy the hungry heart. We notice the higher it grows in the sunlight the farther out it reaches, offering its shade to the weary and often burdened ones of earth, always the same, a shelter from the storm in winter as from the heat in summer.

There are two kinds of spruce. There is the white spruce, a tall and slender tree, which grows in masses, often a whole mountainside covered with it. Because it grows so close together it, like the aspen, is tall and straight, and is much used by the settlers for log houses and almost exclusively for hay derricks.

Our attention was drawn to the children as we came nearer the mountain. We saw they, too, were drinking in the beauty and the grandeur of it all, for when they spoke it was almost in a whisper.

A short turn and we went down a steep, rocky road, not often traveled. In a few minutes we stopped, and father said: "Does this please you?" No one answered, not even the boys, speech seemed so inadequate. On one side a mountain of trees, row on row, until they seemed to reach the sky. On the other a wall of pale red rock, almost perpendicular, while at the top, almost out of sight, were green trees and flowers. At the foot of this great wall lay, as though asleep, a small lake, but the boys soon found something in that lake not asleep. Mother's eyes, as well as those of the boys, danced with pleasure when dinner time came to see the fish, real mountain trout, steaming on the hastily improvised table, and wild red raspberries, which sister had gathered. The boys did not tell mother till later the marks around the bushes were bear tracks—they knew it would spoil her pleasure.

What a dinner! How happy everyone felt. We tried to talk, not so much to say something as to hear ourselves, to break the silence we had never felt before. Then, as though to remind us we were not in Eden, there is a little sense of unrest, an occasional scanning of the mountainside to see if Mr. Bear is not coming, an uninvited guest, to our banquet. We found tracks a-plenty; we wondered from which side he would come, for every side seemed full of possibilities. But father smiled, as though he knew there was no danger.

After dinner we climbed the mountainside for flowers, ferns and moss. This was the happiest time of all. The grandeur, the silence so impressive, even the bear was forgotten.

Very soon—all too soon—father took out his watch. "Time to be going," he said. "Hello," said father to mother as they were busy packing everything snug to make room in the big wagon, "just see those boys!" Sure enough, Will, Bert and their chums came slowly back from the farther end of the lake, each with a string of speckled beauties. How proudly they handed them to father, who looked as pleased as they as he packed them away, bound closely with grass and leaves.

We were soon settled down for the ride home. The dog seemed anxious to stay in the wagon, so glad to be close to its friends, and quickly fell asleep. The horses showed their delight in the way horses can when they found they were traveling homeward. Little daughter was glad to lean in mother's arms, and soon she, too, was fast asleep. While the boys—sleepy? Not they. While there was so much to see—for even though it was the same road, it seemed new every moment. "See that rabbit! Father, wait a minute!" the boys cried, and gave the dog a shake to wake him up, but father said very decidedly: "No time to stop now, boys: we must be getting home." They enjoyed watching the squirrels play hide and seek, their little black eyes fairly snapping with glee at the boys, so helpless to harm them.

When little daughter awoke she was so happy to be still on this lovely trip. Father asked her what she had in her hand. "Something pretty I picked up when we were gathering the flowers. See." Father, taking the rock in his hand, said: "This is

SOME OF MOTHER'S TREASURES.

an Indian arrowhead." "Why," asked the boys, "how did it get up here?" "Years ago this was the Ute Indians' favorite hunting ground," said father. "Yes, but how could they make anything like that?" the boy exclaimed, all weariness forgotten. "We don't know, children, just how, but they would take a piece of flint and chip and chip until they worked it into the desired shape. Men traveling over these hills often found heaps of these chips where they had been at work. This arrowhead," said father with a reminiscent look in his eyes as his thoughts flew back to a like experience, "was used by some Indian as he shot at some unsuspecting deer as it stood sniffing in the fresh morning air." The boys eyed the treasure so longingly even little sister could not but understand. "You boys may have it if you like," she said, and handed it over with a smile. "Good," smiled Bert: "we will put it with the rest of our specimens."

When passing by a grove of trees filled with underbrush, where the sun could not lighten the shadows, back of the brush the boys saw something moving slowly toward them. What could it be? They looked at each other with eyes wide open, and just as they were about to yell to father the strange animal came in sight with a plaintive moo, as though calling attention to the fine young calf at her side. The boys never acknowledged, even to themselves, how frightened they had been. How good it seemed to get out more in the open, where the still bright sunlight reached every nook and crevice. But the sun was getting low, and soon the sunset with its beauty seemed a fitting close to the happy day.

The moon was just peeping over the distant hills, the birds had all gone to bed, the farmers were resting after the day's work, and when we neared our dear old home we felt we had been away a month, so much had been seen and enjoyed. The clean, white beds looked very inviting to the tired children, who were soon asleep, perhaps again chasing the woodchuck or capturing the longed-for bear. While mother with tender hands put the flowers and ferns and moss in water, laying away carefully other trophies, while father stood by watching with keen interest, for he so loved the outdoor life, this "living in the open."

When everything had been cared for, the horses munching their feed, the dog on the door mat gently rapping the floor with his tail, with one eye open watching his master, father took mother's hand in his, saying: "Well, you enjoyed it?" "Yes, dear," she said, her heart too full for words, but later she said: "If we and others would only leave our work more often for such times, how much better it would be for all of us, and how much more we would get out of life."

A Bear Story

In the earlier years bear stories were more plentiful than they are today, probably because the bear were more abundant. The material for the following is furnished by I. N. Traver, of California Mesa.

Having recently reached California Mesa, coming from Silverton, with a number of companions, the company had established a camp and were engaged in looking over the country. One morning Mr. Traver and a companion named Eph, found themselves in the Roubideaux Canon, and across the canon discovered a bunch of deer. Going after them, they succeeded in wounding one, and followed the trail without success until 3 o'clock, when they gave it up and started on their return to camp. Recovering the horses, which they had left when following the trail, they continued their homeward journey down the ridge, pushing along without much regard to the surroundings. Reaching an unusually narrow place on the ridge, with practically perpendicular walls on either side, Mr. Traver, being in the lead, saw in the brush and coming toward them an animal he at first thought was an ox, but second thought reminded him there were no cattle in that section. He was crowding one cliff with the hope of passing without an interview, when the animal suddenly raised on his hind feet and uttered a "woof," which they supposed meant halt. It had the opposite effect, however. Eph, who had not seen the bear until it had raised on its haunches, shouted: "It's a bear!" at the same time putting spurs to his slow, broken-down horse, passing his partner in a twinkling. Mr. Traver's well-bred horse showed his training and refused to let the other horse outrun him, otherwise this might have been another kind of a bear story. Mr. Traver thought the "critter" as big

THE LION CAUGHT BY URIAH HOTCHKISS, FEBRUARY, 1913.

as an emigrant wagon, but to be safe he compromised by saying, "As big as an ox, with paws like a big frying pan." When he rose up on his haunches his head was on the level with theirs as they sat on their horses.

Their rifles were not accurately sighted, they had not many shells, it was getting late and they were some distance from camp, etc., so did not return to dispose of Mr. Bear.

Telling their story on arrival at camp, it was unanimously decided to go and get bruin in the morning, but strange as it may seem, when morning came the appetite for bear meat had disappeared, and the bear was saved to be the meat of some more fortunate being.

The bear got away, so did the hunters, as is often the case.

URIAH HOTCHKISS ROPED BIG LION

Montrose Daily Press, Feb. 26, 1913.

Uriah Hotchkiss, the great hunter, has added another laurel to his crown. Crawling into a cave facing several grizzly bears, which had been driven to their holes by this fearless man, and shooting them down with a trusty six-shooter is no more than climbing a pinon tree and throwing a rope over a mammoth mountain lion which sat on the topmost branch snarling at him scarcely three feet away and threatening to jump into his face any minute.

This latter act is just what Uriah Hotchkiss did

on Wednesday morning about six miles east of Colona. Mr. Hotchkiss heard the day before a big mountain lion had been seen in that vicinity, and he determined to capture the beast, which is so destructive to stock this time of year, if it were possible. Wednesday morning he started on horseback, accompanied by Roy Humphrey with his pack of hunting dogs, and his son, George Hotchkiss, leaving Colona about 4 o'clock.

It was not long before the dogs had struck the trail of the lion in the snow, and they soon came up to him and forced him up a tree about thirty feet high. He was such a fine specimen that Uriah determined he would make an effort to save him alive, even at the cost of his own life. With a rope in his hand, and without a weapon of any kind, he climbed the tree after the lion. The animal was sitting right in the top of the tree. When Uriah got in close proximity to the lion the animal started down the tree after him several times, but Uriah could slide down the pinon faster than the lion, and whipsawed up and down that sapling for some time. George Hotchkiss stood off a short distance holding a bead on the lion with his trusty Winchester to pop him once if he got the best of his father.

Finally the lion decided not to waste his strength in trying to catch Uriah by following him down the tree, so he remained at the top. Uriah gradually worked up closer to him until he was within three feet of him. The lion sat there ready to fly in his face, but Uriah charmed him. One toss of the rope and it landed around the lion's neck. With the two boys at the end of it, they attempted to pull the lion down from the tree, but he was too strong for them. They got him down part of the distance, and Uriah worked around behind him. By twisting the lion's tail he forced him to dislodge from the tree, and when he landed on the ground he kept the boys chasing around for some time before they got another rope over his head.

Finally they succeeded in hog-tying him. Uriah threw him onto the saddle, with the feet over the horn, and he rode behind him into Colona. They now have him securely chained, and it is proposed to bring him to Montrose on Saturday.

He got a swipe at Uriah while he was being untied and scratched his hand somewhat. Uriah says this is the first time he has been caught by a lion.

The animal weighs about two hundred pounds and is about eight feet long, and is the largest seen in that section for some time.

BULL CANON

By Mrs. Annie Philip

My stay in Bull Canon was very interesting to me. I went in the fall of 1912 to cook for the men who were doing the carnotite mining in that place.

Our nearest mail box was nine miles away, our nearest postoffice Naturita, 24 miles distant.

To get to Bull Canon we rode fifteen miles in the stage from Naturita, then nine miles on horseback or on burros over what is known as the "chimney rock trail," two miles long, so named because of a bunch of rock on the side of the trail which rises up about two hundred and fifty feet, formed like a group of chimneys, tan in color.

After climbing a very steep hill we came to a beautiful park known as Deer Park; a little further on we crossed the south fork of the Wild Steer Canon. The trail runs on to the edge of Bull Canon, where there was still two miles to travel before reaching home, some of the way the trail so steep it seemed safer to walk or slide than ride.

It was a very pleasant sight to me to see the boarding house loom up in the darkness with lights in all the rooms.

Mr. Cummings came swinging his lantern to greet the first woman ever known to be in Bull Canon. Others of the men followed. They all looked pleased, for visions of good things to eat, prepared by a woman's hand, seemed very good to these miners. They were all extremely kind to me the fourteen months I was there.

The weather was pleasant during that time of the year. I would often take an interesting book, climb up the rocks on the side of the canon a distance of a hundred feet, and there read aloud to an imaginary audience.

It was not altogether an imaginary one, for the birds flew around me among the pinon and cedar trees. When I whistled they were delighted and answered back. Sometimes a coyote would come near, listen for a moment, then decide my subject beyond his comprehension, leave me without even a farewell bark.

Christmas came with its season of joyous greetings, even in Bull Canon. Hutchin Revlor, one of the packers, brought me a cat Christmas eve all the way from Bed Rock, a distance of twenty-five miles, on a burro's back. How glad she was to see a woman and to me she was a loving companion during the long days I was alone. I named her "Hutchie." Not only did Hutchin bring the cat, but provisions for a Christmas dinner, which consisted in part of an English plum pudding, roast ham and lemon pie. Vance Cloud, an old acquaintance, brought me a box of candy.

Several small plum puddings, which I gave to the men in the neighboring camps, were heartily enjoyed by them.

The miners gathered bunches of cedar with their white berries shining in the sunlight, to decorate the house, making wreathes for the windows and table.

How beautiful it is, no matter how isolated one may be, the loving Christmas spirit is felt and enjoyed!

The latter part of February two hunters—Clarence Ross and his uncle Will—came to the canon to hunt bear meat.

Will Ross said he never was so surprised as when a woman answered his knock, for he never expected to see a woman in that wild canon.

In return for the bread I baked for them they

left me a fine-looking dog, which I prized for his companionship and devotion. I named him Duke.

While these men were with us my son Harry came from Nucla, a distance of thirty miles, to visit me. He came horseback through a fearful snow-storm. He lost his way, for the snow filled the trails, and finally was compelled to leave his horse after feeding it the oats he brought with him.

After hours spent in the cold and darkness—an experience realized only by those who have gone through it—he reached the boarding house at midnight.

During the winter months, when the snow was deep, I would sweep the snow away near the house and feed the birds. The moment they heard me scrape the dish they would whistle and call to their mates in the cliffs and brush, gather near and eat while I was standing by.

From early March till late in the fall there were such an abundance of flowers; I found the maiden-hair fern in all its beauty. This is seldom found in Colorado, I am told.

The latter part of March one of the men brought me the startling news that a cowboy by the name of Lee Bennett, from Norwood, was at his camp with his bride. The thought of meeting a woman seemed good to me. A few days later he brought her to visit me. Some time later another woman braved the ruggedness of this canon, living six miles from me. Often during the summer she came to use my

A SCHOOL TEACHER LEARNING TO FRY MEAT OVER A CAMP FIRE.

flatiron, the only one in the country. It was not an electric, either.

Often during the summer evenings, while sitting outside sewing or reading, beautiful little humming birds came to pay me a visit, drinking out of the four o'clocks growing in the dining room windows so fearlessly they allowed me to touch their soft wings.

One of the pleasures I enjoyed was climbing up the cliffs several hundred feet when the wind was blowing to listen to the wind as it passed through the pinon and cedar trees. Of this I never tired. It was to me the most beautiful music in the world. It sounded like a pipe organ—the great pipe organ of nature.

During the fall my nearest neighbor was a full-blooded Ute Indian. He was called Indian Henry. A kinder neighbor I never saw. He enjoyed coming to our camp and eating pie.

Although I was the only woman around there, I was not lonely with plenty of work and miners coming and going often spent the night at this boarding house. "Chateau de Cummings," it was named. I remember one night the men were telling all the jokes they could think of. They told one on Gordon Galloway, who went into Paradox valley when very young. His father was in the cattle business, and never having been in a town of any size until a young man, went to Ouray and "put up" at the largest hotel there. A room on the top floor was given him. When the time came to retire he sought his room, but could not locate it. He went to the office and asked the clerk for an ax. "An ax! What do you want with an ax?" asked the amazed clerk. "I've lost my room and I want to blaze a trail to it."

Mrs. Martha A. Jerome, one of those pioneer women the whole country holds in loving remembrance for her ready help in time of need, tells of a man named Gilmore who, intent on getting a certain piece of land, lay hidden in the brush near by from the observant eyes of the soldiers and keen eyes of the Indian four days before the Indians left the reservation. Then as soon as soldiers and Indians were gone he crawled out of his hiding place, when lo and behold! four other men with cramped limbs rose up at the same time, with the same expectations, not one knowing of the presence of the others, to take that piece of land.

Fortunately they were good natured and kind, deciding to let the one who was on the ground longest have the land. Gilmore having been there the longest, the men laughingly left him in possession.

THE GUNNISON TUNNEL

The outcome of a man's dream. A short history of the birth and development of one of the greatest examples of ingenuity and perseverance seen on the western slope.

As given by C. E. Adams.

Prior to removal of the Southern Ute Indians from Western Colorado to Utah by a treaty between them and the government, the Uncompahgre valley was a barren waste. It had been traversed by Captain J. W. Gunnison in his exploration trip to Utah, and he had referred to this territory as a desert unfit for cultivation and habitable only for savages.

In 1873 and 1874 the valley was mapped by Professor H. V. Hayden for the United States geological survey, who termed it a part of the great desert between the Rocky mountains and the Wasatch mountains.

The first irrigation ditch taken out of the Uncompahgre river was accomplished by the United States army officers in 1875, when the Fort Crawford Indian agency was established nine miles south of the city of Montrose, and where was stationed for

FINISHED SECTION OF THE GUNNISON TUNNEL,
MONTROSE, COLO.

several years a large detachment of United States troops to keep the Indians in a peaceable attitude toward the whites, who were blazing pioneer trails across the Continental Divide. This ditch was known as the Reservation ditch and served to furnish water for gardening and the succor of many beautiful cottonwood trees the soldiers set out for fringing their parade grounds and campus.

On August 28th, 1881, the Indians were marched down the Uncompahgre valley with their faces toward the setting sun, and the Indian bade a sad and mournful farewell to the land of which he had been in undisputed control, closely followed by a regiment of mounted, blue-coated cavalrymen.

One day later and a band of pioneer "squatters" were released to seek out the new country and "squat" on pieces of land that should be held for their domicile.

This advent of the white man really marked the beginning of agricultural development in the Uncompahgre valley and the opening up of the irrigation systems which have finally culminated in the construction of the Gunnison tunnel.

Naturally enough, the first settlers picked up the land along the banks of the Uncompahgre river, knowing they must raise the water from the river bed to their lands before it would become productive.

The valley settled up fast, and as the choice land in the river bottom became less there was a gradual spreading out upon the higher ground. Soon the mesas, or tablelands, as the Easterner would call them, were invaded by the more venturesome. Here it became necessary for the building of longer and larger ditches in order to reach this land.

Outside capital was sought and the construction of several of the large irrigating canals undertaken, so that in the later '80s the inhabitants suddenly woke up to a realization that the entire flow of water in the Uncompahgre river had been appropriated, and on seasons when the snowfall was light in the mountains or a warm spring carried off the water earlier than usual there was not sufficient water in the stream to supply the demand.

Undaunted by this condition, however, the valley continued to settle up, and more ranches were laid out and crops planted, only to see them burn up in the summer, owing to a lack of moisture.

This condition was still further accentuated by the fact that other pioneers went further up the Uncompahgre river and settled in the river bottom, while others built homes on the small creeks which acted as feeders to the mother stream.

In those days irrigation had not developed sufficiently in Colorado for the passage of laws permitting the establishment of priority water rights and having decrees of court fixing the amount of water one could claim by virtue of prior use, but the fellow higher up on the stream would take all he wanted, and if there was any water for the one below it was all right—if not, he would be up against it, unless he could prevail upon his more fortunate brother to whack up a little.

There was an ample supply of water in the river, provided it could be impounded during the high water period, and let loose gradually. A few talked of building large reservoirs in some of the canons and basins up in the mountains, but capital could not be found willing to undertake this stupendous task.

One night, when all was dark and dreary ahead of him, when he could not see a silver lining to the cloud anywhere, F. C. Lauzon, a rancher whose all had been staked in a little home here, tossed and tumbled on his pillow until finally, after the midnight hour, his worries were bathed and softened in

Nature's sweet restorer. And then it was that he dreamed of bringing the waters of the great Gunnison river underneath Vernal mesa and drop them into the Uncompahgre river.

The following morning Mr. Lauzon arose with a new vision before him. He told his dream to his neighbors and friends. He talked the proposition all the time. Some laughed at him and said it was impossible; others called him a visionary. But there were others to whom the proposition appealed with force.

Not discouraged, Mr. Lauzon spread the idea of bringing in the Gunnison water through a tunnel until he had a considerable following, and in August and September, 1894, Walter H. Fleming of Montrose and Richard Whinnerah of Ouray were employed to make a preliminary survey of this proposition. They ran a line of levels from the Uncompahgre valley to the Gunnison river and found that the Gunnison water could be made to cover practically all of the valley in Montrose and Delta counties.

The report of these engineers not only established the possibility of securing an additional water supply, but disclosed the fact that the cost of the undertaking was far in excess of the ability of the people of the Uncompahgre valley to accomplish.

The agitation was continued, and on August 15, 1896, a meeting was held at Colorow (now Olathe), at which there was a large attendance of farmers and others interested, the object of which was to discuss propositions for an increased water supply. From the files of the Montrose "Press and Messenger" of Friday, August 21, 1896, I take the following account of the happenings at this meeting:

"Lew Ross was voted to the chair and W. J. Horton acted in the capacity of secretary.

"Three propositions were placed before the assembly for increasing the water supply of the valley—the tunnel from the Gunnison, building large reservoirs to store the water of the Uncompahgre and digging down to bedrock and putting a cement dam across the valley to raise and hold the water.

"The first—tunnel to the Gunnison river, presented by Mr. Lauzon—was generally discussed. It was opposed by some as being impracticable. The discussion was general. The drift of the discussion, however, was to investigate the feasibility of the proposition rather than to condemn or indorse it. To this end a committee of fifteen members was decided upon to be appointed by the chair, five members to be selected from Montrose county, five from Delta county and five from Ouray county."

Subsequent meetings were held and gradually the sentiment crystallized into one thought—the construction of the Gunnison tunnel. Realizing that the community could not build such a tunnel, the people began to search on the outside for aid. Private capital could not be interested and the people were somewhat discouraged again; but at last the thought occurred that state aid might be secured from the fact that the state of Colorado had commenced the building of State Canals Nos. 1 and 2.

Meade Hammond of Paonia was a candidate for the legislature from the counties of Delta and Montrose. He was importuned to originate a bill for the construction of the Gunnison tunnel in the event of his election, to which he readily assented. The fortunes of politics traveled with him, and he was elected.

True to his promise, he introduced the bill, which, on April 11, 1901, became a law, carrying with it an appropriation of $25,000 to commence the construction of State Canal No. 3, the object being to carry the waters of the Gunnison river to the Uncompahgre river.

The following December work was actually started upon this tunnel, at a point about eight miles northeast of Montrose and about six miles northwest of the present Gunnison tunnel. This tunnel was driven about 900 feet toward the Gunnison river when work had to be suspended, owing to the fact that the appropriation was exhausted early in the fall of 1902. John J. Tobin of Montrose was a member of the board of control and looked after the work personally.

Prior to this construction, however, the director of the United States geological survey, in the winter of 1900-1901, authorized the expenditure of $4,000 to make investigations in the Uncompahgre valley, which was secured through the efforts of Hon. John

C. Bell of Montrose, congressman from the Second district of Colorado.

The investigation was undertaken by A. L. Fellows, a well-known engineer in the employ of the government, and his labors covered the period of 1901. He concluded that the building of the Gunnison tunnel was a feasible undertaking and that the waters of the Gunnison river could be made to irrigate and reclaim a large body of fertile land in the Uncompahgre valley that would otherwise be of little or no value to anyone.

The following year, on June 17, 1902, the Reclamation act was passed by congress, authorizing the general government to expend money on arid lands to reclaim them, letting the lands be responsible for the payment of the expenditure back to the government in ten equal annual installments, without interest.

As this was the first point at which the geological survey had expended any government money in exploring the feasibility of adding to the water supply of the Uncompahgre valley by means of a tunnel through the divide between the Gunnison and Uncompahgre rivers, it was but natural that the thought of the reclamation service, created in the Reclamation act, should be directed toward this territory for its first effective work.

Following the passage of this law preliminary surveys were ordered to be continued by Mr. Fellows for the development of the Uncompahgre valley. The work of prospecting the field was then begun in real earnest. Up to this time no living man, so far as known, had ever traversed the Black canon of the Gunnison from the mouth of the Cimarron river to the point of the river's confluence with the north fork of the Gunnison, about 30 miles below.

In order to fully explore this deep chasm the, walls of which rise in many places almost perpendicularly to a height of nearly 3,000 feet, men endeavored to penetrate the gorge. Volunteers for this pioneering were few, and it fell to the lot of John E. Pelton, J. A. Curtis, M. F. Hovey, E. B. Anderson and W. W. Torrence to undertake it.

Equipped with two boats used for pleasure purposes at Pelton's lake, on Spring Creek mesa, which were transported to the point of the confluence of the Gunnison and Cimarron rivers in Black canon, and with thirty days' supply of provisions, the boats were launched in the turbulent waters of the Gunnison river.

It was arranged that men should be stationed along the brow of the canon in order to keep track of the movements of these men. The second day one of the boats, "The City of Montrose," was dashed to pieces in a whirling torrent, and the other soon was lost, so all the provisions they could possibly carry were strapped to their backs.

For five days they worked their way down the gorge, over precipices, climbing around cliffs, surmounting huge boulders and swimming rapids, before they were seen by those on the rimrock of the canon, and then they were discovered 1,500 feet below. On they trudged, being in water a large part of the time. At the end of the twentieth day they found they could get no further, for in front rose to a height of 2,500 feet the almost perpendicular chasm, only 28 feet wide at the water's edge. Between these walls of granite the water was a silvery foam, rolling and tossing, and bounding and dashing. To try to swim through this, they felt, meant certain death. They tried to get back up stream, but this was impossible.

The following morning, faint and weakened from lack of food and sleep, bruised from head to foot by being dashed and falling against the rocks, they began to look for a place where they could climb out of the canon. They finally discovered a narrow opening toward the top which offered the only avenue of escape. After christening this particular point in the canon the "Falls of Sorrow," they started to climb up the granite wall, the five being tied together with a long rope. Exhausted, they finally reached the summit on the opposite side of the river from Montrose. They had traversed but 14 miles through the canon in the 21 days.

In August a second attempt was made to fathom the dark mystery of the Black canon, and this was successful, Prof. A. L. Fellows of the U. S. reclamation service and W. W. Torrence of Montrose undertaking the perilous trip. They are the only men who have ever explored the canon the entire distance. Their equipment consisted of a rubber raft, rubber bags for kodak, engineer's instruments, hunting knives and belts, and two silk life lines 600 feet long. Both were expert swimmers and they expected to swim through the places where it was impossible to get around.

When they came to the "Falls of Sorrow" they sat on the edge of the rock overhanging the raging torrent for some time before they decided to try to get past it. Finally they shook hands, bade one another goodbye, and Fellows slid into the water. He disappeared as quickly as though the earth had swallowed him. Torrence waited awhile, and he, too, slipped off, never expecting to come out alive. Six hundred feet below he was cast into calm waters, he knew not how, and succeeded in pulling himself up to a friendly boulder. To his amazement, when he looked around, there sat Fellows on a neighboring rock waiting for him. It was a glad meeting.

They had lost their rubber raft and practically everything they had prior to this time, and they began to be hungry and weak. One day, as they trudged along, they espied a mountain sheep and her young lamb that had climbed down the canon for water, they being able to climb over rocks and precipices insurmountable by man. As they dashed away Torrence overtook the lamb and caught it in his arms. The two then had a good feast of broiled mountain lamb, which strengthened them greatly for the further exploration. The little animal was as manna coming down from heaven, for their lives were doubtless preserved by it.

After ten days of most desperate work they

emerged from the deepest of the chasm at Red Rock canon, where they found a man watching for them with food. There they were refreshed and then continued on to the mouth of the Black canon, which was not so difficult beyond this point. The trip was so dangerous that in all probability no one will ever undertake it again.

But the work of these six men bore fruit. Mr. Fellows was convinced more than ever of the feasibility of building the Gunnison tunnel and he worked night and day to accomplish it.

Finding that the state could not accomplish the great task, on March 16, 1903, the Colorado legislature passed a bill authorizing the conveyance of all its property rights in the Gunnison tunnel to the United States.

Two days prior to this, however, the secretary of the interior approved the general project and authorized the preparation of plans and specifications for construction.

After a series of meetings between the land owners of the Uncompahgre valley and government representatives, the secretary of the interior set aside $2,500,000 from the reclamation fund for the construction of the Uncompahgre project, which contemplated the building of the Gunnison tunnel six miles long and the South canal 12 miles in length.

The first dirt was thrown by I. W. McConnell, project engineer, on January 11, 1905, on the digging of the tunnel, the Taylor-Moore Construction company being the contractor. The company proved to be financially unable to carry on the work and on May 27th the government took charge and finished four years later, the two tunnel headings being brought together, the tunnel being 30,600 feet in length.

The scope of the project has been enlarged constantly since the beginning and at the present writing nearly all of the ditches and canals in the valley are being operated by the government. The ultimate intention is that the entire irrigating system under the project shall be operated by the government.

A CLOUDBURST IN TELLURIDE

Again the people of this city are called upon to witness a scene so terrible and awe-inspiring that mere words fail.

But the effect on this people is always the same—brings out the brotherhood and nobility of man for his fellowman.

Through the courtesy of George R. Painter, editor of "The Telluride Journal," we take the following:

At 12:50 o'clock Monday afternoon, July 27, 1914, following on the heels of one of the hardest rain storms ever experienced in the city, a river of mud, very conservatively estimated at between eight and ten feet in height, swept out of Cornet Creek canon, just north of town, and traveling in a southeasterly direction through town swept everything which was in its path. The largest portion of 15 blocks of the north central, central and eastern residential section, and including one of the most important business blocks of the city, is now wrecked and buried under mud to a depth of from four to ten feet.

A waterspout of unbelievable volume and resulting from a cloudburst near the top of Sawtooth range, directly north of town, was the source of the flood, the water flowing from the pinnacle point of the range almost due north of the Liberty Bell mine workings, and gathering momentum in its mad race through Cornet Creek canon. The water dam owned by the city just north and west from the storage reservoirs for domestic purposes was completely swept from its moorings and its supply of stored-up water was added to the awe-inspiring flood. Boulders were easily carried along on the crest of the big mass of mud and debris forced on by the irresistible force of the onrushing water, which was each second gaining speed as it swept down the mountainside and through the steep, narrow canon. Huge timbers and trees were also carried down with the rush as though they had been mere chips of wood, and these, with the boulders, were driven through houses in the path of the flood and landed high and dry ten blocks from the mouth of the canon.

The old course of the creek flowing from Cornet Creek canon was southeast through the city, but years ago a narrow channel was cut to divert the small stream southwest through the outskirts of town. A small dam was thrown over the old course of the stream and in recent years but little damage resulted from high water. As the river of mud swung out of the canon yesterday afternoon, however, the little dirt dam was as straw, the tons of mud brought down by the flood flowing over the dam and carrying it out. The first buildings taken out by the flood were sheds and a lean-to, the property of Neil Elskamp. A newly remodeled five-room residence, property of Oscar Wunderlich, was next struck and leveled by the flood, which crossed Oak street, and going to the Oscar Bengston residence, occupied at the time by John Johnson and family, crushed it like an eggshell, catching Mrs. Johnson and pinning her arms in such a manner that she was unable to extricate herself and but for the heroic work of Harry Lyle and Johnny Sams would have been carried under the flood. Mr. Lyle supported the weakened woman while Mr. Sams attempted to loosen her arm, and to their everlasting credit let it be known that though momentarily expecting to be carried under by the onrushing flood and being bruised and injured by the boulders and heavy timbers being swirled past them, they resolutely clung to the injured and mangled woman. God in His mercy rewarded their efforts and the woman was removed from the current of the flood and conveyed to the Hadley hospital, where for weeks she was lovingly cared for, mothered by the whole city. Her restoration was marvelous.

As the river of mud and rocks and debris swept past the curve station at the Liberty Bell mine, P. S.

Abbott, a trusted employe of the company, realized what it meant to the unwarned residents of the city, and hurrying to the telephone called up the operator at the telephone exchange in this city and advised her of the danger. The operator, Miss Margarite Kagey, appreciating the responsibility which was thrust upon her, responded most nobly, and through her efforts many of those who resided in the direct path of the flood were warned to leave their homes, doing so and saving their lives.

Mr. and Mrs. Blakley were busy preparing for an outing, when, hearing the roar, they went to the door and saw but one way out—through the chicken yard. Obliged to stop and break the wire-netting gate down, precious time was lost. The young wife was swept away with the flood and not found for some time—the bereaved husband with home and loved one gone in a moment!

Loving ministry was given him, but it is well there is a higher than human to sustain at such a time.

During the night the heavy flow of water from Cornet Creek canon raised, carrying down several immense boulders and necessitating blasting, the heavy detonation of which was heard between 1:30 and 2 o'clock this morning.

A mass meeting of the business men of the city was held in the court house, the meeting being called to order by Mayor Loebnitz. After hearing the opinions of practical men who were familiar with the best manner in which to handle the debris, etc., a general committee of three of the leading citizens of the county was appointed to take charge of the work of cleaning up the city in order that business might be resumed. The committee appointed is comprised of Messrs. F. E. Cristy, Chas. A. Chase and E. H. Sackett.

The suggestion of sluicing out the mud and debris by fluming water from Cornet Creek straight through the city and leading to the river will probably be the one adopted, and, in fact, the flume is already under the course of construction. The boulders and timbers of course will have to be handled otherwise, but the only practical way in which to handle the mud is to sluice it out as has been suggested.

The general committee having the work of cleaning up the city in charge has put a force of 50 carpenters to work shaping timber for a flume which will be run north from the San Miguel river through the alley in the rear of the Telluride Transfer company's barn up to the rear of the Tomkins-Cristy hardware house, through the vacant lot just west of the establishment, and across the street and through the gutted Commercial Club and following the path of the flood to the mouth of the canon. Other flumes will, of course, have to be built later in other sections of the city and the mud sluiced through the flume to the river, Cornet Creek water being used. The big rocks will have to be blasted and smaller ones hauled or dragged away.

The sluicing of mud into the giant flume leading

to the San Miguel river has passed an experimental stage and is now on in earnest. At 1:40 this afternoon the headgate at the dam on the west side of North Oak street was pulled open and a stream of water from Cornet Creek sent through the spillway. Though the stream did considerable work in cutting a channel on the north side of the Tomkins-Cristy warehouse, it was not until the first shift of firemen went on and the magnificent pressure of the city water works brought into play through a fire hose and a three-quarter inch nozzle that real progress was made.

The fire department is comprised of some of the most whole-hearted men in the entire world, and with the experience of the members in handling such matters the value of their service can hardly be computed.

Under the direction of experienced firemen and F. E. Cristy, a member of the general committee, and one of the best posted and most practical placer miners in this section of the county, the mud was forced into the flume and sent on its journey down the San Miguel river.

ALL PRAISE DUE BOY SCOUTS

One of the most generous acts coming to the notice of "The Journal" since the advent of the flood here two weeks ago is the volunteer work of the boy scouts of Telluride. Ten of the big-hearted little chaps are industriously engaged in the work of shoveling the mud out of the Stoermer shoe shop, on

East Columbia avenue. The assistance was voluntarily offered by the little men, who lost no time in equipping themselves with shovels and making the mud fly. And the fact that they are small boys does not detract from the amount of work that they have done. A wide space has already been cleared by them in the building and if they are permitted to continue the entire building will be cleaned. Mr. Stoermer is nearly 80 years of age and without financial means to assist himself, which consideration but adds to the praise due the generous-spirited youths.

The following is taken from the "San Miguel Examiner," through kindness of its editor, F. D. McKown:

Monday noon, July 27, as the writer and his family were sitting at the lunch table, we heard a great roar that did not seem like any other noise made by the elements, and having seen great mud slides run down the mountainsides in places near Telluride this year, without seeing it, we knew that it was either made by water or mud; we knew that it was near, and we felt its danger without knowing what it was or even seeing it, so we went to the door, picked out what we thought a place of safety, then our wife, little girl and ourself went across the street to high ground.

In gaining a place of safety we were also in a place to see the great slide of mud, trees and rock, which was caused by an immense water spout, which fell from the clouds on the Needles, a Sawtooth range of mountains of an altitude of between 13,000 and 14,000 feet above sea level, about a mile, air line, higher than Telluride is, and at a distance to the north of the little city of about three miles, air line.

Ever since the first day of July heavy clouds have hung over the city every day or night, surcharged with rain, with lightning and thunder, the elements seeming at war with one another, yet none thought of a water spout of such immense proportions coming to us. We have had rains almost every day, and on Monday especially the elements were ready and when they broke loose in the great water spout millions of tons of mud and debris was deposited diagonally across a tract of the town five blocks square.

The mouth of Cornet Creek opens into the little valley where Telluride stands on the extreme north of the town and at a point which fairly centers the city. Its opening is between Oak and Aspen streets and the old creek bed, which carried the waters through the town in the pioneer days, was the course taken by the heavy head of water and mud and was followed clear to the river, five blocks below, where it entered the city.

The course of the cloudburst from its source in the hills to the town was down a narrow creek bed, the banks of which in many places have had the wash of ages and are built up with dirt to the height of anywhere from ten to thirty feet. The water spout carried thousands of gallons, or perhaps millions of gallons of water, raising the creek far above its rocky channel into this wash of dirt which formed its banks, and the banks were started to moving and kept moving until they struck the town and crossed it. Rocks weighing ten tons were brought down and deposited at the head of Oak street, where the slide started across town. Trees a couple of feet through and a few to the length of thirty feet were brought down; piles of heavy drift wood added to the great weight, and when the wall came over Cornet falls, down the mouth of the canon and entered the town it was ten to fifteen feet high, and on account of the start it got as it came down the steep mountain, and its great weight, nothing could withstand it.

Two-story frame houses were lifted and turned from their foundations; smaller houses of one story and five to eight rooms which were in the track of the slide were crushed like eggshells; mud was deposited in streets and alleys along five blocks and from a depth of two to eight feet, and all through this mud is huge boulders, trees and driftwood.

In fact, Main street is a sea of mud from the front of the Sheridan hotel to Alder street—five blocks in width—and every place had some damage done, though some a great deal more than others.

This story is briefly told, but it represents a calamity which is the worst by far of anything that has ever happened here. We thought when the Smuggler fire came and the Liberty Bell snowslide that Telluride had its worst calamities, and the loss of life was appalling in both, but this one is of a different caliber, differently affecting the people by the loss of property. True, some have the means to stand the loss, but the percentage of those able to stand it is small compared with the list of losers.

No sooner was the catastrophe over when charity and kindness, inborn and inbred, in the good people of Telluride, began to show up everywhere. Homes were opened by neighbors to the homeless first, then a relief committee was organized and a fund built up, three mining companies coming in, as they always do, with more than their share; there were men named to whom people might go for assistance if destitute.

When the news spread abroad by the medium of the great Associated Press and kindred news dispensing bodies, money began to come in from the outside, and there is still assistance to be had outside if the people will make an effort to get it, or need it later.

The best of all the characteristics displayed was the kindness of one to another and the thoughtfulness which was displayed. Mine managers took picks and shovels and got right in to help dig out family relics from the wrecked houses; lawyers quit their offices, doctors got into the thickest of it; ministers and bankers donned their working clothes, laborers were employed, and the mayor of the city and the aldermen got right in and with shovels and picks helped where help was needed, and they all did heroic work and work which counted.

Just think! ye who sit in comfortable homes and

complain! of the brave heroism of one wife and mother, who, when friends came to condole with her and her husband, right in sight of home filled with mud and debris, she answered with smiling face: "I have not lost anything; you do not need to feel sorry for me; I have my husband and child."

Could there be a grander spirit shown than this?

Oh, Telluride, Telluride! you, surrounded with the grandeur, the sublimity of the mountains, whose gold and silver enrich the world; you, with a people crowned with the spirit of giving, the spirit of large-heartedness and brotherly kindness when the hour of need comes—let the earnest work of removing the debris and obstructions in your streets be a symbol of your desire for the higher lessons the mountains have to give you.

Well may you have the name you bear today as expressed in the hearing of the writer:

"You can depend on Telluride, she is always ready to give and to do—one of the most open-hearted, open-handed towns in Colorado."

Here are words found in one of your papers:

The citizenry of Telluride is composed of sterner stuff than many of the wrecked buildings were, and out of the ashes of our stricken little city will rise a greater, broader and better community.

THE FISHERMAN'S DELIGHT.

CHAPTER XLI

REALIZATION OF THE "PROPHETIC DREAM"

A Birdseye View of Today, as seen with the mind's eye on top of Marshall Pass, the Crest of the Continent.

Here, more than ten thousand eight hundred feet above sea level, with snow-covered mountains in winter clustering so near we feel the touch of "eternal silence." Where the petty things of life disappear while we stand enraptured with the magnificence of the view.

The writer has been over the Pass many times in the last thirty years, but never once has the voice of jest been heard—always the awe-struck whisper, and often the words fail to come at all.

Today we stand viewing the panorama and memory goes back near forty years, when a railroad over the divide was unthought of. We live in the fondest hopes of yesterday and what does our mental vision behold?

Passing through a lovely valley, we reach the town of Gunnison, a thrifty place, where people gather in front of a large, imposing building to welcome the travelers with their presence.

On we go by fields of wild grass, where bunches of cattle enjoy themselves. The river humming a song of sweet content as it flows by. In the summer time one is struck with the idea that all the

CIMARRON, NEAR THE DEPOT.

world has gone a-fishing. Here and there are tents and further on one sees log structures for the convenience of the people who desire an outing. We pass by a fisherman with high rubber boots out in the river by some secluded home of the mountain trout. His basket, which hangs at his side, seems heavy. He smiles at the many eager faces as the train passes by, knowing full well—the passengers' very looks betray their desire to stay with him.

Soon the train stops, taking on an excited little crowd of people who wave an adieu to another group, who evidently are not ready to leave the fishermen's camp at present. Every one in the car is interested in the newcomers, with their tanned faces and repressed excitement over the good time they have had, laughing together over some mishap of one of their number who attempted to cross the stream on a log that proved treacherous; the fixing of stray locks that would not stay fixed, the arranging of parcels that smelled of fish and at last looking around at interested faces as much as to say, "My! we have had such a good time." Everyone in the car senses the breeziness of camp life—feel as though they, too, have been having an outing and forget their weariness.

We soon reach the Black canon, another triumph of man's ingenuity and perseverance in making it possible for a railroad to pass through it, some black rocks in the canon giving rise to the name. Here more of grandeur is to be found. Near the middle of the canon we come to what is named

"Curecanti Needle," a large body of rock towering skyward, tapering at the top. What seems to be a needle is a flagpole placed there, we are told, by a sailor.

CURECANTI NEEDLE, BLACK CANON, COLORADO.

Here again in summer we pass a fisherman's camp with its cluster of tents, right by the railroad, the delight of the fisherman in summer—his dream in winter; where the little, fat chipmunk eats out of the fisherman's hand.

We cannot stop now, but push on to Cimarron. The village is small, but we know the surrounding country abounds with good homes and rich farms and more good fishing. On we move and find more of nature's wonders to admire.

Now we reach Montrose, with its welcoming clasp of the hand. A city of homes, with schools where the young are taught to regard their word as sacred, to be careful what they promise, then stand by it.

A city where, when the touch of sorrow comes, the beautiful flowers of kindness spring up in every direction.

A place where morality is more to be desired than financial gain and where the work of the City Fathers has always been unselfish.

The surrounding mesas fragrant with fruit blossoms in the early spring.

Southward a few miles we reach Colona, a growing little town with a future, the home of Uri Hotchkiss, the fearless hunter.

Some miles further on we come to Ridgway, near which when the early frost touches the foliage on the mountains round about, presents, as a bishop once said, "one of the most magnificent pictures in the world."

Before long we glide into Ouray. No stumps in

SOMEONE ADMIRING THE SCENERY ABOVE THE SMUGGLER MINE, TELLURIDE, COLO.

the middle of the streets now; beautiful homes and a happy people; our old-time friends, the snow-covered mountains, still remain—like the word of God—unchanged.

The mountains on each side of the little city reaching northward are like the arms of a mother, wide open to receive all who may come, but these same arms are just as wide open for those who wish to leave, a symbol of open-heartedness and freedom.

The hospitality of the people illustrated by the scene near the depot, where food is placed for the bunches of wild mountain sheep which come down from the mountains to feed unmolested during the winter months.

Looking in another direction, we see Telluride, the scene of many a conflict in one form and another, but the mountains remain in all their grandeur, while the mills are pouring out their hidden treasures.

Vanadium, twelve miles below Telluride, a pretty little village of twenty-five or thirty homes, where the employes and those interested in the Vanadium's mines and mill live.

Bear Creek, dashing and foaming in early summer, empties itself in the San Miguel river, which flows by, and at night every house and building is lighted with electricity, presenting the appearance of fairyland.

Wonderful changes have taken place in the last few years since vanadium, an ore used for hardening steel, was discovered and brought forth by the Primos Chemical Company.

MOUNTAIN SHEEP COMING DOWN FROM THE MOUNTAINS NEAR THE DEPOT DURING THE WINTER TO EAT THE FEED PLACED THERE FOR THEM BY THE PEOPLE OF OURAY. 1914.

Over to Norwood, Nucla, Paradox, we see nature lavish in her gifts.

North of Montrose, about eleven miles, is the town of Olathe, once named Colorow. It's much like a boy in knee pants, not doing anything but grow. The center of a vast area of agricultural land, including California and Ash mesas, good homes and good schools the ruling thought.

Eleven miles further on we come to the pretty town of Delta—its people hospitable and kind, rich in all that tends towards wealth in man and surrounding country.

Crossing we come to Hotchkiss, Paonia, with their fruit-bearing orchards, over to Grand Junction, which promises to be the size of Denver some day.

Fruita, with its little park of trees and grass in the center of the business part of town—an inviting spot in the heat of the day, a symbol of thoughtfulness for the welfare of others, its surrounding country rich with nature's bountifulness.

Palisades, with its network of ditches and fruit farms, on to Glenwood Springs, where the strawberries make a business of growing, and many, many other places with their surrounding natural advantages.

And now, in the year 1913, comes the completion of what is named "The Rainbow Route," making it possible to take an automobile trip from Montrose to Pueblo in eighteen hours. What cannot man do?

What a contrast to the conditions of nearly forty years ago; we stand awe-struck with head uncovered, as it were, the change seemed so gradual, and yet how swift.

We know all we have seen is true, and yet we are amazed.

The memory of privations fades from our thought—we see a happy people living in the triumph of today.

The question comes, is this beautiful land all utilized? No, No! But from our lofty height on Marshall Pass the fact is seen, that every one who comes, be it in the beginning of this life in the West or now, at the present moment, each one who comes to make for himself a home, is in all respects a pioneer, still blazing the trail for those yet to come, having much the same conditions to meet and overcome—still the individual effort to be made, for overcome he must, wherever he goes.

It may not be so much in the "doing without" or the lack of water, but it's a struggle in some form or other, as some one has said, "there is nothing gained without a struggle."

But, like the parable told by the Master Pioneer, each will "receive a penny," the reward of right effort.

The people of today who feel the call of the mountains moving them to leave the old landmarks and take up the new, need not feel any sense of loss because they were not among the first—it's always morning to the newcomer, full of possibility for good to those who seek good.

But the cry "All aboard!" is heard. We climb on the train, fully aware the "Prophetic Dream" is fulfilled.

When this book with its mission of love was but two-thirds completed it was left for the wife to finish it alone, for the husband suddenly passed over another "blazed trail," which leads not to a country of privation, but to that of greater fruition; where the longing for larger freedom is fully satisfied, and the lessons of the mountains understood. M. R.

www.ingramcontent.com/pod-product-compliance
Lightning Source LLC
LaVergne TN
LVHW050913080826
845145LV00001B/69

* 9 7 8 1 9 3 2 7 3 8 6 7 4 *